"Each character, with individual virtues and sins to make them memorable, is tested in personal trials as well as against the backdrop of WWI and the American Great Depression. If you enjoy Christian historical fiction, and want to be encouraged on how God works on your behalf, I strongly recommend this novel."

—ELAINE STOCK, author of the award-winning
Her Good Girl, and the *Kindred Lake Series*

"Brakefield paints scenes with believable characters who face harsh realities of life. They deal with disease, death, and financial setbacks during World War I and the years that follow. However, like an ever-present ray of sunshine piercing the clouds, God's Word provides a guiding light. The Almighty's blessings are always there for those who trust in Him."

— RICK BARRY, author of *The Methuselah Project*

"Catherine has woven a wonderful epic tale of faith. I love these characters. Following this family is so delightful. Lots of wonderful historical references to the time period sprinkled throughout."

— CINDY ERVIN HUFF, award-winning author of *Secrets and Charades*

OTHER CROSSRIVER BOOKS
BY CATHERINE ULRICH BRAKEFIELD

DESTINY SERIES

Swept into Destiny
Destiny's Whirlwind
Destiny of Heart
Waltz with Destiny (coming in 2019)

OTHER TITLES

Wilted Dandelions

Destiny of Heart

CATHERINE ULRICH BRAKEFIELD

CROSSRIVER
BREWSTER, KANSAS USA

To my readers...
who have inspired me immeasurably
with their words of gratitude!

Cast of Characters

Ruby McConnell Meir   Daughter of Ben & Maggie,
Wife to Stephen

Collina May McConnell Blaine   Daughter of Ben & Maggie,
Wife to Austin Blaine

Franklin Long   Married to Melissa

Maggie Gatlan McConnell   Referred to as Grandma Maggie

Stephen Meir   Married to Ruby McConnell Meir

William Meir   Son of Ruby and Stephen

Esther Meir   Daughter of Ruby and Stephen

Julie Ann Meir   Stephen's twin sister

Buck Briggs   Widower living in Las Animas, Colo.

Myra McConnell Cass   Daughter of Ben and Maggie,
Wife to Clem Cass,
Mother of Sue Ann and Theresa Cass

Clem Cass   Married to Myra

Jane   Widow of Joe Deerhawk,
President Roosevelt's friend

Dawn	Daughter of Jane and Deerhawk
Luke Baker	Son of Doc Baker
Rose Baker	Daughter of Doc Baker
Ruth Jones	Widower/nurse in Las Animas, Colo.
Eric Erhardt	Son of Frances and Anna, Brother to Ann, Grandson of Mrs. DeGrandcamp
Gill McConnell	Cousin to Ruby, Owner of Gill's Dry Cleaners
Skeeder	Shushan's top hand

Acknowledgments

"Where do I begin?" the theme song for *Love Story* is a fitting way to describe my feelings after finishing *Destiny of Heart*. This novel has been on my heart to do for years.

My research took two years, and my companions in writing *Destiny of Heart* were the memories told to me by my mom and gran. The sweet melody of my imagination played a fitting backdrop for my ever-unfolding mission. For this "sweet love story is older than the sea."

My mission is twofold. First, to transport my readers into a nostalgic journey of remembrance, romance, and realism. Secondly, to bring us all to a better understanding of the love story our Savior has for His children:

"In the beginning was the Word, and the Word was with God, and the Word was God... full of grace and truth" (John 1:1, 14).

Only a benevolent God could have brought this wonderful team of the like-minded staff at CrossRiver Media Group and my agent, Cyle Young and his Hartline Agency group, working toward this single goal.

My appreciation is endless for *Debra L. Butterfield* for her willingness to never say "never" to my endless changes to this manuscript! You see, *Destiny of Heart* is special. It is more than a book; it's a legacy of Christ's love to the always-falling-short failings of mankind.

Tamara Clymer, you never fail to awe me in your endeavor to juggle family, work, and your commitment to CrossRiver. You manage to give one hundred percent to everything you do and this shows in your work. You give new meaning and insight into this uncompromising publishing business and to those around you, especially in making your writers a loving part of your family!

Cyle Young, your knowledge of marketing and connections to publishers continues to amaze me. Thank you for your perseverance in inspiring me through the trying times of my writing endeavors and especially the oftentimes too-many commitments I undertake.

To my husband, *Edward Brakefield*, your encouragement and understanding carry me through the rough days and continue to inspire me throughout the valleys and peaks of my life!

Kimberly Warstler, thank you for your unquenchable devotion for reading my novels. Your love for the written word is a constant reminder to me to continue to strive for excellence.

To my prayer warriors, *Linda, Dee, Sue, Carol, Jin, Kathy, Pam*, and *Marsha*, thank you for your prayers, your encouragement, and your willingness to share your love for my books!

To my faithful team of book reviewers who have followed me through the Destiny series years: *Marcia Mitchell*, you inspire me with your insight and thought-provoking reviews. *Cindy Ervin Huff*, you have become a valued friend because of this sequel and have graced me with your wisdom and valuable comments. *Rick Barry*, though historical romance earlier than World War II isn't typically your type of read, I sincerely appreciate your expertise. To *Elaine Stock*, your sincerity and forthright honesty inspires me!

To my precious readers, I pray *Destiny of Heart* will reward you as it did me in writing "a sweet love story that is older than the sea"! That *Destiny of Heart*'s simple truth woven into the characters Collina, Ruby, Franklin, Stephen, Buck, Myra, and Clem gleams the love that Christ Jesus has for us and lights a pathway to the stars and heavens above for you, too! God Bless!

Prologue

hhhh…" Collina cried. "I'm so thirsty." Her tongue touched her cracked and bleeding lips. "Water." She felt her eyelids fluttering. She lacked the strength to open them. It was hot. She had to find Austin. She had to tell him it wasn't his fault. That smell…The swine were back. They were everywhere, pulling at her skirts, keeping her from Austin.

Face down she fell. She'd tripped. The swine were walking on her! Gagging, she clutched her throat, spitting out the mud…no, phlegm. She had to find Austin—but the swine wouldn't let her up.

She couldn't yell. Their smell was horrendous. There was no escape but through the mud, through the long dark tunnel, to that flickering ray of light.

"Collina. Collina, wake up; its Mother."

Austin was waiting for her. He stretched out his arm, his palm open to her. "I know I'm a poor substitute for a husband; you deserve better…always remember that you were loved by me."

"Come back!" She was a fingertip away from him. He leaned closer, his handsome, dimpled grin, his sparkling eyes glowed into hers. Someone shoved her away. She was falling. Twirling into the blackness.

"Oh, you're so hot. Dear Jesus, please, I can't lose her, too." The cool water Mother bathed her face with felt good. "You're burning up. I'll go see if Bugie can overtake Doc."

Mother's footsteps pounded to the beat of Collina's throbbing head. So quiet. The pigs had stopped grunting. Franklin was here. His eyes as

11

blue as the stripes on Old Glory, his hands comforting. "Don't ever take true love for granted, Collina." Tears formed pools in her throbbing eyelids and the salt stung her eyes.

Austin stretched out his hand. "You're my wife." Far, far away she fell into the awaiting abyss.

She was in the cornfield; Franklin was there with her. He was holding the mustard seed. "Nothing is impossible—if you have faith and believe."

She was dancing, dancing in a flowing gown made of starlight white and glistening gold. Faraway, bagpipes played "Minstrel Boy."

"Love, like a budding rose can never too quickly reveal the flower, that is, if it is to last, for all things worth having are worth waiting for...." Back, back into the fog Franklin rode, galloping up Shushan's hills until the mists engulfed him.

Chapter 1

April 7, 1917

unlight swept across Ruby Meir's face. A roar like the rumbling Cumberland Falls vibrated through her bedchambers. Horses neighed, men yelled out orders, and brakes screeched to a halt just below her windowpane.

Trucks at Shushan? No, silly, you're in Amarillo, Texas, in a fancy suite at the Grand Hotel. I must have been dreaming. Her hand touched Collina's letter. She snuggled deeper into the soft bed and drew up the covers. Stephen and she were on their way to Colorado to homestead a section of land near Pikes Peak.

Drums pounded in the distance, followed by a duet of trumpets. This must be the preparations for the parade the bellhop had told them of the night before.

Since her marriage to Stephen, the years had rolled into her world with Stephen's illness baffling the doctors. Now, the chain of war events in Europe had reached America's shores. The Great War did not concern her. Her husband and son did.

She clasped Collina's letter to her bosom. Collina's right; the Lord orders all things. Queen Esther faced her darkest hours at Shushan with perseverance. *And who knoweth whether thou art come to the kingdom for such a time as this?* God carried Queen Esther through her life trials to jubilation. He could do that for her family, too. She wasn't going to allow a silly war or Stephen's peculiar illness or moving to some place she'd never heard of before upset her joy. She just had to keep her faith and hope in God. No matter what happened.

But how was Stephen's fancy book learning from the University of Louisville going to help him out on the Colorado prairies? Neither she nor Stephen had any idea where they would live once they reached Las Animas. Her husband had acquired an itchy foot in spite of the doctor reports.

Cold air swept the bedchambers. She peeked out beneath the covers. The silk curtains fluttered like the colors on a sailboat. Stephen, with their son wrapped in his arms, stepped out onto the balcony that overlooked Main Street. The warbling notes of a trombone followed by more instruments playing a patriotic tune caused her husband to raise his voice an octave. "Are you up?"

She flapped the covers aside. "I am now." She pointed to the partially open french doors. "That's enough noise to raise Lazarus a second time."

He chuckled. "You want to go down and watch the parade?"

"Is it still snowing?" Amarillo's wind had been unrelenting last evening. She wished she hadn't taken William out to meet Stephen's college friend and see the cattle show. The snow was deep in spots, and five-foot drifts had piled up along the roads and walkways. "If you do go out, bundle William and make sure he wears his hat with the ear muffs."

"Give Mommy a kiss."

Little sloppy lips, followed by Stephen's larger ones, found connection with her cheek. William, who'd been riding his father's back, squirmed uncomfortably, his small fist finding solace in Ruby's face.

"Oh me! That's some kiss."

"Ha! Not even eight months old and already swinging a wallop!" Stephen lifted the squirming infant off his back and swung him into his arms amidst the laughter of his son. She opened one eye, attempting to focus, and smiled, swinging her legs over the end of the bed, watching the antics of her child and husband.

William's peals of laughter mingled with the commotion of the parade's preparation outside their window. With blue eyes and light hair, he was a miniature version of Stephen. Both heads came together like two bear cubs romping amidst a clover field. Only William's short legs were not that of his father's.

Ruby frowned. "Do you think that by some quirk of nature William mistakenly acquired my legs?"

Stephen glanced up, one large paw placed firmly on his son's chest, he took one look at his wife's woebegone face and laughed. "Son, I don't think there could be a mother alive that can worry as much as yours." He jumped up and giving her nose a playful thump, said, "Be glad he didn't get that."

"Oh dear!" Covering her nose with her palm, her feet glided across the thick hotel rug and she clutched the edge of the bureau, staring into the mirror. An oval face, large eyes and thick curly hair bounced to her shoulders and down her back. Carefully she uncovered her nose. "Has my nose grown since last night?"

He burst into merry bliss. "Hon, don't take what my sister said to heart."

"How can I help it?" She stared back at her image, turning her head from side to side. Wishing she hadn't eavesdropped on a conversation between Stephen's sister and Emma Glaser. "Your sister's right, my nose is…predominate, and if noses do grow the older you get—oh, why couldn't your sister be wrong?" Ruby pointed to her face. "But she's not. Here's the proof."

Stephen flopped down on the carpet. "All kidding aside, you have nothing to fret about." Seeing her face, he swooped up his son and stood surveying her. He walked over to the bureau with the squirming William wrapped in his arms. "Let this be a lesson to you, son, never kid a worrier."

If she was a worrier, it was because she married the star kidder. "Ever since I confided in you, you've been ribbing me constantly about my poor schnozzle." She wagged an index finger in front of his, giving it a thump. "Is that what a loving husband does?" Her long thick hair flowed down her shoulders in front of her face. She blew one curl away. She was huffing like an over-worked steam engine. Honestly, just when she needed her husband's sympathy, why must he continue to joke?

"You look more like a misplaced angel than a mother of a seven-month-old. A mischievous gleam surfaced to Stephen's laughing eyes, as he lavished them on her. "No, come to think of it," he said, placing William on the carpet, "you are absolutely right, a loving husband should be…" grabbing Ruby in one lunge, "making mad and passionate love to such a succulent and beautiful damsel."

She laughed as he swung her easily into his strong arms.

The sounds of trombones, tambourines, and marching feet boldly announced the parade was moments from beginning.

"I forgot." He kissed her smartly. "I'll get him dressed." He hurried to William's room.

Before she could grab her heavy wool skirt from her trunk, her son came in dressed in a winter coat, mittens, and scarf, and Stephen topped this off with his woolen hat with ear muffs. "Good."

"I might need to stop by the enlistment office. If the rumors are true, the Selective Service Act will require every male over twenty-one to register, only unlike the Civil War's conscription law, this will strictly forbid the use of any substitutes." He sent her a cheeky smile.

Stephen's love for adventure rivaled his dedication to her and William. Blinking, she said, "Are we one or two on your list?"

Stephen laughed. "You and William are and will always be first. Now hurry." The glass panel doors of the balcony banged against the walls as Stephen flung them open.

"You're a grand old flag," the words of the song floated up to them.

"I think the parade has started," Stephen said.

"You're a high-flying flag."

He swept William up. His footsteps pounded like a Cherokee war drum on the balcony.

"And forever in peace may you wave."

Stepping into her wool skirt, she glanced out the window. Snow slapped the glass pane with a vengeance. Oh, men and their fight for valor and honor. When will it end? Dressed, she joined him on the balcony, hugging him to her.

"You're the emblem of…the land I love, the home of the free and the brave."

"Look at them, son. Remember you're seeing a page of history unfold before your very eyes."

The young men below them pounded the pavement with their combat boots. Their stance bold and unyielding, their steps attuned to one another. So many, so willing. "Robert has already left to go overseas."

"Your brother? Yes, Europe's war became America's when that German U-boat torpedoed the *Lusitania* off the coast of Ireland. And five American ships have been sunk this year. That war's too close to our shores and has every red-blooded American in an uproar."

The radio on the next balcony reiterated President Wilson's words. "It is a fearful thing to lead this great peaceful people into war."

Ruby shivered, not due to the cold; she wished it was. Robert had written her from a foxhole in Europe that war was terrible and frightening beyond words.

President Wilson's words blared out. "The right is more precious than peace, and we shall fight for the things which we have carried nearest our hearts."

"Come on." Stephen took her hand and they rushed down the stairway. Bus boys arrayed in flashing red and gold braided suits greeted her. Crystal chandeliers twinkled gaily about the lavishly decorated lobby of the hotel, accenting the deep red and gold drapes and rich mahogany furniture in the lobby.

The doorman opened the outside doors of the Grand Hotel; a gust of cold air greeted them. Snow lined the newly shoveled walkways. The horses' neighs and the tinkling of sabers clashing against the soldiers' stirrup irons mingled with the cheers of the crowd.

A regiment of the cavalrymen rode before them, the insignia of the crossed swords displayed on their sleeves and cavalry blankets. "How dashing." Ruby squealed with delight. "I can envision that gallant Rough Rider Franklin Long there among them."

"Far better it is to dare mighty things…even though checkered by failure," Stephen said, quoting Theodore Roosevelt. "The United States became a world power because of the Rough Riders when America defeated Spain in 1898."

"Ev'ry heart beats true under the red, white and blue."

The horses nodded their fine heads, and their flowing manes caught the sunlight and glistening snow, as they pranced forward as proudly as the foot soldiers in the snow that had fallen last evening and this morning.

17

"Where there's never a boast or brag."

Stephen's eyes gleamed brightly. "See them, son, I wish for one month with these brave men, just for the experience, the elation of being a small part of this history we are now watching march before us."

"Be careful what you ask." One bystander had overheard her husband's remarks. "My son will be unable to purchase another person in his place because of this new law." A plush mink hat covered the attractive lady's powdered forehead. Her thick reddish-brown fur swept her form from neck to boots.

Ruby turned. "I'm so sorry. My husband wants to fight, but he's too sick and past the legal age of thirty to go."

"Sick? He's walking, isn't he?" Her angry eyes stared back at Ruby. "If this war continues more than a few years, you'll see how sick the enlistment office thinks he is. So, your husband is…?"

"Forty-two."

"Well, there's talk about extending the legal age to forty-five."

Ruby pulled on her husband's coat sleeve. "Why would President Wilson sign that into law?" she whispered.

"President Wilson will only do what he must to keep Americans safe." His voice grew louder, she suspected so the lady next to them could clearly hear. "Remember what he said when the crowd below his oval office had applauded after he agreed to a declaration of war?"

Try as she could, she didn't remember. "Was it important?"

"'My message…was a message of death for our young men. How strange it seems to applaud that.'" Stephen looked out at the marching soldiers, glassy eyed. "Such fine outstanding men each and every one. No, President Wilson will only request my service if he must. Americans want the fighting over there in Europe, than to face our foe on American soil. We want those trenches in France and Flanders, far from our shores. Freedom is never without a price." He touched her nose. "Our young men are willing and eager to do what we cannot."

"But should old acquaintance be forgot…keep your eyes on the grand old flag."

She pressed closer to him. Wishing she could give him her health and grant his wish. He had sacrificed all he owned for her and William. "Knowing you, you'll hide the fact you are ill in order to ride in that cavalry regiment." She wagged her finger in front of his face. "Remember what happened to Lieutenant Franklin Long?"

"Have you?" He laughed. "I seriously doubt we have seen the last of that good man." He drew her hand to his lips and kissed it. "Shall we purchase our tickets for tomorrow's train?"

"No, you mustn't," the woman's voice vibrated with emotion. She dotted her eyes. Her embroidered handkerchief was moist.

"We—" a chain of coughs followed. Noting his flushed face, Ruby reached in her pocket for the pills Doctor Luke had given her. "Go inside and take two with some water. I can walk to the train station and get the tickets."

Stephen waved her words aside, wiped his mouth with a fresh handkerchief, and popped in a Luden's Cough Drop. "My mouth was dry, must be the elevation, don't worry."

"I, but," the lady fluttered her handkerchief toward the Grand Hotel. "The porter said the railroad crew just tunneled through a large drift."

Stephen nodded. "He told me that Amarillo's never seen a storm of this magnitude."

The woman dabbed at her eyes again. "True, and this morning I overheard one of the workers on the railroad crew tell the engineer that they hadn't been able to clear all the track, and the engineer said headquarters was aware of this. Said the passenger car could become a steel death trap for those foolish enough to ride the iron horse tomorrow."

Chapter 2

The smoke bellowing out of the big engine spiraled like pale, mystical ghosts against the hazy sky. Mounds of snow standing like cherubim, luminous and bright, their long white robes as soft as meringue, frothy and wind swept, bordered the begrimed gray of the locomotive. Man's invention against the forces of nature and somewhere in-between stood Ruby's family.

"Folks, thought you should know, I haven't lost a train yet. But I gotta tell ya, this is gonna be a testy trip." The stocky conductor buttoned the brass buttons down the front of his dark blue coat absentmindedly. "You'll tell your grandchildren about this trip someday and brag of your experience, just wait and see." He laughed.

The sea of faces didn't smile. One man said, "I never heard of it snowing like this in Amarillo."

The conductor grimaced. "You haven't been to these parts before, have you, mister?" He shrugged. "We don't make the weather. We just do what we can to get people moved."

"Tracks are clean, you say?" Stephen said.

Ruby clutched his arm, recalling what the woman in the mink coat told them yesterday.

The conductor's beady eyes resembled black coals beneath his dark burly eyebrows. "We'll find that truth out for ourselves."

Stephen turned toward the small window next to his seat. "Looks like more snow."

"Yeah." The conductor took out his big gold watch and looked at the hands. "Okay!" he bellowed. "Five minutes and this iron horse rolls. Listen up, folks. Got my orders from the top to move this here train, but I'm warning you, though they tell me the tracks are clear, it'll be a hard trip. Now is the time to get off. Once we start, ain't no turning back. Don't need anyone here to be a melancholy whiner. It ain't no good moping about the weather, no good in wondering about whethers. Either you stay or you go, either you do or you don't…make your decision now and stick to it, that's my motto."

Two people, evidently husband and wife, filled their arms with a sordid assortment of paraphernalia and huffed down the aisle.

"Well, I must say, they should have given us that little speech inside the train station," the woman said as she walked past the conductor.

The conductor did not flinch as an elderly man planted an indignant stare on him before disembarking. "Busboy at the bottom of the steps will help you with that luggage." He tipped his cap. "Have a good day."

The conductor turned to the rest of the passengers, surveying them for a moment. "Okay, so you want to stick it out? You've been duly warned." He strolled off toward the front of the train.

The large locomotive slowly moved forward, lunging and clanging as it pulled the railroad cars along the tracks. The black upholstered seats that faced theirs were empty. Ruby was glad. It gave them more room, and she wouldn't have to worry about conversing with strangers and pretend she wasn't scared.

The big potbelly stove in the far corner of the car gave off a punitive smell of charcoal and hickory but did little to help her cold hands and wet feet. She felt William's. His were toasty warm. His little hands now gripped Stephen's neck. Ruby laughed. "Are you going to let William hold onto you like that all the way to Colorado?"

He smiled over the head of his offspring. "Well, not that far."

As their car gathered speed, Ruby scratched a hole in the frost that had accumulated on the train window. She laid her nose against its cold surface and watched as the landscape sped by faster than she had ever known possible.

Storefronts and houses soon gave way to the vast countryside of white fields and trees. The train maneuvered a series of curves, like the long folds of a snake's body, as it wrapped itself about the tracks. Just ahead, a massive snowdrift, taller than anything she had ever seen, rose and dipped and rose again. It loomed ahead of them like a huge white dinosaur. She could feel the train slow to a crawl, as if hesitating to immerse itself into the belly of this animal of snow. "Oh!" she gasped. Turning to Stephen, she wrapped her arms around his, wishing she, like William, could cling to his neck and be oblivious to her surroundings.

Three blue-suited men each with three or four shovels in their hands came into the car. "We could use some strong backs, anyone game?"

Ten or more soldiers sprang from their seats, grasped a shovel and jumped down the steps of the train. Time seemed to stand still. Would they be forced to stay here for days? A fortnight? Then Ruby felt the engine groan as it moved ever so slowly forward. The men jumped on one at a time. The locomotive wheels gritted against the metal tracks as the locomotive's speed increased, the steam floated past her window, blocking her view of the snowdrift.

Stephen circled her shoulders, feeling her apprehension. The thundering wheels and the thumping tracks echoed their throbbing tune in her ears. The ominous walls of the snow encased their small compartment into darkness. Some passengers cried in dismay. The shadow crept silently across Stephen's face, giving her the allusion of being in a dream. Only his kiss, his firm lips now pressed upon her trembling ones, placed her back into the realm of reality.

💜 💜 💜

They had crossed the Colorado border. The whistle in the engine compartment gave a warning cry. Ruby could feel the smoke billowing about her long skirts as her turn came to mount the iron steps of the train. This had been their second stop. A hurried dinner, a quick toilette, and they were back in their seats again.

"All aboard!" bellowed the conductor as his lantern moved from side to side. She fastened her Monte Carlo coat about her neck and clutched her overnight bag more firmly with her left and with her right hand pulled herself upward. She could feel Stephen's presence behind her, holding the squirming William close to his chest as the wind howled down on her black silk brocade hat, pelting the brim with a mixture of snow and ice.

Reaching the platform of the caboose, she turned before entering the dark interior. Mountains of snow conglomerated into irregular piles, giving the steam from the train no means of escape. Smoke billowed about their heads. She blinked, feeling her way through the opening.

William cried. "Here, Stephen, let me have him." But he had made it up the iron steps and was helping her pull open the door.

"Quick, get in folks; the less smoke in here the better." The conductor shut the door behind them and queried, "You the last ones?"

Stephen nodded, coughing, working to catch his breath.

"Find your seats. The engineer wants to get moving before the snow gets too deep. Humph! Clear they said. Don't know what they're talking about." With that he passed into the other compartment.

Miles and miles of white peaked drifts loomed before Ruby's eyes. They were cast adrift amidst a sea of snow, an ocean of foam, and the hours and miles rolled by with the steady rhythm of steel against steel, as they weaved their way down the monotonous rail. At first she closed her eyes to the drifts that had swept themselves across the tracks, but then she watched fascinated, as one would a sporting event, for the locomotive took the snow banked hurdles in stride, slowing down after the impact, then speeding up to gather momentum for another drift, another hurdle to clear.

In a stubborn frenzy, like a personal vendetta, man's invention fought against the elements of snow and sleet that would preclude it from its preordained destiny. William was lulled by the train's rhythm into a restless sleep as steadily they moved forward, forever forward into the unknown and unseen.

A grizzled old man with long flowing white hair and soft white beard sat directly in front of them. He'd gotten on at the last rest stop and had slept since taking his seat. Not even the cries of some of the more skittish passengers had disturbed his slumber.

But now she felt his eyes staring at her beneath thick bushy white eyebrows. His clothes were made of leather and animal furs, from his cap to his soft black leather boots. He reminded her of someone, but she just couldn't recollect.

He leaned forward, his long beard grazing Stephen's arm, and Ruby noticed how deeply tanned and robust his complexion was. "Worst blizzard in history, they say. But I can recount one back in 1865 that makes this'un look like a kitten beside a bobcat. Yes siree, you kids won't know about that'un; 'twas before you was born.

"Took people in Wyoming weeks to shovel through. Lot of folks died, too." His chewing tobacco issued from one side of his mouth and he took a gnarled finger and wiped it away.

"Sir, is this your first time to Colorado?" Ruby said.

"Why, little missus, you're looking at one of the first prospectors to hit Denver in the gold rush days of 1859. Those were the days when a man was a man if he could keep hold of his scalp. Yes siree."

His eyes gazed past the small compartment, past the fleeting landscape, to a time Ruby and Stephen could not comprehend. "My pa was a young buck then. Got the idea to head west, so out he and Ma came with me." He stopped now, swallowing hard.

"A war party came swooping down on the wagon train and killed them. I hadn't been there when they came, had gone off to the river to fish with my older brother." His weathered mouth puckered. Ruby was moved to tears.

"But you see, they being pagans, they knew no other way but to torture, rape, and kill. They'd mutilate their own bodies, discard their own mother if'n she got too old to be any account. Without Christian morals, that's how civilizations turn out. I hated their…that's when the Lord snatched my coat tails during a tent revival I happened to stumble into. Yeah, I got baptized in the old Mississippi. I married me a nice Christian woman and we settled down and homesteaded a piece of good land.

"Then, when my wife died, and my child was captured during an Indian raid, I couldn't figure God out. But I believed in the Savior. The

Lord led me to my son. He's married now. Just saw him and his missus and passel of young'uns. But ya know," pointing a gnarled finger to his wrinkled eyes, "sometimes, I believe these old eyes has seen too much misery. It grieves me to recollect. People can do some mighty awful things to each other. Then again, they can surprise you, too. Where did you say you're headin'?"

"We're going to Las Animas, Colorado, near Pueblo. We're going to homestead a section there; 360 acres of good farming land will be ours after three years."

"That so, why that's right close to Pikes Peak. During the Colorado Gold Rush of '59 it was 'Pikes Peak or Bust!'" A mammoth laugh erupted from the deep draws of his stomach and swelled through the bellowing hole of his red mouth.

"Santa Claus, that's who you remind me of—"

"Yes, ma'am, I've been heralded that by some children. Well, I'll tell ya, son." He leaned over, pressing his face towards Stephen. "I know that country well. Beautiful and plenty of it.

"But don't let anyone kid ya. It's a hard life, it'll rob your missus there of her youth. That dry air will give her wrinkles before her time, and the backbreaking work will make those broad shoulders of yours stooped beyond knowing. If that weren't enough, there's those darn rattlers and pesky Mexicans to contend with."

Ruby gasped. "Snakes?" She hated snakes.

The man chuckled at her woebegone face. "Pretty gloomy picture I've painted ya." Reaching over, he covered both their hands with his. "But you'll be happy there. It's a good life to raise a family in when you've got the Good Lord at your table."

♥ ♥ ♥

Coming out of the dark locomotive compartment, Ruby blinked. Miles of snow-peaked mountains layered with a sea of snowy landscape dotted with brown buildings that comprised the outskirts of Las Animas met her critical gaze.

"The sky looks as blue as Lady's Lake with not a cloud to be seen," Stephen said.

She gasped as the crisp cool air invaded her lungs. She wrapped William's head in her shawl. "It's as cold as Lady's Lake in winter, too."

Stephen laughed. He grabbed William from her arms and held out his hand to her as she dismounted the train's icy steps.

Ruby shivered in spite of her warm coat.

Stephen hugged her close. "You'll see—my health is bound to improve out here."

"Sure, if you don't contract pneumonia first. Oh, dear." Ruby murmured. "I'm not sure I brought enough warm clothes."

"Let's not worry about that now." Stephen stepped into what he thought was a well-worn path only to sink into a drift up to his knees. "Watch your step, the snow is pretty deep." He pivoted William to one arm and extended his free hand to her.

She took it gratefully, for her long skirt was a definite hindrance in navigating her way up the rugged terrain. She could hear the porter behind her labor with the heavy trunk. His panting breaths told her that he, too, was quickly becoming exhausted. Silently their small caravan trudged up the hill.

Stephen placed a silver dollar in the porter's cold, yet sweaty palms.

"Thanks a heap, mister!" He was back on the snowy trail in a leap. The boy barely managed to jump aboard the big locomotive before the gray steam tinged with soot sent the big wheels to turning down the long miles of track yet to be covered.

"Howdy, strangers, what can I do for you?"

"We need a horse or an automobile to take us to the nearest hotel."

"Humph! There's Myrtle, she's no horse—don't carry much chuck in horses. Myrtle's worth her weight in gold, though, even if she is only a mule. She could take you to any part of town you'd be a needing to go with her eyes closed. During the worst dust storm folks had seen in nearly a decade, she carried me about like she could read my mind. And while those fast cow horses that Will takes such store in were spooking, why, she'd just walk right on by with nary a never mind to the goings-on of his high minded hay burners."

A chain of coughs volleyed to Stephen's throat. Reaching into his pant pocket he said, "How much?"

The proprietor shook his white head, almost knocking his wire-rimmed glasses off the hump on his nose. Raising his hand palm out, he staunchly protested. "There isn't no money in the world that could make me part with my Myrtle."

"But I didn't mean to propose—" Stephen said, stamping his feet, turning his back against a gust of cold wind that was sweeping across the wooden porch of the small depot.

"Now where are my manners? You folks come on in to my little room, got a good fire going in here, you can dry out a little and when I've finished with this here paper work, I'll take you myself to Mary's boarding house."

Ruby heard the latch of the sturdy wooden door slide open. In the nine-by-ten room she observed a large, cluttered pigeonhole desk and a long bench propped up against the back wall. In the opposite corner, glowed a potbellied stove that gave off an odor of hickory bark and cow chips. Ruby put a handkerchief to her nose. *I'd know that smell anywhere.*

Extending his arm, the man said, "Howdy, my name's Jake Rivard."

"I'm Stephen Meir and this is my wife Ruby, and son, William."

Jake plopped down into his spindled office chair so hard it caused the spring at the bottom to complain. "Gotta remember to oil that someday." He motioned for them to take the bench.

"Now, you folks just fill me in on how come you decided to come out our way. I'm fixing on writing me a book someday." He smiled broadly and nodded his head at William. "Figure it'll give my great grandchildren something to read. I've got me near a hundred pages in my diary about folks like you crossing this land." Shrugging his lean shoulders, he peered at them over his spectacles, his sharp blue eyes taking in their appearance. "How far south you hail from, anyway?"

"Emerald, Kentucky." Stephen spread a blanket and placed the squirming William down on the wooden floor with his toy horse. Then producing a clean hanky, he coughed and wiped his mouth.

"Expect this here snow is something new to you." Jake said.

"We get some at home, but you're right, we've not seen the likes before. How long does it last?" Ruby said.

"Oh, it'll probably be gone soon enough. It's just a late dusting. How long you and your missus fixing on staying?"

"We are planning to homestead a section of land," Stephen said.

She shut her eyes to lock out the memories of her husband's attack that had caused the sudden move to a drier climate.

He had come in all excited. The producer from California had liked what he saw. His moving picture machine was a success. They were going to be rich. Then it happened. Red spots of blood dotted the carpet of the parlor floor. Blood was everywhere, all over his freshly starched shirt and his creased trousers. His face had gone white before her eyes. She looked down at her hands, not wanting this man to see the fear in her eyes.

"I sized you up for more of a store keeper than a farmer. Mighty hard work, homesteading. You know anything about farming and cattle?"

"No. Say, you mind if I light my pipe?"

"Na, go ahead, never did take up the habit myself."

Ruby worried her bottom lip. She didn't care for the way Jake shook his head at Stephen. Well, her husband could do anything he put his hand to doing. "My husband is extremely capable. He's a graduate of University of Louisville, and he'll adapt himself to handling a few cows without difficulty."

Jake leaned back on his chair, and his seat bobbed like a cork on the sea. He surveyed her coolly. "I meant no disrespect, ma'am. I'm sure with those credentials he'll be more than equipped for the job.

"But if you came, like some folks do," fixing his gaze on Stephen, "for health reasons, well, farming and ranching is pretty hard work, even for the fittest." His face softened as he watched William crawl toward his parents, clutching onto the long and well-worn bench seat. "If you find that farming gets too hard, let me know, I might be able to find some work in town for your husband."

"I might just take you up on that," Ruby heard Stephen say, and something within her made her grab William and cuddle him a little more tightly.

"Well, I'd best get back to my paperwork so that we can get out of here at a fitting hour." Jake swiveled his chair around to tackle a stack of papers. His arms stopped in midair. "Say, there's a section of land that's abandoned, got a house on it already. Mary, the lady I was telling you about that runs the only boarding house in town, will know how to contact the fella that it used to belong to. You'll probably be able to see it soon as the roads are passable."

He pushed his papers into the various pigeonholes of the desk. "Can't concentrate anyway." He swiveled his chair around. "Can't wait for Mary to see what the storm blew in. There'll be good jawin' tonight round the old stove."

Chapter 3

May 25, 1917

R uby pushed her reticule aside causing William's porridge to topple over the bureau. Milk, sugar, and all. "Ugh…" She lifted her last clean blouse that had fallen with her bag, now wet with the mixture. William crawled over and slapped his fingers together, then swished the milky-white mixture with his hands and knees. The six weeks of confinement in their tiny room at Mary's boarding house had been insufferable.

Mary tried to make her feel welcomed in her house, but she yearned for a home to call her own. She told Stephen if he found a stable with a door—well, Jesus was content to be born in one and she'd be happy to set up housekeeping in it.

William happily slapped his hands in the milk and cereal. She sighed. It had to be better than this. Their hotel door flew open.

"I've found our land and I was able to pick up the homestead rights. See, here's the deed!" Stephen swirled her about the piles of shoes and cases that peppered their small living quarters like mounds of ant hills. William squealed delightedly then muttered, "Da-Da."

Stephen stopped in mid stride. "Did you hear that?"

She smiled with maternal pride at her young offspring. "What do you expect from a smart little boy like ours?" She glanced down at the mess. "After all, he's already finger painting."

"Three blessings in one day." Stephen smiled, holding his son at arm's length. "You want a bath now that you're done with finger painting?"

She felt like a schoolgirl as she probed Stephen with a dozen questions. The noise of William playing in his bathwater didn't hinder her visions of her dream home. Pictures of frilly curtains with matching tablecloths rose like the steam and bubbles of William's coos and laughter about her.

"Wait until you see our new home." Stephen was elbow deep in suds and spattered the small community bath room with water as much as his son.

"We'll leave after we get William dried and dressed."

"Now? I was planning to have you see it after I fixed it up."

Over the next thirty minutes, Ruby dressed William and mopped up the spilled porridge.

"How long has this homestead been abandoned by its former owners?"

"Don't expect much. After all, it took me a month to hunt down the previous owners." Stephen snatched an armload of clothes and dumped them into the trunk. "No one has occupied it for a year, it's run down and it doesn't compare with the big house. It's a square, wood-framed home that, at most, measures nine-by-ten."

"The big house was too big." Ruby planted an affectionate kiss on Stephen's cheek before throwing more clothes into their trunk. "Oh, don't worry. I am sure it is better than what you're telling me."

Julie Ann's scowling face appeared before her. Oh, how well she remembered. Her mind had traveled back in time like a lost refrain of a soulful ballad many a lonely day waiting for Stephen to find their parcel of land. There had been little else to do, and she'd thought plenty about their years in the big house with Stephen's sister, Julie Ann.

Stephen brought her back to reality with a jolt. "I'll go see about getting our horse and wagon ready."

Ruby peeked through the shades of their room. "Why, it's going to be a gorgeous day, just look at that sun. Why not move in now? I'm sure it's bigger than this."

Stephen's thumb and forefinger pulled at his chin thoughtfully. "We could pick up a few household things we'd need on our way out of town. But I was planning on cleaning it up for you and William first."

"Oh, don't worry." She knew full well her husband's cleaning abilities.

"This is our new home, let's clean it together." Ruby laughed. "Do you realize that after eleven years of married life this will actually be our first home together?" She felt his rough wool coat beneath her cheek and hugged him closer. A home they could call their own. God is good.

His thick hair, sharp eyes and strong jaw molded a handsome profile. He was too strong to be sick. Besides, Stephen wore age well. Humph, why couldn't that be said of her? She touched her nose self-consciously. Oh, well. "I know it might not look it, but I have most of everything packed already and by the time you get back with the buckboard, William and I will be ready."

Above the clanging of lids and pots and pans, she heard him chuckle. She turned, blowing a loose curl from her forehead and slammed down the lid of their trunk with a thrust of her wrist. A home on the prairie to call their own; her prayers had been answered. Now she and Stephen could begin their journey of love.

With his hand on the doorknob, he smiled and said, "Well, I guess the decision is settled in your mind."

Stephen strolled across the street to the livery, his silky blond hair blowing wildly in the breezes. She touched the pane of glass gently with her fingertips. Even the sight of him sent chills of delight coursing through her veins. "Oh dear, he should be wearing his hat," Ruby murmured. "Mother always believed in dressing to meet the weather." Tears peppered her eyes at the thought of home and the smell of honeysuckle vines and blossoming dogwood trees and azalea bushes at Shushan. She missed her mother, sisters, and brothers terribly.

She dabbed her eyes with the end of her apron. She'd tried to keep herself busy so thoughts like these couldn't invade her heart.

Her life at the big house hadn't brought any fond memories. Only her staunch loyalty to Stephen bridled her tongue.

What she'd envisioned as married life became a fairy tale dream. She'd grown wiser and had come to realize that happy-ever-after blissfulness was a state earned and reached only after years of understanding and giving on both ends between a man and a woman.

Her thoughts were pulled into the current of memories of her first year of marriage. The pride she'd felt to bear the Meir name, walking from room to room of the huge mansion. Oh, the grandeur of it all, how her friends would envy her. Their bedroom alone took half of the third floor, and their attached bath had a tub and sink made of real marble.

Papa Meir felt the house should rightfully go to his namesake. He'd left Stephen's twin sister, Julie Ann, with the summer home and a trust fund that provided quite a sizeable nest egg, though it had never been revealed to Ruby just how sizeable that nest egg was. Papa Meir had not left Stephen any monetary substance. "A man's not a man if he can't make his own living."

He had provided for his son the foundation for that monetary substance by putting him through the best university money could buy. For the first two years away from home, Stephen had fought the heavy chains of his father's rule and relied heavily on his cousin, Karl, to bail him out of many a hard month when he had wasted away his allowance. Karl faithfully encouraged his carefree cousin to try harder and had stayed up nights helping Stephen cram for exams.

Friction between father and son continued. Upon Stephen's graduation from the university, he decided to begin his own motion picture studio in California. All he needed was a cash advance toward his business enterprise.

Papa Meir thumped his large fist down on the big oak desk in defiance. "You'll not waste my money on such a foolish venture, moving pictures indeed. I sent you to that fancy university to get some brains and here you come back with a head full of foolishness."

When Papa Meir took his last breath, Stephen's name wasn't spoken or summoned. Only Julie Ann heard the last whispered orders of this intolerable Englishman who'd carved his fortune out of an awakening county and controlled his emotions with an iron will.

Not even Julie Ann could change Papa's will. It was unsettling for Julie Ann to learn that the final judgment of their father's would touch her with the icy fingers of realism from the depths of his grave. The big house had been her life, her nucleus, and she wasn't about to give it up so easily. Ruby should have warned Stephen, but she was little prepared for the strong will of Julie Ann.

Smiling down through the window, Ruby watched the golden head of her husband reappear out of the livery. He looked up then and pointed toward the red buckboard and two chestnuts that were being harnessed. *I just wish Stephen hadn't sold the mansion to Julie Ann outright, not until we knew for certain we would like it here.*

Julie Ann had not hidden her delight. Her ample arms encircled Stephen's neck, almost burying him beneath their layered folds. She kissed him soundly. "Oh, dear brother," she clutched the deed to her bosom. "I'll never forget my dear, wonderful brother."

"Humph!" Cousin Karl murmured to her. "With Stephen selling dear sister this house for half its value, I wouldn't forget dear brother either."

Ruby couldn't help wonder where this would lead them. Stephen was so kind hearted and generous. Money was always a secondary item to him. A discerning person could sense this immediately; only Ruby never dreamt they had anything to fear from blood kin.

❦ ❦ ❦

The wind swept across the prairie wild and bold. Ruby tightened her scarf and made sure William's ears were covered as well. He was prone to earaches. His small stubborn chin turned away, and his little hands attempted to snatch the hat off his shaking head. "No."

"Yes," Ruby said, equally obstinate.

Stephen laughed and chirped to the horses. "Giddy up here, William wants to see his new home."

Ruby strained to see past the horizon as the deep crystal blue sky above them melted into oblivion beneath the pale green budding of spring. The land stretched before their eyes in endless miles. No buildings etched a wooden patchwork against the fair blueness of the sky. Only the endless sea of pale green, an aqua-green carpet with only an occasional splotch of bold wild flowers dabbed a splash of color in the sparse landscape.

"Strange," Ruby mused. Only the rattling of their buckboard disturbed the sereneness of the plains. "I've just noticed something." She turned to

Stephen, her palm still raised to her forehead against the bright rays of the sun. "I have yet to see one living thing in the hours of our traveling."

"Mmm." He glanced at her, his eyebrows puckered, as if he'd bit into a sour apple. "When you come to homestead a section like this one, it takes time for people to domesticate it."

"But, Stephen, where are the birds? Why is it so quiet?"

"You got to have trees for birds."

"Yes, of course." She swept her arm across the landscape. "That's why this reminds me of the ocean." A lone building appeared, as if from the ground itself. "Look. Oh, let's stop and see if anyone is at home."

The horses' hooves pounded across the drive and the wheels grated loudly, almost as loudly as her pulsing heart.

"Whoa." Stephen drew up. "Hmm, this is a sod house."

"That's…dirt?" Stacked like cards on a table, the sod walls met a dirt roof. The roof was sprouting prairie grass. There were curtains in the soddy and real paned glass. Ruby jumped down from their buckboard and yelled, "Hello, anyone home?" No answer. A clothes line fluttered in the breeze and a bird cage dangled to the left of the door. She knocked. "Hello? We're your new neighbors come to visit."

Stephen, carrying William, joined her. Only the soft groaning of the wind met her repeated cries. Silence.

"Look here." Stephen pointed to a wooden sign. "This here was recorded to me, being John G. Niehardt's words up Nebraska way and I felt inclined to repeat it here; 'To the sod house settlers. What a breed they were—those sod house settlers. Color, creed, possession did not matter. Everyone was poor, but none a pauper. Can it be they were richer for having little? Can it be they were wiser for knowing less?'"

Stephen pushed opened the door. Dust floated down on them. She observed a dirt floor, a wooden table and cupboard, and bunk beds. Its former occupants were evidently in a hurry to leave. Dust rose about her skirts. She coughed. "How did their food not taste of—"

"Look, they left their plates, even their bedding."

"Maybe they're just away for a time, visiting neighbors?"

"Or else they were city slickers," Stephen said. "And had enough doing without and went back East."

Ruby stepped outside and inhaled deeply. How would they survive out here amidst this sea of grass all alone? "Stephen, is all Colorado like this?"

Stephen laughed. His mirth carried upon the unending wind. "Hardly, most of it is full of trees, like Kentucky, only the part we own is on the prairie. Be patient. We'll be on our homestead soon. We have a beautiful view of Pikes Peak. Folks say that on the hottest summer day, you can look over and still see snow on the top of that peak."

"Oh? Why would I want to see snow?" Ruby replied as Stephen helped her up to her seat in the buckboard. "I never did acquire an attraction for it, especially after our train ride here. But I wonder." She looked down at William and chuckled. "Could we climb up there some time? What an adventure that would be."

"Sure, in fact there's supposed to be a road up there. Only right now the townspeople told me that it could still be impassable with winter snow. There are families living up there right now."

"You mean living up there away from everyone?" She could hardly believe that anyone would want to be shut off from civilization for months at a time.

"Yes." Evidently Stephen shared her views for he stared ahead, shaking his head sadly. "Mr. Yates down at the general store says there are at least three families of white folks and none know how many Indians. They stay up there six, eight months out of the year, not able to come down from the mountain peak till the pass is clear from snow. Sometimes up to June."

"Indians?" she murmured, feeling queasy down in the pit of her stomach. Her mind's eye pictured that grizzled-looking white haired man on the train.

"Oh, you don't have to worry about them; the Indians there are mostly half breeds, part Indian and part Mexican or white. But Mr. Yates said that we should keep a sharp eye out for the Mexicans. Says they're a funny lot, usually don't bother the homesteaders much, but to let him know if we have any trouble with them."

Stephen fell silent. He stroked the thick leather reins with his thumbs. "The livery man in town told me it was a lot harder than most expected, homesteading out here, especially for the women. I just hope I didn't make a mistake, bringing you and William half way across the country, and for what?

"Doctor Luke gave us no guarantees that this climate would help cure me. I may have sold the only thing I had to give you and William after my death."

She hugged him to her, as if to block out his words. He was always the cheerful one, so dependable. He was her and William's anchor in the upheaval of this world they lived in.

"I couldn't live without you, and God knows this. He promises never to give us what we cannot handle. 'There hath no temptation taken you but such as is common to man: but God is faithful, who will not suffer you to be tempted above that ye are able; but will with the temptation also make a way to escape, that ye may be able to bear it.' 1 Corinthians 10:13. So please stop tempting the devil and hush such talk."

"Sorry, I don't mean to worry you." He kissed her forehead. "You have more strength of will than you give yourself credit for. Guess I'm just a little homesick."

Slapping the reins, he said, "Giddy up there. I never dreamt that after four years of college I'd wind up being a farmer, and the worst thing about it is I'm probably greener at it than most eighteen-year-old boys."

"Collina could help you there." Ruby chuckled. Just thinking about her stubborn-headed sister made life brighter. It had the same effect on Stephen, for he laughed.

"It's going to be awful lonely for Mother with Robert gone. At least Jessie and his family are close by and working well with Skeeder."

"I don't think Collina will ever make a farmer out of Austin. His heart just isn't in it. It wouldn't surprise me none if he hightails it up to the Appalachians someday and we never hear from him again."

"Collina would never do such a thing. She'll stay close to home, just in case Mother needs her. But just the same, with us moving to Colorado and Myra and Clem in Detroit, Shushan won't be the same."

"Did you ever think that the McConnells would migrate across these United States?"

Ruby's thoughts wandered back through the span of years she'd not bridged for ages. Back to the time of her father's death and the appearance of Rough Rider Franklin Long. He'd been the first stranger outside of MacDuff County she'd ever met and her sister's first love, only that love wasn't meant to be.

"Shushan." Stephen turned. "That's the name your father named his Kentucky homestead on the climax of the Civil War?"

"Yes, and he took his covered wagon with his six white horses to Tennessee to propose to our mother."

"That must have been some proposal."

"According to Mother, it was a dandy." Ruby sighed. "On Pa's deathbed, he had Collina promise to oversee the estate the way he would."

Stephen's bottom lip pushed forward. "Collina wasn't but a—"

"She'd just turned sixteen years old. But her grit and determination sustained the farm and kept my seven siblings from entering the poor house." Ruby rested back on the wooden buckboard. "I was afraid you might join the cavalry and follow that gallant Franklin Long you were so taken by at Rose Baker's debutante ball."

"Franklin Long had a way about him. I don't blame Collina for falling in love with him. I think every person that shook his hand wanted to be like him or at least have some of his charisma rub off on them."

Ruby looked out over the sea of grass and sighed. "Franklin never returned to Shushan after the war—"

"He was at Shushan's auction."

"He was?"

"He bought Proud Lady. He'd changed. The war does that to men." Stephen searched the horizon.

"I'm glad you were past the enlistment age." The expansive sky immersed their tiny wagon in its omnipotence.

"It's a young man's army."

"Life's consequences often change the course of a person's life." The rough dirt road tossed Ruby to and fro, nearly bumping her offspring from her lap. She moved William onto the seat between her and Stephen. "So Sis married Austin Blaine whom she swore she'd never marry. And him the complete opposite of my ambitious sister."

"Austin's got the charm of a backwoodsman and knows how to spark the ladies. Collina was too naïve to know how to avoid his snare."

"I know," Ruby said. "He'd won himself the reputation of being quite a ladies' man in MacDuff County, much to my sister's regret. She thought she and the Good Lord could change him."

"I approve what Billy Sunday said on that topic. 'You can't measure manhood with a tape line around your biceps.'"

"My favorite is, 'Going to church doesn't make you a Christian any more than going to a garage makes you an automobile,'" Ruby chuckled. That preacher has a unique way of delivering God's message."

The hours bumped along slowly as loneliness swept the endless miles of prairie, a sensation of confusion and uneasiness whirled inside Ruby as dust blew every which way. She tied a scarf about her hat and covered her cheeks. Still, they stung with the sharp minute particles as her eyes teared with the brightness of the sun. Dear Jesus, what would become of them? Now she was the stranger, a foreigner amidst the prairies of Colorado.

Chapter 4

July 11, 1919

Where's Stephen? Late afternoon and still no sign of her husband. He had taken that mail route job Jake Rivard offered him to supplement their dwindling bank account. Stephen lost a sizable amount of cattle during their first winter because of the record snow storms that swept the prairies. He was forced to build a larger barn and more shelters for their horses, dairy cows, and cattle. The hot, dry winds in the summers had parched last year's crops. What next?

Only the noise of the wind sweeping like an iron fist across the plains pounded a reply to her question. Like silent ghosts whisking around the frightened bodies of their cattle, their large, shadowed forms moved about the paddock, their dust-covered heads lowered against the spirals of dirt funneling in and out of their forms, tossing particles of grit into their eyes and nostrils.

She checked on William. How he could manage to sleep through this astonished her. But she thanked the good Lord for small miracles.

"I'm just prolonging the inevitable." Their cow needed milking and their cattle needed hay. Humph! I'll not let some wind scare me from doing my chores. She stepped into her boots and tied a scarf around her head, then bolted out their cabin door.

Ruby threw open the barn door, dropped her bucket, and milked so fast the cow didn't raise an eyelash. She tossed hay to the milk cow and their horses, snatched what eggs there were from her laying hens, and hurried to the barn door. She wedged the barn door shut with her body and then latched it. The wind howled like a lone wolf about her form as it whipped around the barn in a demonic frenzy. She was hard pressed not to fall over. Pure will moved her legs forward. William was alone in the house.

She coughed. Her nose breathed in more dust than air as she wiped at the tears dripping from her eye lids because of stinging particles, she made the last yards as a sprinter would, toward the house, careful not to spill the foaming milk in her bucket and the five eggs cradled in her basket. The door fought her efforts to open it. Once open, she had to lay her body weight against the wooden apparatus to shut it.

A wailing gust of wind rattled the rafters of their little cabin, and dust particles floated downward. Would the roof hold in this wind? William! She ran toward her son's bed. His little snores comforted her and she smiled. Only a toddler could sleep through this. She pressed her face against the one window that graced their cabin. Still no sign of Stephen.

He'd promised her that if the storm became too severe, he'd turn around. The dust storm, now in its third day, had blown and tossed everything not fastened down securely. The hours ticked by. The stormy gloom cloaked their little cabin like a villain's cape.

It felt like eternity to Ruby as she pressed her nose against the windowpane, faithfully watching. Six hours had gone by since Stephen's departure. She'd prayed for her husband's safety and for this storm to end before all the crops he had diligently sown were lost in a sea of grit and dust.

A noise. Was it his truck motor? "He's here!" She danced a jig. Then looked again, the movement flickered away as another gale blew against the house. "Oh, Lord, did I only imagine it?" She stared into the darkness.

"There!" She laughed, there it was. Stephen's truck pulled up in front of the barn. The black Ford was an inch thick in the sandy grit. Stephen climbed out. He ran into the barn, his coat tails flying in the strong gale, his hands laid around his goggled eyes as he fought his way toward the shed. It was just like her husband to think more about the livestock than his own health.

"I can't help worrying about him, Lord." She bustled about her little kitchen nook starting the burner and producing a bucket of water from beneath the sink. Filling the small tea pot, she set it on her lit plate and ran back to the window. "He never knows when to quit." Most farmers on the prairie felt it unnecessary to house their beef cattle, but not her husband.

Money was often hard to come by, hence the reason he took the mail job. That proved an adventure in itself. But with the war rolling to a close, Stephen was thrilled to acquire the first news of what was happening in Europe and more than willing to tell his neighbors about the news. Stephen had become a sort of Paul Revere of Las Animas.

The stamping of feet outside the door told her that her husband had arrived. She flung the door open enjoying the embrace of his tall, thin body against hers. The wind immediately snagged the handle, and they leaned their bodies against the wooden door.

"Whew. That's some wind." Ruby turned.

Stephen was caked from head to toe with layers of the gritty substance, and when he dropped his heavy mailbag, dust rose like a cloud, floating about the room. She removed the dishrag she'd thrown over her shoulder and brushed Stephen off. Dust flew everywhere, caking the wood floor and layering its gritty residue on the table, chairs, and curtains.

The little teakettle, as if not to be outdone, sent its whistling message through the dimly lit cabin interior.

"I'll get that." Stephen hurried toward the sudden disturbance.

Walking toward their bedroom, Ruby peeked into the dim room. William slept soundly through the howl of the wind beating against the wood frames and shutters of the cabin, filtering its fine particles of dust through the cracks of the cabin walls.

"Oh, Stephen, will this wind ever stop?"

He nabbed a bar of soap and a towel and walked toward the sink. "Soon. It has to stop soon. I've got to get some of this grit off my face before it chokes my throat dry. I feel like I drank a gallon of it already." Filling a bowl with water, spilling some in his haste, he lowered his head into the pan and scrubbed, then grabbed the towel Ruby offered. Wiping his face, he said, "Neighbor Stiles said that a funnel cloud was sighted just north of here."

"Wait, don't use that towel, it is full of grit." Ruby opened a curtain and from the bottom of the neatly folded towels, handed him a bright blue one.

Stephen smiled at her rather sheepishly. "Sorry dear, guess I should have listened to you. I didn't really do much good out there."

She stopped what she was doing. For her husband to admit she was right meant he'd come face to face with trouble. "What happened?"

"What you see out that window is mild to what it's really like. Wasn't any way I could get the mail through. I couldn't see five feet ahead of me. If it weren't for the fog lights on my Ford, I wouldn't have found my way back. I did manage to make it to Mr. Riker's, and I gave him the package he'd been waiting for.

"But, as for the others, well, I'll have to try Monday. At least our horses and the milk cow are faring well in the barn. I don't know how you managed to milk them in this! You should have waited for me." He waited for her response. Ruby didn't feel in the arguing mood and shrugged her shoulders.

"The cattle are holding their own. I couldn't get them any water. I did manage to move a roll of hay out to them. That is, if the wind doesn't carry it to the next homestead, they'll have something to eat."

"Stephen, do you really believe our neighbors expected you to deliver their mail in this?"

He kissed her on the forehead. "A man's got to try. It was worth it, just to see Mr. Riker's face." Stephen chuckled. "He went pale as the backside of a ram, and his lower jaw quivered like a jelly fish when he saw me climb up his front steps."

Ruby shook her head, knowing of Riker's itchy gun finger. "Bet you were sorry you scared him, too."

Stephen tilted back his head and laughed.

"Hush, you'll wake William." She placed her hand over his mouth. It's not like Stephen to poke fun at anyone. Bewildered at his condescending attitude, Ruby said, "What's come over you?"

Stephen plopped down into a nearby chair. His head bent over, resting in his hands, his shoulders rocked in stifled mirth.

"Stephen?" Ruby couldn't contain her curiosity any longer. Bending down, she pried Stephen's hands away. "Now tell me what's so funny?"

"He almost made you a widow, Ruby. Said that if I wasn't dead, well then he'd fix it that I soon would be! And then he raised his rifle and got a bead on me."

"Oh!" Ruby gasped. "What's so funny about that?"

Stephen lowered his head, his shoulders heaving with mirth. "That's when my college years paid off. I started reciting the Gettysburg Address, and old Riker said, 'Well, that's got to be Stephen. No other man in these parts knows how to put them fancy store-bought words together.' His eyes nearly popped out of his head. He was looking at me so hard, then he said, 'Nope, don't know anyone down under either that does.'"

Ruby laughed then, shaking her head at him.

"You can't imagine how I looked. I still had my goggles on, and I had an inch of sand all over me, even inside of my mouth, and in that hazy light, old Riker's bad eyesight did the rest."

Ruby wiped the dust off the table before getting out her china. She poured steaming tea into a cup and opened the lid of the pot of stew. "Well, this better let up soon, or else we'll all be looking more like the dust we were made of."

"Oh, I forgot, I've got a letter from home. It's here somewhere… Here it is." He paused only to hand it to her and dipped again into his mail pouch. "And I picked up a paper."

Stephen flapped the creases open as he walked over to the table. He took a bite of stew, chased it down with his tea, then read, "'On June 28, the Treaty of Versailles was signed.' Hmm, I don't like this. The German people are a proud lot and this strips them of some of their choice farmland and some factories." He slapped the paper. "Look here. Their navy is confiscated and they've limited its army. Besides that, the Allies expect them to pay back their war debt because they declare Germany is solely responsible for the war."

"Hmmm…" Ruby mumbled, sitting in her rocker, only half listening to him. Her eyes were glued to Mother's letter, busy reading the news from home. "Ahhh…" She gasped. She dropped the letter in her lap, feeling as if Mother's words had burned her hands instead of her heart. "No! This can't happen."

Stephen hadn't noticed Ruby's upset. He was too occupied with the current news and eating his dinner.

"How in the blue blazes do the Allies expect Germany, a whipped and depleted country, to pay all those billions of dollars back? Congress has refused to ratify the treaty."

The wind howled about the corners of the little cabin; the lantern light flickered. The devil had managed to find a toehold into the McConnells' hearts. "Satan's stomping through Shushan with his dirty boots," she muttered. "What next?"

She covered her mouth. She mustn't say that, nor think it. They weren't Job. God wouldn't allow anything bad to happen to them. Her hand quivered as she picked up the letter. Courage. "Stephen, put your paper down and listen please…

"Daughter, and dear Stephen, I have some grave news. Collina has typhoid. Beatrice had ridden up for a visit and found your dear sister all alone.

"Austin and his two girls were nowhere to be found, and dear Collina was out of her head with the dreaded fever. Beatrice found a copy of divorce papers signed by Austin and a copy of the homestead deed signed off by him and Collina. We just don't know what to make of it all. Pray and pray hard that Collina will find the strength to get well.

"Oh, and in case you have not received my previous letter. Scott had an appendicitis attack. Pray that Doc can save him. Doc and I thought it was typhoid, but sadly, learned too late that it was not. Doc Baker is afraid it has ruptured. May our good Lord give us peace over our terrible mistakes."

Stephen knelt before her, holding both her hands in his. "We will pray for Scott…and your sister. Lord, we ask for Your mercy and Your healing grace on Collina and Scott. Lord, we claim James 5:16 'Confess your faults one to another, and pray one for another, that ye may be healed. The effectual fervent prayer of a righteous man availeth much.'"

Ruby sobbed quietly. Only the beating of the wind on the walls disturbed the stillness between them. Stephen's next words sliced through the distance of years and miles. His words echoed her thoughts. "I never thought Austin would do that to Collina."

Ruby leaned her head back on her spindle rocker cushion and closed her eyes. She wished she could shut out the bad news. That her younger and fun-loving brother wasn't sick and her sister had a happy-ever-after marriage like she. "I just can't believe this. Austin said he'd love Collina till the day he died…and he bespoke his wedding vows at our wedding!"

She squeezed her eyes shut from another onslaught of tears. "Remember that night at Aunt Louise's Christmas Ball?"

"When your aunt asked us about our relationship with Jesus?"

"Yes. You and Bo declared your dedication to the Lord, and Austin said something like 'Always felt it would prove more advantageous for me not to make God too happy, nor the devil too mad.' I got a sinking feeling right here." She cupped her hands around her abdomen, reliving that moment. "It goes to show you what the devil can do to a person's love. What is Collina going to do now? I wouldn't want to live if something ever should happen to you!"

Chapter 5

July 12, 1919

I t was hot, so very hot. Collina didn't have enough spit in her mouth to swallow. "Water, please…" she cried. She was in a pig wallow. She couldn't breathe, her face was covered with slimy mud.

"Collina? Can you hear me?"

She struggled. Someone gently wiped her face, but the stench was in her mouth, her eyes, her nose—such a horrendous smell, and the pigs were all over her, and she was getting pushed down into the mud; it stunk, oh, how it stunk. She fought. Frantic to get out. She had to get out, she had to get water, she had to get away from the pigs and that terrible odor.

"Easy. You're safe. You're at Shushan."

"Mother?" she whispered. The smell was gone now, but the thirst remained. "Water, I'm so… thirsty."

She could feel the rim of a cool glass touch her lips. It stung.

"Remember, just sips."

Obediently, Collina drank, then lay back on her pillow, fighting sleep with all its demons. The smell of ether and lye soap mingled with tobacco and mint whiffed past her nostrils. The combination could mean only one person. "Doc?"

Doc Baker placed a large forefinger and thumb on her right eyelid. She could see the light that explored the depths of her pupil. "My head."

"This will take just a minute. Looks pretty good. Does your chest hurt?"

She shook her head. "Mother?"

"Yes?" she said, taking Collina's hand.

Doctor Baker pulled out his stethoscope, clipped the ear pieces into his ears, and ran knowledgeable fingers along Collina's abdomen. "Tell me if this hurts."

"It hurts." Spasms of coughs racked her lungs; her head throbbed.

"I'm going to make you something to take away that pain in your head. It'll send you to dream land. You'd like that, wouldn't you?"

Collina nodded.

"Sis, it's me, Bugie. Can you hear me? Please get better." Beatrice laid her head on the edge of the bed and wept.

Collina placed her hand on Bugie's silky hair. "Just like an angel's. There, there, don't fret."

Mother cried into her handkerchief. "I've just lost Scott to a ruptured appendix, and I can't lose Collina to typhoid!"

"Scott?" Collina rolled her head. No, not my dear sensitive brother.

"We'll just have to wait and see. Nothing anyone can do until the fever subsides." Doc placed something bitter between her lips. "Good, now drink it all. This should make her rest better. More chance of her body fighting the typhoid if she doesn't toss so much. Just keep her warm and put as much fluids in her that you can. What she needs more than anything now is a desire to live."

"Austin," Collina muttered. She heard Doc, heard her mother. Her eyelids felt heavy; she tried, oh, she needed them open.

"I went through hell when Mary died," Doc said. "I blamed Austin for my baby sister's death for a time. Then the truth hit me like a lightning bolt." Doc threw his stethoscope into his bag with a vengeance. "A little part of me always held resentment for Mary because she married Austin against my wishes.

"I'll never forget how Austin followed me around from cot to cot, wringing his coon hat in his palms, pleading with me to hurry because Mary was in labor and needed me. I loved it. I wanted to humble those proud shoulders of his. But, it turned out, it was me who needed the humbling. Collina, she was a breath of fresh air for me. You know what she said, Maggie?"

Her mother only sobbed.

"'That Mary was ready to meet Jesus, only we needed her goodness here. That maybe some of it would rub off on us.' Why if she hadn't dragged me out of Skeeder's cabin that day, I never would have realized the truth."

Doc's steps reverberated on the wooden floor. His arm knocked the windowpane. Was Doc resting his head on the glass? Was he crying too? She struggled to open her eyelids.

"Austin did love Mary. He tried to do right by her. And Austin loved Collina, too. He risked his life in that swamp to save her. I don't understand why some people can never do right, only hurt the ones they love most. I've got a feeling they end up hurting themselves more.

"Maybe it's a demon, or their own weakness makes them unable to fight temptation when it comes. Maybe they got a sprinkling of God's word, or enough of the Bible to make them feel good, but not enough to know how to battle the evil one and are unequipped to fight the battle against the flesh… 'For the good that I would do I do not: but the evil which I would not, that I do.'

"My own proud heart would not give me rest until at last I sought the forgiveness of my Lord and Savior, Jesus Christ. It was a comfort knowing the apostle Paul had his thorn in the flesh, too. Yet, he considered it a way of growing stronger. 'I take pleasure in infirmities, in reproaches…in persecutions…for Christ's sake: for when I am weak, then am I strong.'"

Collina felt her mother remove the now hot cloth from her forehead, heard the cool water flowing through Mother's fingers. Collina wet her lips. Mother wiped her face with the cloth and then the welcoming coolness met her burning temples.

"'The highway of the upright is to depart from evil: he that keepeth his way preserveth his soul' Proverbs 16:17. God knew your heart, Doc. He knew your conscience wasn't severed, so He could pester the living daylights out of you until you relented and repented!"

Mother removed the cloth and gently kissed Collina on her forehead. "I will pray for Austin, may our Good Lord forgive him. And forgive me for judging him. But I can't help feeling that he and Carrie are formed out of the same worldly mold. They want to use God as their fairy godfather, seeking their own pleasures and not God's will for their lives. They lust after what they don't have and when they get it, it'll always be not enough." Her mother's voice grew quieter. "Was Carrie carrying his child?"

Is that what happened? Collina searched her memory.

"She's pregnant." Doc's voice was low and thoughtful. "I doubt Austin knew what kind of trap she'd set for him, him getting her that way."

Collina turned her face. She had warned Austin about Rosa, but failed to see the snare Carrie planted. Her head spun out of control.

"Come on Doc, we can have some coffee and cake in the kitchen before you leave for home." With her mother's words, she felt herself drifting far, far away.

♥　♥　♥

"I'm so thirsty." Collina moaned. Her tongue touched her cracked and bleeding lips. "Water." She felt her eyelids fluttering. She lacked the strength to open them. It was hot. She had to find Austin. She had to tell him it wasn't his fault. That smell...the swine were back. They were everywhere, pulling at her skirts, keeping her from Austin.

Face down she fell. She'd tripped. The swine were walking on her! Gagging, she clutched her throat, spitting out the mud...no, phlegm. She had to find Austin—but the swine wouldn't let her up.

She couldn't yell. Their smell was horrendous. There was no escape but through the mud, through the long dark tunnel, to that flickering ray of light.

"Collina. Collina, wake up; its Mother."

Austin was waiting for her. He stretched out his arm, his palm open to her. "I know I'm a poor substitute for a husband; you deserve better...always remember you were loved by me."

"Come back!" She was a fingertip away from him. He leaned closer, his handsome, dimpled grin, his sparkling eyes glowed into hers. Someone shoved her away. She was falling. Twirling into the blackness.

"Oh, you're so hot. Dear Jesus, please, I can't lose her, too." The cool water Mother bathed her face with felt good. "You're burning up. I'll go see if Bugie can overtake Doc."

Mother's footsteps pounded to the beat of her throbbing head. So quiet. The pigs had stopped grunting. Franklin was here. His eyes as blue as the stripes on Old Glory, his hands comforting. "Don't ever take true love for granted, Collina." Tears formed pools in her throbbing eyelids and the salt stung her eyes.

Austin stretched out his hand. "You're my wife." Far, far away she fell into the awaiting abyss.

She was in the cornfield; Franklin was there with her. He was holding the mustard seed. "Nothing is impossible—if you have faith and believe."

She was dancing, dancing in a flowing gown made of starlight white and glistening gold. In a faraway distance, bagpipes played "Minstrel Boy."

"Love, like a budding rose can never too quickly reveal the flower, that is, if it is to last, for all things worth having are worth waiting for." Back, back into the fog Franklin rode, galloping up Shushan's hills until the mists engulfed him.

Chapter 6

July 12, 1919

The late afternoon sun fell on Franklin Long's tired shoulders. He closed his eyes, allowing the sun to bathe his face with its warmth. He favored Michigan's summers over the other seasons in Detroit because of the memories he treasured in his heart.

He envisioned the rolling green hills of Kentucky. The warm mists rising from the valleys of MacDuff County in the early morning breezes. The mares and foals neighing to one another. The foals, all legs, frolicking amidst the clover and bluegrass. Upon the wings of spring, breezes of wild honeysuckle and crisp dogwoods had filtered through his cabin window. Oh, he could still imagine its sweet aroma. How the coffee had perked merrily when he entered the big kitchen. The thick bacon and sausage frying in the black cast iron skillet made his belly ache with desire. The soft velvet notes of Collina's laughter as her quick steps tapped the stairway.

What has happened to that man?

Jane often asked him that very question. He still had his Rough Rider's uniform tucked away in the closet. Jane knew of his previous life and ghosts of the past that often haunted his steps.

Franklin blinked. He reached into his pocket for his keys. Looking back was something he'd told himself he must not do. Springs and summers were the hardest. He could never hear the first song of the robin without thinking of Collina. He looked up approvingly at the bold black letters across the door, "Long's Tool and Die Shop." Yes, this was his life now. He wasn't rich, but he was turning a sizable profit. His right hand fumbled in his breast pocket for his watch, 5:45. "Mmm…" His meeting had gone later then he planned. He was already fifteen minutes late. "Melissa will be wondering what happened to me."

He picked up his stride, his walking cane aiding him in hiding the limp he detested. His wife, Melissa, had wanted him to drive their new Dodge four-door sedan the two blocks to work. He knew she was embarrassed over him. That she didn't want the neighbors to see him limping to and from work like some old man.

Still, he preferred his Ford Model T. He didn't care for Dodge's gearshift. Melissa and George, their boarder, said the Dodge sedan was modern and Franklin needed to change with the times. Melissa and George appeared inseparable and enjoyed driving about town. Melissa attracted loads of attention, motoring about in her fashionable furs during the winter months, and her stylish hats during the summer months as she promoted the women's suffragist movement. George, whom Franklin paid to be his wife's chauffeur, drove Melissa around in his dashing motoring togs and provided Melissa with the added allure of prosperity.

"We must keep up appearances with our affluent neighbors and change with the times, Franklin," Melissa had said.

During their earlier years, Melissa was a flighty thing, always looking to him to decide even the most trivial of matters. Even the problem of what to make him for dinner frustrated her beyond words, and there was many a night he had come home to a cold stove and even colder wife. She fussed and fumed at him, begging for a cook to end her frustration. She had complained so about his income being too inadequate for her needs that he had consented to her whim of filling the empty rooms with boarders. Well, not really plural, for Melissa had found just one that met her expectations.

During the first five years of their married life he had hoped for children. But Melissa felt too tied down with all her housewife duties as she called them. So he had hired Clara to do the cooking and cleaning and Jane managed the day-to-day running of the large three-story brick.

Franklin felt assured this would make his wife happy and she would want to settle down to the task of child rearing. He smirked. That had been the beginning of his problems. Melissa, instead, kept coming up with the most outlandish things to fill every waking hour. Parties of every sort filled the calendar, and Franklin was hard put to keep up with her. Her days were spent shopping for the right gown for the evening's festivities. He hardly cared for these new fashions. Narrow skirts and jackets with low waistlines, showed much too much of a lady's figure and left little for the imagination.

He paused his stride, looking with concern down at his gold watch, 5:50. His eyes registered the time but his mind was far from it. "If only I knew she wasn't just looking for an excuse to be with George again." He chuckled. He had nipped that in the bud. He'd given George a loan to go back to Germany. George had talked of nothing else since the war's end. Well, next week, George would be but a memory to the Long household.

Franklin picked up his pace again, his legs easily lapping the gravel sidewalk. He'd told Melissa to be ready by 6:00 and they would have a quiet evening out on the town together, just the two of them. He'd made all the arrangements, dinner at Pierre's and the theater afterwards. Yes, Melissa would be pleased. He didn't want to be late and have her think he wasn't looking forward to the evening as much as she.

As the large Victorian house loomed into view, he hurried up the steps. Clasping the brass knob, he thrust the glass carved doors open.

"Melissa, I'm home!" The large marble foyer echoed her name. Oh, he'd forgotten she didn't like him yelling her name like that.

Hmm…Awful quiet. "Where is everyone?"

"Me? I mean, I'm here, Uncle Frank," came the small voice of Jane's daughter, Dawn. Her long flowing hair flying after her nimble feet, her arms wrapped around her text books. "Oh, Uncle Franklin you've been working much too long." She reached for his hat and cane. "Mother says that's a sure way to sickness. The influenza epidemic at the hospital I work at is seeing more and more cases. Oh, and you'll never guess what happened—"

"Dawn?" Her mother's voice interrupted her from one of the rooms upstairs. "Is that you I hear doing all that chattering?"

Dawn smiled back into Franklin's laughing eyes. "Whoops," she whispered. "I'll tell you later."

Franklin patted Dawn on her shoulder. "Dawn, promise me you'll never cut that beautiful hair of yours into that newfangled bob."

"No, never, I promise."

They were not blood relatives. Franklin was an orphan and had acquired Jane and her infant child, Dawn, after his Rough Rider friend, Deerhawk, died at San Juan Hill. Still, they were his only family.

Reaching into his coat pocket, he pulled out a handful of peppermints. "There you go, for the best girl I know in this whole world. Though I doubt you are as happy to see them as you were as a child."

"Thank you." Dawn kissed him on the cheek. "Oh, Uncle Franklin, I love you so much. I can't believe that Aunt Melissa would—"

"Dawn!" her mother yelled. Her moccasin clad feet making no sound on the hard wood floors. "Uncle Franklin's tired from working all day and being up half the night."

His eyebrows rose in amusement that she had noticed the late hour that he and his wife had returned from a cocktail party. "Dawn's helping me forget just how tired I am."

Nevertheless, Jane's display of emotion was unusual. Without another word Dawn hurried to the kitchen.

Jane took his suit coat, avoiding his eyes.

"Are you holding secrets from me, my dear friend?" Franklin unbuttoned his stiff collar. "I'll never get use to these things. Perhaps I did make a mistake, Jane. I thought I had finally been accepted into high society. But I don't feel it. I feel..." Franklin shrugged, not wanting to say the obvious to a fellow Indian. "Where's Melissa? I promised her dinner and the theater tonight."

"Oh." Jane put a hand to her mouth.

"Something wrong? Don't tell me she's still has a hangover from all that champagne she drank last night?" Franklin smiled, the thought delighted him, for then Melissa became more human and not the snub-nosed society person she'd become. Perhaps she'd prefer to spend a quiet evening home. He knew he could use the rest.

"No, Melissa was fine after her noon supper. She gone."

"Gone? Gone where?"

"My Dawn has been too much in the way this day."

Franklin crossed his arms. Jane was hiding something. But what? "Jane, why don't you start from the beginning?"

"Mrs. Melissa, she say we go or she go." Jane's chest rose and fell heavily. "Mrs. Melissa say she...found my Dawn meddling in Mr. George's room and she told me."

"Let's back up here." George's room was on the third floor. Franklin could see no possible reason for his wife to even be up there. Melissa hated stairs. She had complained more than once about them. "What was my wife doing up on the third floor?"

Jane traced the black pattern in the Indian rug with her moccasin. "My Dawn said she heard a strange noise, so she went to investigate... and found Mrs. Melissa and Mr. George together."

Franklin absently reached into his pant pocket clasping his twenty-dollar bills between his knuckles. His chest ached with remorse. He hadn't known how to tell Jane what he suspected for months. How could he tell her? He looked down at the woman who had saved his life. Glad that the truth was freed. "Yes, Moonwalker, tell me all."

Melissa had wanted to distance herself from Franklin's past and Indian heritage. Especially that an Indian family lived in the same house with an affluent society lady of a prestigious family. Jane smiled. Franklin had not used her birth name for many years.

"Deerhawk would be pleased. You have been good to Deerhawk's daughter, yet my husband's heart would cry for his blood brother now." Her eyes grew moist. "Mrs. Melissa is not a good wife for you. She has committed a grave sin beneath your roof, and now she has run away with whom she committed it with...Mr. George."

Jane bowed her head. "My heart is weighted with the burden of lies I have hidden from my friend. I hoped that Mrs. Melissa would come to her senses and stop the affair she was having with this German." Jane placed her hand over her chest. "My heart is saddened for the love you have abandoned."

He stepped back and sunk heavily into the nearest chair. The truth was now in the open. He had never told Jane, yet she knew.

"Your love for power and wealth has overshadowed your love for this farm girl you have not returned to."

Franklin looked down at his empty hands.

"Your heart has grown old and empty these many years," Jane said. "The love of money has proved a delusion."

"Jane speaks the truth." He felt poorer now than when he had been but a half-breed bound for New York's harbor.

"Well, it's best for everyone that Melissa and George are gone," Franklin muttered, drawing out the wrinkled bills. "I marked my money, I was going to confront her....See, there's my mark. That German was paying me board with my own money." He laughed bitterly. "Imagine that. And I paid him to drive my wife around and then gave him a loan to sail back to Germany—with my money and my wife! What an idiot I am."

Jane nodded.

"Jane, you should have left me where you found me on Cuba's bloody battlefield."

"No. You've made wrong turn, time now to get back on right path."

Franklin grimaced, recalling the green-eyed spirited brunette he had loved most of his life. Collina McConnell. She had married Austin Blaine years ago. "Dear friend, I doubt the path I should have taken still exists."

He quietly exited the back door and strolled around the spacious grounds of his estate, stroking the black leather covering of the Bible Collina had given him before he left for Cuba. He'd worn the pages of it with diligence while convalescing; however, when wealth and position had been obtained, he hardly touched the pages.

He'd forgotten to bring his walking stick and stumbled on a mound of dirt near a boulder. His Bible fell to the ground. He reached to pick it up. Hebrews 4:12 jumped off the page at him. "For the word of God is quick and powerful, and sharper than any two-edged sword, piercing even to the dividing asunder of soul and spirit, and of the joints and marrow, and is a discerner of the thoughts and intents of the heart."

It was finished. His deception was complete. He had duped himself. Jeremiah 20:7 came to mind. He lay prostrate, sobbing. "'Thou art stronger than I, and hast prevailed...' God, You knew the intents of my heart all along. How can I judge Melissa, when the love I held for her was never true? We were two conniving individuals, using each other for social and material gain."

The words he had said to Collina that fateful day after the auction convicted him. You don't love me enough... "Lord, I see now I didn't love You enough to obey and follow You through the laborious recovery of my war wounds. Not even the prosperous years You bestowed to me: why didn't I return to Your loving side?"

He knelt, feeling the wet ground through his trousers. A picture of the young farm girl Collina came unbidden to him. She'd lost her father and bore the weight of a farm and nine siblings on her thin shoulders. She knelt in a desecrated cornfield and asked God's forgiveness. He'd thought it ridiculous. He understood why she wanted to throw away her father's mustard seed—the emblem of Matthew 17:20 and this Irishman's faith. God had not healed her father. What good was God?

Franklin slapped the boulder. The rock's granite mass unaltered, but his hand ached now. "My pride and arrogance are shattered, my worth and work all for naught!" This wretched body of his, his wealth he connived for, an empty tomb of worthlessness.

"I repent, Lord, yes, of all my filthy sins. I ask for Your forgiveness I do not deserve. By faith I receive Your love and grace." He rose to his feet, clutching his Bible and looking up to the heavens. "I have Your peace and the happiness of knowing the promise of being with You in eternity to guide my worthless days until they are extinguished—yes, this hope I have as an anchor of my soul. Amen!"

Chapter 7

July 13, 1919

uby surveyed her house in the first sunshine they'd had in days. She was amazed at how wind could destroy all the efforts she'd made toward cleanliness. She'd finally found something that could do more damage than Stephen to a polished floor. The coffee made a merry bubbling noise on the stove. She coughed from a spray of flour that floated upwards as she pounded the biscuits in a frenzied effort to have them in the oven before—

"Is breakfast ready?" Stephen stomped the dirt off his boots and walked up. "I finished the barn chores. We'd better get a move on or we'll be late for church."

She cut the biscuits and placed them on the cookie sheet and shoved them into her oven. She hadn't planned on going. Her little cabin was in shambles, and she just couldn't leave it that way for one minute longer. "You and William can go without me this Sunday; I've got too much to do." Turning her back on him, she broke the eggs into the ready frying pan. *There, now I said my piece.*

Stephen rested his hands on her shoulders. Giving them a squeeze, he turned her around, smiling down at her with that big lopsided grin of his. "We've all got to go together as a family. We need to thank the Almighty for seeing us through the bad times as well as the good ones. Your work can wait. It'll be there when you get back."

"Yes, I heartily agree," Ruby said.

"Good." Stephen turned to leave.

"But that's what I'm afraid of." She slapped the eggs onto the plates. A quizzical expression filmed his eyes.

She walked over to her curtains and hit them with her spatula. Dust floated aimlessly about the sunlit room. "That this grit and grime will be this way when I return."

There was no swaying Stephen once he got hold of something. God always came first with him. She grumbled to herself as she tried to find something to wear that was not caked in the thick grit that managed to filter itself through the cracks of the cabin. Cleanliness is next to godliness, and she should be staying home and cleaning this mess up, not traipsing off to church.

She climbed in beside Stephen on the black leather seat. A cloud of dust puffed up when she sat down. She coughed, waving her gloved hand before her nose. "I bet they don't even have service today. We'll be the only ones foolish enough to show up."

Stephen ignored her. Instead, he patted William's knee, who sat between them.

"Mommy?" William said, looking up into her furrowed brows.

"Hush, William." She was in no mood for his questions this morning.

"What's wrong, Mommy?" He placed a hand to her protruding bottom lip.

Stephen headed their truck down the road to town. "Nothing that a clean house wouldn't correct, son."

❤ ❤ ❤

Ruby watched Samantha Ferguson's round face grow a deeper shade than normal as she whispered the story told her by Mary Mayas. The congregation knew little about the widow Mrs. Jones. Only what Doctor Walker had told them the week before Mrs. Jones had arrived, that he had hired her as a part-time nurse who would need a place to live. Recently widowed, she had six small children. The men of the congregation had moved a nine-by-twelve one-room house onto a section of land and had stapled it down.

64

Ruby could still hear the apprehension in Stephen's voice as he told her. "They shouldn't have done that house like that. One big wind will blow it over." Ruby nodded, but had secretly thought, I'm just glad that house is done and Stephen's back home.

"Really," Samantha Ferguson whispered, "how could a lone woman hope to succeed out here? Unless she plans to live on the charity of her neighbors. Oh, here comes Widow Jones now."

Ruby took in at a glance Widow Jones' soiled and faded dress and patched shoes.

"Mrs. Jones," Samantha said, slightly winded, "this here is Mrs. Ruby Meir. Her husband helped staple your house like my Jake. I've been trying to tell her what you told Mary Mayas. Well, perhaps you could repeat the news?"

Ruth Jones smiled at Samantha then Ruby with a radiance that seemed to transfigure her homely face. Ruth's tall, big-boned body perched one small toddler on a hip, and another clutched her homemade dress. She patted each head with an absence that told the viewer that here was a woman used to giving without thinking.

Unlike other widows with children, her shoulders weren't bent, nor her head cowed. She met Ruby's cool stare with a smile as she began her story in a soft drawl that matched the cool rushing of a river stream deep in a shady wood. It was the back-home drawl of Ruby's beloved hills.

"Well, I guess I'll begin like I did the first time I told my story. North of here, we didn't get so much of that dust storm you folks did. I was looking out of my east window with my Bible in my lap telling the young'uns a story about Jesus when I happened to look up, and then I saw it. The clouds had been moving along mighty funny for quite a time, and then the old funnel began to appear slow like at first, then its long snake of a tail began to swirl this way and that way.

"I got the children off my lap right quick. But what was I to do? Where was I to go? No storm shed, no hole dug for my little ones. I started to cry. Then I noticed my Bible, it had fallen from my lap, was opened to Psalm 102. 'Hear my prayer, O LORD, and let my cry come unto thee. Hide not thy face from me in the day when I am in trouble.'

"I prayed. I told the children to kneel down beside me, and we all faced the window. We watched it come. The big long funnel was heading straight for us. Well, my heart was a thumping wildly and seemed to be in my throat. Still, I kept right on saying those words.

"My children were as good as gold. Not a one cried or yelled. Guess the oldest might've been too scared and the youngest probably didn't know what to make of the whole thing. I watched and I prayed, then suddenly that old big tail just lifted up. We gasped in amazement, and the oldest children ran to the other side of the house. 'There it goes,' John, my oldest yelled, and sure enough it was moving right on down the same path behind the house."

"Now how could anyone not believe in a God when you hear that story?" Samantha Ferguson retorted, waving her arms.

Widow Jones just smiled that radiant smile and said, "They'd just ask, why didn't He spare my husband?"

After a long silence Samantha Ferguson said, "What do you tell them?"

Widow Jones looked at Samantha with her piercing brown eyes. "I tell them God did spare John. He died of consumption. It's an awful painful illness. We hoped this dry climate might heal him; it seemed to for a spell." Ruth Jones blinked, then said, "He's spared from his pain and suffering. He's with Jesus in paradise now. True, if I had a place to go that would have been safer than where I was, I would have gone. But I didn't. So I prayed to God to spare my life and my children's from that twister. But if He decided not to, that was His decision to make. For I'm only a servant and have no right to ask an Almighty God what His purpose might be."

Widow Jones took Ruby's hand and shook it, smiling. "So nice to meet you, hope to see you again real soon." With that she walked away with her toddler on her hip and her little girl still clutching the folds of her dress.

The Widow Jones' faded dress and worn shoes looked less dingy in that spark of sunlight that filtered around her. The sharp words Ruby had thought rested on her heart heavily.

Suddenly, every nerve in Ruby's body seemed strung to bow tightness. Consumption. She wrapped her arms around her stomach. She and Mrs. Jones had more in common than she had realized. Would the years be kind to Stephen and her, or would Stephen's life end like the Widow Jones' husband's did?

Chapter 8

July 8, 1922

R uby's vegetable patch was coming along nicely. She leaned on her hoe and dabbed her brow with her apron. What she wouldn't give for a tree to give her and her little garden a bit of shade from this hot sun. The little tomatoes and cukes were growing, as were her Kentucky Wonder Beans. She chuckled. Wait till the neighbors tasted her Kentucky Wonders. Mother had sent her the seed. "That is, if I can keep them watered." They needed rain, or else Stephen's wheat and corn crop would never grow past seedlings.

Ruby stroked her bulging stomach. Stephen said with America's economy prospering, he stood a good chance of getting his loan. The stock market was booming.

She'd seen in the *Ladies' Home Journal* that a new dance called the Charleston had become quite the rage. Calling the 1920s "The Jazz Age." All she knew was that she wasn't going to shuck her Victorian undergarments and don those short skirts…at least not until she had this baby.

William, who was helping her, now stopped to rub her stomach. "I want me a little brother, Mommy."

"Really? And how old are you?"

He held out five dirty fingers. "I'm five."

She laughed and kissed the dirty hand. "Remember to ask Jesus in your prayers tonight."

Their neighbors, the Fergusons, on the next section, had two boys, John and James. William would stand and watch them play together and squeal in delight at their antics.

Looking up into the cloudless sky, her eyes fell on the tall mountainous region of Pikes Peak, etching their jagged peaks against the blue aqua of the sky. Her gaze landed like a homing pigeon on the burnt and parched landscape of straw-colored grass and barren dust patches where only the hearty sagebrush would grow.

The lowing of Stephen's cattle moved from one dusty patch of grass to another, their mouths and nostrils caked with dirt, looking for something to eat. Even the affectionate Daisy, the small brown and white milk cow that Stephen had obtained for their dairy needs, struggled to keep the weight on. They supplemented her with a diet of hay.

William ran over to Daisy, his bare feet not making a sound on the dusty ground, and climbed onto her back while she lay in the dust. He lay over and petted her neck, resting his little head pensively down near hers. Oh my, they needed rain badly. Without it, life here would surely wither like their crops.

Stephen and Jake Ferguson had left early that morning for Las Animas to see about obtaining a loan. If this crop should fail, they'd need a loan from the bank to stake them through the winter and money for new seed come spring.

She didn't like accumulating more debts, but Stephen had no choice. Why wouldn't the rains come? Day after day they and their neighbors searched the sky for the clouds. But instead, the unrelenting sun baked down upon the parched land with a ferocity that even Colorado's old timers could not recall.

In 1876 Colorado had received statehood and like the California miners, mining booms at Leadville and Aspen filled their bucket of opportunity to overflowing, and by the 1880s, Colorado's population had increased dramatically. Colorado's virgin soil produced record crops for farmers and this newly formed state became the place to be. Now the rich pockets of Colorado's mines and soil appeared unwilling to release its wealth.

The ranchers blamed the farmer for the miles of barren wasteland, once rich fields of wild grass as far as the eye could see where their cattle could graze and flourish. Now the land wasn't fit for cattle or crops and both farmer and rancher faced a foe, economic ruin.

Much to Ruby's delight, a prairie dog, wide eyed and inquisitive, popped out of his hole just a few feet away from her. He looked up at her, dodged back into his dwelling, only to peek out again and gaze at this strange thing that kept a fixed eye upon him.

"William, come see the little prairie dog." Only the wind moving the dust about the dry earth responded. Looking over at Daisy, she was about to call her son again, but William no longer lay upon the gentle cow. Where could he be? That's not like William. He was a good and obedient boy, but like all children, he did have his times of disobedience. She rounded the corner of the house to see him using Stephen's shovel, hoeing a bit of earth around one wilted and sadly thirsty weed. Ruby smiled and said in her most grateful tone, "My, what a helper William is, but Mommy doesn't like it when you wander and don't tell her where you're going."

"Me want to help." He attacked the hard earth with the zeal and exuberance of youth and in his eagerness, chopped off the top of the weed. He picked it up between thumb and forefinger. "Is it dead?"

Ruby laughed. "Here, I've got a turnip green sprout you can plant."

Across the western horizon, the thunder of hooves sent a cloud of dust behind their steeds. Soon twenty odd riders were pounding the ground near her so hard, she felt the vibration. Dust flew like puffs of clouds, caught in the wind. She blinked, unable to make out who the riders were. William ran to her, clutching her skirts, and it was all she could do to walk, William's hand in hers and her other hand cupping her large abdomen.

She made it to the front of their veranda, into the partial shade that the wooden frame provided. A big black horse rose up on his hindquarters and pawed the air with its hooves. She wrapped her arm protectively around her son.

Brightly clad men with big sombreros cantered up to her. One was very slender, almost feminine in appearance. Ruby grinned. It was indeed a young woman mounted on the most exquisite horse she had ever seen.

The woman smiled back. "Forgive me, señorita, if I do not dismount, but I am afraid that my Eldoblo is a little feisty amidst all these mares."

A man rode forward. "You should not have ridden him this day; he is much too wild."

The girl ignored him. "We are looking for water with which to refresh ourselves and our mounts."

Turning to William, Ruby gave his little hand a squeeze and whispered, "You stay here on the porch. Mommy will be back quickly."

The Mexican girl waved her back. "There are many hands to do the work, see." She waved her arm at the men that accompanied her.

At least a dozen, Ruby surmised, looking into the dark eyes of these long-haired and heavily mustached men. A rough looking group, made fiercer with the pistol each carried at their waist and their long leather-fringed pants creating their own cloud of dust behind them wherever they walked. Their boots were adorned with fancy stitching, and around their heels they wore the largest spurs Ruby had ever seen, shiny and as ornate as the big belts and gold-covered buckles.

"Just point to your well and they will draw the water."

Ruby did as she was told and pointed to the east corner of the house. The well was just a few steps from her vegetable patch that she'd so diligently worked all morning on. "Please have them be careful not to disturb my garden."

The girl turned, and Ruby could see the long thick braid of black hair that fell down her back. "*Mi amigos, el pozo está allí. Por favor dibuja el agua.*"

"Thank you." Ruby understood a few words, and after that, she stood looking after their retreating forms, hoping her wishes would be respected.

They passed her in single file, the clanging of their spurs coupled with the howl of the wind. Ruby suppressed the urge to run into the house and bolt the door as goose bumps sprang up on her wet and clammy skin from the sudden iciness of her thoughts. She was completely outnumbered and totally vulnerable. Clutching William's hand in hers, she followed at a safe distance.

"*Un perro de las praderas, un perro de las praderas!*" One said and laughed, pointing to the small hole Ruby had seen the prairie dog disappear into. Now they took the bandannas from about their necks and plunged them deep into the wooden bucket that one of the amigos had drawn. Most of them did not bother to dismount, but stayed astride their horses while a few did the bidding for the others. One boy, who had not yet reached the age to shave, walked over with a bucket brimmed to the top with the cold newly drawn water, lifting it high so the girl would not need to bend too far over.

"*Mi gracias.*" Then she cupped her hands to drink.

"Oh, wait," Ruby moved as fast as she could toward the house. Inside, she poured freshly squeezed lemonade into a mug. The girl on the black stallion motioned for the boy to take the cup from Ruby's hand and he did.

"Mi gracias," she said.

"Would you like something to eat?" Ruby said.

"Gracias, señorita, but we must be on our way. The cattle, they have strayed much in their search for water. We must get them back before the rains come."

"Rain?" Ruby glanced upward, only one small cloud dared to obstruct the parchment of tranquil blue that met her gaze.

The girl laughed. "It comes. You will see." She motioned with her hands that it was time to depart and as quickly as they had come, they left. Only the dust that flew behind their horses' swift hooves told of the flight and the reality that they had been there.

Ruby's legs were shaking as she climbed down from the porch with the hoe in her hand to see how much damage was done to her garden.

"Mommy, I'm hungry," William whined.

"Okay, Mommy will be back in a minute." The prairie dog came to the rescue. "Do you want to see where a baby prairie dog lives, right in Mommy's garden?"

William held his stomach and looked at Ruby imploringly.

"Oh, dear." Realizing her youth was mimicking her.

Then her son's curiosity got the best of him. "Where is the prairie dog?"

Together they walked to the spot. Ruby moaned seeing her small plants limp and lying on the hot soil, yet relieved that only a small portion had been damaged. She'd forgotten entirely her promise to William and set to work to replant the uprooted plants.

"Mommy!" William screamed. "Snake!" He backed away from the snake that slithered out from beneath the porch.

Ruby's heart was in her throat. Her feet felt like they were made of lead. The baby in her womb bobbed and kicked with every step she took. She felt the world had stopped.

The reptile slithered across the dirt. Ruby's arm went out and with all her strength she flung William away from the danger, attacking the snake with her hoe and dismembering its head.

The snake's tail made a noise. "A rattler! It's a rattler! How dare you come after my child." She swung the hoe high over her head dismembering the snake a second time. Again and again she hit it, jumping back and forth, fearful of the writhing body. Finally, it lay motionless. Ruby surveyed her handiwork. "Good!" Five pieces of the snake lay in the dust.

Her skirts were caked with dust, her face black with dirt and sweat. "Good!" She put a hand to her back; her arms were so tired they couldn't lift the hoe to set it on the porch. She broke down and cried.

William looked at her in amazement, pulling on the folds of her dirt strewn dress. "Mommy."

"William." She took his small body into hers, hugging him tightly. "Mommy."

"Dust storms, droughts, Mexicans, and rattle snakes, what more? Oh, when will this end?"

He raised his head. His brows puckering the way Stephen's did when trying to explain away a problem. Patting the shoulder his head had vacated, he said, "Mommy, can I please have my sandwich now?"

She laughed, hugging him close. A sharp pain in her abdomen shot through her body. She doubled over. "Oh, William," she gasped. "Be…a little man and help Mommy…up the steps."

Chapter 9

R uby concentrated on relaxing her stomach muscles and gathered her skimpy reserve of strength before another contraction started. A clap of thunder split the night and then the rain came, pelting their little house with unrelenting fury. She rolled her back as another contraction gripped her body and above the roar of the wind and rain, Ruby screamed.

Stephen ran to her. "I don't remember your labor being this bad with William. What can I do?"

"Nothing." Ruby panted. What had come over her to scream like that? "I'm sorry. The pain is so intense across my back, but once the doctor gets here, he'll know what to do. He'll be here soon, won't he, Stephen?"

"He'll be here any time now and Ruth Jones is coming too. Ruth volunteered, in case there may be complications."

Ruby didn't like the way Stephen said complications, but after that last contraction, she was glad to have all the help she could. Doc could bring the whole hospital staff if it would help her get this baby out in one piece. But the storm… "Do they have a chance? Making it in this rain?"

"If they started before the rain and made it over the Arkansas River…only Doctor Walker may have had to take an alternate route. That could very well be why they're not here yet."

The cool cloth Stephen had wet with the pump water crossed her hot forehead and cheeks, soothed her frazzled nerves and cooled her brow. "That feels so good." Stephen's scrunched face, with a crisscross of wrinkles on his once smooth brow, brought a half smile to her lips. "I feel much better. How is William?" He'd been such a help to her yesterday. Even helping her into bed and then playing on the floor next to her until Stephen returned.

"You don't have to worry about that boy. He's fast asleep. Mom's screams and the Lord's thunder are not going to rob him of his rest."

She rested back on her pillow.

As if reading her thoughts, Stephen said, "We don't need a hysterical boy on our hands, now do we?"

Something felt wrong. Dear Jesus, please help me, she prayed, remembering Collina and how they tried to help their neighbor, Mary, deliver her baby that turned out breach. Mary and the baby had died. Ruby turned fever-bright eyes toward her husband. "You might have to help deliver this baby."

"I blame myself. I should have been here with you. You've started this labor early due to that rattlesnake you killed."

"No, this baby's on schedule and I'm fine." The moaning of the cabin timbers nearly out yelled her. Her hand sought her husband's, trying not to fight against the sudden contraction sweeping her body.

The new puppy Stephen had surprised them with when he returned from Las Animas barked.

"This may be the doctor now." He laid her hand down on the sheet. "I'll go see before Dixie manages to do what you and the storm couldn't." But it was too late, for her son's cries could be heard distinctly through the closed door.

❧ ❧ ❧

Stephen hurried out and picked up their son, carrying him to the window and pressing his face close to the pane. "It's Doc!"

The shrill bark of the new puppy penetrated every corner of the small cabin. "Hush, Dixie, go lie down. Go on, William, and play with your pup."

Boy and dog romped on the floor together. Stephen sprinted into the rain. Small reservoirs peppered the drive. His ankles plunged into a pool of muddy water. Doctor Walker helped a thin-framed man out of his vehicle. Ruth snatched Doc's bag with one hand and with the other she clutched onto a woman's arm. The rain pounded in wrathful fury on the car roof making a deafening noise.

Turning, she yelled, "Help Mable. You might have to carry her."

Stephen nodded. "Go on in the house. Ruby needs your help." He watched as Doc and the frail-looking man followed Ruth.

The woman stared at him blankly. Her face was smudged with mud. Her matted brown hair fell onto her forehead and into her eyes. She was whimpering; her bottom lip trembled with every inaudible syllable.

"There, there, you're safe now. Come on." There was no response. Half-dragging, half-lifting, he got her up and they started walking to the house. She laid her head on his shoulder and he didn't realize until he had gotten her into the house that she was clad only in a nightgown.

Ruth handed her a cup of hot tea. "Here, Mable, take this."

The woman obeyed. Ruth directed her into a chair by the fireplace.

"What am I going to do? What am I going to do?" moaned the woman.

Ruth patted the woman on the shoulder. Turning to Stephen, Ruth said, "Are there some dry clothes she could put on? They lost their home in the flood."

"Why, sure." Stephen walked into the next room. He paused only to notice the doctor bent over listening to Ruby's stomach.

"How's she doing?" Stephen said, noticing how tiny Ruby looked beneath the blankets, her massive stomach strangely askew in comparison to the rest of her body.

Doc smiled. "Not long until William has a little brother or sister."

Stephen searched the assortment of Ruby's scant dresses. He felt sorry for the woman and man in the other room. He buried his head in one of Ruby's dresses, her scent filling his nostrils. Thank you, Lord, for keeping my family safe. Stephen handed the woman Ruby's charcoal gray with purple stripes. It wasn't one of his favorites, but didn't feel the woman would mind.

"Stephen, allow me to introduce you to Mable and John Sweeney.

"Nice to meet you. Go to William's cot and pull the drapes closed so you can change." His voice cracked with feeling, and he hoped she wouldn't take offense at the pity in his tone.

"We'll need a fire started in the cook stove. Doctor Walker will need hot water and Mable and John will need some hot soup," Ruth said.

Stephen walked over and stoked "Old Unreliable," as Ruby called her stove. He put on the soup Ruby made earlier and filled a pot with water and put that on the stove, too.

William pulled at Stephen's trouser leg, holding out his arms. Little bare toes peeked from beneath Stephen's old discarded shirt. Ruby had cut it down to size but had left room for his son to grow into the nightshirt. Dixie nuzzled the small hand that had momentarily disappeared within the too-long sleeves. "No, Dixie," his son retorted. His tousled blond hair fell across his eyes as he stared up at his father.

Stephen smiled, swooped up his son and hugged him close and carried him to his chair. He glanced over his shoulder. "Can I get you anything until the soup is warm? Tea or something?"

Mable's moans echoed in the small house. Not even Ruby's cries brought her out of her reverie. Stephen covered his son's ears and rocked him, watching their closed bedroom door. Mable's voice rose above the howling wind. Stephen would have preferred the wind.

"I'll never forget those waves as long as I live. Why, the way they came through the windows and doors at us, it was like a huge hand of water reaching out for my little Jane—I clung to her…Had her fast to me when…" Wrapping her arms about herself, she sobbed. John went to her.

"Everywhere you looked was water, huge torrents and sweeping currents of it. I reckon the flood Noah rode weren't any worst. Anyway, me and Jane was doing pretty good when a big timber hit me right in the small of my back. It pushed the breath right out of me and then sent me down under. I thought for sure I was done for, but I got myself straight again, and I still had my little Jane by the hand, only her little face was turnin' blue. I tried to get her to start breathing but I was being

78

tossed to and fro so much I could hardly keep myself afloat. I figured if I could reach the shoreline, she might still have a chance. Only there was no shoreline to reach. I kept drifting down the river, the current and waves pushing me to and fro. Then another piece of kindling got me in the arm, hurt me real bad. I couldn't keep myself afloat without my arm. I looked at my Jane and I realized she was dead. I...I let her go. She floated peaceful-like down the river ahead of me." Mable covered her eyes with her hands and cried. "Why, Lord? Why my Jane?"

What could he say? What could anyone say? The angelic face of his sleeping son met his teary eyes. Stephen slid out of his chair and walked over to the corner of the room where William's little bed was, laid him down, and covered him with the quilt Ruby had made out of scraps of old dresses.

He rushed to the stove and spooned out the hot soup. He pressed a bowl full of the warm broth into Mable's hands, wishing he could do more. Mable ignored the bowl. She stared off in a sort of daze.

"John, do you mind? I need to check in on my wife."

"Sure, no problem." John took the soup and moving his chair near Mable's, he began feeding the soup to her. The distraught Mable pushed the spoon aside and stared at her husband.

"John saw most of it, sitting up in his big Colorado pine. Right, John?"

Stephen stopped dead in his tracks. He turned. John's face turned beet red.

John fidgeted in his chair, then muttered something, seemed to change his mind, cleared his throat, and said, "You almost made it. I got down as quick as I could when I saw you were in trouble."

Mable wasn't gazing out into space any more. She was staring a hole through her husband's heart. "John can't swim. He's afraid of water. But I still can't figure that river busting its dam like that. The noise was like, like something you've never heard before. John climbed that pine to see what had happened; only it was too late, too late for Jane and me. The end of the world. It all happened so fast. One minute we were safe, and the next we were thrashing about in the middle of a flood. My baby was six months old. My little Jane. She had pretty yellow hair." Mable's eyes had left her husband. She stared off in the distance and hummed a lullaby. "That's Jane's favorite."

The first cries of Ruby's baby startled them, and something like normality came back to Mable's blank, staring eyes.

Stephen rushed to Ruby's side. She smiled up at her husband displaying the tiny baby girl, all pink and content, lying in her arms.

"You've got a brave wife, Stephen. The baby came posterior, making delivery difficult. The baby was pushing on Ruby's back instead of the birth channel. With the help of your wife and my capable nurse, I was able to perform a safe delivery."

No one had time to tell Ruby about Mable. No one needed to. When Mable came into the room and asked to hold the infant, Ruby read the truth in Mable's agonized eyes.

Mable cradled the small infant in her arms and walked back into the parlor, sat down, and rocked the babe, gazing into her small face. Taking one small hand into her large one, the tears fell. They came like small streams, and then stronger tributaries worked their way down her exhausted face.

John's eyes met his wife's, and Stephen saw that he, too, was crying.

"I'm sorry, Mable. I built that house too close to the river, didn't you tell me so? I was born lazy. I didn't want to tote that water too far and you always needed water. If you want to know the truth about it, I climbed that tree cuz I knew the dam busted and I wanted to be way away from that water. But I never dreamt that the flood would swoop you and Jane away like that. I thought the house would stay," he said, then bawled like a calf caught in a fence, laying his head in his wife's lap. "Can you forgive me?"

Mable patted the tousled head of her husband, her work-worn hands stroking away his tears. "Why, of course John."

💗 💗 💗

John shook Stephen's hand and thanked him for the clothes and food Stephen had given him.

"Don't forget, when it comes time to build that new house, let me know, and I'll come over and help you."

John looked down at his shoes that he'd been shuffling in his embarrassment and nodded his head.

Mable squeezed her husband's arm. "It's hard for John to accept help of any sort."

"Don't look at it like that. It's one neighbor helping another."

"You've got yourself a beautiful baby girl, Stephen." Ruth smiled at him as she and Doc prepared to leave. Her words were still ringing in his ears as he waved good-bye. He was so happy he could burst a button on his shirt. He was the luckiest guy in the world.

He'd fed the cattle while Ruby and the baby slept. Then he could spend the rest of the day with his family. They had decided to name the baby Esther.

The name fit. He smiled, remembering the little hand, not as long as his index finger. Stephen ran toward the barn. Then it happened. He could feel it come from his chest, then it was in his throat. Blood spurted out like a funnel and the only thought that came to his head was Ruby would learn about this one. He'd managed to keep other times hidden. But this one was staining his shirt something awful.

Chapter 10

September 2, 1922

"Where could your father be?" Ruby gently wrapped the blanket around the sleeping Esther in her little wicker bassinet. She half-listened to the conversations around her as she arranged her pies alongside the others at the festival. This done, she gazed over the heads of people crowding about the tables. "Stephen promised me he wouldn't do anything too strenuous."

So absorbed was she, that she hadn't noticed the small man in the navy and gray pin-striped suit hurrying toward her until he was right in front of her.

"Hi there, little lady. Allow me to introduce myself, Tom Tufner."

His sweaty palm touched her shoulder, and in that instant her husband's face flashed before her eyes. "Stephen?"

"He's next to the cattle tent. He tells me you're from Kentucky; so is my wife. I'd like very much for you to come and meet her."

The man's face was two inches away from hers. His was as dried and brown as the leaves that blew from beneath the maples on Shushan on a sunny October day. He poked a small, stubby finger to his ginger-colored whiskers, thin and scraggly and streaked with gray, stroking it like one of those villains in Macbeth.

"You're too pretty to be worrying yourself this way. How can I help?"

"Did Stephen have a little boy with him?"

"A little boy with laughing blue eyes and an impish smile? He most certainly did. Perched on your husband's shoulders and clapping his hands every time his daddy landed another lad into the dunking tank. That sure is a fine son you have there, and what a beautiful baby." He touched Esther's chin with his index finger. "Coochy coochy coo. Stephen told me all about her. Come now, you must meet my missus."

Esther scrunched her nose at this sudden rude awakening. Her mouth puckered into a round *O*. Ruby sighed. She'd just gotten the babe asleep. Ruby gathered Esther into her arms and followed him toward the quilting tent. "Mary, I want you to meet Stephen's wife. This is Ruby Meir and her daughter, Esther."

"So nice to meet you." Mary extended her hand. Her chestnut hair was brought down a little over her brow from a center part and then swept up into pads at the sides to a chignon below the crown of her head. Ruby remembered her mother wearing her hair like that when she didn't want to fuss with it. Of course, Ruby preferred the latest bob. That is, if she ever had a chance to go to a beauty parlor. The closest one was twenty miles away.

"My, what a lovely baby," Mary said.

Ruby got a whiff of vanilla and honeysuckle. Mary's dress of printed cotton in green and white had full, long sleeves and a white starched collar and cuffs over which she'd worn a white apron that covered the front of her bodice and most of her skirt. *I wonder if she made her dress and her apron herself.*

Ruby's hair flopped in the summer breezes like a banner, announcing to everyone she was as frazzled as her appearance denoted. Her apron, once snow white, now bore the marks of blueberries and strawberries, telling this well-presented woman that she—was not. "Please excuse my appearance. I dumped a whole basket of blueberries on myself on my way here."

The merry gleam in Mary's kind eyes told Ruby she was the motherly type and her next words confirmed it. "Why don't you come sit next to me a while, a young mother needs to rest when she can."

Ruby lowered her eyes and did as she was told. "Thank you." She rested her tired back gratefully on the back of the chair.

"Are you staying for the square dancing later? If you are, I can watch your son and daughter while you and your mister have a whirl."

It would be pleasant to enjoy the festivities for a few hours, but Stephen's last hemorrhage had her worried. "It depends on Stephen. He hasn't been feeling well lately."

"Mary, who's this lovely lady?"

A tall, lanky man clad in buckskin breeches and fringed leather jacket smiled down at her. Pressing a thumb to his wide-brimmed hat, he lifted it back from his face. "She's a real looker, ain't she, Mary?"

Ruby turned around to see whom this stranger could be referring to, but there was no one behind her. Noticing the half-smirk creeping over his face, Ruby felt the color rise in her cheeks. Surely he's not directing his off-handed compliment to me? Pretending indifference, she lavished her attention on Esther. She hoped her preoccupation in tending to her infant would abate this backwoodsman's advances.

He placed one leather boot on the bench seat next to Ruby and leaned closer. The strong earth scents of leather and horses engulfed her senses. His deeply tanned face etched with the stubble of a week-old beard came closer as one tanned hand reached for one of Esther's clinched hands.

"Why, she's the prettiest little thing I've seen in nearly a decade." His eyes went over Ruby in frank assessment. "Yeah, might just be as pretty as her ma someday." He smiled broadly at her. "So you're Stephen Meir's missus."

"Buck Briggs, may I introduce Ruby Meir. Her and her mister came all the way from Emerald, Kentucky. They're homesteading that piece that Mr. Warner vacated," Mary said.

"Don't say. Why it's sure a small world. That piece I marked myself." Leaning closer, he said, "How do you like it here?"

Ruby looked sideways at Mary. The forwardness of this man made her uncomfortable.

"Yeah, I marked all these pieces here about, been here nearly a generation now. Good land, now that the Indians have moved on. Some of them weren't bad. I had me a squaw, right good woman, too. She died of consumption."

"There's her husband coming over now."

"I've met Stephen, known him for some time. I was with him earlier this morning."

Ruby strained her head to see were Mary pointed. Buck took his gaze off her for an instant, then whispered close to her ear, "I'll be talking with you later. Right now I've got to go and get cleaned up a little." Moving his boot away from beside Ruby's skirts, he touched his hat and disappeared into the crowd without a ripple in the tide of bodies that filled the grounds around them. Ruby pushed a strand of hair from her warm face and frowned.

"What's got your dander up?" Stephen said.

Mary laughed. "Buck Briggs. He took a real shine to your wife, never seen him act that way to a white woman. But, you know, come to think about it, Ruby looks a lot like his first wife. Course, his wife's hair was darker and straighter than your wife's, but Ruby and Esther are about the same age of his wife and daughter when they died."

Stephen took William down from his shoulders and placed him beside Ruby, then sat next to her.

Tom Tufner's forehead wrinkled up like a shutter on a window. "You know Buck's not a bad sort. He got the Indians not to create an uprising. They didn't like it much, us taking up their land. But they respected Buck. He got the Cheyenne some real prime land, and a good treaty, too. He's a man of his word, blunt though it may be at times. You can trust a guy like that. Got to know him mighty well when he and I were dividing up the land into homestead parcels. He's got hardly any book learning under his belt, but he makes up for it with Yankee sense." Tom nodded toward his wife's knitting bag.

Mary frowned and reached into her bag. "Tom wants you folks to be the first in these parts to hear about him running for office." Mary handed Stephen a sheet of paper with a picture of Tom and his name in big bold letters. "Tom Tufner for Mayor."

"Why, Tom, you didn't tell me you were running?" Stephen crossed his arms, his eyes peeking from beneath his burrowed brows.

Tom stroked his whiskers absently. "You know, me and Mary

was talking yesterday. Stephen, we sure could use a good campaign manager like you. Need to have me what they call back East an election committee, and I need the right one to head it. How about it?"

"I wish I could," Stephen said. "I'll try to help you as much as I can. Right now I'm up to my elbows in work at the homestead." Standing, he offered his arm to Ruby. "We'd better get back to our pies."

Tom shifted from one foot to the other, scuffing the dust with the toe of his shiny leather shoes. "Do you think you could help finance me? Mighty costly going into politics."

"I'll see what I can do, though, right now, to be honest with you, finances are tight for everyone." Stephen shook Tom's hand. "Good luck to you and the missus." He tilted his hat to include Mary.

"It was nice meeting you, Ruby. You stop by someday so as we can chat a little," Mary said.

Tom glanced over his shoulder at his wife, who hadn't stop eyeing him. "My missus thinks I should tell you that running against me is none other than Buck Briggs."

"You mean that brash westerner?" Ruby replied. She couldn't keep the shock of this knowledge from erupting into distaste.

Tom smiled at her. "Yeah, none other. The way people here like him, I've got my work cut out for me." He raised his hand. "I'll be talking to you all later."

Stephen took Ruby's arm and guided her through the growing throng of buyers. "That Buck Briggs strikes me as a good man. He helped me get that loan this summer. Don't know what the farmers would have done if he hadn't come along when he did."

"Oh, honestly, that Indian lover." Ruby promptly covered her mouth with her hand. After all, her grandmother was half Cherokee Indian.

Stephen looked at her in mocked amazement.

"Oh, I didn't mean it like that."

Stephen's eyes arched in questioned indignation. "I should hope not, because the way folks here are talking, he's going to be our next mayor."

"Oh, Stephen, really."

"That man's character speaks for himself. There isn't a soul around that can say one thing bad against him." Stephen nodded. "Buck Briggs is going places and it's all in the right direction."

❦ ❦ ❦

Ruth Jones scooped the sleeping Esther from Ruby's arms.

"I don't know, Ruth, I'd better keep her with me."

"Now, you go on. Stephen sent me to tell you to come and dance with him. Go on and enjoy yourself with that handsome man of yours—before he finds himself another dancing partner. Your son and I will take care of Esther just fine, won't we?"

William looked up from the piece of pie Mrs. Jones had given him and nodded his consent.

"And you can leave that soiled apron with me, too."

"Oh, I'd forgotten all about it." Ruby laughed and handed it to Ruth. Her son beamed at her and said, "Mommy's pretty."

Ruth gave her a gentle shove toward the dance floor. Dubiously, Ruby smoothed her dress and walked out onto the large wood planked floor brightly lit with colored lanterns and streamers for the festivities. The band consisted mostly of guitars, banjos, and tambourines. Couples had formed on the makeshift dance floor and the band was filling the air with disoriented notes as the musicians tuned their instruments.

Ruby craned her neck, seeking her husband's distinguished gait. Why was Stephen so stubborn? Her mind kept going back to the last hemorrhage he'd had yesterday morning and she'd hoped to take him to see Doctor Walker today. Doctor Walker had been tending the Williamsons over the ridge, but Ruth said he was back. She wanted to confide in him about Stephen's recent attack.

Why did Stephen insist nothing was wrong with him? She had tried to have him see the doctor for a physical, but no matter how she pleaded, he firmly refused. Not even her tears, which usually always got her way, would sway him.

At last she spotted Stephen. He ranked as one of the tallest men she knew, especially next to her five-foot-one height. Only, among these westerners, he blended right in. He was standing next to a man who had to be well over six foot. She smiled to herself; Stephen looked rawboned next to that broad-shouldered, deep-chested westerner.

"Ruby, guess who found me?" Stephen said.

Ruby smiled and extended her hand to the man Stephen was ecstatic over. When she felt the large, hard and calloused hand go around hers, she looked up in amazement. The same dark eyes that had smiled down on her a short time ago now grinned back. His beard gone, a white shadow was visible, though hardly noticeable as his strong jaw creased into a million laugh lines. His eagerness and boyish pleasure were evident as he and her husband exchanged tempered glances.

As the musicians began to play, Ruby looked suspiciously from one to the other. "What are you two up to?"

Buck's deep baritone broke the sudden chillness between the three. "I've been talking to your husband. If it be alright with you, may I have the first dance?"

♥ ♥ ♥

Buck Briggs proved to be a gifted partner, graceful for his large build, and talented in weaving himself and Ruby through the intricate dance patterns. Square dances led into waltzes and waltzes into two steps. Ruby strained to see past the broad shoulders of her partner for those of her husband's.

Though their conversation stayed light and humorous, Ruby noticed Buck probing her for more and more information. Did she like Colorado? Had she adapted to the dryer climate? What did she think about the idea of an improved school system? Could she learn to love Colorado and become less homesick for Kentucky?

Half his questions remained unanswered and the other half received noncommittal retorts. What could she say? She couldn't tell him when she didn't know herself. Frustrated at him as well as with herself, she said, "The love I have for Stephen is large enough to encompass whatever state he chooses for us to live in."

89

The music lapsed. She saw Stephen, and shrugging off Buck's hand, rushed to her husband's side. She pulled him toward her. "I didn't come here to dance every dance with a stranger."

Stephen avoided her eyes, his face strangely pale. His lips were a faint purple color and his arm shook visibly.

"What's wrong?"

He pulled her toward the dance floor. "Till We Meet Again" hummed in the distance of Ruby's tumultuous thoughts. The lyrics sent a sudden chill through her body. "Smile the while you kiss me sad adieu…"

Ruby realized she'd been too wrapped up in her pity-me world to see clearly the strained expression of pain on Stephen's face, his labored breathing. She sobbed.

He placed a gentle finger to her lips and whispered in her ear, "I'm fine, Ruby, really, just a little tired. Enjoy this dance with me, and don't worry, my love. I want you to dance the rest of the night with Buck. He's got a fine head on his shoulders and a willing eagerness to change with the times."

Ruby's vision blurred. Stephen's gaze turned ice-blue. "Stop that, Ruby. There is more to think of than ourselves. Our children need us to be strong and to plan for their futures."

She stifled her cry.

Noting this, he soothed his voice. "'Far better it is to dare mighty things…even though checkered by failure…' In this twilight of my years, remember that my victory over this quintessential life—is Jesus. No matter what happens, remember this when you think of me. I have fought a good fight; I have finished the course God has laid before me and I have kept the faith. If the time of my departure is at hand—"

"Stephen, tell me you're—"

"I don't know." He clutched her hands in his, his mouth firm. "What I do know is you need to dance with Buck. And trust my judgment."

Pools of tears escaped her eyes. She nodded and swept the wetness off her cheeks with the back of her hand.

The dancers who glided beneath the moon's glow conjured a faintly whimsical appearance. The reality of her predicament drew her eyes toward the heavens. The stars sparkling in the velvet night shone down with startling clarity. As clear as day, Ruby thought, thinking of Stephen.

Buck was full of stories about the plains. She tried to concentrate on what he said. But time after time, she heard herself apologize to him, saying, "I'm sorry, Buck, would you repeat that please?"

On one such instance, Buck said, "I'm sorry, what did you say?" He, too, was preoccupied with looking over her head.

Ruby smiled. No wonder some of the things he said didn't completely make sense. "So, you're looking for Stephen, too, aren't you?"

"He's a fine man, Ruby."

As the last dance of the evening ended with the ballad of an Indian love song, a gentle tap on her shoulder made her jump. Ruth Jones was standing there. "Sorry, didn't mean to startle you, but I thought you'd like to know, Stephen's with Doctor Walker. Doctor Walker wants to speak with you now."

❦ ❦ ❦

The smell of ether intoxicated her nostrils and she nearly swooned. Buck's hands went out to steady her. "Stephen, where are you?"

Doctor Walker came out of the cook's tent, closing the curtain behind him. "You got a car, Buck?"

"Yeah, waiting and ready for you."

Ruby looked up in bewilderment. "Does everyone here know what's going on but me?"

Doctor Walker drew her into the tent and reached for his stethoscope, bent over, and listened to Stephen's erratic heartbeat. Ruby knelt down beside her husband's cot.

Stephen took her hand and kissed it. "Doc's given me something so I can sleep."

Ruby watched as his eyelids grew heavier.

Doctor Walker surveyed her beneath his bushy brows. His protruding lower lip retreated to normal as swiftly as a turtle withdraws its head beneath its shell. "How do you want it, Ruby? A nice kind diagnosis full of fancy words, or the ugly truth?"

Ruth rested a comforting hand on Ruby's shoulder.

Ruby patted her hand. "Don't worry, Ruth, I'm ready."

Doctor Walker bent over and checked Stephen's eyes. Then straightened his large bulk, turned to look Ruby straight in the eyes, and forced a smile to crease his lips. "He's asleep now. Do him a world of good." Doctor Walker's face contorted into a complex set of wrinkles. He twirled his stethoscope and Ruby realized he was delaying the verdict on purpose. She took a deep, leveling breath.

"I'm afraid what I've got to tell you is not good. After some extensive blood work, though I'm not a hundred percent sure, I feel I must diagnosis Stephen as being in the advanced stages of tuberculosis. Stephen's symptoms are varied. Sometimes tuberculosis patients' symptoms are varied." Dr. Walker shook his head. "I must say honestly, it's hard to determine whether he has consumption or some other illness. This I do know." Dr. Walker now stood over her as if ready to depart the moment the prognosis was given. "Stephen's dying, Ruby. I'm sorry. There is nothing more I can do. We need to keep him as comfortable as possible. I'm not going to give you any false hopes. There isn't anything anyone can do."

"Thank you, Doctor Walker, for being honest." Ruby glanced at Stephen sleeping peacefully. She pinched her hands together. The noise of the festivities added a backdrop of fiendish merriment to Stephen's prognosis and her disastrous fate. Why, Lord? Why didn't You heal my husband? She never felt so alone.

Chapter 11

Ruby glanced over her shoulder, her little framed house a tiny dot in the landscape of the prairie. Had it been a mere two weeks ago when Doc told her the bad news?

Her shoes grated the dry earth as she shuffled down the lane deep in thought. How could Stephen have been wrong? Ruby rubbed her hand along the smooth surface of a massive boulder, feeling the warmth of the stone generated from the sunlight. Stephen had knelt beside this very rock praying to God. She remembered that day vividly.

It had finished raining and the setting sun gleamed just above Pikes Peak. Sunlight shone through the mist, sending silvery beams of light across the tall stalks of corn, gleaming raindrops on their emerald-green leaves. Ruby had run to her garden to see what the raindrops looked like on her azaleas and roses. That's when she spotted him kneeling beside this very boulder. He'd spotted her and motioned for her to come.

"Oh, Ruby, God is good. I'm going to get well now. I've confessed my sins to our pastor and we are claiming James 5:16. 'Confess your faults to one another, and pray for one another, that ye may be healed. The effectual fervent prayer of a righteous man availeth much.' My healing will be a testimony to all unbelievers. Doctor Walker will have to recognize the miracle that God alone is capable of. Because, Ruby, God has a plan for me. He's calling me into the ministry. I pray I'll be everything in a preacher He wants me to be."

"That's just the type of job you'd be good at, too. What with all your book learning and gentle nature, you'll be a wonderful preacher."

Ruby wrapped her arms around herself, falling back into reality like a thunderbolt splits the air. She could still imagine how his strong arms felt around her, making her feel so secure. What went wrong? What was it Mother always said? "The night is always the blackest just before the dawn."

She remembered doubting Stephen's words, wondering if he'd heard from God—could her lack of faith have caused God not to heal Stephen? She strode back to the house.

The bedroom was hazy and warm in the last glow of the afternoon sun as she entered the room. Ruth looked up from the small homemade paper cups she was working over and smiled. "This is a great idea."

Ruby felt a flicker of pride. "This way, as soon as Stephen spits, I throw them into the stove and burn them. I've also been airing out the room and using a lot of lye soap. If you have any other ideas about what I should do, I'd welcome them."

"Did you enjoy your walk?"

Ruby nodded. "How is Stephen?"

"He's been sleeping peacefully."

Stephen's deeply tanned skin and the stubble on his cheeks seemed unbefitting to this outdoor man lying in broad daylight amidst white sheets and linens.

Ruth rose from her chair and walked over and placed her arms around Ruby's shoulders. "I know this is hard on you, especially with that little babe and all, but remember, if there is anything I or my children can be doing for you, why, you let me know."

How could Ruth, a widow with six children to take care of, help her? Ruby felt guilty allowing her to stay the night with so many mouths depending on her. "You amaze me. With all the work you do with the doctor and having six little ones, I don't know how you hold up."

Ruth laughed. "John and Clare, my two oldest, tend to their brothers and sisters. I'm blessed with a half-dozen of the best children God ever gave a woman. Let's have some tea."

Ruby didn't need any coaxing. The supper hour would come soon enough. Ruby poured the tea into her Sunday cups and felt a twinge of pride when Ruth exclaimed how beautiful they were and how immaculately the cupboard and shelves were kept.

Ruth coaxed her to sit down. "You must remember to be careful of your own health. Buck told me to let him know what needed to be done and he'd do it when he picked me up tomorrow."

Ruby looked up from her teacup. Her fingers tapped the rim nervously. She would need help now that Stephen was ill, but she hated to ask Buck. She felt her cheeks growing warm. What must Ruth think? After all, she'd probably noticed her dancing with him the night Stephen took sick.

Ruth gave Ruby's hand a pat. "Buck understands your predicament, and so do I. We all have something in common now, being that we lost our partners."

Ruby felt a cold chill go up and down her spine. She glanced to the closed door of their bedroom. "God's still in the miracle business. 'For God is not unrighteous to forget your work and labour of love....lay hold upon the hope set before us: which hope we have as an anchor of the soul.' So that is what I'm doing, as Paul, a prisoner of Christ Jesus says in Hebrews 6:10, 18 and 19."

Ruth clutched her hand firmly in her own. "Look here, Ruby, this life is hard, hard enough on men, but harder still on the women and children. You can't afford to shrug away kindness. Buck feels for you. Why, when Stephen approached him—"

"What?" Ruby coughed loudly from the tea she had gulped. Had her husband planned her next partner? "I don't want to hear anymore—"

"Just what are your plans if Stephen should die tomorrow? Are you staying here and fulfilling the dream Stephen had for his children? Or are you going back to Kentucky, where there is little future for you or for them but being a burden on your kinfolk?"

The truth was blatantly clear. Ruth was right. Stephen had put their life savings in this homestead. She had made friends here, good friends, and William had grown to enjoy the prairies and spaciousness

Colorado offered him. To go back now would mean defeat, and besides, what would she do back home? Without Stephen, how could she support herself and her children? Her mother had enough on her without three more hungry mouths to feed.

She grimaced. "I can remember what I thought when I heard about you moving here. I didn't know how you were going to manage alone, but you did. And I guess I'd rather stay put and wait and see if Stephen doesn't get better. We came here for his health, you know."

Ruth's eyes were fixed on the ridge of her teacup, her words hesitant and low. "I understand how you feel. I felt that way when they told me my John was dying. When I knelt down to pray that night, I just knew Jesus was going to heal John. After all, God was too merciful to let a man die that had five little ones and a pregnant wife to support. To this day, I still wonder why the Lord had to take him when he did."

Her tender eyes sought Ruby's. "I wish I could tell you that there is hope, but I can't. That man in there is very sick and he's hanging on by a thread. He's living by shear will. But there's no telling how long… it's up to you to decide what would be the right move for your family. Buck's a mighty good man, men like that don't come by every day of the week. Stephen knows that, and he wants you and the children to be taken care of."

A muffled moan escaped through the door of their bedroom. Ruby gave Ruth's hand a comforting pat before going in to tend to her husband. Ruth didn't know Stephen's determination or her Jesus.

Stephen's eyes looked into Ruby's and a smile creased the corners of his mouth. He coughed and a small red drop of blood filtered from the crease of his lips. This Ruby hastened to blot with her handkerchief.

"How are you feeling? Do you want something to drink or eat?"

Stephen tried to mutter a reply, but a gurgling sound was all that came. He motioned toward the small paper cups Ruby had made. She hastened to retrieve one. This she held up to his mouth and he coughed into it. Ruby tossed it into the wastebasket. She would burn them later, like she had the others.

"Did Doctor Walker tell you?"

Ruby nodded slowly. Her first thought was to play innocent, and then something in his eyes told her he knew. Knew better than she or Doctor Walker or Ruth.

"I…thought for sure… for a time… that I was healed." He coughed, and Ruby held out another cup. He rested his head heavily upon the pillows. "Doctor Walker thinks it's…tuberculosis." Stephen reached for Ruby's hand. "You've got to face…the truth. When I leave for heaven… do you want to stay and work the homestead?"

Ruby opened her mouth to speak, but a lump blocked her vocal cords. Only a gasp escaped. She fought to remain in control of her emotions. She wanted to stay. But she didn't want to stay without Stephen. She didn't want to live without Stephen. It was more than she could bear. God, You promised not to give me more than I… She laid her head down on his chest and cried hot aching tears that refused to stop.

"Stephen, I can't, I can't without you. Please get well. Let's pray. God always heard our prayers before. He doesn't want this. He couldn't!"

"There, there." He patted her heaving shoulders. "I don't believe for a minute that Jesus has deserted us, no, not for a minute. Can you stay here and work the homestead? I'd like to see William and Esther get this land. It'll be worth something someday. Buck has assured me he'd take my place. You could marry as soon as I—"

"Never, never! I could never love any other man but you." She was aghast. The man repulsed her. "How could you ever think I could?" Then, seeing the hurt expression that came over his face, she said, "Oh, Stephen. I…I can't."

Stephen stroked her curls. His soft fingers worked their magic on her frazzled nerves, his low, soothing voice sending solace and hope to her throbbing heart. "You're not able to manage this spread and two little children. This is what we'll do. Tomorrow, go into the bank and place our homestead on their For Sale list. Then get us a one-way train ticket home. It's just as well. I had a dream about my sister; Jesus wants me to tell her something."

Stephen smiled. "I'd like to see Shushan, too, one more time before I die. There I met my true love, and there is something impregnable about Shushan. It's a part of God's promise. Collina will know what to do. She's never failed to accomplish the impossible, and I know God's got a plan that will culminate there for you and the children."

That was it. Stephen had the solution to her woes, the finale to the plaguing questions of what to do. Stephen had answered the yearnings of her heart and given her closure.

"Now I think I'll rest a little. I'm so tired."

Had Stephen heard from God? Stephen thought God said he would be healed. Collina...dear Jesus. Was it right for Ruby to burden Collina with her dying husband and two small children? Maybe she should marry Buck...

Chapter 12

The steam from the locomotive sent pasty gray puffs into the sapphire-blue sky as the hum of the engine blended with the voices of the people. From the train steps, Ruby waved at Ruth Jones and her family, Doctor Walker, the Fergusons, Mable and John Sweeney, Mary and Tom Tufner.

"Are we coming back, Mommy?"

"Someday, William, someday, the good Lord willing." The crispness of this first week in October hung in the air like flapping linen on a clothesline. Esther, cradled in her arms, slept. Proverbs 20:7 murmured in Ruby's thoughts. "The just man walketh in his integrity: his children are blessed after him." She hugged Esther close. Oh, my darling. Stephen would have it no other way but to name you Esther. Are you predestined to carry on Shushan's legacy? Is that why Stephen lived to see you born?

Jake Rivard ran down the steps of his station. The locomotive's whistle blew, sounding like a moan of regret and mirroring Ruby's emotions. She waved. Jake's arms went in the air, his arms sweeping above the others who stood below him. He waved the air furiously.

"Don't forget us. We won't forget you!" Jake had proven to be a true friend, finding that mail route job for Stephen and adopting Dixie. William would miss Dixie. He would miss the gentle cow Daisy, too, but it couldn't be helped. She'd not been able to find a buyer for their homestead in time. But she had left it in the capable hands of Tom Tufner.

Stephen acted somewhat disturbed when she'd told him, her conscious pricking her sharply. No matter now, what was done was done.

The big iron horse belched out a loud burst of steam, and the conductor yelled out over the clamor of voices. "All aboard!"

Ruby hastened to find her seat. There Stephen lay on the makeshift bed that Doctor Walker and Buck Briggs had engineered. Buck was bending over Stephen, reaching for his hand. Stephen smiled weakly, lifting his arm in a determined effort to grasp Buck's strong one.

Buck's voice, thick with emotion retorted, "You take care of yourself." Looking to Ruby he said, "Telegraph us when you change trains. Doctor Walker sent word for the town doctor to be available. If I don't hear from you I'll—"

"I'm sure there will be a doctor waiting." Ruby placed a hand on his arm. "You need not worry." She paused. His eyes searched hers. Kind, caring eyes that conveyed their worry for her and the children. "I cannot adequately tell you how much we appreciate your help." Extending her hand, he took it in his, his strong fingers wrapping around hers, firm and secure.

"It was my pleasure; he's a fine man."

Sudden shyness washed over her. Buck had asked nothing from her. He'd done all the giving, even promising Stephen he would marry her if she decided to stay. Stephen had wanted Buck to take over the ranch and sell it, but she wanted distance between her and Buck Briggs, so she had employed Tufner instead. She bowed her shoulders, speechless, choking on her own insincerity.

He left before she could explain, his broad shoulders bending low before the doorway of the train, then hesitated on the other side. Framed in the open gap before jumping from the deck, he nodded before placing his hat on his head. He turned to dismount the steps.

"No!" William ran to him with his arms outstretched. Buck, with tears gleaming down his cheeks, swept the boy up into a grizzly hug. He gently kissed him on the forehead, like a father might. "You're the man of the house now. Remember what I told you." He relinquished her son and was gone. The gray clouds of smoke floated about the gaping doorway. Ruby rushed forward and threw her body against the door. It whacked shut as the train creaked forward, iron on iron. The shrill whistle echoed its retreat. Ruby knelt before Stephen's cot and cried.

"Mommy, I don't want to be a little man. I wants to go home."

Esther, feeling the tension in the air, cried.

Stephen coughed and Ruby hastened to find one of the paper cups she had made for their trip. The eyes that looked into Ruby's were glassy bright, and when she felt Stephen's forehead, it was warm, too warm. *What if he doesn't make it home—what will I do then?*

❧ ❧ ❧

Ruby clutched Esther to her bosom. She'd left William with his father. William was to watch him and make sure he didn't choke. She stared into the fog for a familiar face. Where could they be? A soft misty rain filled the thick air with more humidity, which didn't make the clothes she'd been wearing for two days smell any fresher. Nor did the heavy humidity help her ailing husband who struggled to breathe. Her body ached for a bath, a soft bed, and sleep. Esther had not stopped crying since the train trip began and had refused to nurse. *Mother will know what to do.* Only, she wasn't going home to Shushan. Stephen had a pressing need to see his sister.

"Mrs. Meir, is that you?"

Ruby would recognize that voice anywhere. "Tom! Oh, I'm so glad to see you."

Tom, hat in hand, his six-foot lanky body leaning forward, and his black face beamed back at her. "Well, it's good to see you back home where you belongs. Let's get you out of this rain."

"Where is Julie Ann? Where is the ambulance I told her to summon?" Tom held out his hand. "She's waiting for you back at the house. Shall I go and fetch Mr. Stephen?"

"You won't be able to handle him by yourself; he's too weak to walk."

Tom's bent and arthritic fingers went to his lips. "You say Mr. Stephen's sick?"

"Yes, Doctor Walker diagnosed it as tuberculosis in its advanced stage."

"Don't you worry." His eyes glanced to the crying babe.

She looked at the Ford sedan and gasped. "Stephen and we can't fit into this."

Tom nodded. "I'll gets the ambulance. Don't fret. I'll go right now."

Ruby leaned back against the leather seats of the depot, checked on Stephen, who was now sleeping, and tried to quiet the sobbing Esther cradled in her arms. The shrill cry of the white ambulance came to a screeching halt next to the train station. Stephen mumbled. Tom was beside her, his eyes wide with concern. Stephen coughed. Blood dripped from the corner of his mouth. "You want to ride in next to him?" She nodded, and as the medics picked up Stephen's cot, she grasped William's small hand and clutched her daughter to her bosom.

❦ ❦ ❦

"Now the neighborhood knows what a state my brother is in! Do you think I want that nosy Laura Jane knowing my business? Well, think again." Julie Ann stamped her plump foot in agitation. Her angry eyes fell on Ruby, then rested on Tom. "What possessed you to call that ambulance?"

Ruby stepped forward, her hands drawn into fists by her sides. "I—"

Tom moved in front of her. "It was the thing to do at the time, Miss Julie Ann."

Her large posterior moved like a disjointed spring as she placed a well-manicured hand to her large bouffant hairstyle. "That is going to cause you a cut in this week's pay check, Tom. Now, if anyone comes to the door this morning, tell them I am not accepting visitors. Get their name and I will call them later."

Tom's forehead puckered worriedly. "But what if they come to see Master Stephen?"

"Stephen is not master of this house! You remember that. I am. And what I say goes. Don't you forget that."

She stared at Ruby, as if daring her to complain.

The sounds of Esther, now awake, reached Ruby. She turned and without a word, hastened up the winding stairway.

Behind her, still fuming, lumbered Julie Ann. "The audacity to bring my brother here; do you think I want to get sick?"

Ruby ducked into the door of the makeshift nursery. There in Stephen's old crib lay Esther, all pink and clean in her white nightie. As soon as Esther saw her, she smiled. Ruby hugged her baby close. Not even Julie Ann could take away her joy. But her peace was not to remain.

The lumbered breath of Julie Ann walking toward them and her shrill voice penetrated the air. "Poor little thing, now what's to become of her?" She stroked the wiggly legs and patted the little arms. Esther's small pink mouth puckered itself in a yawn, and Julie Ann squealed in delight. "You precious thing, may I hold her?"

Maybe there was a soft side to Julie Ann that only her daughter could awaken. Sitting down in the rocker, Julie Ann cradled the small head to her large breast. She watched with amusement as Esther looked for her breakfast. "What you need is to belong to someone who can take care of you properly, someone who can give you all the things a little girl should have."

Realizing an impostor, and not her mother, held her, Esther burst into a piercing cry that told the household she would tolerate no one sleeping in when she had not been fed.

Taking Esther from her sister-in-law Ruby plopped down in the now vacant rocker and soon the cries of anger turned into sighs of contentment as Esther found her breakfast with no trouble. Ruby sighed with relief. "I'm so glad to see you eating again."

Julie Ann grunted in distaste. "Have you given much thought to how you are going to take care of her?"

Ruby shrugged. "Stephen's illness came on us all so suddenly."

"Suddenly?" Julie Ann snorted. "You knew he was sick when you married him, and you still had two children by him. What were you thinking? I really haven't the foggiest notion."

Ruby looked up at her sister-in-law in disbelief.

"Don't give me that look. You know what you were after. Well, there's no money to be had. Stephen spent all his."

"You're wrong, Julie Ann. Stephen gave me untold wealth." Bending down, Ruby kissed her daughter's forehead. "Your brother has left me a legacy of immeasurable riches."

"Humph!" Julie Ann pranced toward the bureau. Looking at its mirror's image, she dabbed at her forehead with her embroidered handkerchief. "Of all the impertinence." Her composure regained, she smiled back at the image and patted her hair. "You thought you'd marry back into the society your mother lost when she married your father, but you never will.

"Besides, your mother's people had it coming. I never did think owning slaves was right and because of plantations like the one your grandparents owned, the South nearly lost everything."

"Living in the city has its drawbacks, too, Julie Ann, so I'll forgive you for your shortsightedness. The slaves were a small issue, next to the larger one of our southern states wanting to secede from the Union. In that issue both my father and mother agreed, they did not want Southern independence."

"What do you mean? Everyone knows Ben fought on the Union side and your mother's family were stanch Confederates."

"Yes, but my mother didn't want to see this great land divided. Like Grandfather didn't want to turn his beloved slaves away. They cried, you know. They didn't want to leave the shelter of their cabins, or the security of knowing they'd never go to bed hungry. But Grandfather wasn't left with much.

"My mother had educated them in the cabin Grandfather and Grandmother had shared in the Glenn. Mother gave those who'd remained a knapsack filled with corn bread and told them what fine people they were and that, with the help of our good Lord, they could accomplish anything they set their minds to doing. Then she sent them away with a page out of the family Bible."

"Then your mother had the audacity to marry an Irish immigrant. Those immigrants did the work your slaves were too valuable to do! I still can't believe Ben would join the Yankees like that."

"Father did what he thought was right," Ruby said with a lift to her chin. "He knew the horrors of war from his roots in Ireland."

A smirk crossed Julie Ann's face. "Well, now you're as poor as you were before you married Stephen, only worse off."

Ruby looked at her questioningly.

"Surely you've read the latest medical findings about tuberculosis. It is thought now to be highly contagious." Julie Ann looked down at her with contempt across her unrelenting lips. "It's only a matter of time when all those people who come down with it will be segregated from healthy people."

"If we bother you so, we will leave. Mother will be happy to have us."

Julie Ann's bottom lip protruded. Silence. Ruby could see the workings of her mind and she worried about the outcome.

"Seeing how this disease is contagious, Esther would be better off with me. Stephen has piffled away all that Papa left him. I could adopt her and raise her as my own. She would have the best clothes, the best schools—"

"Piffled?" Ruby's temper snapped. "You mean like virtually giving you this house? He could have sold it for four times what you paid for it. So he has a kind heart. Now you not only want him out of what's rightfully his, but you want to take his child, too!"

"I can see it's no use talking to you, but maybe my brother has at least acquired some sense after his exile."

"Fine. I will take you to him." They walked the hall to Stephen's room in silence.

Julie Ann hesitated before the ash-colored face of her twin brother.

He stirred slightly. His eyes opened and his lips broke into a smile seeing Ruby. Then his gaze swerved to his twin sister. His smile drooped, then his hand went out to her. He motioned for Julie Ann to sit down in the nearby chair.

"You...look well." He spoke with decided effort.

Julie Ann patted his hand. "Stephen dear, do you have tuberculosis?"

Stephen raised his eyebrows. Evidently, her question had caught him off guard. He glanced up at Ruby. "Yes...so...they...think."

Julie Ann locked her fingers in pious prayer, a small tear trickling down one plump cheek.

"Brother, some physicians believe tuberculosis is contagious. That tuberculosis should be confined like smallpox, and dear brother, that little girl of yours should not be in contact at all with you."

He tried to rise. "What…are…you…"

Ruby rushed to circle her arms around her husband and looked obdurately into Julie Ann's eyes.

Stephen struggled to speak. "Do you know…Jesus?"

"What?" She shook her head. She sent him a cheeky grin. "My dear, dear, brother, you need not worry about me, a faithful church member for over thirty years."

Stephen's eyes did not falter. "Have…you asked Jesus into your…heart? John 3:6–8 commands, 'That which is born of the flesh is flesh, and that which is born of Spirit is spirit…Ye must be born again…born of the Spirit.'"

Julie Ann snorted, leaned forward and with snarling lips whispered, "What is your sin? Pride? Proverbs 16:18 says, 'Pride goeth before destruction, and a haughty spirit before a fall.' Or is it, jealousy, my dear brother? Galatians 5:20,21 tells us that jealousies, outbursts of wrath, selfish ambitions, envy, revelries, and the like…'they which do such things will not inherit the kingdom of God.' God does not punish but for a reason." She spat out her words with venom. "You can well see the fruits of my labor have been blessed." She leaned forward. "But, my dear brother, you are being punished."

Stephen nodded. "As Galatians 5:22–24…states, 'the fruit of the Spirit is love, joy, peace, long-suffering…and they that are Christ's have crucified the flesh.' Yes, I'm…a…sinner. So…are we all."

Julie Ann's eyes widened. "Are you insinuating…" Her composure snapped like a dried branch on a tree swept by the wind. "I was going to take that little girl, going to bring her up in a way you never could. She'd have the things you and your silly wife could never afford to buy her. You've wasted away everything Papa gave you. Now Papa's dead. He can't help you, nor can I."

Stephen smiled, visibly unshaken by her outburst. "No…Father will…he's rich. So am I for all eternity. Sister, have you asked Jesus… into your heart?"

"Oh! This is how you repay my charity. I have more religion in my little finger than you in your whole body. Out of my house this instant!"

Ruby frowned at Julie Ann's retreating back. "What is she so mad about? I should think she'd be elated to see how much you love Jesus and that you welcome leaving this earth for a new life."

Stephen's eyes softened and he shook his head sadly. "Christ Jesus."

Ruby was confused. She knelt down beside him. William was on one side of her, and Esther was asleep in her arms. "But, your sister... She knows Jesus."

Stephen closed his eyes, then opened them. "Satan knows...Jesus is the Son of God...he quoted Scripture to our Lord...but Satan chooses... not to obey...the Bible....true Christians follow Jesus' teachings."

Ruby clutched Esther to her bosom. "Where do we go now?"

"Shushan."

Chapter 13

Ruby's homesick spirit drank in the green rolling hills dotted with brown and black Jersey heifers and marked with row upon row of white wooden fences. The sun made its lazy descent across the sky as deep pink and violet hues streaked geometrically behind its crested beams, golden and glimmering.

There, on the farthest hill, rose Shushan. From the house anyone who happened to glance down the hill could see them coming. They would know it was she. Yes, she smiled to herself, even if they hadn't yet received her last letter. Somehow, they would know. She had tried to call. Julie Ann had a telephone in the big house, only Mother did not. Ruby had called the general store, but Collina wasn't expected down until next week. So here it was the ninth day of October 1922, and she was being chauffeured in a borrowed car. Worst of all, she was coming home to Shushan after five long years with just the clothes on her back, a dying husband, a five-year-old boy, and a baby to live with their aging mother and Collina.

"You sure are a welcomed sight to these old eyes."

Ruby laughed. "Mother, you're hugging me so tight, I'm clear out of breath."

"Well, you've got it coming. It was Collina that sighted you first, coming from the hen house, said right off that she bet it was you."

"Then you got my letter?"

Mother looked over at Collina and then Bugie.

109

Collina and Bugie looked at each other. Collina shrugged her thin shoulders, "No, we haven't received a letter from you since the one telling us you had a baby girl."

Ruby glanced at Tom. "See, what did I tell you?"

He chuckled loudly and opened the trunk for their baggage.

"Can I hold the baby?" Bugie said.

"No, that's grandma's department," Maggie chuckled, as she cradled little Esther in her arms.

"Wait, Tom." Ruby peered into the back seat of the large automobile at Stephen. "Mother, Stephen is real sick. The doctors say he's dying of tuberculosis."

Mother gasped, holding Esther close, as to ward off any illness.

"That's hard to believe. Stephen's always been so healthy," Collina said.

Mother walked toward the car. "How do you feel, Stephen?"

Stephen smiled and said, "Fair to middlin', Maggie."

"Well," reaching into the open window and giving his thin arm a pat, "you and your family are as welcome as the morning sunshine." She smiled down at the little boy who had not stopped looking at her. "So, William, you have yourself a little sister, how do you like that?"

"I wanted me a brother."

"You did!" Maggie laughed. "Come to your grandma, darling. You still remember me? My, you sure have grown."

William buried his head in her apron. Then the unmistakable rustle of something like paper was heard. He looked at her and touched the pockets of her apron.

"Oh, wonder what that could be?" Laughing, Maggie pulled out a hard candy wrapped in bright paper. "I wonder how that got there?"

"For me?"

"Must be. Your sister is too little to eat hard candy." Then, glancing over her shoulder at Collina, Maggie said with tears springing into her kind eyes, "This house will be ringing with children's laughter again. Come on Collina and Bugie, help me tote these things in. It gets dark sooner than we need it to."

"But Mother, there's talk tuberculosis is contagious. Julie Ann says they're thinking of putting people who have the disease into sanatoriums."

Maggie turned around, one hand carrying Esther and the other wrapped around William's shoulders. "Daughter, you can't put Stephen into an institution. No, he'll do better here with us nursing him. My, this little girl feels light for two months. We're going to have to fatten her up."

"But Mother, you, Bugie, and Collina could catch it."

"Do you really think I'd turn you out because those city doctors got some new notions?" Maggie tilted her head, a quizzical look coming into her bright eyes. "Though there might be something to what they say, hear tell up in the mountains whole families were found dead with the white plague. Then people started being a little more careful. But that old consumption would always rear its ugly head now and again.

"But we'll be careful. We'll burn all his spittle and air the house as soon as this cold spell breaks. The children will have to stay away from Stephen. We'll treat it like we did the small pox. Everyone that comes in contact with Stephen will have to wash their hands with soap. We've come through worse, child, and licked it. We'll do it again, the good Lord willing."

"I'll nurse Stephen, I don't want anyone else in contact with him," Ruby said.

Mother made a bed for Stephen right in her fancy parlor room. No one had ever been allowed to use that room unless they were company. But Mother said this way Stephen would be close to the kitchen, and now that everyone was gone and married but Bugie and Skeeder, Maggie nor Collina had any time to spare for wasted steps.

❧ ❧ ❧

Dr. Luke Baker drove all the way in from Louisville to examine Stephen. The two engaged in conversation close to an hour. With Luke doing most of the talking while he examined her husband. Then he checked William and Esther, all the time glancing to the hallway for a glimpse of Collina.

"Why don't you go find her? She's likely in the garden."

"First of all, I'm married now, and second, Collina's changed, Ruby. You can't stand here and tell me that you haven't notice." He let out a deep sigh. "Wish she hadn't given up on men like she has." He plopped himself down in the nearest chair. Leaning forward, he rested his arms on his knees and ran his fingers through his hair.

"I'll not hide the truth from you. Myra was my first choice, Collina my second. Sadly, I don't feel I'm doing my present wife justice. But then, she's happiest when she's shopping or with her society friends anyways. That's why I think I've immersed myself into my work." He rose. "In fact, I'm looking at an opportunity to go north to Detroit and work in a large hospital."

"Detroit? That's where Myra is."

Stephen groaned in the next room. Ruby turned to go to him. Luke followed. Once Ruby made Stephen more comfortable, he slept. Luke patted Stephen's arm and whispered to Ruby, drawing her out of the room. "I do not believe it is tuberculosis, so your baby is safe, as is William.

"Then what could this disease be?"

"I can't be sure without taking Stephen to Detroit for further testing. But I believe it may be lung cancer. The only good thing about that, it is doubtful that cancer is contagious. That's why I want to go to Detroit. There is a new cancer unit opening up." As he walked toward the front door, he paused. "May I ask you a personal question?"

"Certainly, we've know each other since childhood."

"What happened to our dreams? I can remember the night of my sister's debutante ball as if it was yesterday. Stephen so energetic, so full of plans for the future, as I was. I was going to become a famous doctor and make my father and Myra proud." Luke looked up at the staircase. "I will never forget Myra sweeping down those steps on her way to take my hand in hers. I remember thinking. 'I'm the luckiest man alive to have her! God, I don't deserve to be so happy.'" He sighed.

"Well, God must have heard me. That moment in time of youthful dreams evaporated into oblivion and left the stark and naked truth of reality. The only thing the progression of years has held is heartbreak. I lost Myra to Clem. Collina lost Franklin to Detroit. And now you, a soon-to-be widow with two mouths to feed. Life becomes a sequence of years to endure—"

"Until we meet in heaven and reap the fruits of our labors." Ruby clutched Luke's arm. "Don't give up on God. Don't. I haven't, neither have Collina or Myra. Nothing that happens to us gets past the Almighty. 'Now faith is the substance of things hoped for.' Just wait and see!" Ruby shook his arm. "God has a plan for our lives. Never stop believing in Jesus. 'Without faith, it is impossible to please Him.' Like Abraham, Moses, Sarah, and the apostles, we will suffer afflictions." Ruby smiled into his worried face. "We mustn't lose heart, Luke. 'Let us lay aside every weight, and the sin which doth so easily beset us, and let us run with patience the race that is set before us, Looking unto Jesus the author and finisher of our faith.'"

"'Who for the joy that was set before him endured the cross, despising the shame, and is set down at the right hand of the throne of God.' Ruby, I acquire more Bible knowledge from you than I receive from my pastor on Sunday mornings." He kissed her lightly on the cheek and left, closing the door soundly behind him.

If Luke knew the truth. She bowed her head. Oh, Lord, I pray for strength, that I shall not doubt Your infinite will.

Daylight wove into evening and after the supper dishes were dried and Esther and William were fast asleep, Ruby picked up her sewing and sat beside her husband's bed waiting for him to wake up. She didn't wait long.

Stephen stroked his big finger down Ruby's cheek. "Happy?"

Ruby nodded.

"I told Luke…I'm getting stronger." Stephen knew he was welcomed at Shushan as rain on a summer morn, and renewed energy filtered through his wasted body from the effects of Maggie's good broth and herb teas. Only Esther acted discontent with her surroundings. Her husband knew this.

"Why is…Esther fretting so?"

"Mother says she's sore from her trip."

❦ ❦ ❦

Then one morning, with the cardinals loudly singing in the apple tree just outside Stephen's window, Stephen reached for her hand. "Darling…had…a dream. I was looking down on everyone…at Camp Beauregard. Write…Myra. Important she be here…for my funeral."

Ruby's bottom lip quivered. She attempted to stifle her tears for her husband's sake. Stephen patted her hand. "Don't tell…Maggie or Collina. Don't want them worrying…over me. I saw Franklin Long at my…funeral. God said for Collina to trust him."

Ruby gasped. Stephen was unaware of how Collina had changed—how she abhorred marriage.

"Franklin will take care of her…you and the children. He'll know… what to do…"

"But—"

"Shushan will survive." Stephen whispered softly, then nodded off to sleep.

Ruby rose. She turned and saw her mother standing in the doorway. How much had she heard?

Mother wiped her eyes with her apron. Clearing her throat, she said, "It's a miracle he's held out this long. Our Lord has truly blessed you, Ruby. You've got two beautiful children and know the love of a good man. Not every woman is so fortunate."

Yes, Ruby knew what marriage to a good man was like. She hugged her mother close, buried her head in her shoulder, and cried. She felt the weight of sorrow had been lifted from her shoulders, knowing her mother understood her grief.

Maggie patted her head. "Collina nor Myra have been so fortunate." Maggie kissed the top of her head. "Though I shouldn't be saying so because Myra never complained. Still, the signs of a good man versus a bad one are as clear as sunshine and darkness."

"Mother, I feel that way toward Myra, too. I wish there was something we could do. At least she has her two girls. We have worse things to worry about with Collina. She's just a shell of what she used to be. What happened? Luke says she's given up."

"Don't let her know that. Oh, she smiles and laughs and tries to pretend everything is all right. Heaven knows, she works harder than she has ever done before. Her and Skeeder do the jobs that before had taken the clan to do. Collina seems bent on forgetting that she's a woman. Says she feels more comfortable in overalls, and she ties up her hair and roams about the acres without even a care of what she looks like. There was hope for her when Luke came to call. Then when he up and married that society gal in Louisville, well, Collina let on like she didn't care. But I think she wishes she'd not been so cool to his courtin'."

Ruby frowned. "Mother, what are you not telling me?"

She avoided Ruby's look and said, "In little less than two weeks, Lawyer Farlin is going to auction off Shushan and all the land. That's what Collina has been busy doing, collecting the merchandise. I've been told I'll get a child's part. Pray that it includes the house. But knowing Farlin's grudge, it won't be. He won't feel justified until he turns every McConnell out in the street."

Ruby stared at her mother as if in a trance, then over at her sleeping husband. A few moments before Stephen had said Shushan would survive. "Well…I'd better get to writing."

She got out paper and quill, thumbing through a stack of letters; she came across one from Myra. Yes, there was Myra's new address in Detroit. Scanning the letter, it sounded like Myra was taking in boarders. How strange. She'd write her about Stephen. And she'd better tell her about Collina, too, and the auction.

Chapter 14

October 18, 1922

The small bell in the front of the store sent its message to the inhabitants in the rear.

Franklin stepped through the threshold, shoving his hand into his deep brown overcoat. Good, I didn't forget Jane's meat list. The butcher's counter gleamed in the afternoon sunlight. Cupping his walking cane on the crook of his elbow, he waited for the butcher. The man was a busy, untalkative sort. However, if it happened to be the butcher's wife, Ann, well then, it would take a while to attain his purchases. His hand drew out the list. Jane's flowing handwriting met his glance.

The little bell rang its declaration that someone else had opened the shop's door. The woman jumped like a jackrabbit in a snare when she spotted him. She drew her hat down on her forehead, ducked her head, and clutched a young girl's hand, probably no more than sixteen. The girl wore a tam o'-shanter hat. Another girl clutched in the woman's left hand, looked younger, probably fifteen, and wore a military style French beret that complemented her sailor top. Her long, golden curls peeked out charmingly.

The older girl peered out the open shop door. "Mother, I think Daddy followed us."

"No, he's at some speak-easy," the woman whispered, "so don't worry. Now, remember, don't say a thing about your daddy. If he should find out, it'll only bring more trouble."

Just then Ann entered the shop from the back room.

"Mrs. Cass, so glad you came today. I just got in some real nice juicy steaks I'm sure your boarders will enjoy."

Cass? The name sounded familiar, where had he heard the name? He tried to grab a better look of her face.

"I can't manage that this week. But thank you, Ann, I came in for some ground pork and a little bacon. Where's your George this morning?"

"He had to look at some beef up Traverse City way." Ann smiled, and looked up at Franklin. "You have a list from Jane for me?"

He chuckled. "I do indeed." Franklin had only to contend with the butcher's wife, equally intuitive, but bearable singularly. His order shouldn't take too long to fill. The butcher shop was the main headquarters of gossip.

Ann eyed Mrs. Cass with the two children. "My, that is a pretty hat and such a nice bouquet of flowers. I like that nice ribbon and feathers. I prefer these types of hats, so feminine." Ann looked critically to the two girls' hats and laughed. "But what do I know? I still wear my hat with the yellow canary. It's old and looks like my canary's been pawed by a cat before it was stuffed. I still like it." Ann narrowed her eyes. "Let's see, come closer so I can see if Softie got the feathers right."

The woman moved forward.

"Why you got it so slanted? No way to wear a hat like that. See, I show you." She stepped away from the counter, toward Mrs. Cass.

"No. I like it like this."

Ann's eyes widened in alarm, then sadness converted the merry eyes into pity. "Yes, well, perhaps you're right." She turned. "I be right with you, Mr. Long."

"I got a surprise for Theresa and Sue Ann. They will like." Ann disappeared into the back room.

Mrs. Cass let go of her girls' hands and flexed her arm. Franklin bit down on his bottom lip, Cass, Cass that name sounds so familiar.

"Oh, dear, I forgot to check." Mrs. Cass reached into her reticule.

"Is the money from our boarders still there, Mama?" the younger of the two said.

"Hush, Theresa."

The heavy steps of the large, rosy-cheeked Ann reappeared, smiling good-naturedly, with two large pieces of cake in either hand. "I saved these for your girls. They're from my George's birthday cake. You want to eat it in here?" She nodded her head toward the door she'd exited.

Theresa eyed it hungrily.

"Ann, I don't have as much as I thought I had. I think I'll wait to place that meat order."

"No, you take now, come with money when you get it."

Embarrassment and shame washed over her like an opened dam. Franklin looked away. Ann was always performing these types of kind gestures.

"I don't feel right accepting."

"But Mama, what will we eat?" the taller of the girls said.

"Hush, Sue Ann."

Ann's eyes swirled to Sue Ann and then to Mrs. Cass. "I think we need to talk. Come. I will take just a minute."

The kindly woman took Theresa by the hand and led her into her warm kitchen. Sue Ann and Mrs. Cass followed.

"How cute you look in that hat and sailor top." Ann sat heavily down on one of the wooden chairs. "I like yours, too, Sue Ann, you make it?"

Franklin could hear them clearly.

"Yes, I can make you one, if you like."

"You make one for my niece?"

"What color?" Sue Ann said.

"Hmm, I think she would like a blue one." She turned and closed the curtain.

It was hard for Franklin not to eavesdrop. After all, there wasn't much he could do while waiting for his meat order. He knew better not to return home without it. He chuckled. Jane would have his hide if he did.

"You belong to St. Ann Parish like me? Funny I never see you there or the children."

"No, no we're Baptist."

"Baptist? I thought for sure you were Catholic." An uncomfortable silence fell between them. "Then why you stay with that woman beater?

He no good for you."

Franklin heard Mrs. Cass sobbing. "My husband wasn't always like this. I blame Detroit. We should never have moved here during prohibition. There are so many speakeasies for my husband to take refuge from his troubles in."

"What can Ann do to help?" Ann said.

Franklin nodded. An immigrant from Poland, Ann understood a woman's suffering knew no limits and love's compassion no boundaries.

"Thank you for understanding, Ann. Pray. That's all anyone can do."

"Yes, I pray," Ann retorted. Then bustled to her icebox. Franklin heard the rustle of brown wrapping paper and smelled fresh bread. She must be bundling them together.

"I pray someone come along and knock some sense into your silly husband's head. Here. For you and your girls."

"But, I can't."

"You say a Hail Mary for me, please, and you don't tell Father Murray what Ann said." Ann patted her hand tenderly.

Before Franklin had time to turn, out walked Theresa bearing Ann's bundle importantly. "Look, Mommy, this man has a scar on his face."

"Good morning, young lady." He grinned, took off his hat and bowed. She smiled back shyly.

He walked back to the meat counter, slightly embarrassed that he was caught listening.

Sue Ann frowned. "That wasn't nice, Theresa."

"He's got a limp, too." Theresa said.

Sue Ann's curiosity got the better of her. "How did you get that limp, mister?"

Franklin put a gloved hand to his cane. "From the war," he muttered, turning hastily to Ann. "Three steaks, Ann, lean if you've got them."

"Say why do you have that cane? You don't use it."

"Theresa, really. Stop bothering that gentlemen." Mrs. Cass grabbed her and pulled her to her side.

"No problem, madam." Bending over, he smiled into her face. "Many young ladies ask me why I carry it."

"Were you in the Great War?" Sue Ann said. "My girlfriend's father got shell shocked. He's always twitching."

"It was the Spanish American war."

"Really?" Mrs. Cass said, looking at him closer. "I knew someone that fought in that war."

"You mean Uncle Franklin, Mother?" Theresa said. "Did you know our uncle, mister?"

Recognition dawned. Myra McConnell! Collina's older sister who wedded Clem Cass. Of course!

"Did you say Franklin?" Ann beamed at Sue Ann. "That his name, too. He's a war hero. Was decorated with the Purple Heart. Some thought he dead, but he fooled them. Jane could tell you." Ann placed her elbows onto her counter and the palms of her hands on her ample cheeks. "Like Jane tell me. Mr. Franklin too modest to talk about self."

Sue Ann hastened to set the record straight and not have her uncle outdone by this stranger. "Our uncle was very handsome. He had blue eyes and he was real tall. And Aunt Collina said he was as brave as an Indian chief. You know it's not bad to be part Indian. And Mama said—"

"Sue Ann." Myra's face had turned a vibrant red. "My, depend on a child to conjure up a tale from a few hasty remarks between adults."

"Mother." Theresa tugged at her arm.

"We need to be going, girls." Myra gathered Theresa and hastily grabbed Sue Ann's hand and pulled her toward the door.

"Mother." Theresa would not be stilled.

"What is it?" In her haste to answer her outspoken offspring, her hat came dislodged and fell to the floor. Franklin moved to retrieve it. Myra hastened to intercept him.

"Mother, this man has blue eyes like Uncle Franklin." Theresa whispered.

"Ah..."

He stared into her face.

"Yes, I can see he does," Myra said slightly winded. "Franklin Long, I'd know you anywhere."

"Why, that's he." Ann retorted, clasping her hands together and looking up. "Saints preserve us. Jesus thank you!"

He couldn't stifle the amusement that erupted. He embraced her and muttered, "My dear long lost sister-in-law." He looked intently at her. "Saints preserve us, it looks like I've found you just in time. Pray, lead me to the cause of that nasty fall."

Ann chuckled. "See, children, how fast Jesus answers prayers."

❤ ❤ ❤

"Does it hurt?" Franklin said as Myra removed the piece of steak and touched her eye gingerly.

Myra shook her head, relaxing against the soft plush upholstered winged tip chair. "I haven't felt this safe or secure in a long time."

"I insist you stay here the night. I want to meet this husband of yours before he sees you again."

"Oh, no, you mustn't. He's very—"

"Bullish…and I'm not referring to our past president's pet phrase," Franklin retorted. "Do you remember the last time we met? I do. And you are still as beautiful as I remember you from Rose's debutante ball. This type of bully must be dealt with. Trust me, Myra, I know how to handle him." Rising, he patted her shoulder. "I'll go and see how Jane is coming with your room. Then I'll be off. I'll be back and join you and the girls at supper."

❤ ❤ ❤

Franklin smiled. *This is what I hoped Collina would act like.*

Myra gazed in awe at the beautiful cherry wood four-poster bed and stroked the delicately scrolled posts. She picked up the small hand-carved music box, then walked to the window seat and sat down on its plush red velvet seats and gazed out of the window. "Oh, girls, it is so lovely here. Look at the beautifully manicured lawns that stretch out endlessly."

Franklin chuckled.

Jane walked in soundlessly in her moccasins. "Is this she?"

Dawn was suddenly beside her mother.

"No," Franklin whispered.

Myra surveyed the woman and young lady.

Dawn's long shiny black hair was held back with ribbon tied at the back of her head. They were both clad in fashionable dresses; however, on their feet were beautiful beaded Indian moccasins.

"Are you and your daughter related to Franklin?"

He felt the dread in her voice. Did Myra think Dawn was his child?

"My husband met Mr. Franklin in Mr. Roosevelt's army. They became blood brothers. So when my Joe died in war, Mr. Franklin took me and my Dawn in. Franklin's a good man. Like Indians."

Myra laughed. "I can remember a conversation Collina had with us in Luke Baker's heirloom buggy about that very topic."

"Collina?" Jane looked up at him. "It was the name Mr. Franklin said while in the fever's clutches at San Juan. Mr. Franklin spoke about her—"

"Oh?" Myra let out a relieved chuckle. "That is good to hear." She bent down, looking at her girls. "Perhaps Dawn could show Sue Ann and Theresa the grounds outside?"

Franklin watched them leave the room. "Well, I'd best be off, too."

Myra stepped forward. "I'm sorry, Franklin, about that little lie I told my girls. About you and Collina, I'll explain to them that you never married—"

"Big mix up in tribe?"

"Yes. This big." Myra moved her arms above her head to show the hugeness of the error. "Enormous."

"Good thing Mr. Franklin has broad shoulders. Big enough to wipe up problems he's been hoping to fix for many years."

Franklin coughed. "Yes, well, I'll be back for supper."

Chapter 15

The gray haze of cigarette smoke floated around the room like drunken ghosts. Franklin walked into the third speakeasy he'd visited that afternoon. "Have you seen Clem Cass today?"

The bartender, a short, stout, thick haired man, pointed a dirty fingernail in the direction of one table in the far corner of the room.

Franklin took his time. Clem and the girl he had his arm around hadn't noticed him. Yes, it was the same man he'd met at Doc's ball. Same bushy side burns, same large nose, same mean-looking eyes, just older and meaner looking and his curly black hair showed a receding hairline.

"Excuse me," he said, tilting his hat in the direction of the woman, then swerving his gaze to include Clem. "Might you be Clem Cass?"

"Why, yes, that's him," the thin girl replied.

"Shut up!"

"That's no way to speak to a lady."

"Didn't ask to be mentioned and I didn't ask to be interrupted. Now be gone before I make you eat those highfalutin' manners."

"Saw Myra, I hardly recognized her. You beat her up pretty badly. Is that the way you treat your wife? She was such a beautiful thing, before you got a hold of her."

A hush fell over the room.

"Get out of here!"

"I can still remember that night Myra showed us her engagement ring. She was so excited, so in love. I remember that night because Collina was worried about her sister. Worried that Myra might be making a mistake."

"What?" Clem stood, his eyes squinting in the half-lit smoky room. "Who are you?"

"Franklin Long. And if you don't remember me, you soon shall." He nabbed Clem by the collar and hoisted him off his feet. "We need to go for a little walk."

"Let go of me."

"Not yet."

"Let me go, you fatherless ba—" Clem sought the comradeship of his chums. "Hey, you know about this gent? He's a foreigner, came from Canada, a sorry half-breed. Go home to your wigwam. Hey, guys, you ain't gonna let a half-breed bother your friend?" Turning to Franklin, Clem yelled. "I got pals here." Clem pulled his arm up striking Franklin in his jaw.

Franklin sent his fist into Clem's face, which threw Clem five feet into the gutter outside. Clem came up spewing blood and mud. Franklin hit him again, and the men that crowded around yelled. Franklin stood over him, fist readied, with a wary eye on the crowd. "You're coming with me, Clem. That is unless you need more persuasion."

"Hey, you an Injun?"

Franklin turned. A dark burly giant of a man clad in a shirtwaist that emphasized his bronze muscles all the more stood over him.

"I said, you got Injun blood in you?" The man's scowl met Franklin's.

Franklin lowered his jaw and squared off. He'd have to make sure every punch was even. "Can't say. Didn't you hear, I was an orphan."

The man chuckled. "Yeah, me too. Well, now I got me something in common with a red man. Hey, did Clem here do what you say?"

Franklin nodded. "You want to see for yourself? Or are you a woman beater, too?"

"No," the man growled. "I've done bad things, but I ain't scum. It takes one lower than a snake to do that." The man spat on the ground.

Clem rushed Franklin, who landed another punch into Clem's face. "You want more, or are you coming peacefully?"

Clem looked pleadingly at the crowd that circled him. It was clear no one cared to fight his battle. "I'll come."

"What's the matter, Clem, you afraid of gettin' hurt? Does he hit harder than your wife?" crowed someone from the crowd.

Franklin stood Clem on his feet.

"Come on guys, nothing here to see but jelly," the same man yelled.

Clem planted his large hands deep into his pant pockets and hung his head. The crowd dispersed, and Franklin led Clem down the sidewalk.

"Some men would give their eye teeth to have a wife and pair of girls like yours," Franklin said. "What do you mean treating them like that?"

Clem's lower lip quivered. "I'll never be able to go back to that speakeasy again. You want to fight? Well, then come on." Clem pulled away from Franklin and doubled up his fists.

Franklin hit him again, then watched as Clem's anger turned to tears, big tears that fell down his dirty, unshaven pudgy face. "How can you do so much damage to yourself and the people you are supposed to love?" There was only one person he knew that could clean up a mess like this. He pushed Clem along for several blocks then stopped in front of a church.

"What in blue blazes?" Clem looked up in disbelief. "I've not entered a church for years. Myra is a devout Baptist, but I've always stayed home."

"You'll learn a lot here."

Clem tried to duck Franklin's arm. He cuffed him by the neck of his coat. "Pastor, meet Clem Cass."

At the front of the church there was a huge picture of Jesus Christ, below the picture was a large tank.

Clem turned to leave, but Pastor's strong hand captured him. Clem looked up into the face of the largest man most likely Clem had ever seen. The pastor bodily turned him, and Clem turned sheet white. Franklin could see Clem's head swimming from the brandy he had consumed all day as he swayed beneath the pastor's grip.

"I understand, brother, that you've been beating your wife?" The pastor's booming voice echoed in the vast room. "Son, I think with a little time, you will come to see the error of your ways."

An oath began upon his lips. Clem choked it back.

❦ ❦ ❦

Franklin smiled with pleasure as Myra descended the stairs as gracefully as she had in her youth. "Look how lovely your mother looks."

Theresa nodded. "Mother is beautiful."

Myra attempted to cover her black eye.

"It's hardly noticeable, Myra." Franklin extended his arm to her. Myra shyly touched his sleeve.

Throughout supper, Myra kept her eyes on her plate. Franklin kept the conversation active, recalling the recent comments about Germany's problems after the devastating World War. "What was it Roosevelt was quoted as saying? Oh, yes, it went something like, `No triumph of peace is quite so great as the supreme triumphs of war!'"

Myra sighed. "Really? I have my not-too-distant battle with Clem and have never felt any triumphs in that. And speaking about fights, what happened?" Myra glanced over to Theresa and Sue Ann.

"Jane, can you tell the cook that Myra and I will take our coffee in the parlor." Franklin and Jane exchanged glances, murmurs followed, and then the laughter of Theresa and Sue Ann, who both had occupied seats across from Jane and Dawn throughout dinner, filled the silence.

"Mommy," Sue Ann said excitedly, "can Theresa and I go to Dawn's room? She has pictures of Clara Bow and an article about her life."

"Clara Bow? Oh yes, that silent movie actress that is especially popular with the teens and young ladies. Is it all right if the girls go to your room, Dawn?"

"Yes, ma'am." Dawn led Sue Ann and Theresa out of the room, and Franklin, Myra, and Jane strode to the parlor where Cook had already delivered coffee.

Myra appeared nervous. Over him or her husband? "Clem's at a Baptist church on the west side of town. I guess you can say he's on a religious binge."

"Really? I've been trying to get him inside a church for years."

"This preacher is the largest hunk of man you'd ever meet. He was a wrestler once, killed a man, and then he nearly killed himself over the guilt of taking another man's life. That's when he found forgiveness in Christ Jesus and turned into the best preacher a person ever listened to."

Myra touched a finger to her black eye.

The skin around her eye was bruised and Franklin could imagine how sore it felt. Only Jesus can change Clem. "Give Clem another chance, Myra. Happiness could be around the corner for you."

Myra looked up. "He tries; I know he does. What about yourself, Franklin? Why haven't you married? I know that answer, even if you won't admit it. Because you're still in love with Collina. Everyone knows it, even Jane."

"I tried marriage."

Myra rambled forward like a train out of control, acting as if she hadn't heard his words. "The sad thing is, Collina still loves you. She could have married again. Luke was crazy about her and proposed, but Collina wouldn't marry him."

Franklin's expression remained unchanged.

"Don't try to pan that look off on me, or the fact that your first marriage failed. While we're on the topic of happiness, are you trying to tell me you're happy?"

Franklin got up and walked to the window. "What do you expect me to do?" His arms behind his back, he rocked back and forth on his heels. "It's too late for me and for Collina."

Franklin turned. Myra's look spoke of her resolve. "I'm sure your father meant well, but he placed an awful burden on Collina's shoulders when he asked her to keep the legacy of Shushan alive."

"Shushan's going to be auctioned off. There's nothing left of Father's dream. My husband saw to that. Of course, Collina blames herself. She always blames herself. She has an unfathomable well of love for her loved ones, and that includes...you."

"Humph! Does that include Austin?"

"Austin's remarried. Has two little boys and lives in the mountains."

"It'll take more than an auction for Collina to quit on Shushan or that worthless husband of hers."

"You mean, like me?"

Seeing the hurt emotions sweeping her face, he attempted to halt his burning words. Proverbs 16:23 sprang to mind. *The heart of the wise teacheth his mouth, and addeth learning to his lips.*

"I hate the memory of what I allowed Clem to do. From the money we received from Shushan's first auction, we purchased our large house in Detroit. I named it Esau's House. Like Esau traded his inheritance for a bowl of porridge, I exchanged mine for a large run-down house in the middle of Detroit. The rest of my inheritance Clem squandered on his drunken binges.

"After he ran out of money, he'd come slithering back to me. He'd follow me from room to room like a stray dog, fearful that its long-lost home would disappear with its master's presence. Hounding me with his whimpers of past dreams fallen by the wayside, pressing me to ask for money from Mother. 'I felt plagued with the banshees' Clem told Theresa and Sue Ann after one of his binges."

Myra fumbled with her handkerchief. "Will I ever escape from the guilt of what Clem did?" She looked up, beseeching Franklin with her eyes. "The dream Father had for our estate he and Mother had carved from nothing is lost forever, all because of what Clem, with the aid of Lawyer Farlin, did. Why didn't Clem keep his word to me and tell Farlin to stop the court proceedings?"

Franklin stared out the window. He didn't have the answers. What did Myra expect of him?

"I received a letter from Ruby today. Stephen is dying from some mysterious illness and Shushan is to be auctioned off in ten days. How can I face Mother and Collina?"

"You McConnell women are an enduring lot. Don't worry." Franklin patted her on the shoulder. His voice gentle. "Collina's a survivor, like the rest of you. You'll get by."

"Get by? Yes. I'm sure we shall." Myra choked back hot tears. "Where is Jesus? I always believed He'd…it's as if God has turned His back on us."

Chapter 16

October 20, 1922

*C*ollina laid her soiled overalls into a neat pile and stepped over to the pitcher and basin. She dabbed at her eyes and turned to survey the clothes strewn on her bed like cut outs of the *Ladies' Home Journal* and *Vogue*. "Ruby's determined to turn this hayseed into a fashionable lady."

Laying the washcloth over her eyes, she muttered, "Jesus, what will happen to us after the auction?" A drop of rain spattered into the bucket by her bed. "Oh, and then there's the roof. If I'm able to buy the house, I'll need to mend the roofs of the house and barns. And what if I don't have enough money to buy Shushan back?" Collina walked over to the rain-drenched window; streams of water poured down the pane. "There's that tobacco plant in Emerald." She'd heard the pay was good.

Collina felt the folds of her mourning dress wash over her head. The bodice was done in black silk, trimmed Georgette crêpe, and black silk net under black taffeta. The black taffeta hugged her waist and folded demurely to the floor. In sharp contrast to her thoughts, no, God wouldn't want her to feel beaten.

God has a plan. She just wished He'd convey it to her. "Well, Jesus, I know You said that You'd take care of Your children as You do the birds." She walked back to the window. But He doesn't drop the worms in their mouth. He expects the birds to do their part, too. Okay, so I mustn't worry. I'll go to work at the tobacco plant.

She fastened the thick belt of black molded ribbon about her waist, the ends of ribbon mingling in gentle folds with the black taffeta. She slid her feet into the tiny black heels all the while contemplating her next job. How was she going to keep Mother, Bugie, and Ruby and her children safe with a roof over their heads on a meager salary?

The taffeta rustled with her every movement. No way would she go unnoticed in this dress. She paused, seeing her hat. She picked up the black Georgette crêpe and plopped it onto her hair. Its high crown adorned with black nun's veiling gave her face a coquettish appearance.

She turned to the left, then to the right. Amazing what Ruby could accomplish. She couldn't believe the transformation of her personage.

She had told Ruby she didn't feel like competing with the flappers. Hence the reason she hadn't cut her hair into the latest fad, the bob. Ruby politely obeyed and pointed out that because Collina was an old-fashioned girl, she had arrayed her in plenty of fabric and Georgette crêpe. Not the short skirts and hour glass look that many flappers had chosen in *Vogue*.

She shrugged. It didn't matter what she wore. She could be wearing sackcloth, and people would nod and walk right past her as if she didn't matter. And she didn't. What did matter were Ruby and her children... Dear Stephen.

She drew on her gloves and stared at the image in the long mirror and chuckled. "I look like an honest to goodness dignified lady. Hm, maybe we could open up a dress shop. If Ruby can make me look this good, think what she could do with real ladies."

She heard what sounded like a flock of geese landing. Then as the noise drew closer, the roar of an automobile engine muffled everything around. She rushed to the window. "Nothing old-fashioned about that."

As she descended the stairway, the McConnell clan rushed out the front door to watch.

"Yeah, they call this progress. It can't even manage what one horse can climb easy," Jesse said.

The blackened sky above gleamed light and thunder followed.

"Look there, the plate reads Detroit, Michigan. Who do we know from there?" Bell said.

A man clad in raincoat and hat got out of the driver's side, limping heavily on his left leg, and opened the door behind his. Myra and Clem emerged with Sue Ann and Theresa.

"Myra? And my grandchildren!" Mother ran out into the rain, covering her head with her slicker.

Myra glanced back at the automobile and laughed. "I declare, now I know what a fat man on roller skates must feel like skating uphill." Myra hugged her mother close. "I missed you."

Collina started to follow, then hesitated. Broad shouldered and tall, the driver gazed boldly toward the group on the porch.

Ruby turned to Collina. "Uh, Sis, it's much too wet and damp out there for Esther. Would you mind staying here with her?"

Collina hesitated. Oh, how she longed to be a part of the excitement, feel the love of her clan as it had been before they had grown up and left.

Ruby handed her the two-and-a-half-month-old Esther and pushed her toward the doorway before she could decline.

Ruby walked toward the automobile, pausing to talk to the stranger.

"We don't need them, do we, Esther? We can have fun by ourselves."

Esther, her small lips puckering into a rosebud, cooed back at Collina.

Collina laughed. "Why, you're the smartest and prettiest baby in the whole wide world." Pausing at the closed parlor door, she pressed a hand to the large oak doors. "Dear Stephen, I should have known you'd use this opportunity to bring everyone back together again."

"He was a wonderful man, I understand."

Collina spun around so quickly she nearly upset the vase resting on a nearby pedestal table.

The stranger stood before her. His duster, hat, and goggles still in place, as if he proposed a speedy departure.

"Wasn't a better man that lived. Are you a friend of Myra's or Ruby's?"

He removed his smooth gloves, the smell of the rich brown leather intoxicating her nostrils. "I came because Myra needed a way home."

"Then you are sincerely welcomed. Shushan is never the same when one of its loved ones leaves." He had to have a good heart to drive from Detroit to Kentucky for Myra. She smiled. "You must be tired after that long journey—"

"Yes. It was a journey I should have taken sooner."

"There are refreshments in the dining room. Please help yourself. Now, you must excuse me; I must tend to the baby. She's long due for her nap."

"I'm not hungry. May I offer my assistance?" The stranger smiled. "You look familiar. You resemble someone I had once grown fond of. Have you ever been to Detroit?"

Collina shook her head vehemently. "No. And I never intend to. Isn't it funny how a look or a word can remind you of someone? In fact, I was going to ask you that same question."

A crooked, almost jesting smile displayed a strong chin.

Strange. She couldn't understand why. What was so familiar about him? Confusion whirled across her brow like a funnel cloud. "I'm sure you must look better without that hat and those ridiculous goggles."

The slurping noise of Esther sucking her fist broke the silence between them and a wailing scream followed. Collina headed for the stairway.

The stranger stopped her. "Please allow me to carry her up. It will be difficult for you and dangerous for Esther with your long dress and high-heeled shoes. That is, unless the stairway has become shorter with the passing of years."

"What?" Collina stared into the goggled face trying to pierce his veil of secrecy. "Your knowledge of me is unnerving. Just where did you attain it?"

"Uh…Myra."

Esther shook the bottle from her mouth and cried. Collina placed the struggling child on her shoulder. Esther's little fingers caught in the nun's veiling. Collina looked up at the stranger with Ruby's new creation precariously covering one eye. "Perhaps it would be best. But I must warn you Esther does not cotton to strangers and your goggles might frighten her."

Esther quieted her cries into coos of delight upon being clasped to the large shoulder.

"Well, I'm surprised at you, Esther. I suppose there is no understanding—"

"Love." The man had not moved. A sideways look at him made her realize he was studying her attentively. She stepped back, then hastily ascended the stairway. Indignantly she thrust open the bedroom door, and it banged against the wall.

"Shush!" The stranger laid the sleeping Esther in her crib.

Collina reached for a comforter. Esther's little mouth pursed into an O as she nursed an invisible nipple. Collina placed a hand to her mouth, muffling her laugh.

"Thank you. Please enjoy the refreshments in the dining room." Collina headed to her bedroom.

She clicked her tongue against her teeth, her image in the bureau mirror discouraging. The dismal effect of Esther's small fingers to her hat and hair was evident. Removing her hat, tresses of thick dark hair peppered with gray, bounced their way to her shoulder. "Oh, dear." Struggling not to vent her frustrations, she snatched a few hairpins and tried gamely to tame the unruly locks to match their counterparts. Turning, she discarded the unwanted bonnet onto the bed. Her gaze met the doorway in the same instant. "Oh!"

"You never could keep your hair pinned up for long. I'll never forget how it looked when you undid that scarf, how it shone in the moonlight."

With a quick intake of breath and one hand still holding a strand of hair, Collina turned back to the mirror.

"It was beautiful hair then. It's still beautiful."

"Franklin." The name erupted from her mouth without deliberation, as did the longings she sent him from the bureau mirror.

Franklin tossed his goggles onto the Chippendale wing chair. He smiled broadly at her, eagerness written in the creases of his lips. "I was afraid to tell you down there. I wanted more space between the front door and us. Didn't know if you might not decide to give me a boot in the rear." His firm steps ate up the distance, the blue of his eyes deep and intense. "Now, don't go getting mad—"

"Why?" She turned. "Why do you step back into my life now?" She stepped away, as far as the bureau would allow. "I always knew. Or maybe I always hoped, that day of the auction—"

"Proud Lady waits for you at my home." He watched her face

closely. "I was of no use to you working behind a plow. I hoped to make something of myself in the manufacturing business, then—"

"You married that society lady." Half-forgotten memories washed before her eyes, flooding her emotions. Collina clasped her shaking hands. "You must have children of your own, the way Esther took to you."

"No, no children. I'm divorced." Like a cat at a mouse hole, Franklin paused, then said, "If we could only redo those parts of our lives that didn't fit."

She pinched her lower lip with her teeth, the cold hand of reason creeping over her countenance like a shade on a window. "So, you've heard about the upcoming auction."

He frowned. "Perhaps it is silly for me to think we could pick up the pieces of our lives now. That there could be any part of love left. Myra told me what Austin did to you. My wife cheated on me, too. Left me for a big German guy.

"Why did you leave me? I would have done anything for you—"

"But not leave Shushan."

"I, I, couldn't."

"I couldn't farm, and I didn't need your pity. Besides," Franklin stepped closer, "Joseph took the bullet that was meant for me. How do you think that made me feel when they pinned a medal on me for my 'brave service to my country'?"

She clutched the bureau's edge. "You, you didn't give me a chance—"

"To reject me."

Is that what he thought of my love for him? That I would reject him? Collina swiped her eyes and turned toward the bureau. What does it matter? She was just a shell of a woman. "What is done is done."

"I see. I'll stay for the funeral, and then leave tonight."

She looked up. His eyes met hers through the mirror. His strong jaw jutted out like a prize fighter's, daring her. He turned and left. She bowed her head and listened to his receding steps.

"Collina!"

Startled, she turned, surprised to see he had returned. Franklin's brows formed furrows over his stormy eyes.

"God brought me back to the only home I ever wanted. That night at Doc's ball, at Lady's Lake, meant very much to me. I wanted you to know what you said that first night so long ago in the cornfield carried me through a lot of battles. Seeing you in that cornfield again after the auction, with your hair misty with fog, it carried me through another painful rehabilitation period.

"Though I backslid, it carried me through that, too. When Myra informed me Austin and you were divorced…well, she had the crazy notion that—what's holding you back from marrying me now? Shushan is being auctioned off. There's nothing to stop us from becoming man and wife. I'm proposing to you, Collina. Will you marry me?"

Collina traced a scratch in the bureau with her finger. *What can I offer him? I can't have children anymore. I couldn't make Austin happy; what chance do I have to make Franklin happy? Oh, God, I can't bear the thought of abandonment. Another man leaving me for a woman's bed who could give him children.* "Marriage is not part of my plans anymore. And that night in the cornfield was long ago. I'd nearly forgotten it."

There was no movement from the doorway, not even a whisper of a sound. *He must have gone. Surely he realizes there is no hope for us, not now…not ever.* She felt hot tears forming. She squeezed her eyes shut. *No, no, I will not cry; I'm over that.*

"You were the preserver God used to bring me out of my bondage. Strange. You've forgotten that night and I will never forget it. Never forget that because of the love I felt for you, I met my Savior. It was because of you that I met Jesus. I can't explain it, but a part of me always believed this day would come. I've made my share of mistakes but, Collina, I've gotten better than I've deserved."

Her heart cried. She knew what he meant. Suddenly a small voice spoke, her voice. "Is what we're left with worth sharing?"

"What is it that shackles your heart?" He rubbed his hand across his chin. "I thought Myra's marriage would be happy; I know now it wasn't. When I asked her if she had regrets, she said she'd go through it all again for her daughters.

"I remember telling you that one must be patient. That everything worth having is worth waiting for, and love, true love, must sometimes wait, and never be taken for granted."

Confusion whirled about her head like a thunder cloud. Surely Myra told him. He knows, he must. Of course he does. Now that she's barren, it's his conscience that sends him to her side. He just admitted it. And, of course, Franklin, being the knight of old, had to come to her aid. Oh, how humiliating!

"Collina, what is it?"

"Oh, how cruel the thorns of love can be. So you've heard about my hysterectomy from Myra. Well, flowers have their season." Her voice cracked with weariness. "It took me a while to adjust. But I have. I can't believe women can be as silly about such things as passion and love."

He winced as if she'd burned him with hot coals. "Myra didn't tell me."

Collina's hand went to her throat, her cheeks burning before his tormented gaze. She could not bear his pity. She had to get away.

"Enough of this," she said, her look as icy as her words. "They need me downstairs. It's nice to have met an old friend again." She rushed toward the doorway.

He blocked her way. A spark of indignant rage lit his eyes. "Is that all we were. Friends?" He shook. "Now, let me get this straight. You possess no female desires within your bosom? You are frigid as well as barren, passionless, with no ardent desire to love or be loved?"

She tried to push her way past him.

"I think not."

She fought to be free of his arms.

He smiled when she glared up at him. "I have waited a long time for this moment. You have no idea, do you? The torment you've put me through."

His eyes met hers and held them. In an instant he had her in his arms.

She nearly choked on her words when his lips greeted hers. She struggled against him, realizing with a start, he was bending her to his will like a sapling in a whirlwind. "So, you no longer feel like a woman? Then, my love, you need convincing you still are."

She pounded on his back.

"Collina, I love you. I always will. I was too proud, at first, to admit I was a cripple and that I loved you. Too arrogant to change." He cradled her softly in his caress as his lips trailed through her hair, across her forehead, and didn't stop till his lips met hers.

Tears, hot, unwanted tears, streamed down her cheeks as the truth of her undying love for him awakened her passions. "Oh, Franklin, Franklin, but I want you to have it all, children of your own, all the children you ever wanted, and I can't give them to you."

"I'm holding all I'll need on this earth to experience what the joys of heaven will be like," he whispered. He pulled her an arm's length away, looking questioningly into her eyes. "I have caused you so much pain and suffering while I wallowed in my self-pity—"

"I am not without regret," she said. "To my own hard-headedness."

He caressed her cheek. "Yes, my love. We can thank Providence for this moment, but we cannot blame Him for our shortcomings."

Enveloped in his embrace, she closed her eyes, resting her head on his chest. "Lord, I can't believe I'm getting a second chance at happiness when my dear sister has lost hers."

"Collina, you are that earthly love Christ has blessed me with."

"Oh, Franklin. But is it God's will that I should find love and happiness, when I've let Father and Shushan down?"

Chapter 17

hushan had been sold to a wealthy oilman from Texas. Lawyer Farlin gleefully held up an envelope and told the gathering crowd that whatever was bid for the homestead, Mr. Wintworth would double it.

Collina had risen early the next morning. Saddled her horse and ridden away. She needed to think. Surely there was something she could do to change the fate of Shushan.

The bare limbs above her head chattered incoherently and wasted leaves beneath ash-colored trunks fluttered like wingless birds in helpless abandonment. Oh, how will I bear it? Her beloved Shushan divided. Stripped like a bed of its sheets, separated from them forever. Her horse, Magic, snorted and stamped her foot impatiently.

She, Jessie, Robert, Ruby, Bugie, and Bell tried to buy what they could, but the price of the land was steep. Chester and Myra needed the money and they wanted to sell their sections, so she and Jessie bought them out.

Mother had gotten the house and forty acres. Jessie, the good bottomland, and she had the section overlooking Coon's creek. Bugie and Bell had picked up what they could to join hers and Jessie's. But was it enough? Was there enough left for them to farm? And who would be left to farm? Robert was leaving. The Great War had shown him a piece of the world. He had reenlisted in the army. He wanted to be a part of this new America, a part of this new patriotism sweeping the nation.

Franklin's own words floated like the mist below into her troubled thoughts. "Someday the world will look to America for aid, Collina, and America will answer."

Magic pawed the ground impatiently. "Ok, girl, time for our gallop." As they rode up the steeper side of the hill, she felt the tingle of wind greet her freshly scrubbed face, smelled the grass and wild flowers that always grew in abundance here, noticed the dew of the morn sparkle on the leaves of early autumn sunlight and marveled, as she always did, as earth and sky met for one brief moment.

She could see it now, stretched out like one of grandmother's quilts, telling the McConnell's dream, like a history book filled with the pages of her ancestors, the origin of Ben McConnell, a young man, penniless from Ireland who landed on free soil, to now. Collina could just make out the tombstones of the graveyard to the south of her, Camp Beauregard. The land Pa donated to the state. There were only a hundred acres of Shushan left, some of which were too hilly for farming. Hardly enough for five families to make a living on. Pa had entrusted the estate to her, and Shushan was nothing but a shell of her former self.

She gazed out at the rolling hills, the majestic oaks, the cardinals and bluebirds whistling their morning songs to her entreatingly. What should she have done differently? She covered her eyes with her sleeve, the sun too bright for her to gaze upon. There was no changing the outcome. It was finished. How can I leave it?

But there was no softening the hard lines of Franklin's countenance. His eyes could turn from warm to cold, oblivious of emotion, so calculating behind the deep brows that housed the alert mind and determined will beneath. He had looked that way the day Lawyer Farlin came to Shushan. Franklin could have saved Shushan. Lawyer Farlin knew it. So Lawyer Farlin had started the bidding high, much higher than the land was worth.

Franklin would not pay more merely for sentiment. Collina had lost a sizable chunk of her best farmland. She was furious with Franklin. Why were men so stubborn? Why couldn't they live here instead of Detroit? She could remember his very words. Franklin had glanced from the *Southern Chronicle* and laughed at the idea of moving his plant to Kentucky. "There are trees and hills in Michigan too."

"So? They're Yankee hills and trees and Yankee people."

He laughed. "The war's over. Northerners don't have horns and carry pitch forks. Give them a chance. You'll find a large nationality of Irish and Scots as well as English, Italians, French, Dutch, Germans, and, oh, many more in Detroit. New York harbor has seen quite a mixture during our generation. We're swimming in the same kettle now."

"All those nationalities in one country? What kind of a race will Americans turn out?"

"Some coming over on the boat keep their daughters under lock and key. They want a pure strain, I guess. Like marrying like." Franklin shrugged. "So what if we're a nation of misfits who only yearn for freedom and a chance to live as the good Lord intended. Some might call it an inferior race. But what I've seen it only makes the blood stronger."

"You didn't always feel that way."

"I know. I wasted a lot of years worrying about what didn't matter." Franklin's face grew solemn. He bunched up the papers he was reading and threw them down, rising to his feet in such haste that he hardly noticed her cry of dismay in his untidiness. His sure strides carried him toward the window as if hearing something outside. She realized it was only that hidden undertow, a relic of the past always present, always waiting to catch him up into the waters of the deep where she could not follow.

"I thought I did a noble deed when I rescued Jane and baby Dawn from a watery grave. One no account Indian. Only, I saved the person who would end up saving me." His eyes were glassy as they gazed out over the pastureland. "Do you want to know what kind of race Americans will turn out? As Israel was a nation of Jews, America is a nation of Christians.

"Benjamin Franklin was right. God does govern the affairs of man, and a country cannot exist without His aid. For it was only by God's help a handful of cavalry men won San Juan Hill that day."

He had never spoken to her like this before. Had always avoided questions she would ask about the war. She knew little of the Battle of San Juan Hill.

"You never told me exactly what happened that day. I've often wondered how Joe and Joseph McWilliams—" She stopped. Joseph had loved her; she felt a sudden chill.

Franklin watched her closely. "You're entitled to know the reasons behind my moods." He turned back toward the window, leaving her standing there in the middle of the Indian rug.

"The Spaniards outnumbered us three to one. They swarmed on us like buzzards would a fresh carcass. I remember I let go of the reins, using both hands to fight. Then, Joe's black screamed. It's an awful noise when you hear a beast as large as a horse cry out in pain. I fought my way through the smoke until I found him." Franklin turned, his face drawn and tight with pain. "Joe was slit from stomach to thigh from a Spaniard's sword. I pushed his entrails back into his stomach and wrapped my belt around him, then pulled him to a nearby tree. I'll never forget his words. 'I knew you'd come.' As long as I live, I'll never forget those words."

Collina went to him.

He sighed, taking her in his arms. "That's all God gives us sometimes. A kind of sixth sense. No, it's more than that, 'cause you can feel it. It's like the wind; You can't see it, you can only feel it. It bends the knees of the proudest man so he can feel the dirt again. That's when Joseph found me and took the saber that was meant to be mine…I felt guilt knowing how much he loved you. I, I had taken his life, how can I take the only girl he ever loved as well?"

Collina toyed with Magic's reins. Mother said that a good man doesn't come along but once a lifetime. Still, what would Mother do without her?

Franklin would be awake now. He'd find her note on his plate. She didn't want to be around when he read it, so she'd wait here. She hoped he would leave today so she wouldn't have to face him again. Then she, Mother, Bugie, and Ruby would do what farming they could and have a dress shop on the side. After all, she still had some of the farm left. Skeeder said he'd stay on.

Below, a rider entered the lane she'd vacated. Magic whinnied.

Looking down into the mists she could just make out the tall figure in tan coat and breeches. Franklin spotted her, too, and urged his horse into a gallop. Horse and rider bounded up the hill after her.

So that's what he thought of her. Did he think her so weak that he could change her mind at a whim? She turned Magic in the direction of a small bridle path. "He won't be able to find us in here."

Urging her horse into a gallop, she sped down the lane, bending low to avoid the sodden leaves that still clung to their counterparts. She could feel her riding habit grow moist from tree branches, but she sped on. Pausing in the clearing, she listened, her mount heaving from the exertion and thin air of the highlands.

Then she heard him, Franklin and his horse crashing among the thicket with amazing speed. She looked about her for a means of escape. Pines and maples ahead bordered the meadow. If she could make it to their cloaking limbs, then he'd never be able to find her.

Collina bolted from her shelter, leaning over Magic's neck, urging her into a run.

The thundering hoofs of Franklin's horse were just behind them. Closer and closer the hoof beats drew...suddenly, she found herself across his saddle, thrust from her seat like a bag of oats.

"Oh, you scoundrel!"

"What do you mean by writing such things?" Reining his horse up, he slapped her upturned rump.

She turned to slap his swarthy face.

He laughed, holding her hands. "Time hasn't changed that spirit of yours. Why do you fight me so?"

He was exasperating. She tried to put her feelings into words and failed miserably. "You're disappointing. No wonder your wife left you."

Franklin's brows rose in humorous acceptance and chuckled.

"We're rejects, Franklin, both hard to live with. It's best this way. Marriage is not for either of us."

"Don't fret about what God has turned to good." The eyes that eagerly gazed into hers suddenly clouded. "It hurts me to see you hurt. There were unspoken words. Words not written in that sloppy penmanship of yours, but words that I alone could read, because I've shared the same emotions. That's why I know our love will last." He smirked. "It's a love that can put up with the bad things about your character and still find plenty to love."

Collina looked away. But how could she desert those who had comforted her when they now needed the comforting?

A bitter look came over his proud features as he watched her. His eyes hardened as his spirit fought for control. "I don't intend to have another mistake repeated." A groan escaped his taut lips as he pulled her roughly to him. "I love you. Why can't you believe that?" His arms went around her again, so close, so secure.

"It's too late. It's not just our lives that will change."

His eyes rested on her, penetrating her thoughts. She turned away. His finger gently turned her head. "You mean your mother's and sisters' lives will change. And as for the wants of Collina, they are only secondary to the needs of her loved ones. Well, remember me, my love, for I am in need also. My life will be bitterly lonely again if you turn me away. I will gladly take in your family and care for them like they were my own. As for your mother, you surely know how I feel about her. She has always been like the mother I never knew."

"But," she said hesitantly, "what if Mother doesn't want to leave?"

Franklin searched her face, carefully selecting his words, his tone soft and sincere. "How much longer could you have held out trying to run this farm? I'm no farmer. I'm a businessman. Let Jessie and Bell have it. Not even I harbor any hopes in attaining the land back for you. Lawyer Farlin saw to that. It will never be yours or your mother's again." Gently he added, "A home is nothing without the family you love sharing it. With you and your mother and sisters, my home in Detroit can fill our needs as well. I've already purchased the adjoining five acres behind the brick. Can't that be enough for a while? And if that house doesn't make you happy, I'll buy one that will."

Franklin's face blurred before her gaze. "Shushan was Father's dream."

He cradled her head on his shoulder and whispered gently, "Nothing is forever, not wealth, or land, or health. Only love can survive. Only love never ends, Collina. Let's go ask Maggie, Bugie, and Ruby and see what they say about coming home to live with us."

"Are you sure? Well, then if Ruby promises to come with me—"

"Darling, I don't mind if all the McConnells come. I seek your happiness over my own. I always wondered why I was prompted to buy such a large house. Now I know. It's about time those rooms were filled."

"But don't you feel like you're being duped? After all, where else can we go? Are you sure?"

Franklin chuckled. "You don't see God's hand in this? Only our loving Savior could get you to come with me." He kissed her upturned nose. "He knew that you'd have no other alternative. You said the night of Rose's ball, 'God was going to use me for His grand purpose.'" Franklin drew her closer. "This can't get any grander for me, my love!" His lips joined hers in a loving embrace.

❤ ❤ ❤

Collina stroked the long ribbon streamers intertwined with leaves and the late flowers of her bouquet. The soft silk molding around the curved lines of the wide boat neckline gently folded down to her waistline, floating like the wings of a dove to her slim ankles and Mary Jane shoes. She put a hesitant finger to her tiara and the bridal tulle headdress beneath. The cloche veil dragged the floor behind her dress, her train decorated with raised floral forms of roses and buds that Ruby had painstakingly sewn.

Her heart fluttered, unmindful of her desire to quiet it as the soft notes of the wedding march echoed through the house. Family and friends hastened to make an aisle way for her. Except for stooped shoulders and thicker waistlines, they had not changed. Doc Baker, Martha, Neighbor Burns, Skeeder and his mother and sisters, Big Jim McWilliams, Pete O'Riley, Uncle Charlie and Katie, and, oh, just everyone.

Robert hurried around the corner of the parlor and looked up at her. His shoulders appeared broader in his Army dress uniform. His long legs took the steps two at a time. She smiled up into his handsome face, cupping one gloved hand about his pitted cheek. Robert laughed and grasped her hand and kissed it. Collina smiled, realizing what had lain hidden to her in youth. What made Robert different, why did smallpox not dampen his mystique? It was his character that glowed beneath that one always saw first.

He and Franklin were of kindred spirits and she had not realized it until now. Robert, like Franklin, was his own man, a man who must obey, forsaking comfort for commitment, commitment and faith upon which Billy Sunday talked about the day of Father's funeral. Kindred spirits to perform God's will.

"Picture perfect," Maggie said, her eyes brimming over with tears as she watched Collina descend the stairway. "Right down to your shoes and that beaded stitching on your train."

"You clean up might well."

A well-made man with piercing eyes and a stubborn chin met her gaze. "Skeeder, is that you all polished and neat?"

He bowed low and reached for her hand, then kissed it. "I needed that for good luck. Meet your new manager. Your husband-to-be has hired me to farm and maintain Shushan. And the first order of business is a new roof."

"Oh, Skeeder, really?"

"Yes, you can count on it. And I am to hire three more laborers."

There was no doubt in her mind Skeeder would not forsake his job. Memories of a dingy, dirty little cabin flooded her thoughts. Their eyes met; he remembered too.

There were so many beautiful memories in this house. Only, her Father's dream had dissolved into nothingness.

"What was it Pa always quoted from the Book of Esther? I can remember the feeling, just all of a sudden, the words are hard to recall. Esther 9 something?" Robert said.

Then, like candlelight amidst the blackness of a stormy night, she remembered. Her fears dissipated before the truth. Father had known. He'd known how to ensure their survival. Destiny and faith, small as a grain of mustard seed, had gotten them through the trying years. The name Shushan taken from the book of Esther because of a determined soldier's prayer. A prayer for the retribution of his kindred, a prayer that Americans would be united under one flag again, and that this nation under God would become indivisible, an impregnable force to its enemies. And the words of Esther 9:2 came as clear to her mind as if Father stood next to her, his voice as vibrant and firm as it had been then.

"And no man could withstand them; for the fear of them fell upon all people."

The piano vibrated throughout the room announcing Collina's entrance. She strode toward her new hope.

Robert patted her hand, leading her down the aisle. "Thanks, Sis. Father couldn't have said it better himself."

Her younger brother's square jaw was set, his back was straight, his shoulders broad and unyielding. When had he become so sure? When had he grown so wise? "You'll be facing the devil and his demons out there, with no place to come back to."

Robert smiled down at her. "Oh, yes I do, I have Shushan." He removed his arm from hers. "Don't worry, Sis; I won't be fighting the enemy alone. Now go. Franklin needs your help. Franklin and Father are right. Shushan's destiny is ordained by God. It was meant to set its roots throughout America and prove to every Christian that with God nothing is impossible. You go and tell them that up north. Tell them about the southern part of the Union. Tell them about the mustard seed, like you told Franklin that night in the cornfield. Tell them that where faith abides, hope endures, and God's protection prevails!"

Franklin stepped forward, his heart written across his face as he lifted his outstretched palm. She offered him her hand. She felt the strong warmth of his fingers encircling hers. It would prove an adventure, this marriage, an adventure of love.

Chapter 18

October 24, 1929, Detroit, MI.

*C*ollina awoke with a start. Voices outside had awakened her. She felt the pillow next to her. Cold. Franklin had left. He worked morning to evening. The only time he paused was when she forced him to attend a play with her at the Opera House or Fisher Theater.

She draped her robe around her. Viewing the grounds and spacious lawns beneath, she cracked open the window. It's going to be a nice day. But she could not enjoy it fully because of her dream. What did it mean? Her hands went to the chain around her neck with the mustard seed. Her father's words consoling her.

Ben McConnell had wisdom far surpassing his earthly years in prophesying that America must be united beneath one flag, one cause. That cause of freedom, second only to the cause for a nation of Christians to unite against the universal enemies of hatred and greed. Shushan had survived. Would it survive the next generation?

So many wars. The Civil War her father had fought in, the Spanish-American War Franklin had survived; and most recently the Morocco War and World War I that Robert had battled were over. Surely there would be peace now.

Collina recalled her brother's determination to become the best soldier he could. He felt the Germans would rise to fight again. Robert had to be wrong. The Germans had nothing to fight with. So what was this premonition she felt? Why had she dreamed of want and deprivation?

Her family had adapted well to the big brick house on the outskirts of Detroit. At times her life in Detroit seemed a dream. Would she someday awake to the endless chores that followed a farmer's life from dawn to dusk? She never quite understood the course of events that changed the direction of her life.

No longer did she care where she lived, as long as she had Franklin by her side.

The chatter of workers outside her window grew louder. A group of gardeners was coming from the north side of the house.

"How could you take all the money I planned to pay this month's mortgage with and gamble it in the stock market?"

Collina recognized the voice of Alice, their cook. She peeked down through her window. Yes, and there was her husband, Henry, who did their gardening.

"I would have doubled our money if those investors hadn't started selling their stocks. But don't worry, Alice, my friend said to hang in there, the stocks are bound to come up."

"Humph, not much of a friend, I'm thinking. You better hope there's money enough by Monday to pay our mortgage to the bank."

Collina agreed with Alice. Franklin had voiced his concerns regarding the noticeable decline of parts needed for the automotive industry this summer. Production had slowed, but not the stock market. People had rushed to buy stocks before the price escalated further, hoping in that get-rich-quick dream that many of their neighbors entertained.

Franklin felt hard work was the only way to trust your instincts. But he, too, had been caught up into the fever and had invested a sizeable amount of his profit.

Alice retreated through the kitchen door. Collina rushed to get dressed into her riding breeches. Franklin and she agreed not to invest more that they were able to lose. Sadly, many of their friends did not think the same way. They had often confided in her that they, like Henry, had borrowed the money to invest in the stock market.

A soft knock. Collina, now dressed said, "Come in, Jane."

"You must eat before going to the Bloomfield Hunt Club this morning. There will be plenty of time to get your horses ready for the Opening Day ceremonies for Saturday."

"I will. Jane, you promised me you'd come and see that new indoor riding ring. It is truly spectacular! And the new club house is divine."

Kentucky had their fox hunting clubs, but she was always too busy running Shushan to attend. Now it was different. Franklin had a staff of gardeners, a cook, and a house maid, and Jane supervised them to perfection.

Jane chuckled, her warm brown eyes smiling back into hers. "I promise, I will go with you next time." They had grown close, and Collina was glad to have Jane back. Jane's daughter, Dawn, and her husband had their first child, and Jane had gone to visit for a month.

Bugie, too, was gone. First to college and then marriage to a fine man she'd met at college.

Sunlight streamed into the full-length windows. The aqua green grass spread across the rolling hillside in gentle waves of shimmering color as the vibrant yellows, reds, and burnt oranges of October sparkled beneath a clear blue sky. The clang of shovels and hoes met their ears as she opened wide the window and breathed deeply of the fresh autumn air and the smell of turned up dirt and freshly mowed grass.

"You love the smells of the earth like my people do."

"Oh, yes, I do, Jane." The patch of vegetables, pumpkins, and late squash glistened their heavy-laden bounty to her, and the robins and sparrows voiced their merry song.

Cock-a-doodle-do.

Along with their new rooster. "Good thing Franklin bought the adjoining property, or we might have heard some rebuff as to the new addition of a chicken coop." She needed to hurry. "Is everything ready for Buck Briggs? He should be arriving from Colorado today."

"Yes, he has a lovely suite on the east wing. Only, Miss Ruby says he made plans to stay elsewhere."

"Really? Who else does Buck know here?" Collina turned to gaze out the window again, confused. "Jane, what are your thoughts? For five years, Ruby hardly heard from him. Buck gave my sister quite a whirl, coming from Colorado oftentimes this past year to see her? Do you think his intentions are honorable?"

The idea of Ruby and the children leaving Detroit for Colorado frightened Collina. Only, Ruby is not content. "I feel my sister longs for a place of her own." Collina stroked a tendril of hair away from her brow. "Am I being selfish to want her to stay here?"

"I do not think so."

"Life has not been entirely fair to my younger sister. She needs to find a good man and settle down again." Collina plopped down on the window seat. "I pray my experience with my first husband does not have anything to do with my sister's hesitation to remarry. Buck seems like a sincere man, don't you think? Oh, Lord, I just don't know. I've made so many mistakes in my life, I'm afraid to offer anyone advice."

Jane laid a gentle hand on her shoulder. "God knows the needs of the heart better than we."

Startled, Collina looked deeply into Jane's dark eyes, as deep as cool waters. "You think I'm pushing my sister into a relationship she should not entertain?"

"Time will tell about this Buck Briggs. I do not think he knows Jesus the way we know Him. Ruby is wise beyond her years. Trust God."

"Dear Jane. You are my closest confidante next to my dear husband and Mother." Collina turned and laid Jane's brown hand on her cheek. "I would hate to have Ruby and her children leave this house. Franklin and I love to hear the music of children's laughter fill the emptiness. God has given us the children we always longed for to fill our elderly years. I pray God guides my sister's decision. Ruby has too much love inside her not to share it."

Chapter 19

lad in buckskins or suit, it didn't matter. Buck Briggs would stand out in any crowd. His square chin, piercing aqua eyes, and practical horse sense made him one of Las Animas' favorite mayors. Ruby knew if his duties had not consumed his time, he would have visited her more.

Now that his second term was over, there was an eagerness in his steps, a hint of a question in his mesmerizing eyes. He'd grown a special fondness for her children, and they for him. Coupled with his irresistible westerner charm—she was worried.

She walked down the steps to the garden pathway of the Long estate. Her late husband's words engraved in her heart. "Our children need us to be strong and to plan for their futures." She never imagined her future would be without Stephen. But he had foreseen as much, naming Buck his successor.

Stephen wanted her to marry Buck so she could keep the homestead for her children's future. She wasn't sure why God had thrown Buck and her together. But it was evident to her, through their years of letter-writing and visits, that God expected her to meet Buck's dogmatic beliefs armed with Christian virtue.

But since her husband's death and what happened with Collina's first husband, Ruby often doubted if she possessed the kind of faith and commitment she needed to withstand the evil one's advances. She was a disgrace to the McConnell women. She had abandoned her faith and let her dear husband down when he needed her faith the most. She was fearful she would do that again if she should wed Buck.

Buck's broad shoulders broke her vision of the moon's rays pouring over the gardens of her sister's large brick home. He grinned at her. "You haven't said. Did you enjoy yourself?"

"I did. Shows at the Fisher are my favorite." The wind played with a tendril of her hair and swept her scalloped hemline about her ankles. Buck took her arm and they strolled down the sidewalk.

"I'm glad." Buck's other hand went around her fingers. He squeezed them, his words rushing ahead like a runaway horse. "I couldn't believe my eyes, marble floors, marble pillars, and a coach all brimming over with gold accents, a gold crest, and gold adornments." He chuckled. "Every prospector in Colorado would be here if they knew how much gold there was in the Fisher."

Ruby's laughter broke the stillness of the twilight like a boisterous rooster. She slapped her hand across her lips. "I declare, Buck, when I'm around you, your merrymaking gets me in an uproar every time."

"I reckon that's a good thing. I like to see that sparkle back in your eyes and that dab of color there." He pointed to her cheeks.

More color than she'd like often dotted her cheeks when she was with Buck. She'd forget her manners and rise to the pleasures of gaiety he abounded in. Was her sister right? Had Buck managed to fill the emptiness that Stephan had left? Nonsense.

"Is it true the Fisher brothers were sons of a Russian immigrant, without a nickel between them to call their own?"

"I don't know just how much money they had between the two of them, but people who know them say that to meet them on the sidewalks you'd never suspect they were millionaires." The soft breezes tainted with mums mingled with his aftershave. "Perhaps being self-made men has something to do with their humility. They built the Fisher Building as a sort of public monument to their new homeland and to the city that made their dreams come true."

"A pair of sentimentalists." Buck laughed. "Like us." His deep-throated baritone had accompanied hers in duets of laughter throughout the vaudeville show that night. "And they are not afraid to believe in fairy tales. That Cinderella coach sitting smack dab in the middle of the foyer tells all. All it lacked was six white horses." Buck raised his arm to encompass the wide expanse.

"To carry you beyond the realms of circumstance and into the daybreak of a new life." Ruby laughed in spite of her determination not to awaken her mother or her sister who liked to keep a window ajar. Ruby's sense of humor, too long unused, had overcome her better judgment. When had she last laughed so much or felt so happy? For some undeniable reason oblivious to her, Buck Briggs managed to kindle her imagination and spark her enthusiasm. "I think the Fisher brothers convey the sentiments of a lot of immigrants fresh from Ellis Island. The American Dream has come to many in the shape of the automobile."

"Las Animas, Colorado, has a long way to go before competing with Detroit. It's becoming the throbbing heartbeat of this new industrial age, thanks to Henry Ford."

"Oh, Buck, you can't imagine. Manufacturing industries spring up almost overnight like, like giant mushrooms, and I meet southern migrants and midwesterners almost every day. And then there are the Polish, Irish, and Greeks fresh off the boat, all seeking the same dream and finding work and most of all…a chance to make a better life for themselves and their children. Their Cinderella dream."

Ruby was whisked away remembering when she and Stephen had piled what was left of their possessions into a buckboard and headed for their section of land and their little nine-by-ten cabin on the prairies of Colorado. That had been Ruby's Cinderella dream, her life full to overflowing with her devoted husband sitting by her side. Left now with her late husband's words: "No matter what happens, remember this when you think of me. I have fought a good fight; I have finished the course God has laid before me and I have kept the faith."

But what of her faith? It hadn't been strong enough to believe Stephen when he told her Christ was going to heal him. Could it have been her lack of faith that caused Stephen not to be healed by God?

Austin had called her a holy roller every time she quoted Scripture to him. What had happened to her faith when it was tested?

Buck was quick to pick up her change of mood. "Las Animas wasn't without its own families seeking a better life. If I recall correctly that was yours and Stephen's dream."

She ran her hand across a satiny bright red maple leaf absentmindedly. "Stephen had great plans for our section of land." She turned toward him, swimming into the deep emotional aqua of his eyes. The spices of his aftershave floated toward her; his arm swept its way to her shoulder.

She stepped into the shadows of the colorful maples swaying to the melody of the wind. But unlike the graceful folds of the limbs, her mouth worked its way into firm, unyielding lines. "It's getting late, Buck." She hurried toward the steps and doorpost of her home. That was the trouble with Buck versus her other suitors. Her feelings ran too deep for the tall, handsome westerner and he knew this.

"I came over a thousand miles for a reason, Ruby. Aren't you a little bit curious? Wouldn't you like to know?"

Ruby moved from one leg to another uncomfortably, her back against the oak door, not chancing a look into those aqua eyes again. His confidence undermined hers, and that was as clear to her as it was to Buck. "Is it because of business?"

A pause, then the deep tremor of his voice, gently coaxing, as mindful of her emotions as a father might be with a new child, caused her heart to beat faster, as if in tune to his words, unmindful of her desires.

"No, not for business." He stepped closer.

Ruby's heart skipped a beat; she turned the knob and stepped inside. "Please come in." Their footsteps the only noise greeting her. "We must guard our tongues; my sister says these brick walls have ears." Ruby chuckled, the words of her sister elevated her confidence; alone she felt ill equipped to handle the situation.

"Collina?"

"And Mother, her bedroom is on the first floor. Sis warns everyone, especially my impetuous seven-year-old not to say what you do not want repeated." Conscious of her sister's anxiety for her welfare, she added, "I believe Collina often thinks of me more as her daughter than a sibling. Sleeping with one eye open so to speak until she hears the front door open and close behind me after a date.

"But, I think it is Mother whose ears are as sharp as a bat's. She loves to tell everyone over breakfast what she overheard."

"This house is impressive."

The large oak banister and the staircase that swept its way toward the second floor and the lavish cherry wood paneling on the walls and ceiling, greeted his eyes. "I had heard that the Ford mansion is a sizable estate, an absolutely handsome building of great workmanship, but this house is a mansion in its own right. The Brick is hardly a name that does it justice."

Ruby recalled when she'd first seen the leaded glass doors and walked into the threshold of her new home. Her sister refused to marry Franklin or move to Detroit unless she and the children came.

Buck was looking at her, and as usual, seemed to understand her sudden quietness. This irritated her. She turned away so Buck could not read her face. But the action seemed inconsequential, and this practical, blunt westerner continued to plow his way into her turbulent thoughts.

"It had to be hard on you, moving from your little house in Colorado and then here to all of this." His mood serious. "And by the looks of it, you're still having a tough time accepting Stephen's death."

Were all westerners void of tact? "Thank you for understanding, Buck, and yes it was. I am grateful to my sister and brother-in-law. They took me and my children in when I had nowhere else to go."

"I heard a different story from Collina." His long legs covered the distance between them. Buck's sure hands spun her around like she was no more than one of the dry leaves floating in the wind outside. His sharp eyes swept her face. He removed her satin hat. Her heart-shaped face appeared draped like a halo with the golden rays of the lamp. "I can't believe my good fortune," he whispered. "Stephen selecting me to be your husband. You need never live on charity, Ruby, as long as I have a breath in my body." He withdrew a box from his pocket and placed it into her palm.

159

If this is what I think it is…I have only myself to blame. She stepped away. "Buck, it is past midnight, and I must lay out William and Esther's things for school tomorrow."

"I keep forgetting this is Thursday. Are they still attending that Christian school instead of an accredited public school? Don't they learn enough about that Savior guy at Sunday school and church?"

"One can never learn too much about Jesus."

"I am ready to help you with the upbringing of your children…if you accept me the way I am." His arms went out to capture her into an embrace she had no intention of accepting.

Keeping a safe distance, she said, "And I have written you back that unless you accept Jesus as your personal Savior, we really have nothing in common. I have no wish to 'change you into something you are not.' I would appreciate the same favor."

"And what about this token of my honorable intentions?" He puffed out his chest like their proud rooster did on the birth of a batch of new chicks and pointed to the small box. "I specially designed this ring for you and only for you, either to remember me by or to wear with pride as the token of my love. Come now, would marriage be so awful with me?"

She undid the ribbon. Her face grew warm before his ardent stare. Now is not the time. She turned away, her heart pounding an Indian love call. She set the half-unwrapped box on the coffee table. "Where are my manners?"

She led Buck to a settee and walked toward the china cabinet. "Would you like a cup of coffee or perhaps iced tea? We have both."

Buck chuckled. "Oh, right, Detroit's a teetotalling city, too. As dry as the Sahara Desert, that's what Denver is. How do the Detroiters like this?"

Ruby turned, with two glasses in her hand. "I can only voice the elation of my fellow lady parishioners on the rewarding attributes of having one's husband home at a reasonable hour and not squandering their earnings on loose ladies and foul liquor.

"However, Prohibition has brought a confusing array of problems. Gangsters, bootleg whiskey stills, and speakeasies." Ruby sighed. "Of course, our Canadian neighbors are not helping our situation. Alcohol is constantly being smuggled to Detroit. The police can't seem to catch them."

"Did you think trying to turn a man into something he's not was going to be easy?"

"How do you mean?"

"A man has certain needs and one of those is a good stiff drink now and then. You can't take away that right by making a law against it."

Ruby didn't care for the way this conversation was heading. "Did you say you wanted iced tea? Would you like some tea cakes?"

"Yes, that would be fine, oh, and make mine a stiff one."

She poured out the tea into crystal goblets and topped it with a lemon and lime wedge. Collina had been giving Franklin and his associates tea this way, calling it a good-humor cocktail. She turned toward the parlor, feeling more than seeing Buck's eyes on her. Her baby-blue taffeta gown adorned with contrasting bands of fabric, flowed gracefully with her movement, rustling lightly in the still house. She handed Buck his goblet.

"Did you spike it? I could use a good stiff drink right now."

"Take a bite of your tea cake. That's something you can sink your teeth into, it has some brandy in it and is quite spicy."

"Aren't you going to have anything?"

"I'm not thirsty."

Taking a long gulp of his tea, he smacked his lips. "Just the way I like it. You might have done me a favor. After all, I need to keep my wits about me tonight." He smiled back at her, his mouth working over the tea cake as he studied her. "Sure you don't want one?"

She fingered the folds of her gown, which had only a puff of fabric about the shoulders. Etched with black-looped embroidery, it followed a path that dipped modestly around the bodice. The black embroidery then followed its trail to her waistline. She felt the dress had turned out well.

He held up a tea cake to her. She shook her head. Eating was not a social pastime to her; it was merely a means of survival. As was her dress-making business.

It was a shame the lady she had made it for had not liked it. She could have used the money. She sighed. So went the dress making business. This past summer had been layered with disappointments. Competition was plentiful and there were too few ladies willing to wait for her creations to be completed. Besides, amidst this air of plenty, there was an underlining current of want.

Buck gazed at her thoughtfully. "Actually, I know very little about you, Ruby."

She smiled. That was as it should be. She had never disclosed her innermost thoughts to him, her dreams, not even her living preferences. She was certain, not like the other ladies of his acquaintance had. Perhaps that was part of her mystique that drew him like a magnet. "Then why do you want to marry me?"

"Because our union is of a mutual advantage."

"I can tell you truthfully, if Stephen had known of your feelings regarding Jesus, he would not have been so eager for me to accept your marriage proposal."

"I guess I didn't tell him the complete truth." Buck looked down at his glass. "I can't understand why you continue to place your trust in God. Look at you and your children. Your husband is dead, and you are living on the compassion of your sister and brother-in-law."

"When I voice my qualms on that topic, my sister reminds me that God brought Franklin to us at the right time. That she would have refused Franklin's proposal if I had not gone with her to Detroit."

"Your sister said that?"

Ruby stroked the picture of her and her children Collina had placed in the bookcase. "Who can plan one's destiny but God? He loves us and wants all that is best for his children."

Buck continued to observe her.

"If I needed to choose my contentment and happiness over my children's, I wouldn't hesitate. It would be theirs. Esther considers her Uncle Franklin as the father she never knew, and William looks up to Franklin as both father and confidant."

"What happened to you was just a matter of fate. Why Stephen chose me is a mystery to me. Admittedly, it had been Stephen's section of land that had first enticed me to consider Stephen's proposal."

"Really?" Ruby was suddenly alert.

"Your land is prime real estate. Stephen knew that section would be worth something someday. That's why he wanted his children not to lose their inheritance. Tuberculosis may have staked a claim to Stephen's life, but Stephen was determined it would not displace his family's assets."

"So my decision to sell part of the land and have Tufner become trustee over the rest of the estate must have upset you somewhat."

Buck chuckled. "But it became my good fortune when Tufner lost the election and decided to let go of his portion of land and move back east. I was able to grab up a sizable stake to transfer the papers to me and grab up your assets. Trust me, Ruby, I am your friend. Now that you have made me trustee over the section of this prime real estate, watch what I shape it into." Buck twirled the goblet between thumb and index finger. "I am considering running for governor, and I'll need the proper wife by my side to do this."

Was it the brandy Alice had baked into the cake that caused Buck to disclose this truth? Better for her. "Would you like another tea cake?"

Buck held up his hand. "No thanks, I'd best finish this and go."

Ruby smiled, leaning back on her chair, momentarily closing her eyes.

"You are very different from my Cherokee wife, yet, similar. Kindred spirits, so to speak. She was a wonderful bed warmer."

Ruby's eyes flew open. The audacity. Bed warmer indeed. The only warmth he'll feel from me is when my hand comes in contact with his arrogant cheek. She rose, wrapped her shawl around her shoulders, and said, "I need to get to bed."

"Really?" His eyes twinkled back at her.

She ignored his innuendo. "You need to leave. I have much to do preparing Esther for tomorrow. This is her first time to ride on Opening Day.

"Opening Day?"

"The Bloomfield Open Hunt Club. The Longs and I are members. Opening Day is the highlight of the hunt, and usually comes the third Saturday of September. However, because of the unseasonable rain and the completion of the indoor riding ring, the board decided to move the date. It's this Saturday." Ruby glanced at the ring box yet unwrapped. She must politely return it without offending him.

Buck frowned. "Aren't you going to give me the courtesy to open it?"

She handed him the box. "May I tell you a story that Franklin says confirms that God guides our lives and not fate?"

"There are no differences to the Indians' spirits and this make-believe spirit world of the Trinity you Christians cling to so dearly."

"There is no way I can bring you to that understanding. Collina learned that with her first husband, Austin. That choice is up to you and Christ Jesus, whether you choose to obey and follow Jesus or—"

"How could this spirit thing be any different from what the Indians believe?"

Ruby laughed. A bubbly, sparkling noise that lifted her spirits and the somberness of their discussion.

"Collina led Franklin to this truth in a shriveled up cornfield. To this day he tells my children how she led him to the Lord that evening. It took him half a lifetime to bend his obstinate knee to God's will, and he tells my children not to make his mistake."

"Franklin says that, does he? I have great admiration for your brother-in-law."

Ruby walked toward the full-length windows that provided an ample view of the rolling hillside. The colored lights along the distant river never seemed to sleep. The star-lit skies became one with the twinkling earthly lights.

"But he that doeth truth cometh to the light, that his deeds may be made manifest, that they are wrought in God," Ruby muttered.

Buck's hands pressed on her arms. She felt their intense warmth through her shawl. So Buck's first interest in her was her property. She respected him the more for disclosing this truth to her. Perhaps there was something in Buck God wanted her to cultivate.

"I know you are trying to make amends, and I am grateful to you for it. But there are things you have no understanding of. You need not feel guilty. I release you from the promise you made to my late husband."

Buck chuckled, a deep-throated sound. "So it is my heart you have decided to break this month?"

"What are you talking about?"

Buck spun Ruby around so deftly that a startled gasp escaped her closed lips. His eyes searched hers. "You're not being coy, you're being coquettish. And this must stop. You're not setting a good example for your daughter."

"Oh, I see. You've been listening to the latest gossipmongers."

"Two can play this game. It's time you stop shrugging off every suitor's proposal like one of your fancy ball gowns. It's time for you to live again, if not for your gratification, then for your children's." He opened her palm and slapped the ring box into it, then stormed out the front door.

Chapter 20

*T*hat cantankerous westerner. How dare he say she was being coquettish. Humph! I hope he enjoyed his bed on some park bench last night. She wasn't toying with any man's affections, least of all his. She was living and doing it up grandly.

Saturdays in the Long household were never boring. Especially when that day was Opening Day. Esther, dressed in tan riding breeches, skipped down the steps. Her black curly hair bounced about her riding jacket with anticipated eagerness.

"Good morning, Uncle, morning, Auntie, morning, Grandma Maggie! I'm ready for the fox hunt this morning; are you?"

"Oh, to have the energy of youth once more," Ruby said.

"Come here, I want some sugar, sweet one," Grandma Maggie said.

Esther didn't hesitate. She hugged the bent shoulders to her and gave her grandmother a smacking kiss on her wrinkled cheek, then sidestepped to her auntie.

Collina hugged her affectionately. "Now sit down and have your breakfast."

"Wish I could go," William retorted. He'd received high marks on his spelling and math. In fact, he'd received a perfect report card. But that wasn't good enough for Mr. Rode, his teacher, nor Principal Worthington. William now had to study for a test that would promote him to the next grade.

Ruby placed a bowl of steaming oats before him and smiled

encouragingly. "Your father was smart like you. Don't be afraid of using your God-given talents."

"I'm not, Mother. I like to learn. But I want to do what other boys my age are doing, too. Playing ball and riding."

"Why not let him come, Ruby? I've got a horse he could ride," Collina said, looking at her sister hopefully.

Her son's wishful face melted her heart strings and she nodded. "You deserve a break. I'm not sure promoting you to the next grade is such a good idea anyway."

"I agree," Collina said. "You'll have to make all new friends."

Ruby smiled. "Better get dressed."

William slid off his seat. "I won't be long. I've got my riding clothes all on one hanger."

"Ruby, you must come; it's Opening Day," Franklin said.

"You've been working much too hard at your dress shop." Collina leaned over the table. "You need to enjoy yourself."

"I have a woman coming in this morning for alterations."

"On a lovely day like this? Daughter, it won't hurt to call her—"

"Mother's right." Collina nodded. "You could make her appointment early Monday morning. I feel guilty enjoying a life of ease while you work your fingers to the bone. You don't need to pay us rent. I've said that to you time and time again." Collina's carefree laughter floated through the open windows and mingled with the sparrows chirping outside. "I sound like one of those babbling birds outside, I've repeated it so much."

The birds chattered and congregated around the little feeder, which resembled a model of the Brick. They seemed to be quarrelling. Ruby laughed; they reminded her of her children. "You'd get pretty tired of me if all I did was laze around here. Besides, I like to sew. It really doesn't seem like work to me. I enjoy making women look pretty." Ruby kissed her mother on the forehead and sat down, pulling her chair up to the table.

"I don't believe Franklin would have looked my way a second time if not for your gift with the needle!" Collina said.

Franklin looked up from his paper and gave her a wink. "Those skirts at least slowed her down, Ruby, enough for me to catch up to her."

"Good thing, too. I don't mind saying, I'm getting used to living in the lap of luxury, reminds me of my youth," Grandma Maggie chattered. "Franklin, you remind me of my Benjamin, sweeping Collina off her horse like that."

Collina rolled her eyes at him. "You didn't have to tell her that. Well, now back to Ruby. Getting out and meeting people, that's good. And I know I must sound like a broken record, but you don't know what you've been missing these past weeks. The autumn colors are gorgeous, and Kathleen has invited us for dinner and entertainment at her mansion this evening after the hunt breakfast at the club."

"I know. Patrick's invited me to Kathleen's home."

"My sister, the belle of Detroit," Collina said. "How was your evening at the Fisher Thursday evening with Buck?"

Ruby looked up over her bowl, laying down her spoon. "Sis, Buck thinks I'm a...flirt."

"Really? I don't see why you let what people think bother you. After all, Buck's hiding something, proposing to you and then not confiding what home he is visiting."

"How do you know Buck proposed?"

"Humph! If you call that a proposal," muttered Mother.

Ruby looked at her mother pointedly. "Mother?"

Even the sparrows outside knew when to hush to the wise words of the elderly. "Buck needs considerable work on proposing. Now, Collina dear, you need not worry. Ruby has known love early in life, whereas you later. Ruby has the best of Stephen in her children." Grandmother Maggie patted Collina's hand affectionately. "She will never be alone in life. No one is when they know Jesus."

"But what about Patrick? He's crazy about Ruby," Collina said.

Franklin frowned. "I am not sure about Patrick's intentions. So you be careful, Ruby. He is an ambitious stock broker who may soon be out of work by the look of things." He slapped his paper with finality.

Ruby had no intention of allowing Patrick or anyone into her heart.

A change of subject was what was needed. "Collina, you can't imagine; the Fisher is beautiful. And I enjoyed the Detroit Opera House with Patrick last Saturday. I can't decide which I prefer more. Then there is the splendor of the Fox Theater."

Collina leaned forward. "I can't remember how many times I have gone to see an opera or the ballet at the Detroit Opera, but every time I walk in there I am awed by its beauty. Its Italian Renaissance mystique and those Tiffany mosaics…"

"Wasn't that designed by Howard Crane?" Franklin said.

"Was that the architect who designed the Fisher?" Collina asked.

"No, dear, Albert Kahn designed the Fisher. But I believe Crane did the Opera House, Detroit Symphony Orchestra, and this new building, the Fox Theatre. Was it as beautiful as people say, Ruby?"

"Oh, you mean you haven't been to Woodward Avenue lately? Yes, words cannot describe it. You must see it for yourself."

Franklin chuckled. "The Fox opened in September. We are probably the last couple to see it, Collina."

"What were we doing that evening, Franklin?" Collina took a thoughtful sip of her coffee. "Well, we must all go the next time the Fox is showing a vaudeville show. Let's plan it now, shall we? Only, I wonder if one of those silent movies might be playing somewhere; I heard that the *Street Angel* was good?"

"Yes, I'd like to go," Ruby said. "Janet Gaynor starred in it, and I hear she did a superb job. There's talk she may win an Oscar next year at that new Academy Awards program."

"Let us know where it is playing, and we'll take you and the children."

Franklin gave Collina a wink. "What my wife has said is true. You are the family we always desired."

She felt so loved, so needed here. She never wanted to leave that security. Then why did she look for Buck to come strolling through the doorway of her seamstress shop yesterday? Why had she kept Buck's engagement ring? She must return it, wishing, now, she'd never opened the ring box.

The sparkling ruby beset by diamonds that her late husband had given her was gorgeous. However, Buck's ring was a crystal-clear diamond encased with red rubies.

Stephen gave her a ruby ring to signify her chosen name and the rare and precious jewel that she was to him. The deep crimson color signified the love he felt for her. Till death do us part…

Buck wrote that he wished for his ring to complement Stephen's. That he could never replace her first love; he only wished to love her, to keep her secure and safe.

Had Buck returned to Colorado without even saying goodbye?

"What is it, Ruby?" Collina noticed Ruby's preoccupation.

"Nothing."

Collina squeezed Franklin's hand. "It seems like yesterday when I stepped out in faith, believing Franklin's love for me was sincere, and then God did the rest. My life has become a piece of heaven on earth when you, mother, and the children came with me."

Ruby spooned up the remainder of her oats absentmindedly. "I feel I need to make my business succeed."

How could she make them understand she never wanted to feel dependent? Never seek shelter from life through the arms of a man? Perhaps this new age of woman's independence had gotten a hold of her after all.

"Well, I'm back! You all can stop waiting for me." William laughed. He snatched a biscuit and spooned milk gravy over it, sausage and eggs followed. Filling his plate to overflowing and then pouring himself a large glass of milk from the side board, he made his way to the table.

His buff riding pants, white shirt, and canary yellow vest fit into the decor of the paintings depicting stately hunt riders on freshly groomed horses and well-attired ladies perched upon their side-saddles. He glanced up at the picture hanging over his uncle's head and laughed. "Gee, I could eat that horse I'm so hungry!" In one large bite, he consumed half of his biscuit and gravy.

"Is it still warm, dear? Those new hot plates are supposed to keep things warm for over two hours."

"Mmmm, yes, it's perfect."

The rustling of Franklin's newspaper and the chink of the silverware on fine china meant everyone had settled down to eating their breakfast.

The telephone rang, interrupting this peaceful interlude, and then Jane's responding introduction, "The Long house." All eyes turned to Ruby as she was handed the receiver. "A Mrs. Arthur."

"Mummy, tell her you've made plans of your own today," Esther whispered.

"Hello….Oh, you can't? That's fine. How about ten on Monday?"

Chapter 21

Esther was the first up from her chair to hug her mother and then her aunt. Collina gave Esther a hug back. "So, are you going to the hunt with us?"

Ruby nodded.

"Yes!" Both William and Esther, one on either side, kissed her cheek.

Before long, Ruby sat watching the white horse-farm wooden fencing through her passenger window, then the clapboard-and-green shuttered look of the colonial buildings of Bloomfield Open Hunt greeted her eyes. Ruby gave her daughter's hand a squeeze as they walked toward the stables.

Ruby knew Collina meant well, but she could no longer put off the inevitable. "Collina, you needn't worry about me. I don't want you or Kathleen setting me up with any more dates, okay?"

"Oh. What do you mean?"

"I mean, don't tell your friends that I'm in need of male companionship." Ruby kissed her well-meaning sister on the forehead. "You are incapable of being deceptive, my dear sister."

"I keep telling her that," Franklin said, walking up to them. "I told her you'd smell the bait. Now didn't I, dear?"

Collina cleared her throat. "I'm not the culprit this time; it's our dear friend Kathleen. She wants her nephew to wed well, but most importantly, happily. She has been matchmaking this union for a considerable time, and I doubt if you'll get her to relinquish her plans easily."

Buck's face loomed before her mind's eye. Ruby shook her head. "I've had quite enough of matchmaking from Stephen to last me a lifetime."

Franklin's look turned from humorous to concern. "Buck went out of his way to attain your piece of property back from Tufner."

"Hmmm, well, now he's trustee of my interests," Ruby said. The gravel of the drive scrunched noisily beneath her hunt boots, adding to her agitated nerves.

Collina stopped her, searching Ruby's eyes thoughtfully. "Are you sure there is not a little piece of your heart that could learn to care for Buck the way you did Stephen?"

"No. Not Buck or Patrick." Ruby got her horse out of the box stall and brushed her with long energetic strokes.

"Save some of that exuberance for the fox hunt." Collina chuckled.

A half hour went by quickly. Ruby placed Esther's helmet carefully on her head, then secured the safety strap. Collina checked Lea's girth.

Ruby recalled last year's Opening Day. Many visitors came out and thought they could ride like a pro but couldn't. It was best to put safety first, for the sake of her children. Sis agreed.

"Esther, your mommy and I will stay in the back, with the gate crowd," Collina said. "That way you won't have to jump any coops, unless you want to. We can go around them."

"Okay." Esther smiled at her concerned aunt. "What's a coop?"

Franklin's long strides overtook them easily. "It's about three feet high and looks like the top of a roof." He pressed his fingers together in the form of a triangle and grinned, then turned to his wife. "William is ready. How about you?"

Collina nodded. "Come on, Ruby, let's get our mounts."

Going to the stall to get their horses, Collina surveyed her mare's gleaming white coat, stroking her sleek neck. "I remember like it was yesterday the first time I laid eyes on her."

Ruby smiled. "I can remember it, too, wet and slippery with a film of afterbirth and her coat the color of chocolate milk."

Collina had bred Proud Lady, her thoroughbred to an Arabian stallion from England, one of the Domestic Arabians of Lady

Wentworth's. "I had had my doubts about breeding my mare when I saw the compact 14.9 hand high stud."

"I remember what you said about him. 'Why, he's nothing more than a pony.'"

"I know. Lady Wentworth explained to me that Arabians had proven time and again to produce superb get with unequal stamina. A truly good Arabian stallion's offspring always proved to have better conformation than either their sire or dam."

"Kasha has proven true," Collina said. "Broad in chest, her stamina has already far surpassed a normal thoroughbred. Her loyalty as well as her intelligence well equipped her to handle the risky terrain and dangerous footing of Michigan's sometimes slippery woodlands and hills."

Ruby, too, had a share in this unique breeding, with her horse from Proud Lady. She couldn't help thinking that Collina never stopped being the dedicated horsewoman, breeding horses whether it be in Kentucky or Michigan.

She was glad she'd come with Collina and Franklin, glad to have a chance to enjoy this lovely fall afternoon. She took a deep breath of the lush countryside, observing the terrain as she did.

Bloomfield Open Hunt consisted of a plush and rolling countryside of hills, woods, and meadows. Like a bouquet of flowers, the elms, maples, and poplars displayed a lovely array of brilliant crimsons, gold, and rust.

Exuberance electrified the air that beautiful late fall morning as horses promenaded sleek and shiny, their coats glistening in the morning sunlight, their manes and tails braided. Ladies adorned in top hats and tuxedo-style jackets and split skirts perched elegantly on side-saddles. Riders dressed in scarlet rode alongside them.

There was Kathleen dressed in her shadbelly and top hat. Ruby could see the bright golden buttons of her suit from here. She waved. That was all Kathleen needed.

"Collina, Ruby, it's wonderful to see you were able to make it. Esther, William, we've missed you. Have you been doing well in school?"

"Too good," retorted William.

Ruby smiled and said, "They're thinking of promoting him to the next grade level."

"I envy you, William. I was never good at school, especially in math and science. But my father was very good. My husband says your generation will need college to succeed. Can you imagine that? In my generation, if you graduated from high school, you'd achieved more education than most."

Collina turned to her nephew. "Kathleen's father is owner of a large railway. See what getting a good education can do for you?"

"But all work and no play is not good," Kathleen said. "My father worked constantly and never knew when to quit. Now my husband, George, is different. He loves fox hunting and always finds time to do it."

"Was it your father-in-law who owned so much property in Detroit?"

"No, it was George's mother, and her father was a former transit executive. The Bridges were a prominent family back in 1906, so they tell us." Kathleen laughed. "Or should I say they never let us forget it?" She nodded her head toward the young millionairess, Grayson Bridges. "Oh, I almost forgot, George wanted Franklin to know that he's moving his stocks. Said he heard some nasty rumors."

Collina shrugged. "It's nearly the end of the month, why change them now? Anyways, Franklin moved most of our stocks back into our savings. I did not want him to invest our savings in the stock market. I don't mind if he invests some of his company's profits. I have a funny feeling about it. This burst of prosperity could end, look what Europe is experiencing."

"I don't know much about politics, and I'd like to keep it that way. George is constantly reprimanding me about this. Guess I should read the papers more. I prefer the society page. I'm interested in people and relationships." A mischievous smile swept her lighthearted lips. "And a little gossip thrown in for flavor."

"You like seeing your name and picture in the paper and I don't blame you. You always look lovely." Collina chuckled.

"I'm glad Franklin found you. He was so unhappy before. Now he has a perpetual grin on his face, and it was you who brought that into his life." Kathleen sighed and smiled slyly at Ruby. "I wish I could find a helpmate for Patrick that could give his heart that kind of happiness."

Collina winked at Ruby. "I cannot accept full credit. Franklin's sudden commitment to Jesus has much to do with the change you see in him."

"And according to Franklin, you were instrumental in that, too."

"I may have pointed him in the right direction, but it was up to him to take the steps. Speaking of steps, both you and George are two of the best people Ruby and I have had the good fortune to meet here. You both stepped forward and befriended us, when most of society looked another direction."

Ruby nodded. "Kathleen, we felt like hicks from the hills when we first came to Detroit. You and George helped us feel welcome."

"Well, the compliment goes both ways. You and your sister are the epitome of true class." Kathleen sighed. "My mother always said, 'Styles come and go, but true class out-dresses them all.'"

Ruby remembered a time long ago at Shushan when Doctor Baker and Big Jim had said that very thing.

"Kathleen, if you had seen me in my overalls," Collina laughed, "you might not be so willing to say so many kind words about me. Now, Ruby has always been a true lady."

"Especially when I was killing that rattlesnake on the prairies of Colorado. It's comforting to know that there are such kind people in the world like you and George, Kathleen."

"What an exciting life you lead, my dears."

A tall figure broke the sunlight warming Ruby's left cheek. She turned, and stared into the eyes of Patrick, Kathleen's nephew.

"I'm glad you took me up on my invitation!"

Franklin plowed his way through the crowd around his wife and Ruby, then reined his horse to an abrupt halt before Ruby. "Guess who I ran into on the way here?" Turning in his saddle so Ruby could have a clear view, he pointed his crop toward a large man sitting on a gray thoroughbred. None other than Buck Briggs, in white shirt and cravat, black hunt coat, fawn-colored breeches, and black boots.

"Well, good morning." Buck smiled broadly back at her and tipped his helmet. Ruby glanced from Patrick to Buck and said. "I thought you had left."

"I changed my mind."

Grayson Bridges leaned over and handed a pair of white cotton gloves to Buck. "Here. you'll need these to complete the picture. My you do look handsome in hunt attire. Doesn't he, Ruby?"

"I...thought you'd be halfway to Las Animas by now."

"Did I forget to mention that I met Miss Bridges in Denver this spring? She was kind enough to invite me out to Opening Day." He leaned forward, his voice lowered an octave. "I never knew how large Detroit was until our trip to the Fox Thursday evening. What a fascinating city. Miss Bridges volunteered her services as my lovely tour guide yesterday."

Grayson blushed. "Oh, Buck, you must call me Grayson." Turning toward Collina and Ruby, she said, "Buck gave me the time of my life in Denver. That man doesn't tire. I just had to invite him to Detroit. I was shocked out of my nippers when out of the blue he calls me and says he's in Detroit. He got to my house rather late Thursday evening, and we've been out both day and night ever since. What a time we've—"

"The feeling is mutual, Grayson," Buck said, his eyes never leaving Ruby's face.

So that's what he meant when he said two can play this game. Oh, the gall of this man proposing to me and all along planning to stay at Grayson's home.

Patrick chuckled. "Grayson has the means and the knowledge to show a chap a good time."

Ruby turned her attention to Father Kelly walking toward the wooden platform designed for him to give the blessing on Opening Day. Seeing Franklin, he raised his hand in greeting.

Franklin rode over. "Father Kelly, allow me to introduce you to Buck Briggs. He's visiting from Colorado." The Celtic melody of the bagpipe filtered across the well-tended field. Franklin momentarily paused in his conversation with Father Kelly, listening to the tune of "Amazing Grace" floating in the mist through the throng of hunters lifting up glasses of cranberry juice in jovial good humor.

"You know, Father Kelly, some are calling this age 'the era of wonderful nonsense.' Here we are chasing a fox for no real reason, dressed in our fancy clothing, but when I hear those bagpipes playing 'Amazing Grace,' it brings reverence and one cannot help but remember the words. 'Twas grace that taught my heart to fear, and grace my fears relieved."

"How precious did that grace appear the hour I first believed."

Buck chuckled. It was hard for Ruby to decipher his feelings.

The huntsman, hounds, and whippers-in entered the field. Father Kelly stepped onto the platform and opened his Bible. A sudden hush filtered over the riders. Men uncovered their heads. Father Kelly prayed in the name of Jesus Christ for the safety of riders, horses, and hounds and blessed them in the name of the Father, Son, and Holy Spirit.

"Go on with Patrick," Collina said to Ruby. "Franklin and I will stay behind with Esther and William."

The hunters were off to the bays of the hounds and the sound of the horn echoing through the meadows.

Galloping through the woods and across the hills, Ruby was caught up in the excitement of the hunt. Whenever the terrain permitted them, she and Patrick would ride side by side.

Occasionally, she found herself galloping alongside Buck. However, Grayson was always just a horse tail away. The hounds appeared to fly over the hills in full cry after the fox. Horses and riders now in full pursuit.

Resting on a steep hill with the lowlands beneath wrapped in a cloud of mist, Ruby had time to catch her breath when the beauty of colorfully arrayed trees and mist echoed their sonnet to her waiting ears. Her view was suddenly obstructed when Grayson rode before her.

Grayson was enthralled with Buck. On more than one occasion, Buck had to lead her horse safely around the brush that she failed to see. Why doesn't she hook a lasso around him and leave it at that?

"Hi there, gorgeous." Patrick leaned over his saddle, peering at her underneath her safety top hat. His lips parted, displaying a toothy grin. Ruby politely smiled back. "Has anyone told you how gorgeous you look in black? That top hat and cutaway look is fetching on you."

"Really?" Ruby replied, her brows puckered in distress. "I always thought black a morbid color. Something one should only wear for funerals."

Patrick's eyes sparkled into hers. "You'd look good in anything. I can't wait until this evening. Kathleen has planned a delicious dinner and dancing afterwards."

"I'm looking forward to it." Ruby noted Grayson talking to Kathleen, but Buck was not with her.

"Who are you looking for?" Patrick said.

"The—hounds, they look like they may draw again."

"If the hounds should get onto another fox scent, that means at least another two hours with you. Can't say I wouldn't mind it. Being around you, Ruby, is like being on a continuous romp."

"Oh?" Ruby recalled Buck's words. Coquetting? Her conscience poked her uncomfortably. Well, Patrick worked and lived in New York City, and she only meant to show him a good time. He would forget about her once gone. She smiled. After all, out of sight out of mind, so to speak.

"Say, what are your thoughts about my corporation having a branch in Detroit? My sister loves the idea. Think of the advantage living and working in Detroit could give us. We could see each other practically every day."

Ruby felt as if her saddle had sprouted porcupine quills. Her stock tie felt snug, like a noose. She placed a white gloved finger between it and her neck trying to widen it.

Her eyes scanned the landscape. "I wonder how Esther and William are doing. Really I shouldn't leave my sister solely responsible for them."

"I don't see how you have any other choice. There are only two sides to a horse and of what I've seen of late, that Buck guy has been sparring with Franklin and Collina for a spot every time an opportunity arises to be alongside either William or Esther."

"What?" Ruby galloped up the hill. She sucked in her breath. There was Buck, laughing and offering William and Esther a piece of hard candy. A custom on the hunt, for it gave the receiver sugar and added moisture to a sometimes parched mouth. How could she have let this happen? Ruby headed toward her son with Patrick right behind her.

"Buck!" Oh, he was too exasperating.

Buck smiled like a cat would to a mouse peeping out of its mouse hole. "Are you enjoying the hunt?"

"Of course." Ruby retorted, staring at her son. "Are you having a good time?"

"This is great, Mom."

"Can we do it again next weekend?" Esther said.

"We'll see." Ruby craned her neck. "What happened to—"

"Grayson?" Buck chuckled. "She's around someplace. Guess I gave her the slip." He looked sheepishly at Ruby. "You know how it is," he muttered. Looking back at Patrick, he winked.

Chapter 22

*R*uby," Collina whispered. "These are the new electric lights that just about everyone in the city has. The house is also equipped with running water."

"Really? Just like the Fox Theater."

"Yes, and they have a coal burning furnace that's called a stoker that gradually feeds your furnace."

"William would like that," Ruby said. "Less trips up and down the basement steps feeding the burner."

"Kathleen's home was designed by Howard Crane. He seems to be the most sought-after architect in Detroit," Collina said.

"He built the Fox." Ruby examined the high domed ceiling and the intricate scrolled plaster and felt as spellbound as she had entering the Fox Theater.

"Yes! He's built over thirty other masterpieces like these throughout Detroit. His talents and imagination seem boundless. Why look at this foyer, have you seen anything like it?"

White marble floors and pillars of Grecian white and gold crested vines worked their way to a sculptured three-story ceiling. Crystal chandeliers and full-length mirrors completed the glittering white entranceway. The swirling stairway leading to the second level garnished with a gold tipped hand rail added just the right accent.

Butlers dressed in tuxedos waited to carry the coats and furs of each guest. Waitresses in crisp black suits with white cuffs, starch-white aprons and little satin hats adorned with black bows, carried silver trays laden with an assortment of drinks and hors d'oeuvres, and completed the picture of opulence.

"This splendor takes my breath away. Does it yours?" Collina said.

Ruby nodded.

In walked Dr. Luke Baker with a stunning woman draped in furs and jewelry from head to foot. "That must be Luke's wife."

Luke had seen Ruby in the same moment. "So, are you living in Detroit or visiting?"

"We've been here since 1922," Collina said. "It's amazing we haven't bumped into each other sooner. And this must be your lovely wife?"

Luke looked down. "No, my wife passed away last March due to cancer. You know, Ruby, when that disease hit so close to home, it made me more determined to learn how to abate it. I am studying nutrition and the absence of tobacco and alcohol in the body. I really think that proper nutrition and vitamins might be the way to prevent most of our diseases."

Collina patted his arm. "You will, Luke, we have no doubt you shall come across a cure. Now, you must come and visit us. How about Friday evening for dinner, say six?"

Luke smiled. "I shall place it on my calendar."

"And of course your lovely date is welcomed as well."

"Collina, I can't believe you haven't recognized me yet. Rose Baker?"

"Ah…Rose?" Collina's brows went up like a hunting dog's tail on a new scent. "Why of course—"

"There you are. I don't know how I could have missed you." Patrick strolled up to Ruby. He claimed her arm, laying it carefully on his own.

Franklin's tall figure burst through the doorway. He was laughing loudly at something the equally tall man beside him had said.

"You do look divine in that shimmering champagne crepe, Ruby. Doesn't she, Buck?" Franklin said. "But I must confess, I am partial to my lovely lady in red." He smiled into Collina's eyes devotedly, taking her gloved hand into his and sweeping it with a kiss. "I'm glad you took my advice, Collina, you are lovely amidst this glowing white."

"A lovely spark of color, especially with your dark hair done up in that sweeping twist." Ruby shyly avoided Buck's gaze, pulling at the tops of her long, black gloves.

Collina laughed. "My hair is peppered with more silver than black now."

"All the more lovely." Franklin kissed her hand again.

"Franklin, Luke and his sister are here. I have invited them to dine with us next Friday evening."

Suddenly alert, he swerved toward the couple standing off center. "So it is. Nice to see you again."

Buck placed his thumb beneath Ruby's arm and gave it a nudge. "You are equally lovely, Ruby. You resemble a golden angel adorned with a flaming crown. You should wear your hair like that more often. I especially like that ostrich feather; it sets your golden highlights off admirably." A smile creased his dimpled cheeks as he lifted her hand and kissed it.

Patrick's brows puckered. "I think it may be time to take our seats at the table. I do believe that Grayson is looking for you, Buck." Patrick offered Ruby his arm, escorting her to the dining room with Franklin and Collina following.

"How well do you know Buck Briggs?" Patrick asked.

Patrick's feathers were undeniably ruffled. "We met in Colorado when my husband and I were farming a section of land near Las Animas." She disengaged her arm from Patrick's to sit.

The mahogany table with matching chairs sat the twenty guests comfortably. Servants stood at the corners of the room patiently waiting for each guest's bidding. Ruby looked at the plates and silverware in alarm; she had never seen such an assortment of exquisite tableware settings before. Kathleen and George sat at either end of the long table. Their duties as host and hostess displayed admirably their attempt to make each guest comfortable, no matter what the cost.

"Not even Aunt Louise had been this fancy," Collina muttered to Ruby.

Buck sat directly across from her and Patrick with Grayson to his immediate right. He looked the perfect gentleman in a tuxedo that fit him snuggly across his broad shoulders and perfectly at the waist.

"You and your husband owned a section of land in Colorado?" Patrick's voice was marked with curiosity.

"And now the property in Colorado is worth its weight in real estate," Buck said.

Valuable? That prairie land? What is Buck up to?

A tinkling bell brought in the first course, clam chowder.

Patrick, silent, with puckered brows, brooded over his soup as if what Buck had revealed to him took time to digest. Shrimp salad followed. Ruby began to enjoy the pampering and the delicious entrees.

Patrick cleared his throat, as if what he had to say was of grave importance. "Ruby, you are both beautiful and loyal. I knew you were special the first time I laid eyes on you. Now I understand why every gentleman in Detroit wants to marry you."

Ruby's spoon stopped halfway to her mouth. What should she say to her audacious suitor? Painfully aware of her mistakes, her eyes were drawn to Father Kelly sitting a few seats from hers. She could no longer lead Patrick on to make Buck jealous. There. She had admitted it. Now maybe her conscience would quit poking her. She glanced up from her plate. Grayson held a shrimp she had dipped in cocktail sauce to Buck's mouth. It would serve Buck right if he got that white shirt stained red.

Buck noticed her look. Taking his napkin, he carefully placed it across his shirt and bit into the shrimp, taking tail and all.

"Oh," Grayson said, "I just adore a man with a healthy appetite."

"Don't feed me again, Grayson," cautioned Buck. "I'm too independent." He sent her a lingering smile. "Tell me, how do you spend your time when you're not galloping across the countryside in tails and top hats?"

"Oh," she said with a regretful sigh, "this is Opening Day. We do not usually dress this way." Grayson rolled her mascaraed eyes to the sculptured ceiling.

Grayson and Patrick deserved each other. But then, was she implying that she and Buck—?

"Actually, the sport began in the 1700s," Patrick said. "Riders and hounds would hunt the vermin to rid farmers of the pesky fox that stole their livelihood, their poultry and whatever. So the Europeans made it a sport of riding with trained foxhounds across the countryside. Back then they did kill the fox. Today, we just chase them."

"Colorado ranchers and farmers have a time with coyotes and wolves killing their livestock. We shoot the varmints dead. I doubt hunt clubs would thrive in my state. You won't get the men to discard their jeans for these breeches."

"Oh, but they look so good on—some men." Grayson blushed when Buck's eagle look descended on her. She grasped her water glass and immersed her lips around the smooth rim.

"That goes for some women." Patrick smirked, his head tilted toward Ruby.

She rolled her eyes and conveyed her short fuse to her sister. Collina bent over her plate, her shoulders rolling with humor.

Waiters removed plates and filled water glasses, tea glasses, and coffee cups. A scurry of activity filled the large dining room as plates of stuffed flounder and prime rib made their way to the diners.

Ruby didn't remember when she had tasted flounder so delicious. Patrick had chosen the prime rib and equally enjoyed his. The crystal chandeliers above her head were turned off and a flaming cherry soufflé carried in by the tuxedoed waiters created a festive allure to climax the exquisite cuisine.

After a quick toiletry in a gold accented indoor privy that Kathleen called a bathroom—Ruby and Collina had never see the likes of before—they joined a group of ladies who had congregated in the conservatory, where Kathleen began explaining about her tropical plants. Rose drew Collina and Ruby aside as the group moved from the hibiscus to the orchid.

"Get a good look at that!" Rose whispered, pointing to a couple of women with bobbed hair and sequined tiaras perched on their waxed-down curls. "I don't know how they can see with that layered mascara weighing their eyelids down, and get a look at that makeup. They've layered enough rouge on those cheeks to last me a week."

"Who are they?" Collina said. "I've never seen them at the hunt club."

Rose placed a hand to her coiffure and sighed. "No, never, they'd be laughed out of the club if they happened to lose their way and wander inside." She elbowed Collina when one flapper bent over to display the tops of her rolled-up hose. Her short skirts swished in gay pleats to the sudden bobbing of her hips.

Ruby chuckled when the flapper displayed what she sought in the folds of her nylons. She snapped open her cigarette holder, selected one, then perched it loftily on her silver holder and puffed away. Smoke encircled her head like a wreath.

Ruby coughed. Over the breadth of Rose's coiffure, Collina motioned toward the closed doors of the study and gave Ruby a humorous twirl of her eyes.

Ruby understood immediately. Second dessert. It was a term Collina had good-naturedly nicknamed the playful innuendoes of the hunt diners who relish the flavor of digestible gossip after dinner. "Wonder if Franklin is enjoying his second dessert," Ruby whispered. "What do you say we find them?"

The conservatory door swung open and blew in an assortment of leaves as well as Patrick on the multi-brick colored walkway. His gaze swept every woman. Ruby took a step behind Collina, but to little avail.

"I take it you are tired of Patrick's wooing?" Collina whispered.

A punctilious smirk swept Patrick's face when he spotted Ruby. He raised his arm in salutation, striding toward her in purposeful steps.

"Patrick, do you know where Franklin is?"

"Yes. Allow me to escort you lovely ladies to the study." He offered each an arm.

The pungent odor of pipe tobacco and spirals of cigarette smoke blended with the odors of hickory from the large stone fireplace in the east side of the room. George stoked the logs, causing sudden sparks to curl upwards, then returning the stoker to its accustomed place, reached for his packet of pipe tobacco. "Well, fellows, how are your stocks doing?" George drew in a thoughtful puff.

"Great, at the moment," retorted one man. "Do you have any news that might be worth listening to?"

"I heard an ugly rumor that this bull year could end dramatically and tumble over our heads."

Buck and Franklin had taken a seat in the plush leather chairs nestled on either side of the multicolored stones that encased the brick hearth. Buck stretched his head. Seeing them, he elbowed Franklin. He motioned Collina and Ruby to adjoining chairs.

George took a few more puffs. "I think I heard the same rumor, Bill. But that's all it is, just speculation. Someone upset that they haven't the funds to warrant immediate wealth."

"This time last year we had the biggest winning on our stocks ever."

George nodded. "I know, Bill, but Europe is having some real problems with their economy. I hope it stays across the ocean and doesn't affect us."

"Well, as long as we don't invest any money we can't afford to lose, we'll come out all right," Franklin said.

"That's the problem," said Buck. "A lot of people I know in Las Animas think the gold fields are now the stock market. That they can strike it rich and become millionaires overnight. They don't pay off their homes, thinking they can do better with their money in stocks."

"That's true," said George, "I find it beneficial to pay the minimum on my mortgage and invest my assets, instead, in stocks. I made over $50,000 doing that."

"But it's a gamble, George," Franklin said. "No one knows where the stock will be from one day to the next."

George tilted his head up and puffed, in consideration. "The way I see it, it's a gamble every time a farmer sows a crop, or a businessman expands his business. You don't know for sure you'll make that money back. That's why stocks are no different than anything else in life. But at least you got a chance of striking a rich vein."

Franklin shook his head. "As long as I can supply food for the table and don't have a bunch of debts staring me in the face every month, that's riches enough for me."

"That's your prerogative, Franklin, but if it will make you feel any better, Wednesday I'm planning to take most of my assets out and pay all of this off," George said, waving his pipe in the air. "Seems my wife has been talking to yours."

Franklin nodded. "Collina and Ruby have good heads on their shoulders and when the two of them get together, it's like moving the Appalachian Mountains to get them to think differently."

"I think the entertainment is about to begin. We might as well join the ladies," George said.

Ruby felt old-fashioned in her gown. Many of the ladies were adorned in the newest rage of low waistlines, shimmering fabrics, and way shorter hemlines. She glanced down at her ankle length gown.

Grayson's manicured hands were layered on her hips. Her gold silk turban hat with the little tassel flipped to the left of her ear was very modern. Springy curls peaked from beneath her bobbed hair. Ruby's hand went self-consciously to her hair, styled in the newest rage from France called a French twist. She envied Grayson's confidence. She approached every style with charisma and exuberance.

A woman Ruby didn't know pulled Buck toward her, motioning with a bejeweled arm toward the dance floor. Ruby pursed her lips. *Perhaps this new flapper ensemble creates in the wearer a sense of independence.* Grayson crossed her arms and scowled back at the woman.

"Hmm, the music isn't bad." Ruby tapped her toe to the beat.

"Would you like to dance?" Patrick asked.

"Not especially; it's a Charleston and I think this latest rage was created specifically for the younger generation." A lady who had to be in her mid-twenties, swished her hips so energetically it sent her short skirts swinging way past her rolled up nylons. "Such youthful vivacity!"

"Hmm, well it fits your personality."

"The Charleston? How do you mean, Patrick?"

"Oh, no. I meant that it fits your personality that you do not like the Charleston. You're much too, well, vintage to enjoy something so blatantly modern. Look at the way you wear your hair and how you dress. It's a look that would fit in any century."

If Patrick was trying to make her feel outdated, he was doing a good job of it. "I like to dress like the individual I am. I believe in individuality, of course, not to the extreme of being unusual. That is why I pick my clothes very carefully."

"That is you." Buck's masculine voice, placed conveniently behind her right ear, caused her to jump to one side.

"Where did you come from?" She didn't know whether she should be angry or flattered that Buck had managed to escape the claws of Grayson. She felt Patrick's arm go protectively around her waist.

A smile crossed Buck's square jaw. He bowed. "I wonder, fair maiden, if you might consent to having the next waltz with me?"

"That, that would be impossible," stammered Patrick. "You see, Ruby has promised me the next one."

"Patrick, you flatter me. You have hardly left my side all evening."

"Never," Buck chimed.

"Never what?" Ruby retorted.

"Patrick has never left your side for the entire evening, except for the occasional powder room break," Buck burst out angrily.

Ruby smoothed her sequined head band that wove across her forehead to the ostrich feather perched naughtily to the left of her French twist. The fact that Buck had noticed what she did throughout the evening had her cheeks feeling warm.

But that wasn't what Ruby wanted. She wanted to be disengaged and feel the unemotional commitment she felt toward Patrick.

She fanned her hand before her face and turned so Buck would not see her heightened color.

He chuckled deep in his throat.

In low, even monotones, she said, "Patrick is right; I need to dance with him. And I believe Grayson is in need of your services."

Buck bowed and without a word strolled across the ballroom floor.

With the soft notes of the orchestra blending the beginning notes of "Till We Meet Again," Patrick drew her into his embrace. His breathing quickly elevated, perhaps because he was so obviously out of beat with the music. The melody wrapped her into a cocoon of nostalgia from when she danced with Stephen beneath the Colorado stars one last time.

"Smile the while you kiss me sad adieu," came the words.

In an attempt to still her heightening emotions, she said, "Is the Charleston popular in New York?"

"The Charleston is taking over there like it is here. I doubt it will last long."

"Wedding bells will ring so merrily. Ev'ry tear will be a memory..." That was what Stephen had hoped for her with Buck. "I only hope Americans never lose their love for the waltz."

"When a couple can come together as one and blend with the music, it's almost like—"

"Poetry," Ruby said.

"Yes." Patrick's hand closed tenaciously around hers.

With the notes of the instruments lulling to a graceful conclusion, Patrick took her hand and led her to the large veranda. The night wind weaved about the trees in the yard, fingering them ever so gently, which was all that was needed for the vibrant red and golden yellows to fall like snowflakes in the soft light filtering from the open door of the ball room.

"I believe Michigan's perfect season is autumn. It's so beautiful then."

"Has any one ever told you how lovely you are?"

"Me?" Ruby choked out.

Patrick moved toward her with the grace of a cougar.

Ruby felt more like his prey than his companion. Moistening her lips, she contemplated a safer avenue of conversation.

"Your lips, not too small and not too large. I've been wondering what they would be like to kiss—"

"Patrick, we're just friends. You mustn't do anything that might jeopardize that."

"Friends?" He stopped in mid stride. "Wherever did you get that idea?" His arm reached for her before she could move away. She was captured within his strategically placed maneuver.

"I think I need to show you—"

"Patrick, let me go."

A tall, lithe shadow appeared from nowhere. The man wrenched Patrick's arm, freeing hers.

"Guess it's my turn to have that dance." Buck's voice sounded menacing.

Patrick startled, regaining some of his composure, said, "See here.

She is my intended. You have no right to interfere."

"What?" She couldn't have heard right.

"If this abhorrent westerner would give me a chance, you would know that I intend to become your devoted husband."

"I, I, just don't know what to say, Patrick. I—"

"Yes?" Buck tilted his head like an obnoxious owl. His words from the previous night echoed in her head. All that was left was the "who, who...I told you the truth about yourself..."

Her face burned with humiliation. Her life, her reputation would be in shambles if—the word floozy jumped into her thoughts. She'd overheard someone call one of the flappers that. She didn't exactly know what the word meant, but, oh my. She never meant to lead Patrick on. Buck had gotten her into this predicament, him and Grayson.

"I am not looking for a husband, Patrick. I've been married." She glanced down at her ring finger; Stephen's ring sparkled back at her. She squared her shoulders. "I have no desire to wear another man's ring."

Her face felt as if it were burning beneath Buck's acrimonious look. His square jaw resembled one of her brother's traps, and the gleam of his eyes, two dueling pistols. Her cheeks must surely match the scarlet maples.

Buck barred her escape. "I was the one who rescued you from him."

Shaking with rage, the pounding of her heart echoing in her ears, she said, "Good night, Patrick, and good-bye, Buck!"

His hand went to her arm like an iron handcuff. "You talk about your Jesus. Where is your faith, your hope in God to trust your heart? I know you care for me, why do you continue to push me away?"

She struggled.

Patrick reached for Buck's arm. Buck shrugged him aside like he was a bug. "Get out of here, short stuff."

"I can see where I stand now!" He ran out of the room so fast, he stumbled over the doorway. He was scared of Buck.

Well, she could handle this outrageous westerner without anyone's help. "I warn you, let me go."

"That's why you scoff at me over your other suitors. Because I know. Yes, Cinderella is running, running away from every Prince Charming that crosses her path because she can't face the truth about herself. She's afraid to give her heart another chance at love."

The gall! "If you must know, you remind me of my sister's first husband, Austin. He refused Christ Jesus, too, and look what happened." Her eyes stormed into his. "He left my sister! And she was deathly ill with typhoid!" She kicked him hard in the shin.

"Ow!"

The deafening sound of her heart beating its wrenching message to her unwilling mind caused hot tears to blur her vision.

"Hold up you cantankerous woman. Who's Austin? If you're going to brand him as like-minded to me—I have a right to know!"

Chapter 23

uby locked the door of her small shop early, then joined the ever-increasing group of pedestrians crowding Woodward this last Tuesday of October.

"Record Trading Done in First Half Hour!"

Ruby handed the paperboy her coins. She skimmed the headlines: "STOCKS WAVER; UP, THEN DOWN."

"I'm ruined, I'm ruined," said one suit-clad gentleman. "I invested my family's life savings, even this month's mortgage payment, thinking I'd triple my investment like I did in September. What will I tell my wife?"

"Yeah. I became a millionaire overnight and overnight I'm a pauper!"

Ruby hurried past the men and turned the corner. Her heels clipped like a prancing pony on the pavement toward the safety of her domain, the Brick. Collina and Franklin would know what to do.

The ice wagon made its slow descent down her street. The horse appeared indifferent to the goings on. She stopped. The vehicle pulled up to its next customer. She reached into her sack lunch for the apple she hadn't eaten. The soft muzzle of the gentle mare politely picked the apple from her palm. The juice from the fruit foamed on the mare's lips as its large teeth crunched it into applesauce in a matter of minutes. "There is nothing my worrying will do to rectify the situation." She stroked the mare's face thoughtfully.

Jake and his trusty horse made their rounds like clockwork every day filling up his customer's ice boxes with large cubes of ice. A twenty-five pound cube or fifty pound cube was put into the top of the ice box. Behind the wagon was an assortment of young boys, who loved chasing the wagon down the streets, grabbing the ice chips that fell from the ice blocks. It was an unusually warm day for October and Ruby smiled, realizing the boys were working up quite a thirst in their activity. At least some things never change.

"Hi, Mrs. Meir." One tall and very dirty boy disengaged himself from the group. Grabbing his ball cap off his head, he said, "Do you remember me?"

"You're Mrs. DeGrandcamp's grandson, right?"

He nodded, his black hair shining in the bright sunlight like a blackbird's wing.

"How is your dear mother?"

"She's fine. She's at St. Anne's saying the rosary."

"My, I don't know how your mother does it with six children and three little ones. I just have my two and they keep me busy enough." Ruby cocked her head. "I hope you help her with your brothers and sisters?"

"Mostly Ann does, she the oldest girl." The noise of iron shoes grazing pavement, the screeching metal wheels of the old wagon and the scents of horseflesh, damp leaves, and dripping ice broke into their conversation. "Well, I got to be going."

Ruby watched Eric run after the ice wagon. She envied the boys, envied their youth. What would happen next? Mrs. DeGrandcamp had confided in her. She worried about her son-in-law borrowing money to invest in the stock market. Hence the reason Eric's mother was in church, praying.

Ruby remembered Saturday's conversation Collina had with Kathleen McCray.

Who would have suspected that the forewarning Kathleen's husband made that evening of Opening Day would prove true? Still, not even Kathleen or George had predicted Wall Street's crash.

Then the article from wealthy financier John J. Raskob that Ruby read in the *Ladies Home Journal* came sharply to mind. "Everyone Ought to Be Rich!" He advised Americans to invest just $15 a month in the market. After twenty years, he claimed, the venture would be worth $80,000.

Patrick urged her to borrow on the equity of her Colorado property. Stockbrokers like Patrick and even banks funded this reckless expenditure. When she investigated further, sitting before the bank manager, she learned she must pay 20 percent interest on that loan. Patrick said the risk would be worth the rewards.

She'd argued with him that she never had $2 to spare, let alone invest in a gamble. "That's what the stock market sounds to me, just another form of gambling."

Patrick was persistent, so she asked Franklin's advice. He had told her to remain firm. He'd spoken harshly to Patrick after Kathleen's dinner party. Franklin stated that because J.P. Morgan had pooled his resources and was buying large amounts of stock, this should not encourage investors to willingly pay more for a share that might be doomed to fall. Morgan hoped investors would do exactly that.

The fallen stocks had devastated many fortunes. Ruby might as well have invested in the stock market. For the crash hurt her meager income all the same.

She resumed walking. She'd not taken the street car home. She needed to save every penny. She nodded to the man selling his produce from his fruit wagon and paused to give his horse a pat on the neck and hurried on.

She had left her dress shop early, leaving the discarded dresses where she had placed them. One after another, the ladies sadly looked on her lovely designs and shrugged their shoulders. They could not afford to purchase them. Their husbands had lost a considerable amount of money in the market. Could she hold them for a little longer until the stocks went back up?

The milk man suddenly was walking alongside of her, the glass bottles of his milk clanging against each other. She glanced up. His horse was keeping pace with him, and would meet him at the end of the road after he delivered his milk to the houses.

Mr. Tuff tipped his hat.

"Before I make the trip to the Long house, will I be receiving payment for my milk today?"

"Why wouldn't you?"

"I have your eight quarts, but can't afford to give them on credit. That's why I'm later than usual. Been trying to track down customers who promised payment. So far, not one could afford to pay me. Oh, they're positive they'll soon have the cash, but I'm in debt to the milk dealer for my produce."

She shivered. The sun still shone as bright as it had when she closed her shop door. Why did she feel a chill working its way up her spine? "Follow me. I'm heading home now." She reached into her reticule and removed her change purse. Yes, she had the needed money. Mr. Tuff delivered his milk to the last house at the end of the street. His horse waited patiently for him.

"You want a ride? Plenty of room. See?"

Ruby lifted her skirts and climbed into the high perched seat.

The bay horse was not in a hurry. Ruby could have walked the blocks faster. Still she nodded and listened politely to Mr. Tuff's broken English. He apologized for being late with their milk order and not wanting to extend anymore credit. As they neared the large brick, Ruby turned. "I can well appreciate your feelings, Mr. Tuff."

He stopped the milk wagon next to Myra's carriage. Strange, this was not Myra's appointed day for a visit.

Like some Detroiters, Myra still owned a horse and buggy. Most of the cars driven were Model Ts. Although Ford's main selling factor was its affordable price, many families' pocketbooks couldn't afford the vehicle. If you didn't own an automobile, you rode a bike, walked or paid the fare for the street car. If you wanted to go downtown, you caught the Harper car and that would take you through Hastings Street to downtown Detroit and return down Beaubine Street. Usually Myra rode the trolley.

Mr. Tuff helped Ruby down.

"Collina, Mr. Tuff is here with our milk order," Ruby said as she opened the front door.

"Oh, hi, Mr. Tuff, can you take your crate around back to the kitchen? I'll meet you there with your money."

Ruby let out a sigh of relief, but the look in Collina's eyes told her something was amiss.

Ruby didn't have to wait long to find out what it was. Myra sat in the parlor, handkerchief to her eyes, crying.

"Clem lost his job," Collina whispered. "He's gone out to one of those awful speakeasies on one of his binges. Franklin and Buck are looking for him now."

"Buck? You mean he's still at Grayson's?" Ruby, bewildered at the sudden leap of her heart, attempted to cloak her expression.

Collina chuckled. "I don't believe Buck will be run off as easily as your other suitors."

Ruby hung up her coat and patted her coiffure as she gazed in the mirror. She guiltily wished she hadn't frivolously used her money to have her hair bobbed. She sighed. She had two hats she could wear with the fashionable hair style, and she wasn't at all used to seeing so little hair. "Do you think my nose looks larger? I mean, there just is so much of my face exposed." She frowned back at her image.

Collina smiled back into the mirror at her. "Not at all. I think your new hairstyle looks adorable on you…I thought knowing Buck hadn't left might have that reaction. We had an interesting conversation regarding Austin."

"Ah, really?"

"Yes, he seemed quite upset to learn how he left me. I explained how God worked it for the good of all in the end. You've been so moody lately; has it got something to do with Buck?"

"I have not been moody. Buck and I don't see eye to eye about anything. I thought that would make you happy. Do you want your niece and nephew to live in Colorado? If they do, you'll never see them but at Christmas."

"True. Franklin has grown to love them as his own. We'll worry about that later. Come and help me cheer up Myra."

Ruby followed Collina into the parlor. *What made Collina think Buck stayed back for me? After all, he is being entertained by the most beautiful and wealthiest aristocrat in Detroit.*

"Ruby, I love your new bob; only, your face is as red as a harvest moon." Myra dabbed her eyes, and in a pretense of humor, said, "Which one of your beaus caused such heightened feelings? I worried we had a single sister on our hands for sure?"

"Myra, you have more important things to fiddle about than who I'm dating."

Myra shrugged. "I don't care. I can't. I'll go mad if I do. Besides, I have confidence in Franklin. Clem doesn't stand a chance next to that godly man. And now that Luke Baker has taken an interest in our health, I'm sure he'll up Clem's vitamins and minerals, in hopes of regulating his mood swings. I admit, I am worried." She swiped her eyes. "This stock market thing is going to have an effect on everyone."

Maggie entered the parlor leaning heavily on her cane and sat down in her rocker. Myra got up and gave her mother a kiss on her cheek, then sat next to her, accepting one of the glasses of ice tea Collina had brought her and Mother.

"Why would this stock market thing have an effect on those who didn't own stocks?" Collina asked.

"Why?" Myra leaned back in the soft cushiony chair. "It's like we forgot what matters most, with Americans running after the stock market god, looking for a way to get rich quick."

Maggie nodded her silver-white head. "We've forgotten the real wealth—"

"Jesus." Ruby plopped down into the nearest chair. "Now what?"

Maggie looked at each one. "We probably won't know for sure what America will have to go through until a couple more weeks."

Chapter 24

December 24, 1929

Franklin bent his head forward. Woodward Avenue resembled a snow globe, hazy, white, and unreal. It had been a discouraging day. How was he going to tell Collina that their bonds were gone?

Buck's shoulders were hunched. Was he warding off the cold weather or the bad news he'd received? Buck had wired his bank in Colorado only to find the same news waiting for him. His home, lands, and large herd of cattle were now the only things he owned. The bank in Las Animas had closed after the crash.

The Las Animas Bank and Trust had given Buck a small portion of his savings. A couple thousand was all he had received, merely 10 percent of his holdings.

Franklin's money was in the First National Bank of Detroit and appeared to be safe. But he was allowed to withdraw only a couple thousand. He patted his pockets as if to assure himself it was there.

The noise of their boots crunching the snow-covered sidewalk filled the stark silence. No laughter. No muttering. Silence. The pedestrians they passed kept their heads bowed. Dark shadows against a grey and white backdrop.

He and Buck turned the corner and saw a young boy, his wool cap placed sideways on his thick head of hair. His red cheeks told Franklin he'd been out most of the day. The lad's hand, reddened by the cold, raised high in the air, waving the newspaper.

"New York stock brokers jump! Get your papers here!"

"Eric?" He'd seen the youth a half-dozen times before on various street corners. Franklin reached for a paper. "Thanks, Eric."

"Sure, Mr. Long." Eric huddled into the collar of his coat. "Paper! Get your papers here!"

Franklin read the headlines while walking. "What? New York has reported more stock brokers jumping out their ten-story windows! Here's their names—"

"Where is this God you and Ruby talk about? I don't see Him doing anything to prevent this?"

"Where He belongs." Franklin paused his steps, forcing Buck to do the same. "We choose whom we will follow. These big tycoons chose to follow Baal and the god of materialism; materialism failed, and they gave up. Christians know their strength comes from God."

A horse-drawn cart heaped with odds and ends in the alley they were crossing made Franklin hesitate and watch the scene unfolding.

"Wait, I have some good household items here. What will you offer me? I need cash," yelled a women as she ran toward a wagon.

The shabbily dressed man pulled up his tired horse. A cigarette hung from the parched corners of the man's lips. He pushed back his soiled hat with one dirty thumb. "So does the whole country, and it's going to get worse before it gets better. All I can do, lady, is offer you a swap. I don't have any money to barter with. If I did, I would."

The man jumped down from his wagon and placed a feed bag to his horse's head. Giving the animal a pat with his hand, he turned. "Here, you take your pick. If you have any apples or anything my horse can eat, I'll give you anything off this wagon for it. You can't beat the price."

"I don't have anything," the woman sobbed. She held up her empty hands. "But your horse is welcome to eat what little grass he can find in the yard; he can have my vegetable garden if you'll allow me and my children safe passage to Warren. I have relatives there and they have a small farm. We're going to stay there through the winter months."

"Sure, lady. Come on, boy, let's get some dinner."

Franklin took a deep breath. "We'll soon have the same thing in common."

"What's that?"

"Being poor...Come on, Buck, let's find Clem before Myra knows he's missing."

"Now, there's a guy for your prayer book. How many times has Clem repented and then jumped right back into the same pig wallow?"

"Bear one another's burdens, Buck. God knows Clem means well. He's brought it to my attention to give Clem a hand up."

They made their way to Clem's favorite speakeasy. In the dimly lit room, Franklin strained to locate Clem through the perpetual fog of cigarette smoke.

Clem was taxing Franklin's patience. The least little occurrence in Clem's life that he couldn't handle, he'd run to the nearest speakeasy to quench his pain. Going to church had helped. The stock market had brought more woes this month, and only the stoutest and bravest had been able to stand up to their fears.

"Come on, Clem, you got to get back to the Brick before Myra knows you're gone."

Clem wept into his glass. "Go away. I'm a failure."

"If it's because you've lost your job, look around you. Mostly everyone in here are failures. Now get up."

Clem rose, weaving from side to side. Franklin took one arm and Buck took the other, carrying Clem out into the frigid air. "I got me a job, but you see, I've lost everything. Myra doesn't know yet. How can I tell her? I went to the bank and our savings is wiped out. I must have spent it. But I don't remember taking it out. Oh, what did I do with it?"

"This time it wasn't your fault, Clem. It's due to the stock market crash. Your house is paid for, right?"

"Yes, Myra wouldn't have it any other way. And the taxes are all paid. Myra's got a good head on her shoulders."

"Well, then, you're better off than most, Clem."

"What?"

"I'll tell you all about it tomorrow evening at our Christmas get together."

❦ ❦ ❦

Franklin's arms circled Collina's waist. "Are you ready to head to the parlor and face the group now that our Christmas meal is finished?"

"I need to help Jane." She peeked around the corner to where Luke was standing next to Buck. "Do you think Luke Baker was duly impressed?"

Jane placed her hands on her hips. "He seemed to be. He ate like he hadn't for a week. Now, do you mind letting me do my job?"

"Jane, you're too good and I love you to death."

Franklin nodded. Jane was doing all her chores without pay. Placing a hand on her shoulder, he said, "Thank you, Jane." Then offered his arm to Collina, and together they strolled into the parlor.

Clem sat next to Myra, smoking and deep in thought. He caught her glance and guiltily looked away. Coughing, choking on his smoke. Hmm. Franklin mused. What was Clem up to now?

Collina sat down in her Queen Anne chair and Franklin took the seat next to her.

She stroked her dress, tilting her head toward Ruby. "I wonder how Skeeder is doing at Shushan?"

Franklin knew that look. That exchange that needed no words. This Wall Street disaster was worse than they had suspected. And there was always Shushan, where he'd found his Savior, if all else failed, to return to.

Franklin stood. "You are the family I always dreamed of in the orphanage, and like family, I must share with you the bad and good, equally. It seems with Wall Street went our savings."

Collina fell back into her chair. The news had caught her by surprise. "At least I paid the taxes early."

"I hope the check cleared before—"

"I'm certain it did." Collina smiled confidently. "The house is paid for and I paid the butcher and the milkman yesterday with the cash I had on me."

"How about you, Clem?"

"Myra handles the finances. How we looking, girl?"

Myra's brows furrowed. "Taxes are paid and I've got some cash. But, come to think of it, one boarder owes me two months' rent; the others are paid up until next month."

Clem patted his wife's hand. "My friend found me a job picking up milk from a dairy farm in Almont and delivering it to Detroit. That should help us a little."

"How long is this depression expected to last?" Myra said.

Buck and Luke had chosen to stand apart from the family. Buck's arms were crossed as if he was ready for a fight and looking over his opponents for the best option of winning the battle.

Franklin's eyes locked with his. "What's the news?"

"Isn't good. Looks like Wall Street took most of the nation by surprise and no one knows the outcome. It's never happened here before. Over in Europe it's been pretty bad, but none of the politicians thought it would reach across the sea to us."

"We'll have to grit our teeth and hang on," Grandma Maggie said. "This reminds me of what it was like after the Civil War. Our money was no good, our food was all gone. But look; I'm still here to tell about it!"

"And as feisty as ever." Jane chuckled.

"Come sit down next to me; you're every bit part of this family," Maggie said, and Jane complied.

"How's your business doing, Franklin? Mine is gone. Guess I might as well own up. My ladies haven't paid me a cent for all those gowns I did for them." Ruby turned away from Buck's eyes and kept her gaze fixed on Franklin. "People are calling this stock market crash the Great Depression. Well, it depressed me right out of business."

"Be happy you don't have any workers to lay off."

"What?" Collina said.

"I have to let go of ten. Most of my work has been canceled. I can't pay them if I don't get paid."

"You think they might get mad and sabotage the place?" Buck asked.

"Why would they do something like that? It's not Franklin's fault." Ruby glanced at Buck, who smiled back.

"People are funny like that. They look at this grand house and think you have money stashed in your feather bed," Franklin said.

"I've got some there," Maggie said with a cackle. "Maybe I might should move it."

Laughter filled the room. It sounded good, even promising. Franklin realized Maggie had done it purposely, to lighten their hearts. She was good at doing that.

"Mother, how did you survive with no money and no food?" Collina leaned forward in her chair.

"We bartered a lot. You'll find ways. We will all find a way, with our good Lord's guidance. I said Psalm 55:22 so often I memorized it. 'Cast thy burden upon the Lord, and he shall sustain thee; he shall never suffer the righteous to be moved.' Then there's my special verse for my twilight years, 'I have been young, and now am old—"

"Oh, Psalm 37:25, 'Yet have I not seen the righteous forsaken, nor his seed begging bread,'" Ruby said.

"We'll see," Buck mumbled.

Chapter 25

July 2, 1930

Esther swung her leg over. "You have a bony back." The cow
mooed, nuzzling her side where Esther's leg lay.

"What on earth are you doing straddling that cow?" Ruby said.

"If William rode a cow when he was five, I can ride this one at nine."

Ruby laughed. "Esther, you can't believe how silly you look."

"As silly as this cow is going to look in our back yard." Esther jumped
off, her boots scrunching the gravel driveway.

Ruby's eyebrows shot up. This cow is going to look funny grazing on
Franklin's plush green lawn alongside their horses. Still, she could see
Collina's reasoning. Milk was very important to Sis.

"With milk and eggs, a body can live comfortably. Mother approves.
Of course now with pasteurization and homogenization, people don't
milk cows like they used to. But I prefer the way milk tastes right from
the cow."

"Couldn't we die from some disease?" William asked.

"Yes, children die of rickets when they don't get enough milk to drink,"
Collina said. "I'll go and make sure everything is ready in the barn."

Esther frowned at the cow. "My, cows have large heads."

Ruby nodded. "I grew up milking them. Now that I haven't seen one
for some time, you're right. Her head looks too big for her body."

"Who's going to milk her?"

"Collina, I suppose. She used to do a lot of milking."

"Do you think she'll teach me to milk?"

Ruby patted her daughter's shoulder. "She'll be happy to. Why don't you go and ask her?"

"When will Uncle Franklin and Uncle Buck be back from Bloomfield Open Hunt?" William said, watching his sister run toward the barn.

"I don't know. I hope Franklin will be able to buy enough hay and feed for the horses."

"Uncle Franklin and Uncle Buck sure whipped up that barn fast enough. You know, it'll be fun having our horses in our back yard," William said.

"Only problem is feeding them through the winter months." As well as feeding ourselves. Ruby hid her concern from her son and smiled at him confidently. "Why are you calling Mr. Briggs. 'Uncle Buck?'"

"He told me to."

"Well, he's not your uncle. So please address him as Mr. Briggs in the future. Why don't you run after your sister? I'm sure your aunt could use some help preparing the stalls."

"Sure, Mom."

She watched her son leave.

"Hey, what you got there?"

Ruby turned. "Eric, this is our new cow. Mr. Long and Mr. Briggs are bringing our horses. We're going to keep them in our backyard."

"Gee whiz, that is great. Maybe I can help feed them. You know, I've got my own newspaper delivery route now. Maybe I could come over afterwards and you could pay me to feed them, what do you think?"

"I don't know." Ruby placed her hand on his shoulder. "We're trying to cut expenses by bringing Magic, Lea, Kasha, and Proud Lady here."

"Oh." Eric nodded, soberly placing his hands in his pockets. "Can you keep a secret?"

Ruby nodded.

"That's why I've got me that paper route, to help pay the bills. Dad's worried about his job, afraid he might get canned. He's watched a lot of his friends lose their jobs since last year. Figures his time might come this year. You know Detroit's unemployment is at a staggering 34 percent."

"Did you read that in your newspaper?"

"Yeah. I sell papers on Woodward, too, and I need to yell out the news ever so often to get my buyers' interest. Helps if I yell out the important stuff." He popped out his chest importantly. "See here." He thumbed through a tablet loaded with names and addresses. "These are my subscribers. I've got to record each. See those checks by their name? I record if they paid. Pop says not to extend credit past a week, or else I might never get paid." He sighed. "Yeah, I'm hoping to make more money with my paper route. Why, sometimes I stand all day selling my papers for three cents per daily copy and only sell four or five papers." He shrugged. "I end up making five cents profit."

"You're acquiring good business sense at a young age, Eric. Are you saving it up for a new bike?"

"This money goes to my family. They need it to pay the rent and buy food."

"You do all that delivering in this heat?"

"Yup! And some are saying the city is hotter than it's been in twenty-five years!" He stepped closer. "And you better be careful what company you keep, too. The police are planning to make it a lot hotter for these bootleg gangsters." He turned his ball cap around, placing the brim to his back and glanced up at her and nodded. "Well, I got to go. Got to get my homework done before I get my papers. And afterwards me and some of my friends plan on playing a little baseball."

"Homework?" Ruby said. "School's out."

"Not for me. Pop says if I want to get ahead, I'd better study hard, so I can go to college on a scholarship. Well, I'll see ya around, Mrs. Meir."

Ruby's heart was in her throat. Buck had told her that Clem had been seen with some Detroit gangsters lately.

She walked Betsy into her new standing stall. Franklin and Buck had built box stalls for the horses. She retrieved some hay for the cow and then looked in on the chickens. It didn't take Collina long to come up with a number of ways to feed her hungry household.

Myra had done the same, purchasing two hens and a rooster. She was having some trouble with her rooster. She called him too proud for his own good, and if he wasn't careful, first thing she'd do with him was put him into the roasting pan for Sunday supper.

Dear Myra. Should I tell her what Buck said? She hasn't said how Clem is doing at his new job, and probably has no idea he's been seeing men connected with the Mafia. Myra and Clem were planning to be here for a Fourth of July party. That was two days away and, hopefully, she'd get some alone time with Myra then.

The roar of the big horse van coming down the road had Ruby and Collina running out of the barn. BOH's van was pulling into the drive. With a loud thud the truck drove over the curb and into the backyard.

"Did everything go well?"

"Good as could be expected," Franklin said. "I'm glad Buck was with me." Franklin and Buck unhooked the back door of the trailer. Magic neighed. The first horse off was Proud Lady. She fairly blew down the tall ramp. If not for Buck putting his shoulder into the frightened mare, she might have hurt herself.

"Easy, girl, easy. There, that's a good mare."

"What happened, why is she lathered?"

Buck shook his head. "Some horses don't trailer well." Handing her the lead rope, he hurried to help Franklin with Lea.

Collina took her and looked to the ramp for her Anglo-Arab. "Kasha is supposed to be the spirited one; I hope she comes off well."

Ruby and Collina looked on while Franklin and Buck unhooked the last mare. Kasha's ears pricked forward and she snorted at the high ramp.

"Easy, girl," Buck said, petting the sleek neck. "Now you show these other horses how it's done. Come on." Buck took half steps leaning his shoulder into the mare.

"That horse has a head full of sense," Franklin said to Collina.

"She sure does. Look at her, it's as if she understands what Buck is telling her."

Kasha walked down the ramp carefully, then neighed to Magic and Proud Lady when she was safely clear.

"You bred yourself a first-rate horse, Collina," Buck said as he handed her the rope.

"Thank you for your help."

Ruby looked over the railings of the stalls. The horses seemed to know this would be their new home for a while. Not as elegant as the Hunt's, yet it was warm and clean. "How was everything at the Hunt?"

Franklin shook his head, saddened. "Some of the members had to sell their horses. They can't afford to pay the rent and some members may lose their homes. Like Kathleen and George."

Collina looked at Franklin in disbelief. "That can't be. Why, they're millionaires."

"Not any more. George gambled in the stock market heavily. Thought it just a fluke what was happening overseas and didn't want to take his money out when he had the chance of making twice his investment. Lost it all.

"Kathleen was there, in tears over her horse. She begged me to take her. Well, you know her blood line. I was very close to doing it. If it hadn't been for Buck, I know I would have."

"Oh, this is too sad to think about." Ruby blinked away her tears. "We were dining like royalty in that lovely house before this depression. Surely, her rich father can bail them out."

"He lost everything, too, Ruby. The railways, the property, everything. I'm not sure he has a place to live."

"What are Kathleen and George going to do?"

"George is moving their things to that property they own in Metamora. He's got a cabin up in the woods; he and Kathleen are planning on living there."

"What a change from their lavish home."

"Kathleen says she's looking forward to the change. Says that home in the city was too big. Kathleen is not one to flaunt her wealth. I wish I could have taken her horse. She is so worried she won't get a good home."

"Maybe we can, Franklin. We could always ship Kathleen's horse to the homestead in Kentucky. After all, that might be where we'll end up before this is all over. We could raise three crops there and wouldn't have to worry about buying coal. We could always go to the woods and chop down trees for firewood."

Franklin put his arm around his wife, drawing her to him. "You bet!

Now come on; let's go in the Brick and get some lunch. We could all use a little nourishment."

"And, Ruby, we need to prepare our boxes for the festivities at church tomorrow."

"That's right. I'd forgotten. Pastor Brooks is going to donate all contributions to the families who need help," Ruby said.

"That's half of the population of the United States," muttered Buck, disgruntled. "It would be better if the churches stopped holding their hands out and let families alone to deal with their financial problems."

"How can you say that?" Ruby chided. "If it wasn't for the churches and the soup lines they've formed to feed the destitute, I don't know where the people would go."

"I don't think Buck meant it the way you took it, Ruby," Franklin said. "This crash has hurt everyone. No one is immune, and it's hard enough for families without worrying about donations to the church. I'm afraid a lot of people will stop going because they can't afford to give and don't want neighbors knowing how destitute they've become."

Chapter 26

*H*ello, Myra? Is that you? Speak up, I can hardly hear you."
Collina craned to hear over the voices in the background.

"Did you hear what happened at the LaSalle Hotel?"

"No, I don't have our radio on. I've been busy planning for the Fourth of July party."

"Ten men were murdered by gangsters. They even gunned down Jerry Buckley, right in the lobby!"

"You mean that radio commentator? That Jerry Buckley?"

"Yes. I'm so afraid for Clem. He went there to deliver his milk from Almont and he's not back!"

"Don't go anywhere. I'll get Franklin and Buck to check on Clem. Ruby and I will be right over."

❦ ❦ ❦

"You're hooking up Lea? Is that safe, Franklin? What if the gangsters are still out there and she should happen to get shot with a stray bullet?" Collina usually took her carriage, but she didn't want anything happening to her horse. "Ruby and I can walk."

Franklin stopped and turned to survey his wife. "You're more worried about your horse's welfare than your own? Why does that not surprise me?"

She'd not thought of it that way.

"Well, I could use the exercise. If trouble comes, Ruby and I can run into an alley if those gangsters should be around. What do you think?"

"I think you're thinking too much. Now get in."

"I guess. Wait, I could saddle up Kasha, and Ruby and I could ride double. No gangster can get us then. I know we'd be safe."

Franklin smiled broadly at her, then lifted her into the carriage. "Ruby, you stay here and guard the house. I'll take my wife to Myra's. Don't worry. The gangsters have all high-tailed it into their holes. They won't be around now. But I'll bring Myra and her girls back, so prepare the rooms, please."

"Hopefully Clem will already be back at the house before you both get there and have quite a story to tell us."

"I hope so." Collina turned to her husband. "Dear, I know I'm supposed to love, honor, and obey without question, but you usually prefer the automobile, so why did you hook up the horse?"

"Our automobile is out of gas, and I don't think you know it yet, but Lou's Gas and More is out of business."

"No! Not Lou. What will he do?"

"What are we going to do? Can't cruise down Woodward with a bone-dry gas tank. Great invention of Ford's, but during hard times the old hay eater here can run on the grass along the curb."

"The only thing we seem to have a lot of in Detroit lately is gangsters. It gets pretty bad when good people can't carry guns and gangsters can." Collina felt the hot breezes of the July day and patted her forehead dry with her handkerchief. "What a bloody day this turned out to be."

Lea didn't waste any time clip clopping down the road toward Myra's. After pulling into her drive, Franklin helped Collina out and then bounded up the steps.

"Where's Myra?" Franklin asked.

"She's lying down," a man said, closing the door behind Franklin and Collina.

Collina rushed into Myra's bedroom. Kneeling before her, she stroked the loose strands of Myra's brown hair. "Myra, have you heard from Clem?"

Myra nodded. Her stifled cry muffled by her hand. "He's...dead. I can't believe it. The police were just here. They're investigating his death. It's unsure whether he was part of the gang shooting. He, he wasn't delivering milk from that farm in Almont...They were bootleggers who got their whisky from Canada, and Clem was the delivery boy who drove it to the gangsters in Detroit. I can't believe he knew. The farm had a hundred dairy cows. How would he know that some of that milk was whisky?"

"Oh, Myra." Collina rocked back on her knees, closing her eyes. What could she say to Myra that would help? "Do you want some coffee? Something to eat?" She held her hand out to Franklin and he helped her up. If only Myra could know such a love. Myra deserved someone she could lean on, someone who would be good to her.

Myra looked so tired. She'd displayed bravery through all Clem's carousing problems. Buying this house and renting the rooms out to boarders had been her family's main means of income. Now this.

"Franklin," Collina said, "we must help her." He sprang into action.

"Myra, you and your children are coming home with us until this thing with Clem is straightened up. I spoke with a man and his wife boarding here. They seemed a nice sort. They can tell the police where they can find you."

Myra moved to sit up. Collina sat on the bed next to her, putting her arm around her sister's slumped shoulders.

"Do you think that would be okay? I need to get away from here. Here there are only memories of Clem. I want to sleep and not worry."

Franklin nodded. "Collina will help you pack. I'll stop in every day and check on things."

"Mr. and Mrs. Grover are good people. They are the only ones I would consider trusting. Clem wanted me to send Mrs. Wakins and her daughter packing. They haven't paid their rent for six months." Myra turned. "Sis, they have no place to go but to the streets. What am I to do?"

Franklin closed the bedroom door and walked over to her. "See if they are willing to do the cleaning and cooking for your other tenants until they can get on their feet," Franklin whispered. "You're not going to be able to do it for a while. Maybe you can rent your room for more income. I'd rather have you close, in case there is anything to this claim the police are investigating."

Collina stifled her cry. Myra sobbed, leaning her head on Collina's shoulder. Franklin bent down. "Don't worry, Myra, your troubles are almost over. You'll see. Things are going to get better for you from here on. Trust me. I have friends that can find out the truth. Clem wasn't in the mob; it's just a rumor."

"How can you be sure?" Collina whispered.

"Clem didn't have anything the mob wanted. But one of the tenants might know something. I'll find the culprit, rest assured of that. Myra, dry your eyes and get your clothes packed."

Collina felt rejuvenated. She bounced off the bed and drew Myra up with her. "It's going to be great fun, you being at the Brick with everyone. It'll be like the old days again…like our Shushan days. Think of all the work we can get accomplished."

"Oh," Myra groaned. But her smile gave her feelings away. "Franklin, weren't you able to teach Collina how to relax? I thought at least by now, you'd got her to enjoy sitting around without finding something to."

Franklin laughed, his hand on the doorknob. "All I ever accomplished in that respect is becoming a workaholic along with her. Now with this confounded depression, she has taken it upon herself to start what she's always enjoyed the most—farming and raising livestock."

Myra grew serious. "Ten people lost their lives today, murdered in the lobby of the LaSalle Hotel. Some of them, like my Clem, had to be innocent bystanders. You never know for sure where you may be tomorrow."

Collina remembered a Bible passage she'd read that morning. "Life is but a mist that appears for a little while then vanishes. Clem's with the Lord now, Myra, in paradise with Jesus."

"But—"

"Don't worry. He loved the Lord and tried to live a godly life. He's innocent of wrong doing. I feel it."

Chapter 27

Franklin kept his eyes fixed on the preacher. Myra was taking the death of her husband hard and had said she wished she and Clem had never come to Detroit. It didn't make it any easier when the newspapers started to call the day Clem lost his life Bloody July.

Pastor Brooks mounted the steps to his podium, his big form dwarfing the wooden apparatus. Below him stood Clem's coffin. "We all knew Clem to be a red-blooded man who fought a battle with alcohol."

"Pastor never wastes words," Myra whispered.

Pastor Brooks went straight to the meat of the man and the heart of his repentance. He told the congregation that Clem, like them, was a sinner, but had found forgiveness and peace through the grace of Jesus Christ. Clem was at last free from Satan's bondage. They could be, too. Only through His blood could there be redemption for any man or woman.

The large picture of Jesus Christ hung just over the submersing tank, as it had for Franklin when he needed repentance. As it had been for Clem. Romans 8:28 came to mind. *All things work together for good to them that love God, to them who are called according to his purpose.*

When he had stumbled into Myra at the butcher's, she tried to hide the black eye Clem had given her. Through that encounter with Myra and getting Clem to this church to dry out, Franklin thought he'd done a selfless act, especially when he agreed to drive Myra and Clem back to Shushan. But through his supposedly good deed, he found his lost love. He squeezed Collina's hand.

He looked back at Dr. Luke Baker. He was a pew away from Myra. Hopefully, neither would allow this lapse of time to come between them now. He thought of Collina and how she forgave him and he her. Both were granted a second chance and blessings from their Lord and Savior for their simple act of forgiveness. Their desire to follow Christ's teachings had brought them a wealth of untold love.

Collina shifted uneasily in her seat. Franklin bent closer to her.

"Did I do the right thing inviting Buck? I thought it would be a perfect time for him and Ruby to iron out their differences; but Ruby won't even look his way."

Franklin nodded knowingly. "Give love a chance. Look how long it took me to convince you."

She turned, her smile fading on her lips. Her eyes widened, and she discreetly pointed to the black-suited men who had staggered forward and now sat in front of them, while others occupied the back row of the church. Were they here to frighten them or were they out for blood?

Detroit had been the gangster capital for ten years now. People got used to seeing the mobs shoot it out with one another. Usually they left law-abiding citizens alone.

Myra had confided to Franklin about Clem's late-night habits. After accepting that job in Almont, he'd slinked beneath the covers of their bed reeking of cigarettes and cheap perfume.

She had been quick to point out to her wayward husband the error of his ways. A contrite Clem had promised to quit the Almont job, even though it did pay well. He sought the sanctuary of the church over the wrath of God and his wife. For two weeks Clem had walked the straight and narrow. Only, the mob never forgot. How much money did Clem owe these thugs? Or were they here to frighten someone else?

"Clem was a sinner like we all are. A sinner who happened to be in the wrong place at the wrong time that July morning," Pastor Brooks said. "Because Clem accepted Jesus Christ as his Savior he is living in paradise. Do you know for certain that you are going to heaven? Accept Jesus now; tomorrow may be too late." Pastor banged his podium with his fist and stared at the men lining the first and last pews of the church.

"If anyone has any questions, see me after this funeral. If you men are not here to give your condolences to Clem's family, I ask you to leave now." Silence. "Will the pall bearers step forward, please."

Franklin, Buck, and Luke donned white gloves and were the first to reach a handle of the casket. Along with others, they carried it to the waiting hearse and then to the cemetery.

❤ ❤ ❤

"Luke, stay with Myra," Franklin said as the graveside service ended. Luke nodded, eyeing the men.

Franklin and Buck worked their way to the group of black-suited men who had not left their Model Ts to congregate with the other mourners.

"Can I help you gentlemen?" Franklin spoke first.

"We came to pay our respects to the missus," said the tallest man.

"Does she know you?"

"No, but we knew her husband."

"I am the guardian of her estate. How can I help you?"

"We need to talk to the missus."

Buck moved forward. "Move aside, Franklin, I've had dealings with these types of thugs in Denver."

A stocky man with a black mustache withdrew a knife and began cleaning his nails with it.

Buck grinned, lifting out his Bowie knife from the concealment of his boot. "Here, want to try this one? It does a good job on nails, poachers, wolves, and thugs. I can cut them up so small not even a buzzard can find all the parts."

One of the men chuckled. "Yeah, know what you mean."

"What do you want?" Franklin stared back at the man who evidently was the ring leader. A small pudgy man observed them from a distance.

"Look, you see, it's like this. Everyone pays what they owe. It's the American way. If I let one off, then I'd have to let everyone off, see?"

"Yeah. But did you have to kill him?"

The man shrugged. "He got in the way. I don't like killings. What

219

can I say? It happens."

"How much does he owe you?"

"You get me a hundred in cash and we'll call it even."

"On one condition."

The pudgy man stepped forward. "I don't bargain." Like a pack of wolves, his thugs circled Franklin and Buck.

Buck and Franklin stood back to back. "We'll get your money. But here's my deal. You're to never bother my sister-in-law again and get your thugs out of her house."

The tall man nodded.

Franklin looked down the bridge of his nose at him. "I'll have the money for you tomorrow. Where do you want me to meet you?"

The man chuckled. "Give it to Ralph. Myra knows who he is."

The pudgy man walked forward, eyeing Franklin, then Buck. "You Buck Briggs?"

"Yeah."

"You plan to run for that governor position in Colorado?"

Buck nodded.

"My cousin warned you not to. We run Denver. We like it that way."

"A lot of good citizens don't care for the way you run things."

The pudgy man thumped Buck on the chest. "Don't get in our way. This is your last warning."

Buck shoved his hand away. "I don't scare that easily."

"I'll let my cousin know. Oh, and watch your back, westerner."

The seven men in black suits walked away, getting into their automobiles and in a loud cavalcade drove down the road.

"I thought for a moment, we were going to have to fight our way out."

"Me, too." Franklin smiled. "Glad you brought Betsy."

Buck patted the large knife. "Me, too. I'd rather go down fighting than let that slimy bunch of wolves have a picnic at our expense." He looked up hearing running footsteps coming from a nearby tree.

Collina's arms encircled Franklin's arm. Slightly winded, she said, "Does Ruby know about you trying to oust those gangsters in Colorado by becoming governor?"

Ruby walked toward them. She was far enough away that she hadn't heard the conversation. Buck removed his cowboy hat and wiped his forehead with the back of his shirt sleeve. "What should I tell her?"

Franklin chuckled. "The truth. Women can sniff out a lie before you finish telling it."

"But aren't there times you shouldn't be completely honest? You know, the weaker sex due to their fragile—"

"Only if they're laid out in their coffin." Collina's eyes flashed him a warning.

"There are two sides to every coin, Buck, and two ways to a woman's scorn. You've touched on the first. I'll let you figure out the second."

Chapter 28

R uby searched the crowd for a man in a cowboy hat. Humph! At least he showed good judgment in not coming. She surveyed the rows of tables that stretched out with red, blue, and white tablecloths with an assortment of foods ranging from pasta to homemade pies. The aromas filtered across the sultry air, appealing to the hungry and homeless.

Myra's warm smile ensured the wanderer and the destitute they were welcome at her table. "In a way," Myra confined to Ruby, "Clem has managed to give far and beyond what he thought humanly possible. My Clem was definitely the thorny ground person who loved the gospel, but the distractions of life always got him into the wrong crowd."

Violet Mayberry, the head of the ladies' auxiliary, shifted her glasses up her nose. "What did someone do? Put a sign out on Woodward to come here for a free meal?" Clearly, she had not planned to invite the riffraff off the streets to enjoy what she had labored so hard to accomplish. Violet sniffed. "See that man over there? He thought we were having a Fourth of July celebration, and that woman over there thought it was a wedding."

"In a way, we are." Ruby patted Violet's grumbling shoulders. "We are celebrating Clem going home to his Father."

Myra hugged the woman. "Violet, without your sacrifice in organizing everything, none of this could have been possible. Clem's funeral has helped us give a meal to people who needed one and a chance to talk about something other than their own sorrow, a chance to offer sympathy to another."

"We'd hoped to give this food to you, Myra. I doubt if there will be a chicken bone left the way the people keep flooding in here. You have that boarding house full of hungry mouths, and I doubt a handful of them have paid you a month's worth of rent between them."

Myra looked at the crowds of hungry people. "I can't help think that this is God's design. Not that I don't appreciate all that you and the congregation have done for me." Myra placed a hand to her heart; her eyes brimmed with tears. "I feel overwhelmingly grateful."

"There, there." Violet patted her shoulder. "Clem wasn't the best of husbands, but he did love you, Myra. I admire your perseverance."

Ruby recalled Stephen's funeral. All the well-wishers in the world could not wipe away the loneliness she felt. Out of the corner of her eye, she saw him, his wide-brimmed hat and the broad forehead, the square-jawed face of the handsome Buck Briggs. He'd come. He'd written that he would like an answer. He wanted her to go back to Colorado with him, to become his wife. She had asked the congregation to pray for her to make the right choice. All through the church service, he'd kept his distance. He approached them.

"Ruby, do you have a minute?" Buck asked.

"Good afternoon, Mr. …"

"Briggs, ma'am, at your service." He lifted his cowboy hat in greeting.

"Ruby tells us you're from Colorado. Have you heard of Will Rogers? He's a westerner, you know, and part Cherokee Indian." She frowned. "Now, you wouldn't want anyone to force him or you to move out of your state, would you? So why are trying to take our Ruby?" She fluttered her handkerchief in front of his nose.

Ruby drew in a sharp breath. Evidently Violet forgot prayers were supposed to be confidential.

"Yes, ma'am, I can see your point. Will's become a popular person throughout the United States, wouldn't you say?"

"I…yes. In fact, I recall him saying that his ancestors met the *Mayflower*. Do you get a chance to read his column? My, it's in every paper, you know. I look forward to reading it every morning."

"Yes, ma'am, I don't miss a one." His eyes merrily swept Violet and Ruby. What is he up to?

"I especially like the one that goes something like this, 'In the old days there was few things bought on credit. Your taste had to be in harmony with your income....'"

"Yes, yes, I remember that one. Now let me see if I can remember the rest....'Everybody has got more than they used to have, but they haven't got as much as they thought they ought to have.' I think that's what landed us in this depression, don't you, Mr. Briggs?"

"Yes, ma'am, only I think we've been hog swindled by the stock brokers and bankers into thinking we needed more. Will had a good point on this saying: 'He wasn't against bull fighting—'"

"I remember." Violet clapped her hands in glee.

Buck covered his smirk and winked at Ruby. Buck had managed to do what she and Myra could not—get Violet in a happy mood. Buck drawled on.

"Well, then Will continued, 'Some nations like to see blood, and some like to see their victims suffer from speculation...They kill the bull very quick. Wall Street lets you live and suffer.'"

Her laughter sounded like a piglet caught in a picket fence. Ruby joined in.

"Oh, my, that was a funny one," Violet said. "You know, with men like Will Rogers getting us to laugh about ourselves and our problems, we just might get through these bad times."

"Yes, ma'am, I agree wholeheartedly, and you're the person to show this here congregation how simple humor can be found in most familiar circumstances." Buck slowly pulled Ruby away.

"Uh...I'll be back in a moment to help you, Violet."

"Take all the time you need, dear. I have plenty to keep me busy." Violet turned. "Mary, did I tell you about Will Rogers' column?"

Buck pirouetted Ruby through the crowd. "Whee. This is better. I'm not a fan of being bunched up. Feels like being in a cattle bin."

He led her to a garden of roses and petunias. The air smelled divine.

"Meant to ask you what scent are you wearing? It fits you like a glove on a baseball player."

Honestly, what do women see in him? He's as suave as a politician on Election Day. "Lavender soap mostly, and earlier, I was peeling onions. Some of the smell is still on my hands, see?"

Buck took her hands into his large one and bent his head. "Yes, no wonder, I'm fond mostly of food."

His touch sent spasms of goose bumps up and down her arm and spine. She swallowed and withdrew her hands from his grasp. His closeness was always her undoing. Distance was mandatory at all costs.

"What did I do now?" Buck's eyebrow rose like the curve of a question mark. "You don't like to be considered delectable?"

"Oh, honestly, Buck. You need refinement to your wooing manners."

"Wooing?" Buck licked his lips. "Maybe I'm moving in the right direction after all."

Ruby turned. When had her feelings for him changed? When had she started to look for his cowboy hat amidst the crowd? A trembling grin emerged on her sour countenance.

"Now that's the Ruby I remember."

Buck, always adorned in cowboy boots and a cowboy hat, even when dressed in a suit. She had come to expect them. She had never thought the combination could ever complement one another. But on Buck, it fit.

"Then you're not mad?"

"Mad?" She'd been so busy meddling into her own thoughts—what had she missed with his conversation?

"I was afraid to talk to you during the church service, afraid I'd upset you." He stepped closer. "It appears my presence gets you in a tangle at times. Like now."

He mustn't know how his closeness affected her. Lord, help me. A Bible verse pierced her thoughts. *Be ye not unequally yoked together with unbelievers:...what communion hath light with darkness?* He bent his head closer, staring into her eyes. "Why did you come to church, Buck?"

"Franklin needed my assistance with a matter."

"Oh?" She'd hoped he would say because he missed her. That he wanted to learn to love the God she loved and become a better man for her. Why hadn't God tugged on his heart, telling him how he needed to get right with His Son, Jesus? She'd sent enough prayers up to Him.

She turned and strolled along the tree trellis. The wind sent a whiff of pine needles, blending companionably with the roses. She breathed in deeply of their fragrance. "So because of Franklin you returned."

"There's a rumor floating around that the unemployed will be able to register their names for jobs. I'm thinking of suggesting the same for Las Animas. If it wasn't for the gangs and bootleg mobs controlling the liquor trade, Detroit wouldn't be a bad place to live."

"Is that why Franklin needed your assistance?" Her curiosity piqued, she sensed something was amiss. "What did those black-suited strangers in the church want?"

Buck stopped, his face a patchwork of emotions. "I'd rather spare you some pain in not explaining."

Ruby crossed her arms. "I'll learn it eventually, have no doubt. It's up to you to disclose the truth now or later. You decide."

"Ah, yes, Franklin warned me." He stepped closer.

She always felt so short when he did that. His six-foot-four height placed her five-foot height into his shadow. She set her jaw and, like a school madam would do to an unruly student, gave him her most chastising look.

"I'd hoped to gain your approval and not your reproach." He threw his arms out, his look bewildered. "They were part of the bootleggers, the thugs shooting at the LaSalle Hotel. One of them was from Denver. If I valued my life, he warned me not to run for the governor position."

Stunned, Ruby plopped herself down on the settee. "I...they were?"

"What am I to do with you? I try to spare you and protect you, but you will have none of it."

"I..." Protect me? "You're the one who needs protection."

He knelt before her. His lips frowning, but his eyes resembled a puppy being reprimanded by its mistress. "I feel this small when you look at me like that."

She laughed. Warmth, invigorating warmth, ignited her humor a second time and she gaily sang out her happiness. She'd not felt this lighthearted for so long. So very long. And to think gangsters had occupied that very church with her. And gangsters were after Buck. But he was more concerned over her wrath and what she thought of him.

He chuckled deep in his throat.

Oh, he was a rogue and she had grown to like needing him by her side.

Another day in another lifetime came vividly to her memory. Buck lifting Stephen's stretcher up the steps of the train, laying him down in their compartment and then turning one last time to give her his support. Ruby wrapped her face with her hands, trying to block out the memory.

"What is it?"

"You are linked with a part of my life that will always bring back memories I wish never to recall."

Buck circled her with his arms, his strong, binding strength that she had not the will to fight. "Time heals all wounds. I know. For you see, when my wife and child died, I thought I could never stand the hurt of my broken heart."

Ruby felt her body stiffen in his arms. He felt it, too. He released her and she stepped away.

"How long were you married?" Ruby was embarrassed to admit she felt a stab of jealously knowing Buck had had a wife. Perhaps that was a part of the reason that, though she was drawn to him, she felt she could never love him like she had Stephen.

If she could not give herself completely to Buck—

"We were very young when we married."

This woman had loved Buck and he, her. This could come between them like Stephen could come between them. Could she love Buck like she'd loved Stephen?

Buck observed her in silence, then said, "You remind me of her."

"Me?"

"She was beautiful. She had long flowing black hair that came to her waist. Like you, she was dainty and had a waist I could wrap my arm around. Like you, she had fire in her veins and a will of iron in her bones."

"You really know how to sweep a girl off her feet."

He hadn't heard her. Locked in his memories, Buck continued. His voice lowered an octave, more like a rumbling growl deep within his chest. "I am reminded of John Paul Jones' immortal words, 'I have not yet begun to fight.' You've got to be taught to hate a person's color and creed. I hate seeing good people forced to cower like scared chickens before gangsters and the lynching mobs of the Ku Klux Klan…Well, I think it's high time for me to be governor and to make my mark in Colorado. I'm planning to run in '32, and you'll make the perfect wife of a governor."

"Me? Why? I don't know anything about being—"

"You will." She was swimming in his aqua-blue gaze. He reached for her. She melted into his arms and he swept her up into his embrace. Bending low, he whispered, "Did I ever tell you you have kissable lips?"

His lips, soft as velvet, met hers. Tipping her head ever so slightly, she felt her body mold into his arms. Blending into the groove of his chest, she yielded, engulfed in an ecstasy of pure delight.

Parting, his mouth but a whisper from hers, he said, "I think it's about time you admit you want me as much as I want you."

Chapter 29

September 30, 1930

How dare he think she would so easily be taken in by his charms? Ruby pushed back as strangers jostled her for a better position in the unemployment line. Her thoughts lingered on Buck's kiss two months prior. Why hadn't she heard from him? Why did she care?

After all, she was a mother of two. She didn't need Buck in her life. The Nineteenth Amendment had earned her a position on the voting roster and, hopefully, a way to earn her own bread.

She craned her neck to see a glimpse of the open door. Besides, did Buck love her for her? Or was his marriage proposal spurred by his ambition to become governor of Colorado? Still, he was in her prayers nightly. *Lord, I just pray he changes his mind about running for governor. I've lost one husband. Does Buck think I want to lose a second because of a shootout with some gangster?* She had her children to think about.

No. Buck needed someone stronger than she. After all, she'd let Stephen down. She couldn't do that to Buck. She must learn to provide for her children and her.

"Can you believe this? There has to be thousands here this morning," said a man in a black suit. "You'd think they would try to hurry us up."

"Why should they?" said another man in a straw hat. "They figure we haven't got anything else to do."

Another man nearby attempted to strike a match on the bottom of his shoe. Ruby noticed the hole working its way to his sock. He struck the match along the side of his sole and lit his last cigarette and tossed the empty box on the street. "Yeah, I've got a friend in the unemployment office. He told me that the first day this here place was opened they had 19,412 register for jobs."

"For certain?" the suit man said.

"I know because my brother is one of the heads in there, and it's only gotten worse every day since it opened." The man puffed on his cigarette like a steam locomotive.

Ruby pressed back into the crowd, determined not to lose ground.

"The next day brought forty-six, and yesterday brought nearly seventy-six thousand more registered," cigarette man said.

"Can't be. There couldn't be that many Detroiters looking for work," the man in the straw hat replied.

"Yeah, maybe they're coming in from other counties."

Cigarette man shrugged. "All I know is what my brother tells me."

"Then what's the use in waiting in line? There ain't no jobs." The man in the suit tugged on his tie.

"Stay put," hat man said.

"Yes," said Ruby. "My neighbor registered the first day, said the people inside were friendly and seemed willing to help find him employment."

"Yeah, that's right, lady," hat man said. "There's a rumor going around that these apple growers in Washington State need some place to market their produce."

"How did you find that out?" cigarette man said.

"What's it to you? You think that only your brother knows the goings on in Detroit?" suit man said.

"You got to have some money up front in order to sell apples, and you got to be a Detroit resident for at least one year," hat man explained.

"That right?" Suit man scanned the crowd.

People with angry faces, some bearded, others clean shaven, shoved Ruby without noticing. She rubbed her shoulders.

"They're strict," whispered the man in the straw hat. "That's why if these people here aren't from Detroit, they won't qualify."

"Gee whiz," said suit man. "What's a gent going to do with their wife and children crying from hunger?"

Ruby bit her bottom lip. Maybe the man was an out-a-towner. Quickly she scribbled the address of her church on a piece of paper. "Here, there are free meals and beds available for the asking."

"Thanks." The man shoved the piece of paper into his trouser pocket.

"Will women be able to sell them?" Ruby asked cigarette man. The men turned to survey her.

"Don't you have a mister who can do the peddling for you?"

Buck's face flashed through her mind's eye. She recalled his kiss and how she'd felt leaning within the security of his arms. She'd melted like swiss cheese on that July day…What's wrong with me? Why am I here when I don't have to be? Am I doing the right thing? It would be so easy to give up these burdens and become Mrs. Buck Briggs. Is that what I should do?

"I…well, no," Ruby stammered. Buck's kiss had wilted away her convictions. But his smug smile afterwards instilled a conflict within her bosom. She would never know if she could stand on her own two feet if she didn't try now. Besides, how dare he think she was like all his other women? She refused to be a shrinking violet whenever Mighty Buck Briggs wiggled his baby finger at her…Like his wife indeed!

The man with the straw hat shook his head. "I don't know, Miss; mighty lonely work for a woman on some street corner all day."

"Say, that won't be fair. Some gent will get Woodward Avenue and some other gent, most likely me, will get some lonely street corner in some back alley," suit man said.

"No. That's not the way it's going to work. Busy corners will be rotated, that way every man gets a chance at the hot spots."

Ruby bit her lip. This wasn't a good idea. She looked around. Most of the people standing in line were men.

She wasn't going to get a job over a man, even though she was the head of her household. In fact, someone on the Zenith last night asked all women to give up their jobs to men. What did they expect her to do for a living?

A woman with bright red lips came up to her. "I was looking for you."

"Back of the line, girly, no cuts."

The man with the cigarette puffed harder. "Let her stay. What's it going to hurt? It'll give the lady here some female company."

"Much obliged, mister," the woman said.

The man with the straw hat tipped it, a little less enthusiastically than for Ruby previously.

"Thank you. I do appreciate the advice you supplied me, but it would be nice for some female companionship." Ruby smiled. "It's going to be a long day."

The woman looked across the street, then waved to two other girls standing on the street corner. She snuggled into Ruby's side and whispered, "Say you're a looker. Why spend your time waiting in line with a bunch of losers?" She rolled her large expressive eyes, then whispered in Ruby's ear, "This isn't going to give you anything but bunions on your toes. Come with me and my friends. We can show you how to make some real cash and have some fun doing it."

Ruby wished she'd never said one hospitable thing to this woman. She shoved her arm away from Red Lips' grasp. "I have two children, a boy and a girl. What would they think about their mother walking the streets? If you need help, my church is willing to help anyone in need. You needn't feel you have to peddle your—body to any Tom, Dick, or Harry."

"What? I'm giving you the chance to experience the finer things of life, not diapers and a sink full of dirty dishes." The woman readjusted her satin hat and put some spit to her curl, which feathered one rouged cheek. "You don't know what you're missing, girlie."

Ruby chuckled, thinking what Anna, Eric's mother, had said about such women. "Never, not for a million dollars."

"A million dollars can buy a lot of happiness. Think about that when your stomach is turning inside out for something to eat." The woman dashed across the street to her waiting friends. They all conversed for a moment, turned and laughed in Ruby's direction, and then walked down the street into a building of questionable proprieties.

The man in the straw hat whispered, "Don't you have a relative or two that could give you a decent job?"

Cousin Gill. Why hadn't she thought of him earlier? Ruby looked down the street. He was just a block away. Should she?

"Don't give up your place in line, Miss. You never know what's through those doors."

❦   ❦   ❦

Today has got to be better than yesterday. Ruby's ears pounded to the rhythm of her heels as they tapped into Gill's dry-cleaning shop with more confidence than she felt. Franklin had to lay off more employees, and things weren't looking good for the Long household.

"Hi, coz, great to see you. How's it been going?" Ruby said.

"Fair to middlin'. How's business?"

"You seem kind of down, what's wrong?"

Gill walked to the counter. He'd been bagging up some cleaning he'd just finished pressing. His hair was moist from the steam irons and presses, and he still had a yard of fabric loosely hung around his neck. "My seamstress quit on me. Can you believe that? In this depression she ups and quits."

Ruby felt a thread of hope. Her toes ached from the hours of walking the pavement looking for work. "What does the job entail?"

Gill stopped mid-stride. "You wouldn't be interested; I can only pay ten cents an hour."

Ruby hoped her face didn't convey her disappointment. Well, it's a job.

"Yeah, with bread and milk going up, ten cents don't go far. Besides, why are you looking for work? I thought Collina and Franklin were taking care of you and your children? You don't need to work. You're not going to be kicked out on the streets like some families."

Ruby pressed her hands on the counter. "I need to help with the bills. I'm not a moocher. As soon as these hard times are over, I'm planning to start my dress shop up again."

"Maybe some of your clients would come over here if they knew you were working for me?" He was pensive for a moment. "Your Mother was good to me. I don't know where I woulda lived those ten odd years if it wasn't for her taking me in when Ma died. But, Ruby, I hate to see you working in this hot place for pennies. It's like Hades in here when all the presses are going, and then when they stop, you freeze." He shrugged. "Ain't no help for it. Just the nature of the beast, I guess. And I'm barely keeping the doors open."

"I don't mind the work."

"Are you sure? If'n you're like me and got to work to keep body and soul together, I'm willing to help. But these heavy drapes feel like they weigh a ton at times, and I'm stronger than you are. My muscles are worn out. One lady told me her body was falling apart with arthritis and sickness because of my working conditions. You sure?"

"I'm willing to try, if you'll let me."

"You've got the job, if you want it. The girl I had in here before decided the dance hall down the street didn't look so bad. She said her shoulders and arms ached something awful after the end of the day."

"The dance hall. Isn't that place a pick-up spot for—"

"That's the rumor going around."

Ruby stopped, embarrassed to say more. Anna, due to her experience in Detroit, had been a ready source of information. She had told her not to darken the door there. It was a notorious spot for the worst type of women.

Ruby smiled, remembering Anna's words, "Why would any woman risk getting pregnant for a few dollars?" Anna, a good Catholic, enjoyed attending church and often was one of the first parishioners in the pew on Sunday mornings. She had confided to Ruby she felt the priests and nuns should marry; that way they'd have first-hand experience on raising a flock of children.

Ruby chuckled. "When can I start?"

"How about right now?"

❤ ❤ ❤

Ruby walked home with fifty cents jangling in her pocket. Since this was Friday, Gill paid her like his other employees. Everyone seemed very nice and Ruby's spirits were high.

"Would you like to buy an apple, ma'am?"

Ruby stopped, recalling the conversation she had waiting in line at the unemployment office. "How much are they?"

"Five cents." The man smiled. His white dress shirt and red tie made a nice contrast. His overcoat was a bit shabby, but his black shoes were clean and polished.

Ruby looked at him curiously. "You weren't here yesterday. What happened to Max?"

"Max is at the Fisher building today; we rotate the best spots."

"Where do you get your apples from? How can I be sure they're as fresh as Max's?" Ruby said.

"All the apples are from Washington State growers. We have to be licensed to sell these apples, and Detroit residents for at least a year." He swept his hat off his head and bowed. "We take our work serious, small as it may be." He held up a shiny red apple. "It's a job."

Ruby laughed. "And you do it well, too." She handed him a nickel.

"Ah, it's good to hear laughter. Say, did you hear what Will Rogers said last night?"

Ruby had little time to listen to the Zenith what with making sure both her children knew their studies for the next day and had clean clothes to go to school in. "No, what did he say?"

"Said, 'We'll be the first nation in the world to go to the poor house in an automobile.'"

Ruby laughed and the man joined her.

"Yeah, when you think things couldn't get worse, they surprise you."

Ruby jiggled her pocket. "No, things are getting better, you wait and see. The year 1931 will bring an end to this depression; it's all a matter of believing it will." Her sister, Myra, needed it to end. So did Collina. They all did.

Chapter 30

July 25, 1931

"Ruby, it's your turn to invite someone over for Sunday dinner."

She forced her thoughts from the reverie of the charismatic westerner and chuckled. *I wonder what his next move will be when he reads my letter.*

"Ruby?" Collina said.

"Oh, I pick Anna and her family. Her husband lost his job."

"Aren't they a family of eight?" Collina and Myra exchanged glances.

"Anna hasn't gone to church either. Eric says his ma is embarrassed not to have any money to put in the offering plate," Ruby said.

Myra walked over to the icebox. "There's two quarts of milk left. What's ailing Betsy?"

"Poacher," Collina replied. "I have to leave a little for the calf Betsy is nursing. But I haven't been able to catch the thief that manages to milk her before I get up in the morning."

Myra opened the lid and peeked into the pot of stew she was preparing, then stepped over to the counter full of tomatoes, green peppers, and carrots. "Praise the good Lord for Collina's green thumb. I think I could make it stretch to include another eight. But there won't be much meat in it. Come take a look."

Collina and Ruby walked to the stove.

"I'm glad July had more rain than last year. My vegetables had a chance to ripen without drying out. But what are we going to eat for the rest of the week until the other tomatoes are ripe?" Collina said.

"What would Mother say?"

"We'll make do," all three chimed and laughed.

"Did I hear my name?" Maggie said, a twinkle in her eyes.

"Ruby, go invite our neighbors over for some good old Southern stew. Myra, you'd better make another dozen sour dough biscuits," Collina instructed.

"Mother, I promised my friend I'd eat supper with her today. Remember? I asked your permission last week," Esther said, her look pleading.

"So you did! Then I will drop you off to your friend's home and then ask our German neighbors to dinner." Ruby shrugged, reaching for her hat. "Maybe they'll not come. After all, they might have plans."

"Humph," Grandma Maggie retorted, leaning heavily on her cane. "The only plan a body makes nowadays is to move to Hooverville." She lifted up a recent letter. "Mrs. Brown lost her house. I told her to go to Shushan and check with Skeeder. Maybe he has a cabin they can stay in and sharecrop."

"Hooverville?" William said. "We have one in Detroit, too. It's for the people who don't have homes. Terrible looking they are, made up of cardboard and such."

"I know, son. There are Hoovervilles across America now."

"Why do they all have the same name?"

"In honor of President Hoover," Grandma Maggie replied in a whiny voice. "People don't give our president the respect he deserves. After all, he didn't twist anyone's arm to buy in the stock market. He wasn't the one that caused the stock to crumble like a day-old newspaper into the garbage."

"I know, Mother." Myra cut up some more vegetables and dumped everything into the big kettle. "But some politician in Washington says this depression wasn't caused by the stock market crash."

"Well, it sure didn't help it! People wanted to get rich in a hurry and didn't mind buying on time to get there. Humph, I think the idea of borrowing your way to wealth is…foolishness." Grandma Maggie stamped her cane. "William, where's your manners? Your grandmother needs to sit down a spell." She jiggled her apron pocket reproachfully.

"Yes, Grandmother." William reached for the nearest chair and helped her sit down. Grandma pulled at his sleeve and gave him a wet kiss on his cheek, then reached into her apron pocket and placed a hard candy in his palm.

"Mother, really, before dinner?" Ruby shook her head.

"Hush, daughter; it's a grandmother's job to spoil her grandchildren."

Collina chuckled as she added some bits of chicken to the kettle. "Give it up, Sis. You can't change some things, and the things you can change take more energy than you have, like this depression our nation is in. This reminds me of the time after Father's—"

"Demise." Grandma Maggie stomped her cane on the wooden floor. "Let's not waste time talking about the past. We need to get the table set for our company. Now who's not working hard enough?"

Jane picked up the silverware and dishes. Grandma Maggie looked around and sniffed, then cackled like an old hen. "Humph, that'd be me!"

The roof fairly took off that time with the laughter that erupted.

Ruby stepped outside with Esther, walked her to her friend's home, and then headed to the Erhardts' to invite them to dinner.

💙 💙 💙

"Come right in. Here, let me take that for you," Franklin said.

"I thought you could use this."

"My Anna never crosses a threshold without bringing something in her hands," Francis, her husband said.

A carefully wrapped present was cradled in her arms, and her husband proudly bore a four-layer German-chocolate cake. Ann, their oldest daughter, carried in a large pot of German potatoes.

"It's the way we Germans like them." Francis was clearly proud of his wife's cooking and his German heritage. "We might as well get a flavor of each others' cultures."

"Thank you, Francis. We are so glad you and your family could come at such short notice," Franklin said.

"We were sorry to hear about your Clem dying at the hands of those gangsters. It's been a year now, I know, but the heart still remembers,"

Francis said to Myra as he eyed the tall man standing next to her.

"Luke Baker." He stretched out his hand. "Nice to meet you."

"Luke, please take our guests to the parlor," Franklin said. "I'll show Anna and her daughters to the kitchen."

Like a colony of bees, the women were scurrying about making the last preparations for dinner. Coming from the kitchen, Franklin caught up with Luke.

"Myra tells me she is over Clem's death. I wish I could believe that."

"You are helping her to do that, Luke, by being here for her. Collina is keeping her busy with the church and getting her estate in order. It has been a year since Clem's death." Franklin laid a fatherly hand on Luke's shoulder. "We all need to move forward. Concentrate our energy on getting through this Great Depression." Franklin motioned for Francis to take a seat.

Luke looked over at Francis and said, "Were you listening to the radio when Dewey was talking against capitalism and for socialism?"

"No, and I'm glad I didn't. Americans don't need his propaganda at a time like this. President Hoover has enough on his plate right now."

"You know everyone is pointing their fingers in his direction." Franklin held up his hand, turning his folded fingers around. "But there are three fingers pointing back. After all, Hoover was inaugurated in March of '29. The crash came in October. We've only ourselves to blame for the mess we're in. People were buying on credit, trusting in the stocks to make them rich. Why, the stock market is nothing but a socially accepted betting ring. I know more neighbors that chose not to pay off their homes and, instead, invested in the stock market. That was foolish."

Francis shook his head. "Yeah, the unemployment relief demonstrations back in January only made things worse. It didn't help anyone's spirits when the U.S. Census said Detroit was the hardest hit in the country."

Franklin rested back in his chair. "Auto production went down over 1,300,000 units in January. The Fisher plant went idle. But look what the Fisher brothers did. They turned their plant into the City Municipal Lodging House with heat, lights, showers, and meals."

Luke smiled. "There are a lot of good-hearted people in Detroit, despite the gangsters and this depression. I and 1500 other physicians are donating free medical care under the Medical Relief Committee."

"Those thrift gardens we planted in the spring have helped my family," Francis said. "I heard some politician say, can't remember his name for the life of me right now, that if more of the middle class would have invested, the crash wouldn't have happened. You think there's any truth in that?"

Franklin grunted. "It's easy to speculate after the bucket is empty of water, but hard to figure, at times, where the leak is."

Francis nodded. "I got a letter from my friend in Berlin. Says Hitler is one crafty devil. He's got his own ideas, forming his own party, calling it the Nazis. Of course, Hitler's been a rebel for years, threatening the partisan for some time. But my friend feels it's only a matter of time before Hitler and his Nazis take over Germany."

"I don't trust that fellow. I hope the German people don't back him," Franklin said.

"Germany is not like America." Francis fingered his chin. "Most of the people do not like to get involved with politics."

A soft rap on the door, then William's face appeared in the open doorway. "Mom says to come and eat."

"Then we'd best not be late, or there won't be anything left to eat."

💜 💜 💜

Ruby looked around at the seventeen people crowded around the dining room table. Five loaves and two fishes came to mind. Jesus fed the multitude. And that's what they needed right now, a miracle.

"Franklin, will you please say grace?" Collina said.

"Guess I best make it a good one. Francis, you can pray your prayer of thanks, as well. I don't think God will mind hearing two prayers for the feast set before us.

"Lord, we humbly thank You for Your blessings, for this food, the roof over our heads, and we ask you to bless and help others who are not so fortunate, amen."

Francis nodded his head and said, "Bless us, O Lord, and these thy gifts, which we are about to receive, from thy bounty, through Christ, our Lord. Amen." With that Francis' family made the sign of the cross.

"With car production down, how has that affected your business, Franklin?" asked Francis.

"Not good. Ford's cut down their vendor list from 300 to 100. Luckily, my tool and dye shop remained on their list. Smart move, seeing how I'm the only one with the castings they need for their engine blocks. Still, I hope production will pick up. I don't want to lay off any more people."

"My parents came over from the old country and were lucky to have a roof over their heads," Anna said. She seemed determined to lighten the atmosphere of gloom that had spread across this country and table.

"What did your father do?" William asked.

"He did a lot of jobs, but mostly he worked for the brick yard. We lived on State Road between Eleven and Twelve Mile Road for a while, then we moved in with my father's sister, where I was born. Then my father had to move away for a while, and mother got work wherever she could find it. When my father returned, we moved to Rinke's place on State Road between Ten and Eleven, where my sister Irene was born, then to Eight Mile Road and Mound where my brother Paul was born; then to Eleven Mile Road and Ryan where Norbert was born."

"You moved a lot," William said, "and remembered all the addresses."

Anna took a few mouthfuls of food, chewing it down thoughtfully. "It was hard, at times. But I recall the time I spent one year with my grandparents so I could attend Catholic school in order to make my First Communion.

"That was the hardest year of my life. I was so homesick for Mother and Father and all my brothers and sisters. We even lived in a saloon one year at Six Mile and Conant. Mom got a job cooking for the men who worked on the roads, and my older sister served.

"Oftentimes we lived in a tent near Seven Mile and Gratiot so we could move easily to where the men worked. I had to tend to the babies. But Mom made my older sister share her tips with me.

"On Saturday evenings my dad would go to the different barn raisings and parties and play his accordion. I had to go along and drive the buggy. Pa was too tired to drive back, what with working a ten-hour day, five days a week as part of the road crew."

"How many brothers and sisters do you have? Afraid I lost count, Anna," said Franklin.

"Five and I was the oldest. We did settle down. My mother's sister, Mary, and her husband, William, owned a lumber yard and built a house for my mother and father on Erbie in Detroit between St. Cyril and Van Dyke. Mom stayed there until she died, had the wake right in that house. Mother sure loved that house."

Collina noticed Anna's half eaten plate of food. "Do you want me to warm your plate?"

"No, it's fine, but my coffee has gotten cold."

Ruby got up. "Here, give it to me," motioning for Collina to remain seated.

Myra looked up with tears forming in her eyes. "You know, Anna, I think God placed you at our table for a reason. I was feeling sorry for myself. Clem wasn't all that good of a provider. Still..." Myra put a hand to her chest. "I wish I could have helped him. I didn't know he was trying—"

"Clem's death was not your fault, Myra." Luke leaned closer to her.

She put her napkin to her eyes. "I know."

Luke glanced down at his plate, then reached for Myra's hand and squeezed it. Myra pulled away.

Ruby felt frozen in place. Then coming out of her trance, handed Anna her coffee. Luke's undying love for Myra spoke agony to everyone who knew their story. Luke had forgiven Myra for eloping with Clem and leaving Luke looking foolish at the dance. He'd accepted Myra's daughters as if they were his own. He'd even stood by her the following year making sure the mafia did not bother her or her boarding house.

Ruby bit her lower lip. Buck had taken care of her holdings in Colorado without complaint. He'd come to Detroit a half-dozen times during this past year. He continued to woo her and said his ring was hers no matter what she decided...But he'd refused to consider her plea and not run for governor. Did he love her or not?

Her face burned with the remembrance of his kiss upon her lips.

Still, he refused to see the reason why he needed to come to the Lord or listen to her advice.

Clem was in heaven along with Stephen. Franklin, Collina, and Myra had shown the way to Jesus through their actions. Why hadn't Buck seen his way to the Savior through her?

Grandmother Maggie cleared her throat. Her black satin lace dress with the large cameo fastened below the intricate lace collar bespoke of her commanding presence. "Myra, you know I wish you only the best in life, as does your loving Savior. It was He that chose to take Clem when He did.

"I could have spent my remaining years with one foot in the grave when my Ben died. I could have wondered what sin I committed to have my beloved Ben leave this earth before me. I chose to live. To be an example to my children of what a godly woman does when hardship befalls us."

Her sharp eyes looked from Myra to Luke. "I pray you give God… and love a second chance. You can trust God too little, but you can never trust Him too much."

Myra blinked. Then she shyly reached for Luke's hand and smiled into his hopeful eyes.

Collina moved to speak, but Anna captured the lapse in conversation first. "Death is hard to overcome, like my Francis said earlier. But we must trust God's judgment. I wouldn't trade places with the richest woman in the world living in a palace if it meant missing my dear mother's kind voice and understanding arms. That's all anyone of us needs in life—love. It's enough. I'm blessed to have a good man like my Francis. He is a good provider."

Francis beamed beneath her praise, then looked down at his plate and shuffled around the stew. "With the good Lord's help, I'll keep providing."

"Papa tried to keep a roof over our heads and provide for all our needs, but we were like the gypsies, forever wandering. My brothers enjoyed it during the summer months." Anna's laughter filled the room, encouraging others to join her.

Anna had stored up warm memories about her loving family who had learned to share and make do in their new homeland. "We had our good times, and our bad times.

"Learning English was difficult for Father, but he persevered, telling us children to embrace this American culture and go to school and learn all about freedom. Our French and German languages were not spoken in the home. When it got real cold in the winter months, a family relative would take us in and be glad to do it."

Ruby saw the look Collina and Franklin exchanged. Oh, how she longed for a love like that again.

"When's dessert?" William asked.

Franklin reached over to ruffle William's hair. "The only thing on this guy's mind is food. I don't know where he packs it away, but he carries it well."

Francis laughed, looking at his broad-shouldered son. "It's hard to figure out how such thin bodies can hold so much."

"Ah, gee, Pa, I'm not so thin," Eric said.

"No, son, guess you're not. What with all that exercise you get, delivering papers before you go to school and getting up at midnight to take your eldest sister to the bus stop. You put to work everything you eat."

"How are you going to do that when school starts? When are you going to sleep?" Ruby asked.

"I'll manage." Eric looked down at his plate of cake.

His sister, Ann, moaned. "I don't know why I took that midnight shift. It was foolish of me and now I can't afford to quit."

"It's okay, Sis," Eric said.

Grandma Maggie had more questions and looked over at Francis. "How did you and your wife meet?"

Francis looked over to Anna and smiled. "We met at Stroh's Brewery. Everyone wanted to date the beautiful Anna, but she would have nothing to do with them—"

"I decided to date Francis because he always walked out of the brewery sober while most of the men left work stone drunk."

"Myra and I were childhood sweethearts," Luke said.

Tears floated into Myra's eyes.

Anna smiled. "A woman has a large heart; that's the way God made her."

"When do you want to get married, Myra?" Luke said.

A cry went up from Collina and Mother.

"Well, it's about time," said Franklin.

"October 1, that has a nice ring to it, and speaking about rings…" Luke scooted off his chair, knelt down on one knee, and grabbed Myra's left hand. "Myra, will you do me the honor of marrying me?" He produced a ring box from his suit pocket and opened it. A diamond solitaire sparkled in the glow of sunlight and gaslight.

Tears flowed down Myra's cheeks. She whispered a shy yes. Luke placed the ring on her finger and enveloped her like a cocoon with his love.

Ruby glanced down at her hands clutched in her lap. Her fingernails cut into her flesh like sandpaper.

William poked his nose out from his piece of cake and said, "Mother, when are you going to marry Mr. Briggs? You already have his ring stuck in the back corner of your desk drawer."

Collina cried, clasping her hands together and then clapping. "Maybe we can make it a double wedding. What do you think, Ruby?"

"I, I'm not sure if I will accept Buck's proposal of marriage."

"Oh?"

"There's no need to rush into anything—"

"Sometimes a thoroughbred needs a little nudge out of the starting gate, so to speak." Grandma Maggie chuckled.

Everyone laughed. Grandma Maggie cleared her throat. "However, Ruby has known the best, and sometimes it's hard to fill such large shoes. Ruby, you take your time. The Good Lord will let you know when to step into another commitment."

"Buck wired that he'll be here next Friday on some sort of business matter," Franklin said. "He'll be staying here. I told him to bring his Sunday best and plan on attending the church social with us. We need as many people to come to this fundraiser as we can get, church attendance being down and all."

Ruby felt the heat rise to her cheeks. Business matter indeed. She'd written Buck that she wished to sell her property in Colorado. She could use the money, and she felt no desire to return.

Chapter 31

August 1, 1931

The church was half full. Ruby and Collina exchanged glances. Neither had noticed the dwindling number of attendees. However, last night Franklin had brought up that very concern. Why had so many of their beloved congregation stopped attending?

Buck was quick to say because people were realizing that God doesn't care. His arrogance had reached new heights, with even Collina and Franklin exchanging worried glances.

"Or more to the reality of our dire situation," Buck said, puffing on his smelly cigar, "there is no God."

"There is a God and He cares," Franklin replied. "I believe many Detroiters are embarrassed they have no money to drop into the offering plate. They are too proud to let their congregational family see how destitute they have become."

And that had ended the conversation.

Ruby stole a backwards glance at Buck sitting in the last pew. His arms crossed, his lower lip out, his scowl fixed on the large picture of Jesus and the tank that sat just below. She turned back and shook her head sadly.

Jesus, only You can work Your miracle in Buck's heart. There. She'd given Buck over to the Lord. She had work to do for those Christians who would accept her help.

Ruby had volunteered to head the charitable clothing drive for the destitute. Her sewing skills came in handy with mending the rips and holes in the donated clothing. Most of the lower to middle class had no

249

problem accepting the church's help.

The more well-to-do of their congregation refused. She would knock on their door, hear whispering inside, her arms laden with clothes and food. No one responded. One such family was the Joneses who lived on Walnut Street. She'd told pastor and had yet to hear what had happened.

Pastor climbed the pulpit steps as if he bore the weight of the world on his shoulders.

The congregation rose and sang, "Onward Christian Soldiers."

"Onward Christian soldiers, marching as to war, With the cross of Jesus going on before. Christ, the royal Master, leads against the foe; Forward into battle, see his banners go!" The words echoed against the walls, reverberating from the ceiling, lifting the spirits of the congregation.

Pastor smiled his radiant smile. "These empty pews are not an affront to me. I'm not up here to extol myself. But I am concerned about those who have chosen to not seek Him who can help in this time of need. It is not a sin to be poor. It is not a sin to need. It is not a sin to feel rejected. In an effort to help those families that can no longer give a portion of their wages, I have decided that we will no longer pass the offering plate.

"If you are able to give, there will be a box in the back of the church. Money is inconsequential to God's fruit." Pastor Brooks opened his Bible. "Please turn to Luke 8:5–8...'A sower went out to sow his seed: and as he sowed, some fell by the way side; and it was trodden down, and the fowls of the air devoured it. And some fell upon a rock; and as soon as it was sprung up, it withered away, because it lacked moisture. And some fell among thorns; and the thorns sprang up with it, and choked it. And other fell on good ground and sprang up, and bare fruit an hundredfold...He that hath ears to hear, let him hear!'"

Collina leaned closer. "Ruby, this is the parable Billy Sunday told the day we buried Pa."

"The sower in this parable is Jesus and the seed, the Word of God." The pastor stepped away from the podium. "The hard ground is that person with a hardened heart; sin or worldly pursuits blind his thoughts. He can't hear God for the coins or the want of them jingling in his pockets and refuses to believe in God's life-changing message."

Ruby held her breath. If there was any time in the sermon Buck would balk and storm out of church, it would be now. Silence.

"Now the stony ground is that person who's aware of the gospel; he may own a Bible." Pastor lifted his Bible in the air. "Even pick it up and read it a little, but his heart isn't fully convicted. So when troubles like these we're going through happen, his faith isn't strong enough to stand against the devil's doubting whispers." Pastor sighed, his head down as he returned to his podium.

"The thorny ground is that person who receives the word of God but then the distractions in life—worries, riches, lusts, whatever they are—they take over that person's mind and heart and that person won't grow in the truth of God's holy Word."

Pastor leaned over his podium. "Ah, but good soil...True salvation burns in his heart and he bears much fruit.

"Now what is that fruit? Is it money, prestige, fancy clothes and worldly positions? No! God doesn't want or need your money.

"Please turn to Galatians 5:22–24. 'But the fruit of the Spirit is love, joy, peace, longsuffering, gentleness, goodness, faith, Meekness, temperance; against such there is no law. And they that are Christ's have crucified the flesh with the affections and lusts. If we live in the Spirit, let us also walk in the Spirit.'"

The pastor laid down his Bible. "This reminds me of one such incident. Paul Jones and his family are not here, as you can see. Paul lost his job and so did his wife, Marge. Ruby and I have tried to help this family to no avail. I saw him on the street corner one day holding up a sign saying, 'Work is what I want and not charity. Who will help me get a job? I will furnish references.' So if anyone here knows of some work he can do, please contact him. You can't help admire the Detroit spirit. Most Detroiters would rather give than receive!"

The pastor slapped his Bible shut. "God will keep our door open if we do the will of Jesus Christ. Franklin will go door to door to find out which of our families would like help, and in the meantime give assistance in the way of doing church work for food and clothing to the less fortunate.

"This is not charity. It is the barter system that began during America's colony days. This is not about pity. This is about helping one another in the spirit of Jesus Christ."

Collina often said Franklin knew the Bible better than a clergyman. Ruby believed that to be true; she'd catch Franklin reading his Bible way into the night

Recalling the first time she met Franklin when he was a soldier for the Rough Riders, Ruby couldn't believe the change in him. That change could only be worked by the Holy Spirit.

She had heard the Scriptures before she knew how to read them, yet had never experienced the "wake-up call" that Franklin had. Pretending to adjust Esther's bonnet, she turned in her seat to sneak a look at Buck.

He had chosen not to sit with the family. He looked up at that same moment. She sucked in her breath and turned back to the preacher.

"Is Buck still back there?" Collina whispered.

"Yes, and he looks as mad as a passel of hornets."

"Good, I was afraid he sat in the back so he could leave without anyone noticing." Collina continued her whispering, "It's a wonder he didn't leave last night, what with the verbal thrashing Franklin gave him after you retired."

Franklin nudged Collina and put a finger to his lips.

The pastor held up the first box. "What am I bid for this box?" One after another, boxes were purchased.

Ruby felt her cheeks grow warm when the pastor held up her box. "What am I bid for this delicate little thing tied with the pink ribbon that matches the pink hat worn by our dear Ruby?"

Collina nodded at her. As if pastor's words were not enough to embarrass her. No wonder Sis made her go up and change her hat before departing for church.

Two dollars someone chimed, five dollars another retorted. Ruby could feel her face growing uncomfortably warm. Looking at the floor, she wished she could climb beneath those very boards.

Ten dollars, Bill Peterson retorted in his deep base. Earl Endwood, who had chosen to sit behind her, poked her shoulder and whispered,

"What did you put in that box? Must be something scrumptious; that's a lot of money for these times."

"Fried chicken, potato salad, coleslaw, sourdough biscuits, and a piece of chocolate cake that Ruby made," Collina said.

"That right?" Earl leaned forward. Ruby refused to look at any one. "Chocolate is my favorite. Twenty dollars!"

Ruby rubbed her ear. My, that was loud. "Oh, it's not that good, Earl, I wouldn't want you to spend what you have left of your savings on me." Ruby glanced back.

Earl's smile covered his broad face. "It's worth every cent just to have an afternoon with you, Ruby."

"Thirty dollars!" came a booming voice from the back of the room. Everyone turned to see who had yelled that outrageous sum.

Buck Briggs stood up, legs spread apart and his muscular arms crossed against his chest. He'd perched his cowboy hat over one eye and now placed a thumb to the brim and set it off his forehead. Ruby turned and crossed her arms. His overrated self-esteem had raised her temper to the boiling point. And how dare he place a hat on his arrogant head in the house of the Lord!

She smiled back into Earl's eyes and coquettishly puckered her lips. "I'd been looking forward to having lunch with you, but I guess I'll have to spend it with that westerner."

Earl frowned. Raising his arm, he chimed, "Forty U.S. dollars!"

Buck walked forward. She stared straight ahead. Her chin defiant.

Earl placed a protective arm around Ruby's shoulder, and she smiled into his eyes. That should send the signal to Buck to back off.

Buck chuckled. "One hundred dollars."

Like the strong current of the ocean, a rumbling wave of response met Buck's offer.

"Did I hear you right, son? Did you say one hundred dollars?"

"I don't recollect you standing at my baby crib, but, yes, pastor, you heard correct."

"How do you intend to pay? Now or in payments?"

Buck drew out his wallet. His cowboy boots slammed the wood

flooring like a sledge hammer.

"Sorry, Ruby." Earl withdrew his arm.

"Oh, don't worry, Earl. Some people have money to burn."

The pastor cleared his throat. "We shall conclude by singing the last two verses of 'Onward Christian Soldiers' and dismiss for lunch."

Earl and she rose with the congregation.

Ruby joined in with, "Crowns and thrones may perish, kingdoms rise and wane; But the Church of Jesus constant will remain. Gates of hell can never 'gainst the Church prevail; We have Christ's own promise, which can never fail. Onward then, ye people! Join our happy throng; Blend with ours your voices in the triumph song. Glory, laud and honor unto Christ the King; This through countless ages men and angels sing."

❤ ❤ ❤

Buck picked a secluded spot in the far back of the parish estate. Upon a hill, it overlooked the church and parsonage, surrounded by maples and elms. The soft breezes of summer added to the beauty of their surroundings. Many of the congregation had chosen to remain indoors because of the heat. Ruby was glad Buck had picked this spot to have their picnic lunch. Her pride didn't permit her to allow Buck to know this. Onward Christian Soldier—after all, she had her foe sitting across from her. She moved uncomfortably on the blanket.

"Now let me see what you've packed. I am hungry enough to eat a whole cow."

Ruby removed the pink bow and opened the lid. "I hope chicken will do." She spread the checkered napkin and placed the chicken onto a plate. There were five pieces: two breasts, two legs, and a thigh. "Which piece do you prefer, white or dark?"

"It doesn't matter; I like all equally." His eyes were studying her, and she tried not to let the secluded spot or his closeness bother her. She opened the potato salad container and placed a spoon into it. She did the same to the baked beans, and then placed a plate, napkin, and silverware before Buck. "There, help yourself. I really don't know your appetite."

"And I thought by now, you did." His eyes sparkled merrily.

Ruby felt a flush work its way to her cheeks.

Buck chuckled. "Go ahead and fill my plate."

She did as she was bid, placing a breast, leg, and thigh on one plate and giving him another plate filled with potato salad, baked beans, coleslaw, and biscuit. "I have brought a small container of honey if you'd like some on your biscuit."

"Where did William and Esther go?"

"They are eating with their friends in the church. William is growing up so fast. I hardly have time to catch my breath. The principal has accelerated him a grade level. I was worried about that, but William is handling the curriculum just fine."

"Stephen would be proud of them. They are both fine children. You have done a good job raising them."

He could be so charming when he wanted to be.

"What I said earlier is the truth. You need to hold onto your investment in Colorado."

"I don't see how that is possible. I've taken a part-time job at my cousin's dry cleaners, and I am still having trouble keeping body and soul together with what sewing I can find. I sold my dress shop. Franklin was kind enough to give me the attic to use as a sewing room to make dresses for the ladies who still have enough finances to buy one. But the money isn't much, just enough to clothe us."

"Colorado taxes are being waived. You won't have to pay them for ten years. Everyone is having the same trouble. The good thing about your investment is that Stephen had enough foresight to pay off his dept. And because I've been planting crops these years, you own the land free and clear. I can find some family who needs a place to live to continue farming it. You will be able to make a little rent off it. Someday that land will be worth something for your children."

What Buck said made sense. Still, the dust storms, prairie fires, droughts, and those terrible rattlesnakes came vividly to her mind. "I can't believe you think that destitute prairie land could be worth anything. Oh, I worked alongside Stephen believing in his dream. But now that he is gone, I can't believe in it any longer. That dream died with Stephen."

Buck looked out over the hillside as if he wasn't seeing it. She struggled to keep her emotions in check. Why did what he feel, what he thought affect her? Did he care what she felt, what worried her?

"It's a hard land. Not easily given to the plow. But some day, mark my words, it will be prime real estate." Buck bent forward, his eyes glassy bright. "Think of it, Ruby. Your land annexed to mine. Why, we'd be some of the biggest land owners in the county." He bit off a huge piece of chicken leg and chewed slowly.

She should have realized there was something in this for Buck. His ambitions knew no limits. Did he think she was that naive not to see through his plans? He must have seen the disgust register across her face. For his next words were aimed at her heart.

"Don't take what is left from Stephen's dream and discard it. It's like taking the only part of Stephen's life that meant something."

Ruby huffed, shook the crumbs from her dress, and jumped to her feet. She must resemble an avenging warrior by the startled look on Buck's face. "What Stephen left behind that will amount to something is his children. Not a piece of worthless land."

Chapter 32

October 1, 1931

R uby, her mouth full of straight pins, looked up, hearing her sister enter the room.

"What a lovely day for a wedding." Collina hurried in with the wedding bouquet. "Don't you think so, Ruby?"

Her needle poised over the loose lace on Myra's wedding gown. "Umm."

Myra's fingers traced the intricate lace and mother of pearls that graced the yoke of her gown. "When Clem and I eloped, I lost more out of my hasty marriage than I stopped to think about."

Collina handed her snow-white elbow high gloves to Myra.

Mother's slow shuffling gait could be heard coming through the doorway. She stumbled on the edge of the colorful Indian rug. Quickly Collina took her arm and helped her to the nearest chair, a Queen Anne that had a bright floral arrangement that swept seat, arms, and back with bright red, pinks, and yellows.

"Mother, you should consider that wheelchair Luke brought you. It could save you from a nasty fall."

Mother slapped the arm of the chair and rested her cane, like an afterthought, on the arm. "Franklin has provided me with that elevator contraption so I can visit everyone up here when I have a mind. If I sit any more than I'm doing, I'm afraid with my memory, I'll forget how to walk completely. Nope. I want to go out of this world standing on my two good feet." She laughed her shrill cackle and everyone joined in.

"That is, if our Good Lord is willing. Your Aunt Louise warned me not to succumb to a wheelchair, unless you absolutely had to."

"When did Aunt Louise die?" Ruby asked.

"Hmm, while you and Stephen were living in Colorado; 1919 I think, but don't quote me on that. She was bedridden for a few years, you know. Told me she'd be happy to leave this earth for her eternal home. That she was born to serve not to be served."

Collina knelt beside her. "Mother, do you remember what Aunt Louise used to tell us about marriage?"

Mother puckered her lips. Her wrinkles contrasted sharply with her sparkling brown eyes.

Ruby rested in a chair next to her, thinking Mother had captured the youthful heart. Her unfailing spirit, her willingness to see the good in a predicament made her a treasure to be around. Ruby chuckled. Mother had acquired a wealth of wisdom, with her well of good works.

Some would call that being a survivor, able to withstand the storms of life and always coming up head first and not feet first. *Favour is deceitful, and beauty is vain: but a woman who feareth the Lord, she shall be praised. Give her of the fruit of her hands; and let her own works praise her in the gates.* The words of Proverbs 31:30,31 sang through her thoughts.

"Most likely it was the same thing Aunt Louise said to me. Now let me see." Mother put a thin finger to her cheek, deep in thought. "How does youth know when love is forever? Or is it commitment, one to another, that binds the heart after romanticism is replaced by reality?"

Myra grimaced. "Well, at least I can say I wasn't too young when I entered matrimony with Luke Baker."

Mother looked sharply at her eldest daughter. Seemingly satisfied, she rested back in the cushioned chair. "We become young a second time when love awakens in us."

Myra blushed.

"You see, my dears, there are no old people in heaven." Mother's sharp eyes lit on each daughter gently, and then she nodded her snow-white head. "Because of the love Jesus has for each and every one of you."

❦ ❦ ❦

Mother gave Ruby much to contemplate. The balcony of the guest room overlooked the gently sloping drive that curved like a horse's silky mane about the rows of maple trees. The trees, brightly arrayed with their colorful foliage, swayed to and fro like dancers promenading to the tunes of the autumn wind.

Was she in love with Buck? Collina said she felt love for Franklin before he'd become a Christian. That she felt God tell her He was going to use Franklin for the glory of His name. Though it took over a decade to fulfill, God's promise had come true.

Ruby lifted her face, feeling the breezes sweep her brow. To the south, the green lawn spread like a carpet beneath the neatly assembled chairs. The wooden platforms, complete with their brightly colored ribbons tied in the traditional wedding knots, were picture perfect. A small disturbance fluttered past her ears like a passel of cawing blackbirds in the midst of hummingbirds. Two big bays pranced up the drive, nervously flinging pebbles from their small, neatly trimmed hooves, much to the dismay of the pedestrians lining the driveway.

"Sorry, I do apologize," Buck said, fluttering the reins for the horses to pick up their pace. The open carriage was glistening white, with white satin streamers and bows decking its carriage parts and red-velvet seats fat with cushions inside. Buck glanced up and impulsively stood. Taking off his top hat, he smiled up at her and gave her a gallant bow. "For the bride and groom!"

Wherever did he get such a fancy coach in such dire times like these? This will prove an interesting wedding, with Buck standing alongside her. She laughed. He was full of surprises. She prayed she'd keep her wits about her this day. "I thought I heard you out here laughing." Collina waved at Buck. Seeing her pot of roses on the window sill, she plucked one and held it up to her nose.

Myra joined them. "This is like it was when we were growing up at Shushan."

Collina nodded. "I remember something Franklin said at Rose

Baker's ball. It was about you, Myra. I was so afraid you were making a mistake marrying Clem." She held up the flower. "It was about a rose bud and why a rose takes longer to bloom than other flowers."

Ruby listened. She could use some good advice.

"Franklin said, 'Everything worth having is worth waiting for.' I think that is like the fruit of the Spirit. It takes time to see the harvest." Collina chuckled. "I didn't know it would take nearly twenty years to know about Franklin's love. I would have rejected him that day he brought you home, Myra, if not for two things."

"What's that?" Myra asked.

"He told me I could take Ruby with me to Detroit, and that through all his failures and blunders, God had given him better than he deserved." Collina looked out over the vast landscape.

"Austin blamed God for his failures—and mine. Now I see that Austin was the seed on the thorny ground. I think I was like that, too, for a time, with all the distractions life threw my way. Thank God, I got back on my knees, and felt my way to the good ground!"

Ruby crumbled. "Oh, help! Buck's both the hard and the thorny ground. He doesn't believe in Jesus, and I...I'm in love with him!"

Myra and Collina exchanged glances. "Well, time for us to get busy and pray," Collina said. "After all, Ruby, remember, Buck hasn't a prayer in this old world!"

Myra nodded.

"That's true enough." Ruby sniffed.

"I thought I could bring Austin to the Lord with my faith. I learned the hard way that a person has to walk that road to salvation on their own. It was a hard pill to swallow, but Jesus got it down. I received a lesson from God on forgiveness and grace when I allowed Franklin into my life."

Chapter 33

Franklin threw down the paper and tumbled into his chair. "I'm ruined."

Collina's mouth gaped open but no words came forth. She picked up the discarded paper. Across the front page in huge bold headlines: "Auto production down to 1,332,000 units."

"What does this mean, Franklin?"

"It means I've got to lay off everyone and close my plant." Franklin rubbed his face. "I've been hoping for some miracle. Actually, I didn't need the newspaper to tell me how bad it has gotten. You can see it in the faces of everyone in Detroit.

"I should never have brought you here…We could move back to Kentucky. We would have enough to eat and someplace warm, but here, the winters are cold and the growing time is short."

"We can still do that."

Franklin gathered her up in his arms. "My love, I don't know how in the world I ever managed to get through a day without you."

Collina melted into his embrace, savoring it, drinking like a sailor the turbulence of his embrace. "And I don't know how I managed to make it all those years without you." Their lips entwined for a moment lost in the oneness that was theirs to cherish.

"Oh, excuse me." Ruby put a hand over her eyes.

"Mommy," William said, "what's wrong? They're married; they do this a lot."

"You're not around enough to notice." Esther chuckled.

Ruby smiled, slightly flustered. "How did you do in school? You know, you can be at the top of your class like—"

"William?" Esther stamped her foot. "Maybe I don't want to. School work comes easy to William. I have to struggle for every grade I make. And he says he's surpassed you."

"No, Mother, I haven't. You'll always be wiser than I because you're so old."

Ruby tapped his sandy-colored head, so much like Stephen's. "Old! I like that, with all your vocabulary skills, couldn't you pick a better word than old?"

"Mature? Vintage?"

"Oh! Why I have half a mind to—" Ruby started after her son. William hadn't expected her to retaliate as she had. Around the chairs and then the couch they playfully ran. Ruby caught up with her son and gave him one good swipe across his behind. "There, see, your mother isn't too ancient to do that."

She laughed, glancing at Collina, who pointed to the newspaper.

"What happened?"

"Auto production fell and Franklin has to close his plant." Collina wrung her hands. "I've learned that families are being evicted from the Regency Hotel. There's a rumor the Welfare Department might renege on their offer to pay for the destitute. The landlord of the Regency is sending the people out on the streets."

"You mean another Hooverville, don't you?"

"How terrible to bring up children in this."

William stepped forward, glanced from his aunt to his mother. "What about that Fisher building? Maybe there's room there? They have showers and a cafeteria set up for the homeless."

Esther followed. "You mean the City Municipal Lodging House?" Esther looked hopefully from one adult to another. "My best friend is living there with her family, and she says they have electricity for the lights and heat. They even have showers and meals.

"Nope. All full up," Franklin said.

"What about the church?" Esther looked to her mother.

Ruby shook her head. "I know the pastor would be happy to take them in, but we don't have floor space available. Pastor has put some families in the sanctuary and moves them every Wednesday and Sundays for services." Ruby plopped herself down in one overstuffed chair, resting her head on the comfortable head rest. "Just when you think you've housed the homeless, then something like this happens."

Ruby sprang up, her face showing a gleam of hope. "I forgot to tell you, children; come sit down please. I want to tell you a story, an honest-to-goodness true story about the generosity of the human heart."

"Really?" Esther was first to sit at Ruby's feet. William followed. Collina smiled and urged Franklin closer. They all could use some good news for a change.

"On Friday this man came by looking like a frozen scarecrow. He didn't have an overcoat on, and all he wanted was a clean shirt to put on for a job interview," Ruby said. "So I drew one out and handed it to him, along with an overcoat and some gloves. I was so busy; I didn't have time to check the pockets.

"He accepted the shirt gratefully and went out to his interview. Well, yesterday he came back, and you'll never guess what he gave me."

"What?" Esther said.

"There was something in the pocket of the coat? Right?" said the practical William.

Ruby nodded. "In his hand he held two diamond cufflinks. He'd found them in the coat's pocket and returned them."

Franklin looked at Collina. His tired face broke into a smile.

"I still cannot believe it. No one would have been the wiser. He didn't even have enough change to buy himself a cup of coffee, and I had given him the shirt and coat. He could have reasoned that the clothes were his to do with as he desired. But he didn't."

Collina dabbed her eyes with her handkerchief.

"There are a lot of good people out there." Ruby blinked away her tears. "They may not have much, but they aren't willing to steal. Surely, God will bless Detroit."

Franklin drew a paper from his pocket, looked at the address, then handed it to Ruby. "Here, I almost forgot; this is addressed to you. Someone handed it to me."

Ruby hesitated before opening it. Unfolding the letter revealed a woman's handwriting. The paper was stained with water marks. Tears? It was from the widow, Mrs. Burns. She had six children.

"Do you know of any place we can go? We are being evicted from the Regency tomorrow."

Chapter 34

March 7, 1932

ow, Mrs. Meir, I tried to be patient. I've given Mrs. Burns and her children free rent for months. I can't continue any longer. You understand. I run a business; I need paying renters."

Ruby tried to silence the angry words that flooded her thoughts, anger with this depression that would not release its death grip on Detroit. She had filled out the numerous papers, but to no avail.

The landlord puffed on his cigar as he walked around the small, two-bedroom apartment, clean and tidy. In one corner of the room huddled Mrs. Burns and her family. The children, washed and neat in their threadbare clothes, said not a word. The rumbling motors of the cars outside the window captured their attention. Families were piling their few remaining possessions onto the last thing they owned, their car.

"Look," a man in a worn-out overcoat yelled. He was passing out flyers. "They need fruit pickers in California. They say a cabin and two square meals are provided for every worker."

"That's where me and my family will go. I'm through with factory work." A man with a passel of towheaded children climbed in the back of their pick-up truck.

The landlord smirked, puffs of smoke fogging Ruby's view of his face and the happenings below. However, his contemptuous words would follow her like a lost pup in a rainstorm for years to come. "They print out thousands of those handbills when all they need are a hundred migrant workers." The man guffawed. "That work lasts for a season, sometimes less than a week or two, at best."

Mrs. Burns looked at Ruby.

She put a finger to her temple. The First Baptist Church had no available room left. But Annie said Father Murphy had an available spot for a couple. She looked over at Mrs. Burns, and counted. Six. The number hadn't changed. Well, the baby and the toddler took little space. Suddenly, she was furious at this pudgy landlord who had enough money to waste on smelly cigars. "So you are going to cast this good woman and her children onto the streets?"

The landlord shrugged. "Your brother-in-law is wealthy; ask him for the money."

Franklin had just taken in Dawn, her children, and husband who had lost his job. Speaking of which, Collina confided in her that now that Franklin had to close the plant they would have to rely on their savings to feed everyone.

Ruby stood a little taller. "All you'll do is leave this apartment empty. You'll still have to pay for the heat. What does it hurt to let them live here until you find a paying tenant?"

The landlord removed the cigar from his mouth and blew a puff of smoke in Ruby's face. "They are not my concern. I've been patient. I've got bills to pay. All you do-gooders do no good to me. How will I pay my taxes? What am I supposed to live on? Air?" His heavy steps made the floor vibrate beneath her feet. Putting his hand on the door handle he turned it and said over his shoulder. "I'll give her till the end of the week and then she and her kids are out of here." He opened the door and stormed down the steps.

Ruby turned to the woman huddled in the corner with her children. "I might have a place where you can move to. Give me a little time, Mrs. Burns. I'm going to go see Father Murphy. He had an available room a couple days ago."

"We're not Catholic."

"That doesn't matter."

Mrs. Burns nodded. "We've got a few more days. Meanwhile I better get to packing." She turned to her eldest girl. "You follow Mrs. Meir down the steps and take this bucket. I need some water. We need to wash the floor and the walls. I don't want the next tenants to move into a dirty place."

"But Mama it was dirty when we got it."

"That is none of our concern. We're not like that. Someday when I get a job, we will pay every cent we owe. It's only right. I don't like living on charity."

"Don't worry. I'm going to find you a better place than this."

Though March, winter did not want to release itself from Detroit. The wind swept around the corner mercilessly, and Ruby buried her head deeper into her wool coat. A commotion the next street over made her stop. Looking up, she saw men and women running to join the ever-increasing crowd marching down Woodward.

"What's wrong?"

A woman turned and yelled. "It's a hunger march; we're marching clear to Dearborn."

Ruby hurried on toward St. Ann's Church. She walked into the office, only to note the Father watching the marchers below. She joined him at the window. "My, there must be thousands down in the street."

Father Murphy nodded. "They're headed by that communist candidate running for mayor, Albert Goetz."

"But don't they understand everyone is out of work? Who do they expect will help them?"

"Ford Motor Company. Ford just had some massive layoffs. Workers are asking for union recognition, full employment, and a six-hour work day with no reduction in wages." Father Murphy turned and smiled at Ruby. "Be nice, wouldn't it?" Walking over to his desk he sat down with a heavy sigh. "What can I do for you?"

"Is that room still available? I have a family being evicted at the end of the week and no place to go."

"Yes, I still have it. It's very small. You said family. I told Anna that this room is only big enough for a man and wife to share." Father Murphy set his blue eyes on her.

She took a deep breath. "You are my only hope. Mrs. Burns is a widow with six small children. I can't let them go to another Hooverville. We need…" She collapsed into a nearby chair. Father Murphy's kind eyes looked into hers.

"Don't worry; we'll make do. Bring me your family. Don't fret now, Ruby. It won't be as bad as you think. I've heard talk that come July there may be another place for the homeless. The National Guard might donate tents. My congregation, along with others, are starting a sewing circle and a food drive.

"Some of the men of the congregation are organizing a work detail for sanitary conditions and playgrounds for the children. Some of the teachers are pooling their time to make sure the children continue their education. We've even started a group right in these Hoovervilles to organize those ladies and gentlemen with skills."

"So, will you allow the homeless to make the meals and disperse the food and clothing?" Ruby looked up, drying her tears.

"They're homeless, not helpless. They all had homes and jobs. Some of them gave too much to others and have found themselves depleted of savings and funds. They want to be useful. We've found out that given a little incentive, they manage themselves. They even have designated policemen and volunteer firemen."

Tears flowed down her cheeks, happy tears. But she felt a pang of apprehension for Franklin and Collina. Their hearts were often bigger than their pocketbook. How much savings was left? Would they be joining the others in a new Hooverville? Mother couldn't go, she was too old.

She thanked Father Murphy and left. She rushed down the sidewalks, her head bowed, fearful that at any time an angry rioter would hurtle himself at her, a lone woman. The crowd swept her along, like a rush of flood waters. Like a piece of driftwood, she was powerless, dragged, and pulled in a massive flow of smelly bodies and yelling voices.

"Let me out of here!"

A man shoved her. A burly man with foul breath and a long beard grabbed her. She fought him. "Let go of me!"

The other man pushed the bearded man aside, then he flung her into his arms and held her tightly. She couldn't see her assailant; he was holding her too close. The yelling increased to ear-shattering levels. She cried out, thrusting her fists into his chest.

"Ruby, my love, it's me, Buck."

"Buck! Oh, Buck, I'm...so scared." She sobbed, clawing at his coat. "Hold me close. I'm so tired of fighting, tired. I—"

"There now, don't worry. You're safe with me." He picked her up and carried her to a bench. After wiping the tears from her cheeks with his handkerchief, he then had her blow her nose. She looked up. His face swept hers, assuring for himself that she was relaxed and in her reasonable mind.

"I could have been in Dearborn by now. When did you get here? You wrote me you couldn't leave Colorado until April."

Buck put a thumb to one teardrop, then held her close. She crumbled into his embrace. She couldn't remember a time she felt so exhausted.

He buried his head in her hair. "I heard you cry. I ran up and down the sidewalks wondering where you were. Oh, Ruby!" He held her at arm's length, his eyes searching her face. "Never, never, do that to me again.

"I blame myself for not being here sooner. You need me as much as I need you." He seized her to him in a crushing hug. "I don't know what I'd do if something should happen to you."

Could it be? Is it possible that something besides ambition managed to work its way into Buck's heart? Could it be that Buck did love her? Lord Jesus, please let it be true, please show me the truth.

"Come on, let's go home."

They huddled around the radio that evening. Four marchers were killed, trampled to death. Ruby shuddered. She could have been one of them. Hundreds were injured when the Dearborn police attempted to stop them at the border of Detroit and Dearborn and a riot began.

Franklin and Buck decided to go to the funeral.

❦ ❦ ❦

The band played a tune unfamiliar to most Americans. Franklin looked over at Buck.

"I hope that isn't what I think it is." He turned to the man singing along with the band. "Is that the communist workers' anthem?"

The man nodded, not breaking rhythm.

"Look at this crowd," Franklin whispered.

"There's got to be over ten thousand here. The funeral march is from the 1905 Russian Revolution."

"You're kidding." Coming to the grave site, Franklin pointed to the people congregated there. "There's got to 30,000 here."

Buck shook his head slowly. "Herbert Hoover got a bad break, entering the presidency eight months after the stock market crash. This new guy, what's his name? Roosevelt something or other, who's running against him, will have a better chance at the people's confidence."

"We have to do what we can to endorse Roosevelt. If he's half the man his cousin was, well then America has a fighting chance getting back on its feet."

A man approached carrying a large sign. "Work is what I want and not charity. Who will help me get a job?" For an instant their eyes met and held.

Franklin extended his hand and a wiry smile, nodding his head in salutation. "How you doing?" That was a silly remark. It was obvious as to the state of this man's situation.

"Not very well. Do you remember me? I worked at your plant. Joe Proskow is the name."

"Joe, right. That was some time ago. What did you do after you left?"

"My wife and I went to work for a restaurant. We got the leftovers free. That is, until the restaurant closed."

"Did you try Mama's Home Cooking on Union Street? Sometimes she can use extra help."

"Already been there. They've got all the help they need."

"Well, we'll walk with you a while, if you don't have to be somewhere."

Joe looked at the crowd milling around the funeral procession. "I don't. Don't think much of communism or socialism. My parents left Russia because of it. That is not the way out of this mess. Yeah, I'll walk with you."

The three walked together, heads bent against the bright sunlight shining down on them. Franklin stole a sidelong glance at Joe.

He'd turned his sign face down as he walked, the print facing away from his and Buck's view, as if embarrassed he didn't have a job. His shoulders bent, he pulled his hat even further over his eyes.

"Say, did you try Bud's? They use cooks at times."

"I've been up and down this street at least a half a dozen times."

"The church on the corner has cots and gives everyone one square meal a day."

"Me and my misses aren't looking for handouts. We're looking for work and a decent place to live with our children."

Buck looked up at him and nodded. "So is a third of the nation."

"Well, here's my car." Joe opened the door of his model T and thrust his sign inside. His wife was in the front seat. His three children in the back. On the roof, were boxes and a rocking chair strapped down. Joe stretched out his hand. "Thank you for listening."

There was something about the way he shrugged his shoulders that made Franklin worry he may have reached the end of his rope. Unable to face their wives and children, many men had chosen suicide as the alternative to seeing the heartbreaking faces of their loved ones starve.

"Wait!"

Joe turned. "I'm not looking for charity, Mr. Long."

"Yeah, I know."

Joe's face looked blankly into his.

"Look, I've got a real nice stable and all the running water you need, and plenty of chickens. You could be my caretaker. Come to church on Sunday and we can talk more about it."

"Franklin," Buck whispered, "you've already taken in Dawn and her family."

"We don't need—"

"This isn't charity. I had to close my plant. But I'm thinking. I moved my equipment to the tool shed. And, well, if I can find some work—"

Joe banged the steering wheel. "I see your point, boss!"

Franklin chuckled and stretched out his arm. "It's a God thing that I happened to see you with that sign."

It was as if new blood had started pulsing into Joe's veins. The color came back into his face and a large grin swept his lips. "When can we move in?"

"Any time after Sunday." Franklin smiled. "I'll take you over there after church. That will give me time to clean you and your missus a spot and to tell my wife."

"You sure are asking a lot of Collina," Buck muttered. "I'm not sure Ruby would be so understanding if I didn't ask her first."

Chapter 35

March 13, 1932

Buck pointed to the back pew of the church as they entered. Ruby wanted to be front and center to see if what the Lord had revealed to her the day of the riot was of God. Had the Lord finally picked the strings of Buck's heart? Did Buck love her for her and only her?

"Oh, have it your way." She pushed past him and sat down, her arms crossed. He smiled, plopping next to her. Collina and Franklin walked forward. She nodded to her children to follow their aunt and uncle. Right behind her children, the family Franklin had invited to church followed.

All she knew about the Proskows was that they were going to live in the stable for a while until Franklin either built them a cabin, or they found somewhere else to stay. Now she'd never get to know what more Collina had found out, all because she had to partner herself with the most stubborn man in the world.

"Our reading will be from Romans 9:20–23...'O man, who art thou that repliest against God? Shall the thing formed say to him that formed it, Why hast thou made me thus? Hath not the potter power over the clay, of the same lump to make one vessel unto honour, and another unto dishonour? What if God, willing to shew his wrath, and to make his power known, endured with much longsuffering the vessels of wrath fitted to destruction: and that he might make known the riches of his glory on the vessels of mercy, which he had afore prepared unto glory.'"

Pastor paused and surveyed his congregation. "These are hard words, words not often spoken before a congregation, let alone during times like these when our nation has so many people in need.

"Why did these terrible times happen? Why does our loved one die when we prayed for him or her to live? Was our faith not strong enough?"

Ruby moved uneasily.

"The Potter decides! Look what the Potter had His Son go through? Jesus didn't do anything wrong. He had a mission to do here. He patiently endured, showing His mercy to those people who nailed Him to a cross! Do you think He enjoyed that? God chose the Jews but He included us, the undeserving Gentiles, to become part of His kingdom, children of the living God. Jesus, knowing the truth, racked with pain, bleeding from head to toe, cried out, 'Lord, why hast thou forsaken me?' If the Son of God felt that way and had to suffer, do you think you're too good to? Don't remain a lump of disgusting clay! Get out of your pity-me wagon and become a child of God! 'For whosoever shall call upon the name of the Lord will be saved.' This life is all the hell I want to experience.

"Don't push off the Holy Spirit when He prompts you into action. 'To day if ye will hear his voice, harden not your hearts.'

"'For the Word of God is quick and powerful, and sharper than any twoedged sword, piercing even to the dividing asunder of soul and spirit...and is a discerner of the thoughts and intents of the heart.'"

The pastor leaned over his podium. "We all know that it is in our hearts we hide the truth. Thinking things we ought not, going places we shouldn't."

Ruby was glad the podium was between her and the pastor; she was afraid he'd come right off the stage after her.

Buck enveloped her hand in his.

"But we have Christ Jesus, who in all points was tempted like we are, yet did not sin." He motioned with his hands to step forward. "Let us therefore come boldly unto the throne of grace, that we may obtain mercy, and find grace to help in time of need."

Ruby squeezed Buck's hand. "I have to go forward, Buck."

"I feel like a roped calf." His voice cracked with emotion. "I, I never experienced—"

"I know. I've been freed from my miserable burden."

The pastor's voice boomed louder. "If you have felt the Holy Spirit, or if you have doubts about your salvation, don't allow the devil to get a toe hold into your heart by not responding to Christ's call."

Buck rose. He extended his hand. Together they walked forward.

❦　❦　❦

Ruby and Buck spent the afternoon walking the grounds of the Brick. He confided to her the dark crevices of his life that had kept him from seeing the truth.

She wanted to tell him everything. All her secrets, her inhibitions. She was at a crossroads on how.

Buck's fingers tightened around her hand. Somehow, he knew. And then she saw it—the boulder. She'd found it one day when she'd gone for a walk. It had become her personal prayer rock after that. It reminded her of Las Animas, where Stephen knelt and prayed so many years ago. She rested her hand on the rock, feeling its warmth from the sun.

"What's wrong?" Buck looked from her to the boulder.

The gentle breezes whispered through the grass and leaves of the trees. Her eyes filled with tears.

"It was at a boulder like this one that I found Stephen one morning. When he saw me he sprang from his knees, his Bible still clutched in his hand. His face all aglow. He'd heard from God. He felt God had promised him he would be healed and he'd become a preacher.

"He was so excited, and I tried to be, too, but inside I doubted. Buck, I doubted Stephen! I always felt that it was because of my lack of faith that Stephen wasn't healed and died. It haunted me. Stephen was a good man. It wasn't because he lacked faith. It had to be because of mine! My smug declaration of Christian virtue was a facade covering the weak-kneed faithless creature I was. When Stephen needed me…I was no help to him. It was easier to hide behind my church clothes than to wear Christ's armor! Easier to do all those charitable acts, than to face reality."

Buck's face mirrored her own agony. Her heart leapt, and she ran to him enfolding herself into his embrace. "Why has God made me thus? What the preacher said at church today made me realize that God is stronger than me—and Satan."

"He patiently endured the cross for our sake, Ruby."

Ruby looked up at Buck, his face unreadable.

"He was the spotless lamb offered up for us."

"God can't wipe away a person's past," Ruby said.

"No, but He can help us rewrite the ending." He drew her to him, his arms soft and inviting.

"I used to think that was all stupid religious ideological mumbo jumbo. Not anymore. Too much has happened to make me see a greater good in those people who know Jesus." He chuckled. "You are at the top of my list. You church-going Bible thumper! I thank God that Stephen called me out. I thank my Savior, Christ Jesus, you thumped that Bible at my head hard enough to make a dent! Can you forgive me for being so hard-headed and obstinate?" He drew her away and smiled down at her. "And forgive yourself for not believing God can heal all wounds—including your lapse of faith?"

In a few words he had summed up what had troubled her for years. She looked up at him baffled. "You have taken hold of what Christ's message is." It was like Buck had changed from inside out in an instant. "What about your plans to become governor of Colorado?"

He turned away from her, bent over to pluck a blade of grass and rubbed it between thumb and finger. The noise of a car motor came to her ears. That new family was moving into the stable. Their voices drifted across the lawn along with their exclamations of joy and laughter. Ruby watched Sis hand them a large platter of something. She couldn't make out what from here.

"I'm not sure if becoming governor is what God has planned for me anymore." He stared at the people who had vacated the Ford truck. His sloping forehead, high cheek bones, and strong jaw etched like granite in the setting sunlight. "I'm a little confused to be honest with you. All of a sudden, I don't care anymore about position, land, or wealth. What do any of those things matter if you have no one to share them with?"

He turned then, his brows puckered. "Can you ever love me like you did Stephen?"

Ruby reached into her pocket and slipped on Buck's ring. "I already do. My love for you is different from the way I felt about Stephen, but as meaningful."

He swept her into his embrace and twirled her around the gardens.

Her laughter mingled with the songs of the blue jays and robins overhead. "All this time, love and forgiveness were a repentant prayer away."

Chapter 36

March 4, 1933

"Hurry everyone, the president is about to speak." William ran through the house, then halted before the partly opened door and gaped. "Is Grandmother Maggie dying?"

Grandmother Maggie whispered weakly, "I came into this world without anyone of you helping, and I guess I can leave the same way. Now, you go on in the parlor and listen to this new President Roosevelt. If he's anything like his cousin, the nation will be in good hands."

Franklin bit his lower lip. There wasn't any time left. If he was going to do this, it was now or never. "Might I have a moment with Maggie alone?"

"Certainly." Ruby clutched her children's hands. Buck followed. She led her children out, glancing over her shoulder. Collina rose to leave. Franklin extended his arm. "Sorry, I need my better half to stay."

Franklin knelt. "Maggie, I've lost the plant and all my money I had in the bank. Hopefully, President Roosevelt will give us some compensation." He looked at Collina. "Darling, I didn't know how to tell you. I found a buyer for the Brick. I paid over ten thousand for the buildings and the additional property. He offered to pay four thousand. Do we stay? Or do we all go to Kentucky to wait out the depression?"

A noise came from the parlor, chairs and tables scraping across the floor. Suddenly the noise of the Zenith, static, and then a loud voice filtered through the closed door. Collina hurried to the door and opened it a crack.

"Buck said there's no reason why you can't hear some of Roosevelt's speech," Ruby said.

Collina looked back. Franklin glanced down at the prostrate Maggie, who nodded. "Great contraption, this radio. This progress I like."

The deep voice of President Franklin D. Roosevelt said, "I am certain that my fellow Americans expect that on my induction into the Presidency I will address them with a candor and a decision which the present situation of our Nation impels. This is preeminently the time to speak the truth, the whole truth, frankly and boldly. Nor need we shrink from honestly facing conditions in our country today. This great Nation will endure as it has endured, will revive and will prosper. So, first of all, let me assert my firm belief that the only thing we have to fear is fear itself—nameless, unreasoning, unjustified terror which paralyzes needed efforts to convert retreat into advance. In every dark hour of our national life a leadership of frankness and vigor has met with that understanding and support of the people themselves which is essential to victory. I am convinced that you will again give that support to leadership in these critical days.

"In such a spirit on my part and on yours we face our common difficulties. They concern, thank God, only material things. Values have shrunken to fantastic levels; taxes have risen; our ability to pay has fallen; government of all kinds is faced by serious curtailment of income; the means of exchange are frozen in the currents of trade; the withered leaves of industrial enterprise lie on every side; farmers find no markets for their produce; the savings of many years in thousands of families are gone."

Franklin laid his head down on the bed, tightly shutting his eyelids. God, tell me what to do? Suddenly he felt Maggie's hand gently stroke his hair.

"You know what to do...son."

"I thought I wasn't materialistic. But now that everything is gone... I'm scared. It was alright when my decisions only affected myself—"

President Roosevelt's voice interrupted his words. "Only a foolish optimist can deny the dark realities of the moment.

"Yet our distress comes from no failure of substance. We are stricken by no plague of locusts. Compared with the perils which our forefathers conquered because they believed and were not afraid, we have still much to be thankful for. Nature still offers her bounty and human efforts have multiplied it."

"That…is the way it was after the Civil War," Maggie said. "Our money was worthless, but we had our land. Then the carpetbaggers came."

Roosevelt's voice rose an octave, as of with vitality of truth and purpose. "Practices of the unscrupulous money changers stand indicted in the court of public opinion, rejected by the hearts and minds of men.

"True they have tried, but their efforts have been cast in the pattern of an outworn tradition. Faced by failure of credit they have proposed only the lending of more money….They know only the rules of a generation of self-seekers. They have no vision, and when there is no vision the people perish…."

Franklin lifted his head. "When there is no vision—"

"The people perish…' That is what old honest Abe Lincoln said and my Ben, too. Said we'd been fighting Satan and it was time to put that devil in his place." The door opened. Franklin motioned for everyone to come in.

Roosevelt's words blared through the open doorway. "Happiness lies not in the mere possession of money; it lies in the joy of achievement, in the thrill of creative effort. The joy and moral stimulation of work no longer must be forgotten….Small wonder that confidence languishes, for it thrives only on honesty, on honor, on the sacredness of obligations, on faithful protection, on unselfish performance; without them it cannot live."

Maggie chuckled. "From out of the abundance of the heart, the mouth speaks."

"Our greatest primary task is to put people to work. This is no unsolvable problem if we face it wisely and courageously. It can be accomplished in part by direct recruiting by the Government itself, treating the task as we would treat the emergency of a war, but at the same time, through this employment, accomplishing greatly needed projects to stimulate and reorganize the use of our natural resources."

"God hasn't abandoned us; we've abandoned Him," Buck said.

Roosevelt talked on. "The task can be helped by definite efforts to raise the values of agricultural products and with this the power to purchase the output of our cities. It can be helped by preventing realistically the tragedy of the growing loss through foreclosure of our small homes and our farms. It can be helped by insistence that the Federal, State, and local governments act forthwith on the demand that their cost be drastically reduced."

"Maybe we should return to Kentucky. We can grow three crops a year, next to Michigan's one," Collina said.

Static filled the air waves momentarily, then Roosevelt's voice continued. "Finally, in our progress toward a resumption of work we require two safeguards against a return of the evils of the old order: there must be a strict supervision of all banking and credits and investments, so that there will be an end to speculation with other people's money; and there must be provision for an adequate but sound currency."

"A little late," Franklin grumbled.

"Yeah," Buck said. "Hopefully, Roosevelt will find a way to honor what some of us have lost."

Roosevelt's voice rose higher, as if talking over Buck's. "If I read the temper of our people correctly, we now realize as we have never realized before our interdependence on each other; that we cannot merely take but we must give as well; that if we are to go forward, we must move as a trained and loyal army willing to sacrifice for the good of a common discipline, because without such discipline no progress is made, no leadership becomes effective....

"With this pledge taken, I assume unhesitatingly the leadership of this great army of our people dedicated to a disciplined attack upon our common problems.

"Action in this image and to this end is feasible under the form of government which we have inherited from our ancestors."

Grandmother Maggie sighed. "Father thought the South would perish. I thought we'd perish when my Ben died. Well, we have survived with less than this."

Roosevelt's voice broke to a whisper. "That is why our constitutional system has proved itself the most superbly enduring political mechanism the modern world has produced. It has met every stress of vast expansion of territory, of foreign wars, of bitter internal strife, of world relations...."

"We face the arduous days that lie before us in the warm courage of national unity; with the clear consciousness of seeking old and precious moral values; with the clean satisfaction that comes from the stern performance of duty by old and young alike. We aim at the assurance of a rounded and permanent national life....

"The people of the United States have not failed....They have asked for discipline and direction under leadership. They have made me the present instrument of their wishes. In the spirit of the gift I take it.

"In this dedication of a Nation we humbly ask the blessing of God. May He protect each and every one of us. May He guide me in the days to come."

Maggie sighed. "It is going to be like the old days again, bartering your way back to your dignity. Bet the old house will stand a little taller and look pretty good to you all. Ah..." Her veined hand covered her heart and she gasped. "I'll be going now...don't want to wear out my welcome....Do you hear that lovely music? It sounds like harps...in the distance. There's my Ben..."

Collina sobbed, kneeling at her bedside, with Ruby and Myra kneeling beside her. Maggie blinked. "Tears of joy, daughters... remember what my Ben said about the mustard seed...a bit of faith with hope mixed in to carry you through. Hope in...the Lord." Her eyes glassed over and her jaw dropped.

Franklin reached over and gently closed her eyelids, then kissed her on the forehead. "She was the mother I never knew."

Chapter 37

April 14, 1933

R uby dabbed her eyes. The train whistle blew out its warning. Steam fogged the air and the locomotive lumbered to a screeching stop before them. Black smoke filled the sodden air. Buck's warm fingers caressed hers. "Ruby, I believe this Roosevelt fellow is the guy for the job to get America back on its feet again. 'We have nothing to fear but fear itself.' I have to admit, it resonates."

"I know. Franklin is expecting great things from Roosevelt. Even with him declaring a bank holiday, Franklin didn't appear to worry." She chuckled. "Still, he made that man give him cash for the Brick. Collina has already made a list of seed she needs for planting once we're back in Kentucky. She's in a hurry to leave."

"It's been over two weeks since the banks reopened." Buck moved his baggage closer to the train entrance.

"I know. Detroit's two largest banks were liquidated and two new ones founded in their place: Manufacturers and National Bank of Detroit."

"More importantly, men and women want to feel needed. I believe that the Civilian Conservation Corps Roosevelt signed into law will give the people that."

"What exactly is the CCC?" Ruby was bumped and she felt Buck's arms go out protectively.

"Some are calling it Roosevelt's Tree Army but it will mean more than that, you wait and see. Male citizens between the ages of eighteen and twenty-five will be paid $30 a month and given supplemental basic and vocational education while they serve. They'll plant trees, clear and maintain roads, reseed grazing lands, just about everything."

"Eric's excited, though he's too young to participate. He told me the other day, 'It's a job that needs to be accomplished, and it's a hand up, not a hand out.'"

"No truer words were ever spoken." Buck cupped his hands around hers and kissed them. "I would never have found my Savior without you."

"And I would never have found complete peace or love again without you! I'm sorry now you didn't run for governor. You had your mind set on that, and you would have made a wonderful governor." She hugged him close, finding solace. "I was afraid something might happen to you with those—"

"I'm glad I didn't. I'm not going to run for any government position, unless my wife says so."

Ruby's heart leapt within her bosom. "You're not?"

"Jesus has shown me that the only thing that matters is Him." A look of pure joy swept his countenance. "Him and those He gives us to share our lives on earth with. I want to share my life with you, darling, be it in Colorado, Detroit, or Kentucky."

"You mean that? What about your land speculations?"

"I'm leaving to make plans to sell our portions, if that is what you want, or I can lease our holdings out. So, pray tell me, Ruby. I'll call you when I get there."

Her mind revolved like a whirlwind. Buck loves the Lord—this is what I've dreamed of, prayed for. She felt undecided. She never cared for farming life, and now that Franklin had sold the Brick, she was uncertain what to do.

No telling with prohibition ending what the bootleggers were going to do now. Would there be bars on every street corner like some people said? Franklin wasn't going to wait around and see. "Oh dear, tell me what to do, Buck."

"My love." Buck knelt. "Nothing can destroy what we have together. And until Jesus decides to separate us by death, let our hearts remain forever one."

Ruby sniffed, "Oh—"

"Excuse me," a woman said.

"What are you doing down there?" One man huffed, dragging a large suitcase and glaring down at Buck, kneeling on the ground.

People bumped into them. The smell of smoke and coal dust filtered across her nostrils. Of all the places Buck could have picked to declare his love for her…this one had to be the worst. Yet the love she saw in his eyes. His earnestness wrapped her in a cocoon. Suddenly her heart knew before her mind could. "Buck, let me go with you!"

"No. I'm not sure what kind of soup I'll find myself in Colorado, with beer and wine being legalized—our thugs might declare all-out war. I've made a few people mad at me not running for the governor position. But I'll handle them; don't you worry about that."

"But I thought you would be safe from those gangsters now."

Three black-suited men ducked into the train station. They reappeared with tickets clasped firmly in their hands.

Buck eyed them. "I'm not going to let the organized crime thugs get away. I know enough to send them all to prison for a very long time. We've got a president in the White House now that is willing to do something about it, too. But don't you worry about me." He kissed her finger that bore his ring. "Write me and let me know your wedding plans."

"Oh, Buck, you decide. I don't care anymore where we live, as long as we're together! Let me go with you. My sister can watch the children. We can get married in Las Animas."

"No, darling, you'll be safer with Franklin and Collina. Stay with them until I come for you and our children." His eyes earnestly gazed into hers. "I love you."

One long mournful sound and then two small toots of the whistle blew. In a heartrending embrace, he caressed her to him, his kiss long and lingering, mingling with her tears.…He wiped them away with his thumb. "'Smile the while you kiss me sad adieu…,' remember?" He was gone. Caught up in the black smoke of the locomotive, its large iron wheels somersaulting like her emotions, groaning as her heart did, aching for her lost love. *When we meet in the after…No!*

Ruby clutched her throat. Like Stephen! She ran after the train. If Buck saw her, he'd fly to her side. His strong arms would encircle her. His laughing eyes would tease her back into a good mood for acting like a silly, frightened child.

The compartments rumbled by her, the wind from the train sweeping her skirt. "God, where is he?" She searched the bystanders. It would be just like him to be standing somewhere on the other side of the train, observing her…waiting for her…

"I'll come for you…you and our children. I love you!" His vibrant words whispered a timeless message to her aching heart. "'Smile a while…' Remember?"

Unleashed tears formed on her cheeks. "I will never forget, Buck. 'Wedding bells will ring so merrily… Ev'ry tear will be a memory… So wait and pray each night for me…Till we meet again.'"

Chapter 1

*A*round and around the couples danced. Their laughter rose and fell in response to the tides of notes from Glenn Miller's orchestra. Their steps were in perfect rhythm as if for one purpose, one desire.

Esther stepped away from the Vanity's balcony. Her gaze traveled to the multi-paned windows flanked with draping sheers. They offered the dancers a peek of the stars outside, while crystal chandeliers cast a golden glow on the Mayan ceiling inside.

If she was dreaming, she hoped to never wake. She stared into one of the glinted full-length mirrors adorning either side of the three promenades. A man smiled back, his eyes resting on hers.

"Oh." She whirled around to find herself inches from the stranger who had to be at least six-foot-four. Thick jet-black hair waved around a strong masculine face. But his eyes—intelligent, attentive, holding within their hazel depths a mischievous twinkle.

"Be careful; there are men here who'll take advantage of a beautiful woman."

"Do men staring into a mirror count?"

"Only if they stare back." A laugh escaped his lips. "Has anyone ever told you your eyes sparkle and get as big as saucers when you blush?"

Who is he?

His black tuxedo with a shiny satin lapel emphasized his broad shoulders and slender waist. An amused glint crinkled the corners of his eyes. "I'm Eric Erhardt, a junior draftsman at Taylor and Gaskin. I'm taking night courses at Lawrence Institute and plan to own my own engineering firm someday. And you are?"

Besides being irresistibly handsome, the man was a mind reader. "Esther Meir."

His eyes didn't leave her face. It was unnerving.

"So, Esther Meir, what do you do besides looking like a porcelain priestess in this palace of the Aztecs?"

If he knew, he wouldn't be calling her a priestess. Three hours ago she was sweating like a field hand. The palms of her hands still felt clammy. Hope he doesn't ask me to shake his. "My brother and I are attending college. I attend night courses at the Detroit Business Institute. William, my brother, is a junior accountant at Ford Motor. He goes to night school at the University of Detroit. He earned a scholarship."

"U of D, what's he studying?"

"Accounting. He made the Dean's List and won an all-expense-paid vacation to a dude ranch. He's taking me and my friend along."

"Really?" He chuckled deeply. "So, you're, eighteen, nineteen?"

She felt like leaving him talking to the mirror behind her, but she was wondering his age, too. "I'm nineteen."

"That makes you two years younger than me." His eyes bore down on her like a hawk hunting a chicken. Ridiculous. Here they were immersed in the splendors of geometric stones, gleaming bronzes, and ivory pilasters, a scene fit for King Solomon himself, and he was looking at her like she was his next meal.

"What's your opinion of the Vanity? Some say Charles Agree made a mistake designing it after an Aztec theme."

She'd read about Agree in the paper. "The theme sort of embodies America's hopes—prosperity and purpose."

Eric's voice dropped an octave. "You fit this palace mystique. I can't pinpoint why exactly; maybe it's your gown." His gaze traveled downward. "It fits you perfectly, as if made just for you. I especially like the way that gown gathers at your...um, waist and...Well, it drapes your...everything well. Say, there's something on—" His hand brushed her bare shoulder, his palm lingering there a second too long.

She slapped his hand off her shoulder. "Are all northerners as brazen as you?" He'd better be happy it wasn't his face.

"Northerner? I thought I heard an accent. You're not from Detroit?"

"I'm from MacDuff County, Kentucky."

"You needn't get in a lather. I thought I might have known you." He shrugged. "But I've never been to Kentucky." A look of polished suaveness bathed his face. "I like meeting a girl on the up and up." His warm hand cupped her elbow, guiding her toward the balcony.

"So you're not just new to the Vanity. You're new to our big city ways. Guess it's up to me to educate you."

A wrought-iron railing separated the onlookers from the dancers below. "The Vanity is one of three ballrooms in Detroit. Each one shows its beauty differently." He closed the gap between them. "Like a beautiful gal."

His breath tickled her ear. Resisting the urge to step back, she craned her neck up. "Does that line work on most uneducated women?"

He chuckled and sent her an audacious smile, displaying dimples symmetrically placed on either cheek. "Usually."

She'd never met a guy so insultingly frank. Yet his smile was infectious. She found herself smiling back. The sound of the trombone broke through their conversation as the rise and fall of a Glenn Miller intonation of clarinet, horns, and strings echoed about the ballroom.

Couples made their way down from the promenade and onto the gleaming maple floor in a flood of blues, reds, and golden full-length gowns against the black tuxedos.

"Eric. Down here."

Alert as a bird dog on a new scent, Eric turned toward the woman's voice on the dance floor below. A tall, attractive woman, her champagne-colored hair rolled in an upsweep, stood on the edge of the ballroom floor. "Glenn Miller's going to play our song."

Eric's eyes swept Esther like a warm summer breeze, lingering on her upturned face. "I promised my friend Marge that if she could get Glenn Miller to play 'In the Mood,' I'd dance with her."

Did regret cause him to hesitate before leaving her side?

"Esther." Dot McCoy yanked her out of her reverie. "I'd like you to meet my neighbors, Robert and Mary Rizzo. Robert's leaving Monday for England to join the British aviators."

Mary stared at her wedding ring, twirling it around her finger.

Dot cleared her throat. "Mary's in the family way. Isn't that wonderful?"

Robert nodded. "I'll be back, though, before Mary has the baby, that's if—"

"America doesn't declare war first," Mary said.

"Oh, now, don't believe what Senator Wheeler from California said on the radio last night." A shake of Dot's head started her thick auburn curls bobbing across her brow.

"Which part?" Robert kissed Mary's forehead. "The part that Europe wants more tanks and planes and American lives? Or the part that American Jewish filmmakers are 'Hollywood Hitlers' and unpatriotic because their films encourage involvement in Europe's war? I got an earful. No offense, Dot."

"No offense taken, Robert. Our Jewish roots are embedded deep in American soil, and I've stopped worrying about what some senator in California says."

"That's a relief. Mary and I couldn't have better neighbors, and we think highly of you and your parents." Robert kissed Mary's ring hand. "Come on, darling; dance with me. I don't want our last evening at the Vanity to be sad. And I'll bring back souvenirs for you and our baby."

A gust of cool wind from the full-length windows laced with the fragrance of petunias and roses sent the sheers flying madly into the room, breathing the coming autumn. Mary rested her head on Robert's shoulder, waltzing below Esther to the enchanting melody of "The White Cliffs of Dover."

Esther shivered, but not from the sudden chill sweeping the room. She wished it were. Mary's child would miss her father terribly if he didn't return.

"Poor kids." Dot wrapped her knuckles around the railing.

"You're afraid, too, that Robert won't—"

"You're the Christian, so you'd best pray a lot, kiddo. Europe hasn't seen the worst of it. Americans haven't a clue." Dot should know. Some of her Jewish relatives still lived in Berlin. According to the newsreel, British Prime Minister Winston Churchill broadcast that 'scores of thousands of executions of civilians are being perpetrated by German police troops.'"

Never able to stay serious for long, Dot turned her attention on Esther. "Your dress is darling, even though it is homemade. In this light, it's not really scarlet, right?" Dot snapped her fingers. "I've been wondering why you remind me of that person in *Gone with the Wind*. You know, that Scarlett girl. Your hair's even the same shade as hers. And you wear it down, like she did, except without those funny little bow things."

"I didn't have time after work to—"

"Looks perfect for you." Dot glanced out at the ballroom. "Oh, look, there's William. That blonde he's dancing with is out of step. It's a two-step, not a jitterbug. Well, William's having a good time. All I need is to find you your Rhett Butler." Dot waved. "Well, look at that. I've found him. You're perfect for each other."

Esther glanced over the banister. Right into Eric's upturned face. He smiled back.

Dot whispered, "I bet you haven't anyone like Erhardt in Kentucky. He's tall as an oak with shoulders as broad as a football field. Per-fect." Dot stressed the two syllables like smacking her lips over a particularly scrumptious pastry.

A nervous titter escaped Esther's lips. Never in her lifetime could she imagine that she and this Eric guy would lock eyes at that particular moment. She was acting like a moonstruck kid from the hicks.

"Eric's the handsomest unattached male in Detroit. When he takes you into his embrace," Dot hugged her arms, skimming them down her shoulders, "it's like nothing you've ever experienced."

When the last notes of Glenn Miller's trombone ended, he held up his hand to the applause of the dancers. "The next dance is for our beautiful ladies. The Robbers' Dance will now begin." With a flourish, the orchestra began "Chattanooga Choo Choo."

Dot squeezed her arm. "Isn't this swell? I love being flirted with. I'm planning not to get serious about anyone for a couple of years at least."

"How else would we figure out what kind of man we want to marry?"

Dot followed Robert and Mary jitterbugging about the dance floor. "Marriage is the lifelong bond between a man and woman. We need to know what we're getting ourselves and our future children into."

The couples swirled and dipped around the dance floor. "If America is thrust into Europe's war, falling in love could be heart-wrenching, Dot."

"Tragic."

"I pray Jesus will guide me to His choice for my husband-to-be."

Dot slapped the railing with the palm of her hand. "Oh, jeepers creepers, that Jesus stuff again. Esther, when are you going to stop leaning on that crutch?" Dot tugged at her arm. "Come on; we've got to hurry before another Robbers' Dance begins."

"What is a Robbers' Dance?"

Dot looked at her in disbelief. "You steal a dance with the man of your choice."

"You ask the man for a dance?"

"Don't give me that high-hat look. It's perfectly proper." Her blue eyes twinkled into Esther's worried glance as she grabbed her arm. "Then again, with your goods…What I wouldn't give for a figure like yours."

Esther dug in, pulling back. "You go. I'll have more fun watching from here."

"Come on, Esther. It's not unladylike. Surely, you've been to Sadie Hawkins dances in Kentucky. You didn't just milk cows down on that farm."

Esther laughed. "Thanks for the invite. You go, I'll wait here." The soft, poetic notes of a waltz sent the couples dipping and swaying around the dance floor. Eric guided his partner, and her flowing taffeta gown feathered as gently as a bird in flight around her slender legs. The woman glided effortlessly to Eric's lead as if she were on ice skates.

"I wish I could dance like them," Esther muttered. I wish I could forget that terrible night I tried.

Discussion Questions

1. The United States entered the Great War in 1917. How long did it last? What other name is the Great War called today?

2. Ruby is frightened sick of snakes. However, she attacks the rattlesnake to save her son. Have you ever had a similar experience?

3. Were you shocked to learn that Austin was unfaithful to Collina? Doc used an analytical approach to handle Austin's sin. Maggie a practical no-nonsense approach. Which one are you more like? Which biblical passages spoke to you?

4. Franklin put wealth before God. Do you know someone who has done this? What happened to their relationship with God? What incident brought Franklin back to the Lord? What Scriptures did he cite?

5. "We can thank Providence for this moment, but we cannot blame Him because of our shortcomings." What does this mean to you? Have you ever experienced what Franklin and Collina have? Have you ever gotten a second chance at happiness?

6. Collina rejects Franklin's first proposal. What changed her mind? Ironically, Collina did not go with Franklin to Detroit the first time because of her duties to her family. Amazingly, this second time Shushan has been sold and her duties to her family caused her to go with Franklin. Did you find the hand of God in this?

7. Shushan became a haven for the Jewish people as Esther 9:2 states. "And no man could withstand them; for the fear of them fell upon all people." Benjamin Franklin said, "God does govern the affairs of man, and a country cannot exist without His aid." As Israel is a nation of Jews, America is a nation of Christians. Who said this? Do you think this is true of America today?

8. The Great Depression began in what year? For what reason? Do you think it could happen again?

9. Clem was in the wrong place at the wrong time. He often visited speakeasies and repented later. Can you think of people who do that?

10. What Bible verse or verses cause Buck to believe in God? What causes Ruby to feel guilt free over her husband's death and see that her faith had been enough? Have you ever had an experience like Ruby's?

CATHERINE ULRICH BRAKEFIELD

Catherine is an ardent receiver of Christ's rejuvenating love, as well as a hopeless romantic and patriot. She skillfully intertwines these elements into her writing as the author of *Wilted Dandelions, Swept into Destiny, Destiny's Whirwind*, and *Destiny of Heart* inspirational historical romances; and *Images of America, The Lapeer Area*. Her most recent history book is *Images of America, Eastern Lapeer County*. Catherine, former staff writer for *Michigan Traveler Magazine*, has freelanced for numerous publications. Her short stories have been published in Guidepost Books *Extraordinary Answers to Prayers, Unexpected Answers* and *Desires of Your Heart*; Baker Books, Revell, *The Dog Next Door*; CrossRiver Publishing, *The Benefit Package*. She spent three weeks driving across the western part of the United States, meeting her extended family of Americans. This trip inspired her inspirational historical romance, *Wilted Dandelions*.

Catherine enjoys horseback riding, swimming, camping, and traveling the byroads across America. She lives in Michigan with her husband, Edward, of forty years, and her Arabian horses. Her children grown and married, she and Edward are the blessed recipients of two handsome grandsons and two beautiful granddaughters.

www.CatherineUlrichBrakefield.com
www.Facebook.com/CatherineUlrichBrakefield
www.Twitter.com/CUBrakefield

Hostile indians,
raging rivers,
and treacherous trails
are nothing
compared to
marrying a man
she does not know.
Wilted Dandelions
Available in bookstores and from online retailers.
CrossRiver Media
www.crossrivermedia.com

FIND MORE GREAT FICTION AT CROSSRIVERMEDIA.COM

ROAD TO DEER RUN
Elaine Marie Cooper

The year is 1777 and the war has already broken the heart of nine-teen-year-old Mary Thomsen. Her brother was killed by the King's army, so when she stumbles across a wounded British soldier, she isn't sure if she should she help him or let him die, cold and alone. Severely wounded, Daniel Lowe wonders if the young woman looking down at him is an angel or the enemy. Need and compassion bring them together, but will the bitterness of war keep them apart?

SWEPT INTO DESTINY
Catherine Ulrich Brakefield

As the battle between North and South rages, Maggie Gatlan is forced to make a difficult decision. She must choose between her love for the South and her growing feelings for the hardworking and handsome Union solder, Ben McConnell. Was Ben right? Had this Irish immigrant perceived the truth of what God had predestined for America?

LOTTIE'S GIFT
Jane M. Tucker

She's a little girl with a big gift. Lottie Braun has enjoyed a happy childhood in rural Iowa with her father and older sister. But the quiet, nearly idyllic life she enjoyed as a child ended with tragedy and a secret that tore the two sisters apart. Forty years later, Lottie is a world-class pianist with a celebrated career and an empty personal life. One sleepless night, she allows herself to remember and she discovers that memories, once allowed, are difficult to suppress. Will she ever find her way home?

POSTMARK FROM THE PAST
Vickie Phelps

In November 1989, Emily Patterson is enjoying a quiet life in west Texas, but emptiness nips at her heart. Then a red envelope appears in her mailbox with no return address and a postmark from 1968. It's a letter from Mark who declares his love for her, but who is Mark? Is someone playing a cruel joke? As Emily seeks to solve the mystery, can she risk her heart to find a miracle in the *Postmark from the Past*?

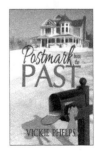

CPSIA information can be obtained
at www.ICGtesting.com
Printed in the USA
BVHW040212150520
579740BV00006B/70